W9-AHF-954

Highlander in Her Dreams

Highlander in
Her Dreams

Allie Mackay

A SIGNET ECLIPSE BOOK

SIGNET ECLIPSE
Published by New American Library, a division of
Penguin Group (USA) Inc., 375 Hudson Street,
New York, New York 10014, USA
Penguin Group (Canada), 90 Eglinton Avenue East, Suite 700, Toronto,
Ontario M4P 2Y3, Canada (a division of Pearson Penguin Canada Inc.)
Penguin Books Ltd., 80 Strand, London WC2R 0RL, England
Penguin Ireland, 25 St. Stephen's Green, Dublin 2,
Ireland (a division of Penguin Books Ltd.)
Penguin Group (Australia), 250 Camberwell Road, Camberwell, Victoria 3124,
Australia (a division of Pearson Australia Group Pty. Ltd.)
Penguin Books India Pvt. Ltd., 11 Community Centre, Panchsheel Park,
New Delhi - 110 017, India
Penguin Group (NZ), 67 Apollo Drive, Rosedale, North Shore 0632,
New Zealand (a division of Pearson New Zealand Ltd.)
Penguin Books (South Africa) (Pty.) Ltd., 24 Sturdee Avenue,
Rosebank, Johannesburg 2196, South Africa

Penguin Books Ltd., Registered Offices:
80 Strand, London WC2R 0RL, England

First published by Signet Eclipse, an imprint of New American Library,
a division of Penguin Group (USA) Inc.

Copyright © Sue-Ellen Welfonder, 2007
All rights reserved

ISBN-13: 978-0-7394-8953-6

SIGNET ECLIPSE and logo are trademarks of Penguin Group (USA) Inc.

Printed in the United States of America

Without limiting the rights under copyright reserved above, no part of this
publication may be reproduced, stored in or introduced into a retrieval sys-
tem, or transmitted, in any form, or by any means (electronic, mechanical,
photocopying, recording, or otherwise), without the prior written permission
of both the copyright owner and the above publisher of this book.

PUBLISHER'S NOTE
This is a work of fiction. Names, characters, places, and incidents either are
the product of the author's imagination or are used fictitiously, and any resemblance to actual persons, living or dead, business establishments, events, or
locales is entirely coincidental.
    The publisher does not have any control over and does not assume any
responsibility for author or third-party Web sites or their content.

The scanning, uploading, and distribution of this book via the Internet or via
any other means without the permission of the publisher is illegal and punish-
able by law. Please purchase only authorized electronic editions, and do not
participate in or encourage electronic piracy of copyrighted materials. Your
support of the author's rights is appreciated.

*In loving memory of my mother-in-law,
Annegrete "Anna" Welfonder, née Lemke.
A kind and soft-spoken gentlewoman, she was
the heart and soul of her home, beloved by
her family and all who knew her.
She made every meal a feast, every visit a
celebration, and had the most beautiful
smile I've ever seen. While her cheesecakes
could have topped New York's finest, and
her laugh was warm enough to melt the hardest
hearts, I remember her best for her quiet,
unassuming ways. She was the mother-in-law I
would wish for every bride and I feel blessed
that she was mine.*

ACKNOWLEDGMENTS

Scotland inspires every word I write, and although I have enjoyed a love affair with Scotland all my life, a few well-loved places there mean more to me than others. The Isle of Skye, now officially known as Eilean a' Cheò, pronounced "ellan-uh-ch-yaw" and meaning Island of Mist, is one such place. I always spend time there on my visits to Scotland, and it was on Skye that I found the inspiration for this book.

Castle Wrath actually exists and is a favorite Skye haunt of mine. Its true name is Duntulm, and the ruins there are very much as described in *Highlander in Her Dreams*. Only the medieval arch is missing, although it, too, can be found on Skye. I simply borrowed the arch, transplanting it to Castle Wrath from another very special Skye castle ruin, Dun Sgathaich.

Like Kira, I have enjoyed picnics atop the grass-grown arch at Dun Sgathaich. I've also spent time at Duntulm, my attention always drawn to a certain deep, dark opening in the earth. One that I strongly suspect leads down into Duntulm's haunted dungeon where Hugh, a one-time Duntulm laird's evil cousin, was imprisoned. His cries and rantings are said to be heard to this day and I can vouch that Duntulm does indeed echo with the *possibilities* of such ghostly residents.

Many legends are attached to both Skye ruins. A

particularly colorful one concerns a clan feud between the MacDonalds and the MacLeods, a tale known as "The War of the One-Eyed Woman." With so much tradition and lore, it would seem far-fetched to expect more, but Scotland never fails to surprise and delight.

I found further inspiration on a lonely stretch of a northern Scotland beach during this book's deadline. While walking this isolated shore near sundown, I spotted a lone man atop the high dunes, looking out toward the North Sea. Tall, striking-looking, and kilted, he appeared to own the strand. The word "guardian" struck me as I observed him. I also thought of Aidan, imagining that he would stand atop Wrath's cliff in very much the way this man claimed his high dune. I took three photographs of "Aidan." Two show him as I saw him. The third photo shows only a brilliant globe of glowing light. To this day, I wonder who, or what, he was. In any event, seeing him made me feel good about writing this book.

I must also credit three women for their help in making this tale shine. My agent, Roberta Brown, best friend and trusted confidante. She reads every line I write almost as soon as it's typed. Although she'll deny it, I *know* she is an angel. As always, heartfelt appreciation to my amazing editor, Anne Bohner. There aren't words to thank her for her keen insight and ability to zero in on just what needs fixing. Special thanks to Liza Schwartz. She, too, offered invaluable suggestions. Thank you, ladies. I appreciate your input and support so much.

Last but not least, my deep appreciation to my handsome husband, Manfred, for his devotion and enthusiasm, and my precious little dog, Em. The world's sweetest Jack Russell, he rules my life and keeps me happy.

"Time is of little importance in the Highlands, a magical place of picturesque beauty, languorous and seductive, where you can easily believe the distant past was only yesterday, the faraway and long ago not lost at all but waiting to be discovered by those with eyes to see."

—Wee Hughie MacSporran, historian, storyteller, and keeper of tradition

First Prologue

Castle Wrath, the Isle of Skye, 1315

"May the devil boil and blister him."

Aidan MacDonald, proud Highland chieftain, paced the battlements of his cliff-top stronghold, fury pounding through him, disbelief and outrage firing his blood.

Fierce blood, easily heated, for he claimed descent from a long line of fearless Norsemen as well as the ancient chiefs of the great Clan Donald, a race of men famed and respected throughout the Hebrides and beyond. A powerful man who believed that Highlanders were the equal of all men and better than most, he cut an imposing figure against the glittering waters stretching out below him.

Topping six foot four and favoring rough Highland garb, he was a giant among men, turning heads and inspiring awe wherever he went. Just now, with his dark, wind-tossed hair gleaming as bright as the great sword strapped at his side and his eyes blazing, the very air seemed to catch flame and part before him. Certainly, on a fair day, few were the men bold enough to challenge him. On a day such as this, only a fool would dare.

Aidan of Wrath had a reputation for turning savage. Especially when those he loved were threatened.

And this morn, he wanted blood.

More specifically, his cousin Conan Dearg's blood.

"A pox on the craven!" He whipped around to glare at his *good* cousin, Tavish. "I'll see the bastard's tender parts fed to the wolves. As for you"—he flashed a glance at the tight-lipped, bushy-bearded courier standing a few feet away, against the parapet wall—"if you won't tell us your name, then I'd hear if you knew what is writ on this parchment?"

Aidan took a step toward him, his fingers clenching around the damning missive.

"Well?"

The courier thrust out his jaw, his eyes cold and shuttered.

"Perhaps a reminder is in order?" Aidan's voice came as icy as the man's expression. "See you, this missive is scrawled with words that would have meant my death. My own, and every man, woman, and child in my clan."

Had the scroll been delivered to its intended recipient and not, by mistake, to him.

Anger scoring his breath, he let his gaze sweep across the choppy seas to the steep cliffs of nearby Wrath Isle, its glistening black buttresses spray-washed with plume. He fisted his hands, his eyes narrowed on the long, white-crested combers breaking on the rocks.

He would not be broken so easily.

This time Conan Dearg had gone too far.

He swung back to the courier. "How many of my cousin's men knew of this plot?"

"Does it matter?" The man spoke at last, arrogance rolling off him. "Hearing their names changes naught. All in these isles know you've sworn ne'er to spill a kinsman's blood."

"He speaks true." Tavish gripped his arm, speaking low. "Conan Dearg is your cousin, as am I. He—"

"Conan Dearg severed all ties with this house when he sought to arrange our murder." Aidan scrunched the parchment in his hand, its rolled surface seeming almost alive. Evil. "To think he planned to slit our throats as we sat at his table, guests at a feast held in our honor!"

He stood firm, legs apart and shoulders back, the edge of his plaid snapping in the wind. "I canna let it bide, Tavish. No' this time."

"We can put him out on Wrath Isle. His man, too, if he refuses to speak." Tavish glanced at the nearby islet's jagged cliff face. "With the tide rips and reefs surrounding the isle, they'd ne'er escape. It'd be the closest place to hell a soul could find in these parts."

Aidan shook his head. He knew Wrath Isle, a sea-lashed hellhole as wicked-looking this fair morn as on a cold afternoon of dense gray mist. But the isle's brooding face deceived. With cunning, a man could survive there.

It wasn't the place for Conan Dearg.

He drew a long breath, hot bile rising in his throat.

"He'd not find much foraging on the isle." Tavish spit over the parapet wall, the gesture more than eloquent. "No women, either."

Aidan shot him a look, his frown deepening.

Conan the Red's handsome face flashed before him, his dazzling smile as false as the day was long. Not lacking in stature, charm, or arrogance, he was a man to turn female heads and win hearts.

Men, too, easily fell prey to his swagger and jaunty airs.

Foolish men.

As he, too, had been. But no more.

Fury tightening his chest, he turned back to the courier. "I ask you again—how many of my cousin's men knew of this perfidy?"

The man rubbed the back of his neck, his face belligerent.

He said nothing.

Aidan cracked his knuckles. "Perhaps some time in my water pit will loosen your tongue? 'Tis an old, disused well, its shaft open to the tides. Greater men than you have spilled their secrets after a night in its briny depths."

"I'll see you in hell first." Steel flashing, the man whipped a dirk from the cowled neck of his cloak and lunged. "Give my regards to the dev—"

"Greet him yourself!" Aidan seized the man's wrist, hurling him over the parapet wall before the dirk even fell from his fingers.

Snatching it up, he tossed it after him, not bothering to look where man or knife landed. In the sea or on the rocks, the result was the same.

Beside him, Tavish coughed. "And Conan Dearg?"

Aidan dusted his hands on his plaid. "Have a party of men set out at once. Send them to his castle. To the ends of the earth if need be. I want him found and brought here alive."

"Alive?" Tavish's eyes widened.

"So I have said," Aidan confirmed. "Out of deference to our kinship—and my oath—I'll no' end his life. That he can decide on his own, whene'er he tires of the comforts of my dungeon and a diet of salt beef and soured water."

"Salt beef and soured water?" Tavish echoed again, comprehension spreading across his features. "No man can live long on suchlike. If he doesn't die of hunger, his thirst will drive him mad."

"Aye, that will be the way of it." Aidan nodded, feeling not a shimmer of remorse.

"And"—he took Tavish's arm, leading him from the battlements—"we'll have a feast to mark the craven's capture, the thwarting of his plan. See you that Cook makes preparations."

Tavish gave a curt nod as they stepped into the shadows of the stair tower. "It will be done."

"Indeed, it shall," Aidan agreed.

The moment he slid the bolt on Conan Dearg's cell, he would treat his clan to the most raucous celebration Castle Wrath had ever seen. A lavish fest sparing no delicacies or merrymaking revels. With free-flowing ale and women equally generous with their charms, he'd make it a night to remember.

Always.

Second Prologue

The Isle of Skye
Many Centuries Later . . .

Only a few months after her eighteenth birthday and in the unlikely environs of a crowded tour bus, Kira Bedwell fell in love.

With Scotland.

Passionately, irrevocably, never-look-back in love.

Not as one might expect with a strapping, kilt-wearing hunky, all dimpled smiles and twinkling eyes. A powerfully built Celtic giant able to melt a woman at twenty paces just by reciting the alphabet in his rich, buttery-smooth burr.

O-o-oh no. That would have made things too simple.

Kira Always-Take-the-Hard-Way Bedwell had fallen in love with the land.

Well, the land and a few choice secret fantasies. Delicious fantasies that set her heart to pounding and made her toes curl. The kind of things that would have made her parents regret every dime they'd doled out for her graduation trip to Scotland.

Land of her dreams.

A place to stir and kindle female desires if ever there was one. Hers had been simmering for as long as she could remember—tartan-clad fantasies sparked by the colorful tales spun by one-time Scottish neighbors. The MacIvers had moved elsewhere, but the magic of their stories stayed with Kira, as did her dreams of misty hills, heathery moors, and bold, sword-swinging men.

Frowning, she crossed her legs and stared out the window, the image of a braw, wild-maned Highlander striking out across that untamed, heather-covered land a bit too vivid for comfort.

She moistened her lips, determining to ignore the nervous flutter in her belly. Prickly little flickers of giddiness that whipped through her each time she imagined such a man looming up out of the mist to ravish her. Her pulse escalated and she needed a few slow, deep breaths to compose herself. Amazing, what the thought of a hot-eyed, handsome man in full Highland regalia can do to a girl.

Especially if such a man is bent on making a woman his.

But the only kilties she'd encountered so far on her holiday coach tour through the Scottish Highlands were men over sixty. Each one ancient even if he did speak with a deep, bone-melting burr. She recrossed her legs, her frustration minimal but definitely there. Not a one of the over-sixty gallants even had had cute knees.

Forget sexy calves.

As for filling out their kilts . . .

Pathetic.

She frowned again and looked out her window at Eilean a' Cheò, Isle of the Mist. Better known as Skye, and one of the highlights of the tour. A rapidly vanishing highlight, as today was the tour's only full day on the misty isle and she didn't want to miss a single moment.

They were driving north along the cliff-hugging, single-track road through the heart of Trotternish, a landscape of rock, sea, and brilliant blue sky almost too glorious to behold.

The glistening bays of rocks and white sand, the black-faced sheep grazing the greenest pastures she'd ever seen. Shining seas of deepest blue and dark, rugged coastline. Cliffs, caves, and ruined croft houses, the fire-blackened stones squeezing her heart.

The woman next to her touched her elbow then, offering potato chips, but Kira ignored her, making only a noncommittal *mmmph*. She'd eat later, when they stopped at Kilt Rock for a picnic lunch.

For now, she only wanted to drink in the views. She was branding the vistas onto her memory, securing them there so they could be recalled at will when the tour ended and she returned to Pennsylvania, leaving her new love behind.

The MacIvers had been right. They'd sworn that no one could set foot in their homeland without losing their heart to Scotland's mist and castles. The wild skirl of pipes and vibrant flashes of plaid. She'd certainly fallen hard. Crazy in love, as her sisters would say.

Crazy in love with Scotland.

And crazily annoyed by the constant drone of the tour guide's voice.

A deep and pleasing Highland voice that she would surely have found appealing if the speaker hadn't been such a bore. She glanced at him, then quickly away. That he seemed to be the only kilted Scotsman close to her age only made it worse.

Rosy-cheeked, red-haired, and pudgy, he bore a rather strong resemblance to a giant tartan-draped teddy bear.

Leaning back against the seat, she blew out a frustrated breath. If she'd harbored any illusions about romance on this tour, Wee Hughie MacSporran wasn't her man.

". . . ancient seat of the MacDonalds of Skye, Castle Wrath stands empty, its once formidable walls crumbled and silent." The guide's voice rolled on, at last saying something that caught her attention.

She sat up, perking her ears.

Castle Wrath sounded interesting.

She could go for crumbled walls. Especially if they were silent, she decided, trying not to notice that her seatmate was opening a second bag of potato chips.

"Some say Castle Wrath is haunted," Wee Hughie went on, seemingly oblivious to crackling potato chip bags. In fact, his chest swelled a bit as he looked round to see the effect of his tale. "To be sure, its walls are bloodstained, each stone a reminder of the past. The turbulent history of the ancient warrior-chiefs who once dwelt there."

Pausing, he pointed out the ruin on its cliff, clearly pleased by the tour-goers' indrawn breaths. Their appreciative ooohs and ahhhs.

Kira ooohed too.

She couldn't help herself. Etched starkly against sea

and sky, Castle Wrath, or what was left of it, looked
just as dark and brooding as Wee Hughie described it.

Shivering suddenly, she rubbed her arms and nestled deeper into her jacket. She'd seen a lot of castle
ruins since arriving in Scotland, but this one had her
catching her breath.

It was different.

Romantic.

In a spookily delicious sort of way.

She turned back to the guide, for once not wanting
to miss a word he had to say.

"Castle Wrath was originally a Pictish fort," he told
the group. "A *dun*. This first stronghold was seized by
invading Norsemen until they, in turn, were dislodged
by the Lords of the Isles." He looked around again,
pitching his voice for maximum impact. "These early
MacDonalds were fierce and powerful. Their sway
along Scotland's western coast was absolute."

He paused, his hands clenching the green vinyl
satchel that Kira knew held his scribblings on Scottish
history and lore.

Looking ready to impart that lore, he cleared his
throat. "Deep grooves in the rock of the castle's landing beach attest to the MacDonalds' prowess at sea,
for the grooves are believed to have been caused by
the keels of countless MacDonald galleys being drawn
onto the shore. These fearless men were the ones who
raised the new castle, and it is their ghosts whose foot-
falls, knocks, and curses can be heard—"

"Have you seen our guide's beanstalk?"

Kira blinked. *"Beanstalk?"*

She looked at her seatmate, certain she'd misunderstood.

But the woman nodded, her gaze on Wee Hughie. "It's quite impressive."

Kira could feel her jaw drop. True, she hadn't seen that many naked men, but she'd seen enough to know that Wee Hughie's beanstalk was the only part of his anatomy that lived up to his name. She'd caught a glimpse of his *Highland pride* when some of the tourgoers photographed him at Bannockburn. Striking a pose beside the famous statue of King Robert the Bruce, he'd looked regal enough until an inopportune gust of wind revealed what a true Scotsman wears— or doesn't wear—beneath his kilt.

A wind blast that proved Wee Hughie MacSporran to be anything but impressive.

Wincing at the memory, she shot a glance at him. "I didn't think he was all that—"

"He's descended from the MacDonalds, Lords of the Isles," Kira's seatmate enthused, poking her arm for emphasis. "From the great Somerled himself. I know genealogists back home who'd sell the farm for such illustrious forebears." She paused to press a hand to her breast and sigh. "He carries a diagram of his lineage in that green satchel. It goes back two thousand years."

"Oh." Kira hoped the other woman hadn't guessed her mistake. She'd forgotten the guide's ancestral pedigree. His supposed claim to noble roots.

Kira didn't believe a word he said.

Any descendant of Robert Bruce and other historical greats would surely be dashing and bold, with dark, flashing eyes full of heat and passion. Beautiful in a wild, savage way. Sinfully sexy. Well-muscled rather than well-*fleshed*—and definitely well-hung.

She squirmed on the seat, certain that her cheeks were brightening.

Certain, too, that she wouldn't be picnicking at Kilt Rock with full-of-himself MacSporran and the tour group. As if drawn by a force impossible to resist, she stared through the bus window at the ruin perched so precariously on the cliff-top. Bold men, mighty and strong, had called the romantic pile of stones their own, and if their echoes still lingered there she was of a mind to find them.

Or at least enjoy her packed lunch surrounded by the solitude.

The bus could return for her later. If she could persuade the driver to indulge her.

Determination urging her on, she approached him a short while later during the obligatory roadside photo stop. A pleasant enough man about her father's age, he turned when he sensed her hovering, his smile fading at the lunch packet clutched in her hand.

"My regrets, lass, but there won't be time for you to eat that here." He shook his head. "Not if we're to make the craft and art shops on our way to Kilt Rock."

"I'm not interested in arts and crafts." Kira plunged forward before she lost her courage. "I'd rather picnic here than at Kilt Rock."

"Here?" The bus driver's brows shot upward. He eyed the clumpy grass at the roadside, the peaty little burn not far from where they stood. "Do you have any idea how many sheep pats are scattered hereabouts? Och, nay, here's no place for a lunch stop."

Looking sure of it, he glanced at the other tourgoers, some already filing back into the bus. "I canna see anyone in this group wanting to picnic here."

"I didn't mean the others." Kira seized her chance. "I meant just me. And not here, along the roadway," she added, casting a wistful look toward Castle Wrath. "I'd like to spend an hour or two out at the ruins. Eat my lunch there and do a bit of exploring."

She looked back at the bus driver, giving him her most hopeful smile. "It would be the highlight of my trip. Something special that I'd cherish forever."

The driver stared at her for a few moments, then began rubbing his chin with the back of his hand. He said nothing, but the look he was giving her wasn't encouraging.

"You could pick me up on the way back to Portree." Kira rushed the words before he could say no. "Two hours is all I ask. More if you'd need the time to come for me. I wouldn't mind the wait."

"That ruin really is haunted," he warned her. "Wee Hughie wasn't lying. Strange things have been known to happen there. The place is right dangerous, too. It's no' one of those fancy historical sites run by the National Trust."

He turned piercing blue eyes on her. "Everything at Wrath stands as it was, untouched by man all down the centuries. Och, nay, you canna go there. The cliff is riddled with underground tunnels, stairwells and rooms, much of it already crumbled into the sea."

"Oh, please," Kira pleaded, feeling as if the ancient stones were actually calling to her. "I'll be careful. I promise."

The bus driver set his jaw and Kira's heart plummeted when he glanced at his watch. "Come, lass. Think with your head, no' your heart. We'll tour Dunvegan Castle in the morning, before we leave for Inverness. You'll like Dunvegan much better. It's furnished and has a gift shop—"

"Which is why Castle Wrath is so special." Kira's throat began to thicken with her need to reach the ruins. "It's not overrun with tourists. It hasn't been spoiled." She paused to draw a breath. "My parents worked overtime for a year to give me this trip and I can't imagine ever getting back. Visiting Scotland again doesn't figure in my budget."

The driver grunted. Then he nudged at a cluster of heather roots, his hesitation giving her hope.

"I've ne'er had anything happen to anyone on one of my tours." He looked at her, a troubled frown knitting his brow. "One false step out there and you'd find yourself in some underground chamber, maybe even standing at the very wall of the cliff, the earth opening away at your feet and falling straight down to the sea."

"Nothing will happen to me." Kira lifted her chin, tightening her grip on the lunch packet. "Believe me, anyone used to walking around downtown Philly can poke around Scottish castle ruins."

"Ach, well." The driver gave a resigned sigh. "I still dinna like it. No' at all."

Kira smiled. "I won't give you cause to be sorry."

"I'd have to double back to fetch you," he said, rubbing his chin again. "It's a straight shot from Kilt Rock south to Portree. The others might not like—"

"I'll make it up to them," Kira exclaimed, her heart soaring. "I'll never be late getting back to the bus again, and I promise not to ask for extra time in the bookshops."

"Just have a care." He looked at her, his brow still furrowed. "Wrath is an odd place, true as I'm here. I'd ne'er forgive myself if harm came to you."

Then he was gone, striding away and herding his charges into the bus as if he needed a speedy departure to keep him from changing his mind.

A distinct possibility, she was sure.

So she didn't release her breath until the big blue and white Highland Coach Tours bus rumbled away, finally disappearing around a bend in the road.

Alone at last, she allowed herself one doubtful glance at the nearest sheep pats, certain they'd suddenly increased in size and number. But she steeled herself as quickly, putting back her shoulders and lifting her chin. Making ready for the long march across the grassy field to get to the ruins.

Ahead of her was an unhurried world of hills, clouds, and mist.

Mist?

She blinked. She'd heard how quickly Highland weather could change, but this was ridiculous.

She blinked again, but the mist remained.

The day had definitely darkened, turning just a shade uninviting.

She peered over her shoulder, scanning the road behind her, but the sky in that direction stretched as clear and bright blue as before. Cozy-looking threads of smoke still rose from the chimney of a croft house not far from where the bus had parked, and if the sea glittered any more brilliantly, she'd need sunglasses.

Only Castle Wrath had fallen into shadow, its eerie

silhouette silent against waters now the color of cold, dark slate.

She took a deep breath and kept her chin lifted. Already, sea mist was dampening her cheeks, and the chill wetness in the air made the day smell peaty and old.

No, not old.

Ancient.

She started forward, refusing to be unsettled. She liked ancient, and this was just the kind of atmosphere she'd come to Scotland to see.

So why were her palms getting clammy? Her nerves starting to go all jittery and her mouth bone-dry?

She frowned. Bedwells weren't known for being fainthearts.

But *bone* hadn't been a very wise word choice.

It summoned Wee Hughie's tales about wailing, foot-stomping ghosts, but she pushed his words from her mind, choosing instead to dwell on the other images he'd conjured. Namely those of the great and powerful MacDonald chieftains, preferring to think of them as they'd been in their glory days rather than as they might be now, skulking about in the ruined shell of their onetime stronghold, bemoaning the passing centuries, their ancient battle cries lost on the wind.

Thinking that she could use a battle cry of her own, she marched on, looking out for sheep pats and huddling deeper into her jacket.

Scudding mists blew across her vision, and the pounding of the waves grew louder with each forward step. She could still see Castle Wrath looming on the far side of the high, three-sided promontory, but the rocky spit of land leading out to it was proving more narrow and steep than she'd judged.

Kira's heart began to pound. She quickened her pace, her excitement cresting when she caught her first glimpse of Wrath Bay and the deep grooves scoring the smooth, flat rocks of its surf-beaten shore.

Just as Wee Hughie MacSporran had said.

Then she was there, the heart of the ruins opening up before her. All thought of the medieval landing beach and its ancient keel marks vanished from her mind.

A labyrinth of tall rough-hewn walls, uneven ground, and tumbled stone, the ruins stopped her heart. The remains of the curtain walls clung to the cliff edges, windswept and dangerous, but what really caught her eye was the top half of an imposing medieval gateway.

Still bearing traces of a beautifully incised Celtic design, the gateway raged up out of the rubble, its grass-grown arch framing the sea and the jagged black rocks of the nearby island she knew to be Wrath Isle.

Without doubt, she'd never seen a wilder, more romantic place. A onetime Norse fortalice. Vikings once walked and caroused here.

Real live *Vikings*.

Big, brawny men shouting praise to Thor and Odin as they raised brimming drinking horns and gnawed on huge ribs of fire-roasted beef.

Kira drew a deep breath, trying hard not to pinch herself.

Especially when she thought about the Norsemen's successors. Wee Hughie MacSporran's Celtic warrior chieftains, the kind of larger-than-life heroes she could only dream about.

Bold and virile men who could only belong to a place like this.

A place of myth and legend.

Looking around, she was sure of it.

Shifting curtains of mist swirled everywhere, drifting low across the overgrown grass and fallen masonry, softening the edges and making it seem as if she were seeing the world through a translucent silken veil.

And what a world it was.

The constant roar of the sea and the loud *whooshing* of the wind were fitting, too, giving the place an otherworldly feel she would never have experienced on a clear, sun-bright day.

She set down her lunch packet and stepped into the sheltering lee of a wall, not quite ready to spoil the moment.

Nor was she reckless.

Rough bent grass and fallen stones weren't the only things littering the ground that must've once been the castle's inner bailey. Winking at her from a wild tangle of nettles and bramble bushes, deep crevices opened darkly into the earth. Silent abysses of blackness that could only be the underground passages, stairwells, and vaults she'd been warned about.

Almost tasting her need to explore those abysses, she took a deep breath, drinking in chill air ripe with the tang of the sea and damp stone. She felt an irresistible shimmer of excitement she couldn't quite put her finger on.

She pressed her hands against the stones, splaying her fingers across their cold and gritty surface, not at all surprised to sense a faint vibration humming somewhere deep inside them.

She felt a distant thrumming real enough to send a chill through her and even lead her to imagine the sounds of loud masculine laughter and song. The sharp blasts of a trumpeter's fanfare. Barking dogs and a series of thin, high-pitched squeals.

Excited *feminine* squeals.

Kira frowned and took her hands off the wall.

The sounds stopped at once.

Or, she admitted, she recognized them for what they'd been: the rushing of the wind and nothing else. Even if the tingles spilling through her said otherwise.

An odd prickling sensation she knew wouldn't stop until she'd peered into one of the earth-and-rubble-clogged gaps in Castle Wrath's bailey.

Her lunch forgotten, she considered her options. She wasn't about to march across the nettle-filled courtyard and risk plunging into some bottomless medieval pit, meeting an early grave. Or, at the very least, twisting an ankle and ruining the remainder of her trip. But the shell of one of Castle Wrath's great drum-towers stood slightly tilted to her left, a scant fifty feet away.

Best of all, in the shadow of the tower's hulk she could make out the remains of a stairwell. A dark, downward spiraling turnpike stair that filled her with such a sense of wonder she didn't realize she'd moved until she found herself hovering on its weathered threshold. An impenetrable blackness stared back at her, so deep that its dank, earthy-smelling chill lifted the fine hairs on her nape.

Something was down there.

Something more than nerves and imagination.

The sudden tightness in her chest and the cold hard knot forming in her belly assured her of it. As did the increasing dryness of her mouth and the racing of her pulse, the faint flickering torchlight filling the stairwell.

Flickering torchlight?

Kira's eyes flew wide, her jaw dropping. She grabbed the edges of the crumbling stairwell's doorway, holding tight, but there could be no mistake. The light was flaring brighter now, shining hotly and illuminating the cold stone walls and the impossibly medieval-looking Highland chieftain staring up at her from the bottom of the stairs, the vaulted hallows of his crowded, well-lit great hall looming behind him.

That it was *his* hall couldn't be questioned.

She'd bet her plane ticket back to Newark that a more lairdly man had never walked the earth. Nor a sexier one. A towering raven-haired giant, he was clad in rough-looking tartan and calfskin, and hung about with gleaming mail and bold Celtic jewelry. Power and sheer male animal magnetism rolled off him, stealing her breath and weakening her knees.

Making her question her sanity.

Perhaps someone on the bus tour had slipped something into her tepid breakfast tea.

Something that would make her hallucinate.

Imagine the hunky Highlander who couldn't really be there.

Just as she couldn't really be hearing the sounds of medieval merrymaking.

Feasting noises, she was sure. The same raucous male laughter and bursts of trumpet fanfares and song she'd heard earlier, the collective din of a celebrating throng—not that she cared.

A marching brass band could stomp past and blast her right off the cliff-top. As long as *he* stood glaring up at her, the world as Kira Bedwell had known and loved it ceased to exist.

And he *was* glaring.

Every gorgeous muscle-ripped inch of him.

He locked gazes with her, glowering at her as only a fierce, hot-eyed, broadsword-packing Highlander could do. A truth she hadn't known until this very moment, but one she would take with her to her grave.

If she lived that long.

The too-dishy-to-be-real Highlander might have a patent on sex appeal, but he was also armed to the teeth. A huge two-handed sword hung from a wide leather shoulder belt slung across his chest, and a glittering array of other equally wicked-looking medieval weapons peeked at her from beneath his voluminous tartan plaid. Not that he needed such a display of steel. O-o-oh, no. Such a man probably uprooted trees with one hand for exercise.

Big trees.

And at the moment, she felt incredibly treelike.

She swallowed hard, pressing her fingers more firmly against the stone edges of the door arch. Any further movement wasn't an option. Her legs had gone all rubbery, and even if she could have taken a step backward, away from the opening, she just knew he would charge up the stairs if she did.

Stairs that no longer looked worn and crumbling

but new and unlittered, wholly free of fallen rubble
and earth or the thick weeds that had clogged the top
of the stairwell mere moments before.

She squeezed her eyes shut and opened them again.
"This can't be happening," she gasped, jerking her
hands off the now-smooth edges of the door arch.

"Nay, it canna be," the Highlander agreed, his voice
a deep velvety burr as he angled his head at her, his
gaze narrowing suspiciously. "Though I would know
why it is!"

The words held a bold challenge, the suspicion in
his eyes changing swiftly to something else.

Something darkly seductive and dangerous.

"Och, aye, I would hear the why of it." He tossed
back his hair, the look he was giving her almost a
physical touch. "Nor am I one to no' welcome a
comely lass into my hall—howe'er strange her raiments."

"Raiments?" Kira blinked.

"Your hose, sweetness." His gaze dropped to her
legs, lingering there just long enough to make her
squirm. "I've ne'er seen the like on a woman. No'
that I'm complaining."

Kira swallowed. "Y-you can't be . . . anything.
You're not even there."

"Ho! So you say?" He looked down at his plaid,
flicking its edge. "If my plaid's real, than I vow I am,
too. Nay, lass, 'tis *you* who canna be here."

"You're a ghost."

He laughed. "Since I haven't died yet, that's no'
possible."

"I was told anything is possible in Scotland and now
I believe it!" Kira stared at him. "Whatever you are."

He flashed a roguish grin and started forward, mounting the tight, winding steps with long, easy strides. " 'Tis laird of this keep I am." His deep burr filled the stairwell, rich, sonorous, and real as the chill bumps on her arms. "I'm also a man—as I can prove if you wish!"

Reaching her, he seized her shoulders, his grip strong and firm, warm even through the thickness of her jacket. He stepped close, so near that the hilt of his sword pressed into her hip. "Now, lass," he said, his gaze scorching her, "tell me. Do I feel like a ghost?"

Kira sucked in a breath. "No, but—"

"Exactly." His mouth curved with a triumphant smile. " 'Tis you who is out of place, no' me. Though I vow you dinna feel like a ghost either."

Then his smile went wicked, his eyes darkening as he pulled her tighter against him, lowering his head as if to give her a hard, bruising kiss. Instead, his lips only brushed hers lightly, just barely touching her before he disappeared into darkness.

Kira screamed, but only the wind and the crashing sea answered her.

That, and the stairwell's emptiness. The same total blackness, icy cold and dank-smelling, that she'd been staring into all along.

Her imagination had run away with her. There could be no other explanation. She'd wished for a Highlander with a wolfish smile and a honeyed tongue, and so she'd conjured him.

Simple as that.

She would just lean against the ruined wall of the drum-tower and wait until her knees stopped knocking before she gathered her untouched lunch packet and returned to the road to wait for the tour bus. It wasn't until she was halfway there that she realized she'd picked up more than her picnic goods.

Her heart still beating wildly, she looked at her left hand, slowly uncurling her fingers to reveal the squarish clump of granite she must've grabbed when she'd held so tight to the crumbling edges of the stairwell's door arch.

She frowned.

The stone seemed to stare at her in mute reproach, but rather than taking it back, she hurried on, clutching the stone like a precious treasure.

And to her it was.

A memento of her Highlander.

With a sigh, she paused a few feet from the road, looking back over her shoulder at the ruins. The sun had burst through the clouds, burning off the mist and gilding the tumbled walls with the bright blue and gold of the late-spring afternoon. Even the wind was lessening and the dark, jagged cliffs of Wrath Isle no longer looked quite so menacing.

The ruined castle no longer a home to ghosts.

An empty shell was all it was, she made herself believe, choosing as well to ignore the thickness in her throat and the stinging heat jabbing the backs of her eyes.

Whoever or whatever he'd been, her hunky Highlander couldn't have been real.

Never in all her dreams.

Chapter 1

Kira Bedwell had a dirty little secret.

A towering plaid-hung secret, masterful and passionate, impossibly addictive.

Maddening, too, for he came to her only in her dreams.

Deliciously heated dreams that called to her now, teasing the edges of her sleep and flooding her with tingling, languorous warmth until she began to stretch and roll beneath the bedcovers. She reached for an extra pillow, hugging it close as the walls of her apartment's tiny bedroom shimmered and shimmied, taking on a silvery translucence. As always, her pulse leapt at the transformation, the rippling luminescence giving her a view of the cliffs and the sea, a sheep-grazed hill and tumbled, mist-clad ruins.

Ancient ruins, well loved and remembered.

Kira sighed, her heart catching. She bit her lip and splayed her fingers across the cool linen of her bed-

sheets. She could imagine him so well, her darkly seductive Highlander. If she concentrated, she could
almost see him in the shadows, waiting. Mist swirled
around his tall, strapping form, a strong wind tearing
at his plaid and whipping his raven hair. His hot gaze
would make her burn, the raw sensuality streaming
off him flowing over her like pure, molten lust, rousing her.

He'd step closer then, a slow smile curving his lips,
the sheer eroticism of him and his own insatiable need
almost letting her forget she'd fallen asleep in her
clothes.

Again.

The third night in a week, if she wished to keep
note, which she didn't. Once was more than enough
and three times bordered on seriously bothersome.

If she weren't mistaken, this time she'd even kept
on her shoes!

She frowned and flipped onto her side. Yearning
still swept her, but she cracked an eye, her dreamspun
ardor vanishing as she peered into the darkness.

Her silent bedroom stared back at her, cramped,
cluttered, and shabby chic. Pathetically empty of hot-
eyed Scotsmen. But the pale glimmer of a new moon
fell across the little polished brass carriage clock on
her bedside table, the piece's stark black hands showing the hour as three a.m. Give or take ten minutes.

She blew out a frustrated breath. Like so many of
her carefully accumulated treasures, the antique clock
wasn't perfect, keeping time to its own rhythm. Sometimes accurate, sometimes ahead or behind, and every
so often not at all.

Like her dreams.

They, too, couldn't be forced.

Aidan MacDonald, medieval clan chieftain extraordinaire, slipped into her fantasies only when it suited him.

Or so Kira thought.

Just as she assumed her bold dream lover could only be the MacDonalds' legendary leader. After her one trip to Scotland years ago, she'd spent months researching Clan Donald and Castle Wrath, finally determining Aidan as *her* Highlander.

The tantalizingly gorgeous Celtic he-god she'd glimpsed so briefly.

And never forgotten.

A man of any less mythic status couldn't possibly invade her sleep and ravish her with such wild, heart-pounding sex. Just the imagined scent of him made her dizzy with longing. Remembering the cool silk of his glossy, shoulder-length hair, or the hardness of his muscles, was enough to make her breath quicken. Thinking about his kisses, the skillful glide of his hands on her body, did things to her she never would have believed possible.

Watching him stride toward her, his sword hung low on his hip and a predatory gleam in his eye, positively melted her.

He was the essence of her deepest, darkest fantasies.

Her secret lover, he'd ruined her for all others.

Kira sighed, her fingers curling into the bedcovers. Warmth pulsed through her just thinking about him. More than just a fantasy lover, he had influenced her life in ways she'd never have believed possible. He'd initiated her into her special gift of far-seeing, the ability to catch a visual or mental image of the distant past. An inherited talent kept secret in her family and one she hadn't been aware of at all until the day she'd hoped to picnic at Castle Wrath and had peered down a ruined stairwell, looking straight into Aidan's torchlit hall and his dark, smoldering stare.

Kira shivered. She wanted that stare on her now.

Ached to see him.

Instead, nothing stirred except a chill wind whistling around her old brick apartment house. The faint *tap-tap* of tree branches against her window. All was still and quiet. Through a chink in the curtains she could see that the sky was low with clouds, the night cold and damp.

She stared out the window and sighed. Any other time she would have smiled. She liked cold and damp. Throw in a handful of mist and a bit of soft, thin rain and her imagination could transport her to Scotland.

That other world where she longed to be, not here listening to the night wind sighing around Aldan, Pennsylvania's seen-better-days Castle Apartments, but hearing Hebridean gales blowing in from the sea. Long Atlantic breakers crashing on jagged black rocks.

Rugged cliffs and slate-colored seas, the tingle of salt mist damping her cheeks.

That was what she wanted.

Needed.

Unfortunately, on her budget, the closest she could hope to get to Scotland was dusting the framed tea towel of Edinburgh's Royal Mile that hung above her sagging sofa. Frustration welling, she twisted onto her side and pulled a pillow over her head. Truth was, she cherished that tea towel. Like the small tartan-covered armchair beside her bed, she'd found the tea towel at a garage sale. Along with the worthless wooden frame she'd used to mount it.

A thin purse sparked creativity.

And penning supposedly true tales of the strange and inexplicable for *Destiny Magazine*, a popular monthly focused on all things supernatural, didn't generate enough income for luxuries.

Even if some of her stories were fact.

Like her most recent. The reason she'd barricaded herself inside her postage-stamp-sized apartment and wasn't answering her phone or e-mail.

Kira groaned and knocked the pillow aside. Impossible, how a mere week could turn someone's life upside down. One excited phone call to *Destiny* from a group of wannabe archaeologists, and there she was, using her far-seeing ability to help them locate the remains of a Viking longboat resting proudly at the bottom of a river-bisected Cape Cod lake, her discovery proving beyond a doubt that Norsemen were the first to land on the New World's shores. Overnight, she'd become everyone's most celebrated darling.

Or their worst nightmare.

Depending on whether one favored horn-helmeted sea marauders or the tried and true. Either way, even if *Destiny* raised her salary to match her sudden and unwanted notoriety, the proponents of a certain Mediterranean mariner weren't too keen to see their hero's glory dinted.

A shudder rippled down Kira's spine and she

clutched the covers tighter. She'd lost track of how many historical societies wanted her head, each one raking her over the coals for her blasphemy.

Christopher Columbus may have died centuries ago, but his spirit was alive and well in America.

His fans active.

Out there, and sharpening their claws.

She frowned. No, a raise wasn't going to help her. The means to purchase an air ticket meant tiddly-squat if she ended up tarred and feathered before she could ever reach the airport.

Not to mention a Glasgow-bound plane.

Judging by the hate mail she'd been receiving, such a mob might even seize and burn her passport. Already, she'd found two nails thrust into her car tires, and some exceptionally witty soul who clearly lived in her apartment building had smeared some kind of unidentifiable goo on her doorknob. Icky, foul-smelling goo. Kira swiped an annoying strand of hair off her forehead. At least fretting about such nonsense took her mind off him.

The gorgeous, incredible-in-bed medieval High-lander she shouldn't be fantasizing about when she was in a pickle.

She sighed and shut her eyes, doing her best to forget him. The alpha Gael who not only could melt her with one heated, sensuous glance but knew better than any real man how to ignite her passion.

A fool's passion, imagined and *un*real, regardless of how exquisite.

She pressed a hand to her forehead and massaged her temples. The broadcast reporters and television cameras camped in the Castle Apartments parking lot *were* real and she'd had enough of them. As the daughter of a ceramic tile salesman and a high school art teacher, she wasn't used to the limelight.

Nor did she like it.

Especially when they all seemed determined to make sport of her.

"Sleep." She breathed the word like a mantra, repeating it in her mind as she rubbed two fingers between her brows. A good eight hours of oblivion was what she needed.

Maybe then she'd wake refreshed, the snarl of television crews and other suchlike long-noses gone from outside her apartment's ground-floor windows, the world a new and bright place, free of problems and cares.

Yes, she decided, settling an arm over her head, sleep was just what she needed.

Lass . . . your raiments.

Deep and rich, the mellifluous words seduced the darkness, pure Highland and buttery smooth. Familiar in ways that slid right through her sleep to curl low in her belly, warming and melting her. Making her tingle and sizzle in all the right places.

Aidan MacDonald's sinfully sexy burr could do that.

That, and many other things.

All delicious.

Her eyes snapped open. He stood in the dim moonlight near her window, his hands on his hips and his head angled as he looked at her. All male dominance and breathtakingly handsome, he caught and held her gaze, the heat of his own already stroking her, making her burn.

"The raiments," he said again, stepping closer. "Have done with them."

Kira's breath caught. Her heart leapt. Somewhere in the distance a siren wailed. Not that she cared. Her body refused to move. She could only stare, desire and need streaking through her, embarrassment flaming the back of her neck, scalding her cheeks.

He wanted her naked, as was his wont.

But unless she was mistaken, getting that way might dampen his ardor.

She was wearing her comfy granny-style panties. High-waisted, white cotton, and boring. Equally bad, she had on her favorite oversized training suit. The baggy one with the little tear in the knee.

She swallowed. "I wasn't expecting you tonight . . . It's been a while."

He shrugged. "I've had matters to see to," he said, flicking a speck of lint off his plaid. "That doesn't mean I haven't hungered for you. I have, and my need is great."

"I missed you, too," she stalled, trying to calculate how quickly she could rid herself of her less-than-flattering clothes and assume a seductive pose.

In dreams, anything should be possible, but her limbs remained stubbornly frozen, her fumbling fingers impossibly clumsy.

He started toward her, his own hands already unbuckling his sword belt. His eyes narrowing, he paused just long enough to set aside his great brand and whip off his plaid. Then, as was the way with sexual fantasies, he flashed a smile and was naked, without even having to stoop to yank off his rough-leathered brogues.

"Ahhh . . ." Kira's palms began to dampen. "Maybe tonight isn't a good time."

Towering over the bed now, he cocked a brow. "Sweetness, I've told you," he began, his gaze flicking the length of her, "*any* time we have is good." For an instant his face clouded. "It isn't always easy to find you." He folded his arms, looking serious. "I dinna ken what powers let us come together. Only that we must seize the moments we have."

Kira swallowed, her heart pounding. "But?"

"But you know I have ne'er cared for your way of dress." His eyes narrowed on her sweatshirt. " 'Tis passing strange."

Kira burrowed deeper into the covers. Wait till he saw her granny panties!

"Clothes shouldn't matter in dreams." She met his gaze, her heart still hammering. "Besides, they're all I have—"

"You have an . . . *abundance*." He reached for the covers and whipped them off the bed, some Highland sleight of hand or dream-inspired magic leaving her unclothed.

Just as naked as he was.

She blinked. So much for cotton underwear and baggy sweatpants.

He looked at her, the covers dangling from his hand, her clothes nowhere in sight, and an expression of intense satisfaction on his handsome face.

"That's better," he said, letting the blanket fall.

No, it's better than better, Kira wanted to say, but the words lodged in her throat. She moistened her lips, her gaze flicking over his magnificence. Her heart swelled, her chest tightening even as her tender places went soft and achy. Just looking at him tantalized her. Need flamed through her, throbbing and urgent as his dark eyes heated, flaring with passion as they swept her own nakedness.

"Sweet lass, were you not a *bruadar*, I'd keep you in my bed for a sennight." He reached to smooth strong fingers along the curve of her hip. "Nay, seven days wouldn't sate me. I'd double that, ravishing you again and again for a fortnight."

Kira sighed, her limbs going liquid.

But one thing he'd said troubled her. A word she didn't know.

"A broo-e-tar?" She had trouble speaking, the effect of his touch and his rich burr, working the usual magic on her. "You've never called me that before."

"Mayhap I do not speak the word for I wish it were not so. *Bruadar* is the Gaelic for a dream. I would have you as a full-blooded woman, hot and alive in my arms." He folded those arms now, his eyes darkening. "Hot, alive, and mine."

"I am yours." Kira's heart pounded, the truth of those three words slashing across her soul. The impossibility of them damned her. "You are the dream," she argued, meeting his stare full on, her own challenging him to deny it. "You're here in my bedroom. I'm not in yours."

"Say you?" One raven brow arced in a look of sheer male authority. "Yon walls look like mine to me," he said, flashing a glance at the windows.

Windows no longer there.

Kira gulped, unable to deny that her windows were gone. Likewise her carefully sewn tartan window dressings and even the entire wall. In their place, proud whitewashed stones gleamed with the soft glow of candles, and the tasseled edges of a richly colored tapestry fluttered gently in the draught of an unshuttered window.

A tall arch-topped window.

Very medieval-y.

Definitely not hers.

Her eyes widened. She could even feel the chill night breeze here in her bed. Catch the brisk tang of the sea; the pounding of waves onto a fearsome, rock-strewn shore. Then the illusion faded, leaving only the fragile luminescence of her dream, her plaid-patterned curtains faintly visible again, staring mutely from behind the shimmering silver. And instead of the roar of Hebridean waves, she heard only the tic-ticking of her clock.

The familiar light branch scratching at the glass of her apartment windows.

Irrefutable evidence of just where she was and that despite the intensity of his stare, she was indeed only dreaming.

"Dinna fash yourself, lass. It doesna matter. No' where we are." He looked at her, his gaze going deep. "All that matters is that I want you. And"—he paused, desire blazing in his eyes—"that you want me. You do, don't you?"

"O-o-oh, yes." She reached for him and he obliged her, gathering her close for a hungry, lip-bruising kiss. Tightening his arms around her, he plundered her mouth, the mastery of his tongue blotting out everything but sensation.

The wild thundering of her heart and the slight creaking of her secondhand bed when he stretched out beside her, the full hot and hard length of him pressed skin to skin against her own trembling softness.

The creak made her frown, its intrusion reminding her this was all fantasy. A dream that could be so easily shattered—and often was.

She moaned. Determined to hold on to him as long as possible, she slid her hands up his powerful back, gripping his shoulders as he rolled on top of her, that very special hot, hard, and glorious part of him already probing her, seeking their bliss.

Not breaking their kiss, he slipped a hand between them to cup her breast. His fingers splayed over her fullness, teased her swollen nipple. "You are mine," he growled, his breath warm against her lips. "I will ne'er let you go. No' if I must search to the ends of the earth to find you."

Something inside her broke on his words and she clung to him, returning his kiss with all the passion she had, refusing to accept the futility of his vow.

Aidan the magnificent, as she sometimes thought of him, could search for her through all time, even turn the world on end, and never would he find her.

Not really.

Too many centuries stretched between them.

That truth scalding the backs of her eyes, she opened her mouth wider beneath his, welcoming the mad thrust of his tongue, needing the intimacy of his soul-searing kisses.

Needing all of him.

Understanding that need as only he could, he deepened the kiss, swirling his tongue over and around hers as he eased himself inside her, the silky-smooth glide of each rock-hard inch deeper into her eager, clutching heat sending waves of pleasure spilling through her.

She matched his thrusts, losing herself to the elemental fury of their joining, reveling in the sexy Gaelic love words he breathed against her lips. Dark, lusty-sounding words, full of an untamed, earthy wildness that thrilled her, his every passionate utterance driving her closer and closer to an explosive, shattering release.

Her own cries loud in her head, she writhed and arched her hips, her need breaking even as her cries turned shrill. Sharp, jangling cries so annoying and harsh they could never be coming from her throat.

Not now, on the verge of her climax.

The noise continued, growing insistent, seeming louder with each passion-zapping shrill until she came awake with a start and recognized the sound for what it was.

Her telephone.

Kira groaned.

Aidan was nowhere to be seen.

If he'd been there at all—a peek beneath the covers proved she was still wearing her comfy training suit. The whole grungy works, complete with tennies. Worse, if her heavy-eyed grogginess and the bands of light sneaking in past her drawn curtains meant anything, she'd slept way too late.

Almost afraid to look, she groped for her little bedside clock, glanced at it, and then groaned again. Ten thirty a.m. A new record, even for her, notorious *un*-morning person that she was.

And still the phone rang.

Wishing she'd slept with earplugs, she scrambled to a sitting position and grabbed the phone. Squinting at the caller ID display, she almost put down the receiver.

Much as she loved her, her mother wasn't someone she cared to talk to before at least two cups of coffee.

Strong black coffee, the kind you could stand a spoon in.

Bracing herself, she drew a deep breath, determined to sound awake. "Hello?"

"Carter Williams called, dear," her mother gushed. "He wants to speak with you." She paused for a breath and Kira could hear her excitement bubbling through the phone line. "I told him we could have coffee at three. Here at the house. He—"

"Wait a minute." Kira sat up, warning bells ringing in her head. "Who is Carter Williams?"

"Kira." Her mother gave an exasperated sigh. "Would I invite him over if he weren't important?"

No, she wouldn't, but Kira wasn't about to point that out to her.

"Who is he?" she repeated instead.

Blanche Bedwell hesitated.

A pause that made Kira's stomach clench.

The only men wishing to speak to her lately were icky-pot media hounds. Worse, her mother not only worried about status, she was also a notorious matchmaker who believed every female under thirty should be married and having babies.

Like Kira's sisters.

"Well? Who is Carter Williams?" Kira was sure she didn't want to know.

"He's with the *Aldan Bee.* A nice young man who's going places. I play bridge with his mother. He only wants to ask you a few questions about your Viking ship."

"It isn't *my* Viking ship. It's what's left of a foundered Norse longship and a few ancient mooring holes and other artifacts that prove—"

"Whatever." Kira could almost see her mother waving an airy hand. "Carter Williams might give you an in at the *Bee* if you—"

"An in at the *Bee*?" The tops of Kira's ears started getting warm. "I don't want to work for the *Bee*."

"It would be a real job, dear."

"I have a job." Kira glanced at the papers and books piled on her tiny desk across the room.

Research for her next assignment: *My Three-Month Marriage to a Yeti.*

Suppressing a groan, she threw back the covers and stood. "*Destiny Magazine* pays well enough for me to cover my monthly bills. And"—she shoved a hand through her mussed hair—"writing for them lets me stretch my imagination. The readers who buy the magazine are entertained and I can pay my rent."

"Making up tales of alien abductions."

"If need be . . . yes." Kira shot another glance at her stack of Yeti books, not about to admit that she, too, was growing weary of penning such drivel.

But not weary enough to barter her soul by working with the kind of wolf pack presently prowling the Castle Apartments parking lot. They were still there, the snarkies, as a furtive glance out her window revealed. If she weren't mistaken, they might even have increased in number overnight.

Like the plague of the giant toadstools she'd written about a few years ago.

Cringing at the memory, she turned away from the window and dropped onto the edge of her bed, not knowing whether to laugh or cry.

"Kira, child, Carter Williams is—"

"Not all my stories are about aliens," Kira cut in, thoughts of aliens and mutant toadstools making her testy. "The Norse longboat is an important discovery. The excavation has drawn some of the nation's top archaeologists. *Destiny* understands my special gift. No other magazine or paper would let me—"

"Carter Williams is single."

That did it.

Kira shot to her feet. "And so am I. Happily so."

Her gaze slid to the glittery clump of granite sitting in a place of honor beside her computer's keyboard. At once, Aidan's face flashed before her and she could almost hear his deep burr again.

You are mine.

I will ne'er let you go. No' if I must search to the ends of the earth to find you.

Crossing the room, she picked up the stone. "Carter Williams will just have to do without me," she said, closing her fingers around the piece of granite. "You know I've gone off men for a while. I told you that the last time you tried to set me up with someone."

Her mother made an impatient sound. "There was nothing wrong with Lonnie Ward. Your father says he's certain Lonnie will be the next manager at the Tile Bonanza. You could have done worse."

Kira glanced at the ceiling. "Lonnie Ward doesn't like dogs." She tightened her fingers around the granite. "You should have seen him brushing at his pants after a dog ran up to him and sniffed him in the park. You know I could never be happy with a dog-hater."

"You don't have a dog, dear."

"I will someday."

As soon as she didn't live in an apartment the size of a fishbowl.

Her mother drew a breath. "I believe Carter Williams has a dog. I've seen him about town with a spaniel. And his mother has two—"

"It won't work, Mom." Kira puffed her bangs off her forehead. "I'm not biting."

"You're still mooning over that Highland chieftain," her mother said, and Kira almost dropped the phone. She'd never told anyone about her dreams. Not even her sisters. And especially not her mother. "It isn't healthy to obsess over someone who lived centuries ago, poring through history books and decorating your apartment like the set of *Brigadoon*."

"Lots of people love Scotland," Kira returned, relief sweeping her that her mother hadn't somehow guessed the truth about Aidan. "Even Kerry and Lindsay devour romance novels set there."

Blanche Bedwell sighed. "Your sisters are also well-balanced young women who have other interests."

Kira rolled her eyes. Her younger sister, Kerry's, only goal in life seemed to be squeezing into clothes too tight for her under-five-foot Rubenesque figure, eating sweets, and producing babies. And her older sister, Lindsay, was a hypochondriac tree hugger and such a clinging vine, Kira wondered how she managed to spend enough time away from their parents to run her own household, much less raise her two children.

"You should follow in your sisters' footsteps," her mother added. "Marry and raise a family."

Kira set down her stone and glanced at the drawn curtains. She couldn't see them, but she could feel the Carter Williamses of the world out there, clogging the parking lot, waiting for her to show herself.

She shuddered, her stomach knotting at the thought of facing them. But then she put her shoulders back and stood straighter. Silly or not, she knew Aidan wouldn't approve of a spineless woman.

Not in his century and not in her dreams.

As soon as she'd showered and had her coffee, she'd go outside and tell the long-noses to buzz off. Find someone else to be the centerpiece of their snarkfest.

She wouldn't cooperate. Nor would she be intimidated.

"Perhaps you're right—in part," she admitted. "Maybe I do need other interests. But don't forget, it was your own great-aunt Minnie's *inheritance* that got me into all this." She left out that her life might've taken an easier course if her mother hadn't kept mum about some females in the family having far-seeing talents.

A trait that had lain dormant for generations and that Blanche Bedwell had hoped would never surface again.

Unfortunately—or not—it had, and its startling arrival that day at Wrath Isle had changed Kira's life.

"Great-aunt Minnie lived in a different time," her mother sniffed. "People were more impressionable then. You have the means to channel your talents into a more sensible direction."

Kira bristled. "Maybe I like the direction I've taken. I'm interested in the paranormal, though I wouldn't mind a better-paying job where I wouldn't have to spend half my time making up nonsense about angels amongst us and Bigfoot sightings. It's the *true* supernatural that fascinates me. Ghosts, reincarnation, that sort of thing."

Her mother sighed.

Ignoring her, Kira began pacing. "I'd like to work quietly and behind the scenes, without being plunged into the limelight."

"Limelight isn't necessarily bad," her mother countered. "Such attention could draw the notice of—"

"Just the kind of man I'd not be interested in," Kira finished for her. "Not if flash and brass topped his list of the important things in life."

Her mother tsk-tsked. "You've set your sights too high, my dear. Phemie's stepdaughter is the only soul I've ever heard of who married a Scottish laird and went off to live happily ever after in a castle. Such things don't happen every day."

No, they didn't. Kira knew that.

The quick flash of green-tinged heat jabbing needles in her heart proved it.

A Scottish laird and living in the Highlands. In a real castle. She shot a glance at her desk, the silver-framed photo of the ruins of Castle Wrath claiming pride of place right next to her piece of granite. Her heart squeezed and the green-tinted heat began spreading through her chest, making each breath difficult.

"Phemie and the girl's father went over to see the couple last year," her mother was saying. "Though

Phemie couldn't stomach sleeping in the castle, saying it was too damp and musty and full of ghosts.
She—"

"Phemie as in Euphemia Ross?" Disbelief washed
over Kira. "The sharp-tongued little wisp of a woman
in your bridge club? The one everyone calls the Cairn
Avenue shrew?"

"Now, Kira." Blanche Bedwell used her most pla-
cating tone. "She's Euphemia *McDougall* these days
and, yes, her stepdaughter, Mara, married a real live
Highland chieftain. Sir Alexander Douglas, I believe
Phemie called him. Their castle is somewhere near a
place called Uban or something."

"Oban," Kira corrected her. "The gateway to the
Hebrides. It's on Scotland's west coast. My tour years
ago stopped there. We had a whole hour's look at
Dunstaffnage Castle."

"Well, dear, if ever you go back, I'm sure Phemie
would give you Mara's phone number and address.
She'd surely be pleased to see you. Just—"

She broke off as the doorbell trilled in the back-
ground. "That will be Lindsay. She made a batch of
organic brownies for your father. Call if you need
me."

"I will," Kira said as her mother rang off.

Not that her mother—or anyone—could help her
with what she needed.

Knowing she couldn't even help herself in that regard, she put down the phone and began peeling off
her rumpled clothes, making for the bathroom. Naked,
she yanked back her thistle-covered shower curtain
and made to step beneath the steaming, pounding
spray.

Until her phone rang again. Pausing, she listened as her answering machine clicked on and *Destiny Magazine*'s executive editor's voice rose above the sound of running water, the man's tone giving her pause.

Dan Hillard sounded excited.

Kira, girl. His booming voice filled the bathroom. *I know you're in hiding and may even want to quit, but I've got a new assignment for you.*

"O-o-oh, no, you don't." Kira grabbed a towel and slung it around her as she hastened back into her bedroom to click off the machine. "Not for a while anyway."

This is one you won't want to miss, Dan's voice cajoled, almost as if he'd heard her. *It'll get you away from this media circus.*

Kira hesitated, her fingers hovering over the answering machine. Something in his voice was getting to her, making her heart skitter.

Faraway, Kira. All expenses paid.

She closed her eyes, breathed deeply, ready to reject—

Another voice broke in, interrupting Dan. *Come, lass, I'm waiting for you.*

Kira whirled around, the towel dropping to the floor. But only her empty bedroom stared back at her. Even if the echo of Aidan's voice still rang her in ears. Dark, rich, and sexy, and so full of longing her knees weakened.

He'd called to her.

She was certain of it.

Trembling, she stooped to pick up her towel, waiting for Dan to say something else. But he, too, was gone. Nothing remained of her boss or his cryptic message but the insistent little red light blinking on the answering machine.

Not that she needed to hear the words.

Her heart already knew.

She was going to Scotland.

Chapter 2

"Come, lass, I'm waiting for you. Burning for you."

Aidan MacDonald stood at the tall arch-topped window of his bedchamber, one hand clenched around his sword belt, the other clutching the tasseled edges of a richly embroidered tapestry proudly adorning his wall.

A brilliantly colored display of bold knights and fair, half-naked ladies romping in a wood, their erotic playfulness so explicitly depicted that he could scarce bear looking at it.

Truth be told, if his temper didn't soon improve, he might just yank the thing from the wall and send it sailing out his window.

Letting go of it, he shoved a hand through his hair and scowled. For well over a sennight, he'd been unable to reach his *bruadar*. The comely, well-made vixen of his dreams he'd glimpsed but once and ne'er been able to put from his mind.

Or his heart.

Not to mention what she did to his body.

"Hell and damnation." He blew out a breath, the scent and feel of her haunting him. A bittersweet torment so real and vibrant he hurt inside. Ached with a deep, lancing pain that knew no healing.

Not without her. Her soft, lush lips parting beneath his, her bountiful curves, warm, silken, and smooth, crushed tight against him as he held her in his arms. Made her his again and again.

This time never letting her go.

His scowl deepening, he curled his hands to fists. "I burn for you, lass," he growled, staring out at the cold, wind-whipped waters tossing so indifferently beneath his tower chamber's window. The jagged cliffs of nearby Wrath Isle, each frowning, black-glistening fissure suiting his mood, firing his frustration.

His fury at such a foul turn of fate.

Setting his jaw, he braced his hands on the edges of the window arch, leaning out so the night wind could cool him. Take the heat out of his face if not his blood.

"Saints, lass, I need you." The tightness in his chest let him know just how much. "For the love of the Ancient Ones, where-are-you?"

"She is long gone, that's what," a deep voice reproached from behind him. "God's eyes, man, what did you do to her?"

Aidan spun around. "What did I do to who?"

Tavish MacDonald merely cocked a brow. Aidan's most trusted friend and cousin—though some whispered half brother due to their strong resemblance—reached to pinch out the wicks of a hanging cresset lamp.

Aidan fixed him with a withering glare, trying for the life of him to recall if he'd e'er fallen so deep in his cups as to regale his friend with tales of *her*.

"You ought know better than to have a lamp burn-

ing so close to the window on such a windy night."
Tavish waved a hand through the dissipating smoke.
"As for who I meant"—he slid a narrow glance at
Aidan—" 'twas the MacLeod widow. She herself and
all her men."

Aidan relaxed. But only for a moment.

Turning back to the window, he clasped his hands
behind his back and drew a deep breath, his gaze on
the moon as it came and went through the clouds. He
might not have spilled his heart to Tavish in a long
ale-filled night in his great hall, but the departure of
the MacLeod woman presented an entirely different
kind of problem.

He'd counted on her men to help him scour the
hills and surrounding islands for Conan Dearg.

Trouble was, the price of Fenella MacLeod's men
and galleys was one he hadn't wished to pay.

"She left in a huff," Tavish informed him. "Away
with the tide and a scowl darker than some of your
own."

Aidan turned from the window and made straight
for a polished oak table across the room, well laden
with cold breast of chicken, oatcakes and cheese, and
a freshly filled ewer of ale. The table's offerings were
meant to be his evening repast, but circumstance had
stolen his appetite.

Truth was, if his days didn't soon take a better turn,
he might ne'er regain it.

"Lady Fenella was quick to offer aid." Tavish hovered behind him again. "Few in these isles have a
larger flotilla of longships. Or better-kept ones. Her
men are fierce and strong-armed. She would have
served you well."

Aidan almost spewed the ale he'd just poured for himself. Frowning in earnest now, he tossed down the rest in one great swig, slamming down the cup before he wheeled around.

"A God's name, Tavish! The lady *wished* to serve me." He glowered at his friend, felt heat surging up his neck. "She came here dressed in her bed-robe and naught else, her hair unbound and hanging to her hips."

Aidan clamped his mouth shut, decency keeping him from revealing how she'd swept into his bedchamber, shutting and bolting the door behind her, then flinging open her robe to display her full, large-nippled breasts and the tangle of thick jet-black curls topping her thighs.

"She made no mistake in letting me know why she came knocking on my door so late of an e'en." Aidan's brows knit together at the memory. "The woman was bold, Tavish. Overbold."

To his annoyance, rather than answer him, Tavish moved to the table, taking his time to help himself to a towering portion of sliced chicken and a brimming cup of ale.

Worse, he then lowered himself into a chair beside the fire, setting his victuals on a nearby stool before he stretched his long legs toward the warmth of the softly glowing peats. Looking irritatingly comfortable, he pinned Aidan with an all-too-suspicious stare.

"Fenella MacLeod is an ardent woman. Generously made and vigorous, her eyes *knowing*." Tavish leaned back in the chair, his own gaze too knowing for Aidan's liking. "Seldom have I seen a larger-breasted female. She has fine legs as well. I caught a glimpse of them once when she hitched up her skirts to board one of her late husband's galleys." He paused, lifting a hand to study his knuckles. "Indeed, many are the men in your hall who would bed her gladly."

Aidan quirked a brow. "Yourself included?"

"Nay, I, too, would have turned her from my door."

"I am glad to hear it. I would have doubted your honor otherwise." Aidan nodded, well pleased that his friend, too, drew the line at lying with the widow of a onetime ally. "Though I would not begrudge the men of my garrison such a dalliance. Not if the lady desired it."

"She comes and goes here at will, as you know. There are surely men amongst us eager enough to enjoy her charms. But the specter of her late husband is not the only reason you refused her."

Aidan lowered the cup he was about to refill. "What are you saying?"

Tavish looked up, his knuckles forgotten. "We were born and bred together," he said, holding Aidan's stare. "I know you as few men can claim. I know the depth of your honor, the privilege of your trust, and the pleasure of your friendship. I've seen the rage of your battle-fury, felt secure knowing you were at my back. And"—he paused, sitting forward in the chair—"I know you are a well-lusted man."

Aidan folded his arms. "So? I would not call myself a man were I not."

"To be sure, and neither would I," Tavish agreed, studying his fool knuckles again. "Nor," he added, looking up quickly, "did I abstain from the plump bed warmer that robber baron on Pabay thoughtfully provided for me when we sailed there to look for Conan Dearg."

Aidan frowned.

His friend's stare grew more penetrating. "Despite the roughness of the men, the wenches on that isle of marauders were more than pleasing. Frang the Fearless offered you the comeliest of them all, yet"—he paused, lifting his ale cup to take a sip without his gaze leaving Aidan's face—"if memory serves, you slept alone."

"Leave be," Aidan warned him, unpleasantly aware of the muscle beginning to twitch in his jaw. "I am thinking you could not have enjoyed your night on Pabay overmuch if you were so occupied observing mine!"

Seemingly calm as a spring morn, Tavish crossed his ankles. "Lady Fenella is not the first female to leave here looking soured in recent times," he drawled, brushing oatcake crumbs from his legs. "Nor have you tumbled Sinead, the Irish laundress, in longer than I can recall."

Aidan felt his face coloring. "Who I *tumble* and when is my own business and no one else's," he snapped, especially furious to be reminded of the flame-haired Irish girl. There was only one fiery-tressed lass he hungered for and it wasn't Castle Wrath's light-skirted laundress.

Tavish lifted his hands in surrender.

Mock surrender, Aidan was sure.

"I am only concerned for you," the lout declared, proving he wasn't about to let the matter lie. "You've been missed in the hall. Everyone knows you're up here brooding, locking yourself in your privy quarters or prowling the battlements at all hours, snarling like a chained beast."

I'm feeling like a chained beast! Aidan almost roared at him.

A deprived beast, trapped, ravenous, and filled with fury.

And about to do bodily harm to the one soul he loved above all men. If the great buffoon who looked so like him and knew his heart so well didn't soon have done with his badgering.

Turning away, lest his friend eye him any deeper than he already had, Aidan stalked back to the window and glared out at the expanse of dark water stretching between his own cliffs and the inky-black bulk of Wrath Isle. A strong swell was running, the swift current reminding him of the *other* matter weighing so heavily on his mind.

A matter he suddenly knew the answer to.

He almost smiled.

Under other circumstances, he would have.

As it was, it sufficed that he now had a clear enough head to squelch Tavish's concerns. Drawing a deep breath just in case he needed it, he returned to the fire, deliberately striking his most formidable pose and not for the first time silently thanking the saints for the one-inch advantage of height that he boasted over his friend.

"I haven't been brooding," he lied, blurting the untruth before the other had a chance to speak. "I've been thinking."

That, at least, was the truth.

Tavish looked at him, unblinking. "I daresay you have."

"Not about wenching." Another lie.

Knowing Tavish would see through a third, he put his shoulders back and shot another glance at the window, remembering well the treacherous journey the two of them had made to Wrath Isle but a few days before.

A dangerous crossing that had led to naught, their hours spent searching the isle's caves and tumbled ruins turning up little more than angry seabirds and moldering sheep bones. Of Conan Dearg, there'd been nary a sign.

It'd been an undertaking he'd meant to make alone, not wishing to endanger anyone else's life but his own. Tavish, great and beloved meddler that he was, had declared himself of another mind, vowing he'd swim after Aidan's boat if he didn't let him board.

And Tavish MacDonald, may the saints e'er bless him, always kept his word.

Reason enough to welcome his company, however grudgingly.

Looking at him now, Aidan heaved a great sigh and spoke the only part of his heart he was able to share. "It grieves me to have caused the MacLeod widow distress, but it troubles me more that we haven't yet found Conan Dearg," he said, his hand going almost absently to his sword hilt. "We've upturned every stone on this isle and others, even sailing to that notorious robbers' den, Pabay, then scouring every tainted, treacherous inch of Wrath Isle as well.

"So-o-o," he concluded, reaching down to scratch

his favorite dog, Ferlie, behind the ears when the great beast lumbered up to him, pressing his shaggy bulk against his legs, "while I regret losing the support of Fenella MacLeod and her birlinns, I doubt we will have needed them to find Conan Dearg."

Tavish tossed Ferlie a bit of roasted chicken. "Indeed?"

Aidan nodded. "Since we've looked everywhere the double-dyed bastard could have hid, there's only one place he can be," he said, growing more certain by the moment. "Ardcraig."

"His own holding?" Tavish blinked, for once looked nonplussed. "But we've already gone there, even searching his keep from the undercroft to the parapets."

"And seeing what we expected to see," Aidan said, his thumb caressing the jeweled pommel of his sword hilt. "Next time we shall look for the unexpected. Then we shall find him. 'Tis a feeling in my bones."

"Then let us drink to your *feelings*." Tavish pushed to his feet, a smile tugging at his lips. "I have ne'er known them to be wrong."

"Neither have I," Aidan agreed, watching his friend pour them both a generous portion of ale.

He only hoped his feelings about his *bruadar* were as accurate. That the shapely, hot-blooded woman he'd been thinking of as a dream vision wasn't that at all, but a *tamhasg*. Nightly visitations of the woman meant to be his future bride.

As soon as Conan Dearg was found and locked in his dungeon, his people safe from treachery, he meant to find out.

No matter what it cost him.

Nothing was surer.

*   *   *

Worlds and an ocean away, Kira stood in the middle of the Newark Liberty International Airport check-in area, almost oblivious to everything but the precious Newark-Glasgow boarding pass clutched in her hot little hand. Gate C-127, seat number 24A. A window behind the wing, left side so that she could see the sun rise over Ireland and then the endless sweep of the Hebrides as the plane descended into Scotland.

She remembered it well. The views that had stilled her heart and stolen her breath as she'd stared out at the isle-dotted coast, feasting her gaze on soaring cliffs, deep inlets, and sparkling, crystal-clear bays. Long Atlantic rollers crashing over jagged, black-teethed reefs and tiny crescent-shaped strands of gleaming white sand, inaccessible bits of paradise, pristine and almost too beautiful to bear looking down upon.

Then at last the Highlands stretching away to the horizon, each ever-higher rising hill bathed in the soft, rosy-gold glow of a new morning.

The new day she'd yearned for so long.

A place of mist-hung peace and splendor so different from the hectic lifestyle she loathed that just thinking of being there soon nearly set her to swooning.

Ignoring the airport chaos, she traced a fingertip across the fresh black print on her boarding card. She kept her finger on the word *Glasgow*, certain each letter held magic. Truth was, she could feel it. The boarding card vibrated in her hand, its pulsating warmth making her fingers tingle.

Until she realized it wasn't the boarding card causing the sensation but the trembling of her own fingers, her hands as they shook with giddy excitement. Whether in the flesh or not, Aidan was there waiting for her. She'd felt him call to her, could feel him calling her now.

Chances were, once there, she'd catch another true glimpse of him. A *daylight* glimpse without the smoke-and-mirror effects of her dreams. If it had happened once, it could again, and that knowledge, combined with the thrill of finally getting back to Scotland, was pushing her over the edge.

Making her light-headed.

She took a deep breath, then shoved her boarding card deep into a side pocket of her purse, wiping her damp palms on her one great splurge: a fine and stylish, many-pocketed, weatherproof jacket complete with hood.

"Kira, you've gone pale. Are you okay?" Dan Hillard gripped her elbow, his blue eyes filling with concern. "We can still get your luggage back. You don't have to go if you don't want to."

"Don't want to go?" Kira blinked at him, all the whir, noise, and haste of the airport filtering back into her consciousness, pulling her into its crowded, bustling reality.

"*Of course* I want to go. More than I can say." She placed her hand over his, squeezing his fingers. "I'm fine. It's just too warm for me in here. I don't think they ever run air conditioners in this airport."

"You're sure?"

"I'm positive."

A tall, middle-aged man with an open, ruddy face and an unfortunate haircut that made him look more like an army general than the executive editor of a magazine that specialized in paranormal oddities, Dan slung an arm around her shoulders, drawing her near in a fatherly hug.

"What about driving on the left?" He stood back to look at her, the simple question making her stomach flip-flop. "The last time you were there, you were on an escorted coach tour. This time there's a rental car waiting for you at the Glasgow airport. Will you be able to manage?"

Kira straightened her back against her belly flutters and hitched up the shoulder strap of her carry-on. "Of course I'll manage," she said, willing it so.

To get to Castle Wrath, I'd drive on water if need be.
Left, right, or upside down.

Leaving those sentiments unsaid, she forced her brightest smile. "Americans drive in Scotland all the time," she added, the words meant for herself as well as to reassure Dan. "I've also studied maps and"— she paused, stepping aside to make way for a young woman tugging two wailing children behind her—"if I recall correctly, about the only traffic hazard to worry about over there is sheep jams."

"As long as you're sure." He still sounded doubtful.

"I am."

"Sure enough to make it all the way to those three fairy mounds I want you to investigate?"

"The Na Tri Shean?" Kira smiled, her exhilaration returning, banishing the little niggles of doubt about driving. Dan's three conical-shaped fairy hills were thought to open into the Other World, providing access to the Land of the Fae. Not that she cared where the hills might lead or what mythical entities might dwell there.

More interesting to her was that Dan claimed the
Na Tri Shean were also rumored to be time portals.

A possibility he wanted her to explore.

And an opportunity she couldn't refuse. Not with
the three supposed time-portalling-fairy-mounds located not far from the Isle of Skye.

More specifically, Castle Wrath.

The image of those cliff-top ruins blazed across her
mind, and her heart skipped. She could see her Aidan
standing there, so fierce and tall, his plaid slung
proudly over one shoulder, his gleaming raven hair
whipped by the stiff sea winds. He was looking west,
searching for her, she was certain.

Catching her sigh before it could escape, she flashed
Dan a confident smile. "I'll make it to your fairy
mounds," she assured him. "I'd crawl on my knees to
get there. Driving will be a breeze."

Seemingly mollified, he harrumphed, his gaze flickering to her carry-on. "You have all the information
I gave you? Eyewitness local and tourist accounts of
the strange goings-on around those three hills? Copies
of the ancient Celtic legends that mention them?"

Kira nodded. "I have everything," she said, patting
her bulging satchellike bag.

Including a dog-eared copy of *The Hebridean Clans*,
a slim but fascinating volume, its pages dominated by
Clan Donald, Lords of the Isles and undisputed rulers
of Scotland's medieval western seaboard.

She'd found *him* in that book and she wasn't about
to leave it behind.

"You've read the stories?" Dan was watching her.
"The stress of the last days hasn't kept you from going
over them? I don't want you running into anything

unprepared. There's always a kernel of truth in old legends. Who knows what—"

"I'll be fine." Kira leaned up to kiss his whiskered cheek. "And don't worry, you'll get your story. One way or the other. If the Na Tri Shean don't speak to me, I have a few other ideas for sure-winning tales."

His smile returned. "What? You visit Culloden and run into a handsome six foot four Highlander and discover you're soul mates? Reincarnations of long-dead star-crossed lovers? Maybe that infamous Wolf of Badenoch and his great love, Mariota?"

A hot little rush shot through Kira. She wasn't planning on going anywhere near Culloden, but she had hung her heart on a six foot four Highlander.

At least she was pretty sure her sexy medieval warrior chieftain was about that height.

"I'm surprised you've even heard of the Wolf and his Mariota," she said, hoping Dan couldn't hear the thundering of her heart.

He shrugged. "I dated a girl from Inverness in college. A bit of a history buff, always going on about those two. She was obsessed by Scotland's most legendary love pairs." He paused to rub his chin. "So if not the notorious Wolf come back to life at Culloden, what other ideas do you have?"

Kira felt a jab of self-consciousness but brushed it aside. Dan and *Destiny* had been good to her. "O-o-oh," she said, shifting her carry-on again, "something along the lines of *I Was Seduced by a Selkie* or *I Found the Big Grey Man of Ben MacDui Sleeping in My Holiday Cottage.*"

"Ben Mac-*Who-ee*?" Dan shook his head.

"A *ben* is a mountain. The Big Grey Man is like

Bigfoot." Kira smiled. "He's the Yeti of the Scottish Cairngorms."

Dan laughed. "I'll be happy with any story you bring back. You just take care of yourself." His eyes took on that worried look again. "I have a feeling those fairy mounds might be the real thing. Like that lake in Cape Cod."

"If they are, just don't forget your promise."

"A time portal would be a bigger story than a sunken Viking boat, Kira." He hesitated. "You'd be world-famous."

"Not if you keep your word and leave my name off the story." Kira lifted her chin, not willing to budge. "I've had enough fame in recent days to last a lifetime. Give the honors to one of the horn-tooters who'll love the glory."

Dan looked uncomfortable. "You're sure?"

"Absolutely."

"Then off with you and be quick about it." He clutched her to him for a quick hug. "I hate long good-byes."

So did Kira, but before she could say her own, he was gone. Vanished into the teeming maze of hastening passengers and harried-looking airport personnel.

Shifting her carry-on yet again, she remembered what else she hated. Namely carting around unnecessary take-alongs pressed on her by her well-meaning family. No wonder her bag was digging a groove into her shoulder.

Determined to lighten her load—and avoid excess calories she really couldn't afford—she made for the nearest waste bin, then unzipped her carry-on, plucking out the bulky plastic bag stuffed with Lindsay's crushed and crumbling organic chocolate chip cookies.

A fat wedge of some kind of soybean imitation cheddar cheese and a mysterious home-baked energy bar her sister had sworn would keep her from suffering jet lag. Half a poorly wrapped hoagie her father must've secretly slipped into the bag after seeing Lindsay give her so much unappetizing health food.

Pitching it all, Kira dusted her hands and rezipped her now much lighter bag. But not before her gaze fell upon her book, *The Hebridean Clans*.

Her heart thumped. Catching her lip between her teeth, she retrieved her boarding card and headed for the long line at the security checkpoint, thoughts of catching a glimpse of her own Hebridean chieftain in real live waking hours quickening her steps.

With a bit of luck and if her special gift of far-seeing didn't let her down, it just might happen.

She couldn't think of anything sweeter.

Chapter 3

Many hours and even more transatlantic miles later, Kira pulled her fine-running hire car into a so-called lay-by, and rested her head against the steering wheel. She'd made it past Loch Lomond and even Crianlarich, carefully following the A-82, the most scenic route into the Highlands. But she wasn't sure she could go much farther. The many twists and turns were getting to her, each new one bringing her closer to defeat.

She'd lied to herself about left-handed driving.

It wasn't a breeze.

It was horrible.

Worse, she'd been sorely disillusioned to think that sheep jams were the only hazards of Scottish roads. Truth be told, to borrow the language of her medieval Highlander, the only sheep she'd spied so far were pleasant-looking woolly creatures seemingly content to keep to the verdant pastures rising from the impossibly narrow road.

She sighed. Leave it to her to make such a journey at a time when tiredness fogged her brain and heightened her fright factor.

Trying hard not to tremble and absolutely refusing

to cry, she rolled down the window, hoping a good blast of clean and brisk air would bolster her confidence. Instead, the opened window only brought the approaching roar and passing *whoosh* of yet another speeding sports car.

A locally licensed car, flying past the lay-by at breakneck speed and disappearing into the wilds of Rannoch Moor before she could even blink, much less wonder why she'd ever thought she could tackle such a drive without a good night's sleep to recover from jet lag.

And if she wished to ponder her plight, the equally speedy *whooshes* of two coach tour buses and an over-wide recreational vehicle dashed her hopes of wallowing in self-pity.

"Holy guacamole," she breathed, clutching the steering wheel.

Maybe she would have to crawl on her knees to Castle Wrath. Pulling over to tremble and catch her breath each time some impatient driver zoomed up behind her wasn't getting her anywhere. But maybe her handy-dandy map of the Highlands would. That, and her mother's carefully written instructions to the Cairn Avenue shrew's stepdaughter's castle near Oban.

Ravenscraig, the place was called if she remembered rightly, and it even boasted a re-created Highland period settlement—One Cairn Village—with craft shops, a tearoom, and tourist lodgings.

Loosening her grip on the steering wheel, she twisted left, reaching for her purse, then digging inside its voluminous side pockets, searching for the folded piece of paper with her mother's notes. A quick scan of them and a glance at her map brought her an instant boost. She need drive only a bit farther north, then veer west onto the A-85, straight through Glen Lochy and the Pass of Brander before continuing along Loch Etive until she reached Ravenscraig Castle. According to her mother, she couldn't miss it, as the castle and its One Cairn Village were clearly signposted.

Kira smiled. Signposted was good.

Better yet, the A-85 would also take her along a short bit of Loch Awe, allowing her a nice view of that loch's picturesque Kilchurn Castle. Her smile widened. Might as well enjoy the touristy stuff along the way.

And Ravenscraig was a good deal closer than the Isle of Skye, where she'd booked a room at a small family-run inn. With her eyes feeling like sandpaper, sleep riding her hard, and her jaw beginning to ache from repeating the words *stay left*, a hot shower and a soft, clean bed sounded like heaven.

Just how much like heaven astounded her when, a long but scenic stretch of Highland roads behind her, she stood in the heart of Ravenscraig's One Cairn Village and felt herself transported to Brigadoon.

This was Celtic whimsy at its finest.

Fine enough to blunt the worst of her jet lag.

"Oh-my-gosh." She stopped beside a large memorial cairn topped with a Celtic cross, the clutch of thick-walled, blue-doored Highland-y cottages surrounding it taking her breath and delighting her. A profusion of late-blooming flowers and heather rioted everywhere, spilling from rustic-looking halved wine barrels and crowding winding, moss-grown paths. Curling wisps of fragrant peat smoke rose from several of the thatched cottages' squat chimney stacks, and although the afternoon light was failing, there was enough to cast a golden autumnal glow across the whole old-timey-looking village.

She glanced about, letting the place's magic close around her. It was like stepping into one of her books on Highland life, as if she'd blinked and suddenly found herself inside the sepia photographs of days long past and forgotten. The kind of photograph she was always mooning over.

"Oh-my-gosh," she said again, her eyes misting.

The strapping young Highlander beside her chuckled. Setting down her bags, Malcolm, as he'd introduced himself, flashed her a dimpled grin. "That's exactly what Mistress Mara said the first time she saw the castle," he told her, his soft Highland voice almost as exciting as the *Brigadoon*-like village. "Looks like you have a greater heart for the simple things?"

A greater heart. Kira sighed. Just the phrase, so old-fashioned and Scottish-sounding, thickened her throat. She blinked, tried to wipe the damp from her eyes as unobtrusively as possible.

Seeing it anyway, the red-haired Malcolm reached to dry her cheeks with a strong, calloused thumb. "Dinna shame your emotion, lass. I've seen grown men shed tears hereabouts. Scotland does that to people."

Kira nodded, his words making her eyes water all the more.

"I've always loved Scotland." She blinked, unable to keep the hitch out of her voice. "The mournful hills and deep glens, heather-clad moors and hidden lochs. And, yes, it's the simple things that stir me. A drift of peat smoke on chill autumn air or the laughter and song at ceilidhs. *Real* ceilidhs in crofts and cottages, not the kitschy Scottish song-and-dance evenings you see in big touristy hotels."

She paused, swiping at her eyes again. "I sometimes think I belong to another age. The time of clan battles and Celtic legends, back when a skirl of pipes and a war cry roused men to whip out their swords and—"

She broke off, heat flaming her cheeks. "I'm sorry, I get carried away—"

"You feel the pull o' the hills is what it is." Malcolm-of-the-red-hair picked up her bags again. "And I'm a-thinking if you don't have Scottish blood, then you did . . . at one time," he added, the notion warming her like the sun breaking through clouds.

Before she could say anything, he nodded toward one of the cottages, its blue-shuttered windows glowing with the flickering light of what looked to be candles. "That's the Heatherbrae. Yours for the night, and nay, those aren't real candles in the windows," he said, as if he'd read her mind. "They're electric. The cottages may look of another century, but they have all the comforts of our own.

"And that up yonder"—he indicated a well-lit cottage at the end of the path, one slightly larger than the rest—"is Innes's soap-and-candle craft and workshop. If you pop up there, you'll find she keeps a platter of shortbread and fresh-brewed tea ready for visitors."

Kira cast a longing glance at the Heatherbrae. "But—"

"I need a few minutes to ready your cottage." The young man offered an apologetic smile. "We didn't know for sure if you were coming, see you, and Mistress Mara and her Alex insist on a true Highland welcome for their guests: a warming fire on the hearth grate and a waiting dram at your bedside."

"That sounds wonderful and so does Innes's tea and shortbread. Still"—Kira glanced at the large memorial cairn, according to its bronze plaque, dedicated to some long-dead MacDougalls—"I don't want to trouble the woman," she finished, her gaze also lighting on a nearby wooden signpost marking the beginning of a woodland walk.

An evening walk she was sure would give her a second wind.

Following her gaze, Malcolm's rosy-cheeked complexion turned a slightly deeper red. "Sorry, lass, but Innes will be expecting you. She . . . er . . . watches out her shop windows, having nothing much else to do the day. Just smile and nod if she mentions Lord Basil."

"Lord Basil?" The words had no sooner left her lips than the image of an elegantly dressed, hawk-nosed man loomed before her, his aristocratic stare haughty and cold.

Kira blinked and he vanished, leaving her with a rash of goose bumps, alone on the path.

Malcolm-the-red had left her, too. The cracked door of the Heatherbrae and the wedge of warm yellow light spilling out into the cottage's little garden left no doubt as to where he'd gone.

She also had no doubts that they'd been observed, for unless jet lag was playing tricks on her or her far-seeing gift was showing her yet another resident of Ravenscraig's past, there was a white-haired woman peering at her from behind one of the soap-and-candle craft and workshop windows.

A *tiny* white-haired woman, she discovered upon stepping inside the shop a few minutes later. A frilly-aproned, birdlike woman who beamed at her with a cheery, welcoming smile and a telltale faraway look in her bright blue eyes.

"Come away in!" she enthused, scurrying from the window to a plaid-draped table set with a tea service and an array of what looked to be home-baked short-bread. "I'm Innes, maker of fine soaps and candles. And you'll be herself, the young American Lord Basil told us we might be seeing," she added, pouring the tea with a shaky, age-spotted hand. "Lord Basil likes Yanks." She paused, her voice dropping to a conspiratorial whisper. "He even married one."

Kira looked at her, guessing she must mistake Mara McDougall's Highland chieftain husband for someone named Lord Basil. No doubt the stuffy-looking aristocrat she'd glimpsed on the path. She was pretty sure her mother had said Euphemia Ross's stepdaughter's husband's name was Alex.

Sir Alexander Douglas.

"You are a Yank, aren't you?" Innes came closer, holding out a rattling teacup and saucer.

"I'm Kira Bedwell. And, yes, I'm American. From Aldan, Pennsylvania, near Philly." Kira accepted the tea and took a sip. "Philadelphia," she added, just in case the old woman had never heard the term *Philly*.

"Lord Basil comes from London," Innes stated, as if she hadn't spoken.

Determined to be polite, Kira opened her mouth to reply, but the words lodged in her throat, all thought of Innes and her apparent delusions forgotten as she blinked at a small display of books on local history and fauna.

A familiar face stared back at her.

Wee Hughie MacSporran. The puffed-up peacock of a tour guide who'd accompanied her long-ago coach tour and repeatedly regaled the company with his claims to lofty ancestry.

And there he was again, preening with self-importance on the cover of a book titled *Rivers of Stone: A Highlander's Ancestral Journey.*

Kira blinked again, half certain that this time jet lag really was getting to her. But when she looked a second time, there could be no mistaking.

It was the tour guide.

Even if he looked a bit more portly than she remembered. His name was on the book, too: Wee Hughie MacSporran, historian, storyteller, and keeper of tradition.

Kira almost dropped her teacup. How like the swellhead to tack on so many distinctions to his name.

Curious, she set down her tea and reached for the book, clearly a vanity-press job. Her fingers were just closing on it when a richly timbred voice spoke behind her.

A deep Highland voice that sounded so much like *him* that her heart leapt to her throat.

"A fine book," the voice said in endorsement, "written by a local man well versed in our legends and lore. You can have a copy if you like. A wee welcome-to-Scotland gift."

Kira spun around, the book clasped to her breast.

"Thank you. I know the author. He guided a tour I was on years ago. And you must be—"

"No' Lord Basil," the Highlander returned, stepping aside to make way for an aging collie when the dog shuffled in, then plopped down at his feet. "He was the late Lady of Ravenscraig's English husband. And this"—he cast an affectionate glance at the collie—"is Ben. He's the true master at Ravenscraig."

The dog thumped his tail and looked up, his approving brown eyes saying he knew it.

"Myself, I'm Alex. Mara's husband." He took one of the shortbreads off the table and gave it to Ben. "You have to be Miss Bedwell? My regrets that we were unable to greet you, but"—he glanced at his kilt and shrugged—"we were having a folk afternoon for a gathering of schoolchildren at the Victorian Lodge."

He looked over his shoulder at the semidarkness framed by the shop's half-open door. "You may have seen the turrets of the lodge on your way here. It's a rambling old pile just the other side of the woodland walk."

Kira gaped at him, well aware he was talking, but hardly registering a word he said. Indeed, she was quite sure her jaw was hanging open, but she found herself unable to do anything about it.

Sir Alexander Douglas had that kind of presence.

Tall, well built, and handsome, he had rich chestnut brown hair just skimming his shoulders and the kind of deep, sea green eyes she would've sworn existed only in the pages of historical romance novels.

She blinked again, surprised by his kilted perfection.

And he wasn't just wearing a kilt. Not like the kilt-clad Americans she'd seen at stateside Highland Games. O-o-oh, no. This man really *wore* his tartan. He was the genuine article, decked out in full Highland regalia, every magnificent inch of him making her weak in the knees.

Not because of himself, but because he reminded her of *him*.

Her Aidan.

Alex Douglas had that same medieval-y air about him. The only thing missing was the sword.

But then that, too, was there. A great, wicked-looking broadsword flashing silver at his hip as his plaid seemed to stir in some unseen wind, its eerie passage even riffling his hair.

Kira swallowed and the image slowly faded. The wind vanished quicker, but the sword lingered to the last. Then it, too, was no more, and the only flashing silver left on him was the large Celtic brooch holding his plaid at his shoulder and the cantle on his fancy dress sporran.

A MacDougall clan sporran of finest leather and fur with tasseled diamond-cut chains—just like the assortment of various clan sporrans hanging on the wall behind the shop's till.

Kira's heart thumped. Imagining Aidan wearing such a grand sporran nearly made her swoon. If ever a man's best part deserved such an accolade it was his.

She swallowed again, feeling heat blaze onto her cheeks. "I'm sorry, I—"

"It's okay. Women always react to him that way." A pretty auburn-haired woman with a Philly accent stepped forward, extending her hand. "Especially mad-for-plaid American women," she added, her warm smile taking any sting out of the words. "I'm Mara—pleased to meet you. My father called and told us you might be stopping by. I'm glad you did."

Kira took her hand. "I am, too," she said, her blush deepening because she hadn't even noticed the woman standing there. "This place is like *Brigadoon*. Amazing."

Mara McDougall Douglas looked pleased. "That was our intent."

She threw a smile at her husband, then slipped behind the till to straighten a large framed print of three sword-brandishing Highlanders captured in the midst of what appeared to be a medieval battle fray.

The print hung beside the display of clan sporrans, and on closer inspection, Kira saw that the sword-wielding Highlander in the middle was none other than Mara's Alex.

"That's you!" She swung around to look at him, but he only smiled and shrugged again.

"Yes, that's him," his wife confirmed, clearly proud. "Alex, and two of his best friends, Hardwic— I mean, Sir Hardwin de Studley of Seagrave—and the big, burly fierce-looking fellow, that's Bran of Barra."

Kira's brows lifted. "Hardwin *de Studley*?"

Her hosts exchanged glances.

Alex cleared his throat. "An old family name. Goes back centuries."

He glanced at the print. "I've known him for . . . years. Bran as well. They were among the most fearsome fighters of their day, their sword skills second only to a certain Sassunach I also had the privilege to call my friend."

"Were?" Kira looked at the men on the print again. "You mean they're dead?"

"No." Mara came out from behind the till. "He means they're expert swordsmen. Alex and his friends are reenactors. They stage medieval battles for our visitors. Mostly in summer when we're full up here."

"Oh." Kira tightened her hold on Wee Hughie's book, certain she'd caught Mara shooting her husband a warning glance.

"I'm surprised Euphemia didn't mention the reen-actments to your mother." Mara hooked her hand through her husband's arm. "Alex and his company put on quite a show when she and my father visited last year."

Innes tittered. "Ach, that biddie was too fashed about bogles to pay much heed to aught else," she asserted, pinning her gaze on Kira. "Be you afeart o' bogles?"

"Bogles?"

"Ghosts," Alex explained, a smile quirking his lips. "Innes is asking if they frighten you."

"Maybe a better question would be if she *believes* in ghosts." Mara glanced from her husband to Kira. "In America, people aren't as receptive to such things as over here, where every house, pub, and castle is simply accepted as having ghosts."

"Indeed?" Alex looked amused. "So, Kira Bedwell, what do you think of them?"

"Ghosts? I rather like them. Or rather, the notion of them." Kira smiled, leaving it at that. She wasn't about to mention her talent and especially not having already glimpsed the previous Ravenscraig lord.

If he'd indeed been a spirit.

She could usually see through ghosts, so she sus-pected she'd only caught a brief glimpse of the past again, an image imprinted on a path the man often frequented.

Sure that was the way of it, she turned to Mara. "Do you have ghosts at Ravenscraig?"

"None that would bother you," Alex answered again, this time clicking his fingers at Ben, then holding open the door so the dog could trot outside. "You'll sleep well enough at the Heatherbrae. It should be ready now if you'd like us to see you there."

Opening her mouth to say she would, Kira was horrified when a ferocious yawn snatched the words. Blessedly, her hosts had already stepped out the door, and Innes appeared too busy humming to herself to notice.

Not wanting to intrude on the old woman's obvious happy place, she did allow herself a quick glance at Wee Hughie's book before she started after Alex and Kira. Skipping what looked to be long passages of flowery prose about his illustrious ancestors, she flipped right to the illustrations and photographs in the book's middle, nearly dropping the thing yet again when the words *Na Tri Shean* leapt out at her.

Captured in a glossy black-and-white photo, the three fairy mounds sent an immediate shiver down her spine.

She'd either been there before or would be at some point in the future.

And in a way that had nothing to do with her assignment for Dan Hillard and *Destiny Magazine*.

Giving herself a shake lest her hosts look at her and think she'd seen a ghost, she shut the book and left the shop, walking straight out into the next surprise.

Scotland's world-renowned *gloaming*.

In the short time she'd been inside the soap-and-candle craft and workshop, the evening had turned a deep bluish violet and soft, billowing mists were descending, sliding silently down the hillsides. The whole *Brigadoon*ish scene was now bathed in a gentle, never-to-be-forgotten luminosity she knew Highlanders thought of as the time between the two lights.

A special and magical time full of mystical promise.

Her heart jolting at the notion, she made her way down the path after Alex and Mara, hoping that the proximity to Castle Wrath and One Cairn Village's own magic might let Aidan come to her in her dreams that night.

He hadn't visited her in weeks, and she needed him badly.

Almost feeling his hot and hungry gaze on her, she hastened her steps. Heatherbrae Cottage and her bed loomed just ahead. Soon she might feel his heated touch, lose herself in the mastery of his kisses, and glory in the deliciousness of the Gaelic love words he whispered against her naked skin.

Kira sighed.

O-o-oh, yes, she needed him.

Even if having him make love to her on Scottish soil might prove a greater sensual pleasure than she could bear.

She just hoped she'd have the chance to find out.

Only a few hours to the north by car, but many centuries distant in time, Aidan MacDonald prowled the lofty battlements of Castle Wrath, his features set in a fierce scowl. He was feeling every bit the harsh and embittered soul his good friend Tavish had accused him of being. A dark-tempered, coldhearted beast, some of his younger squires had called him when they hadn't known he'd heard. Remembering the incident now, he raked a hand through his hair and stifled a scornful laugh. Soon the wee kitchen lads would be claiming his eyes glowed red and he hid a tail beneath his plaid.

Even his guardsmen had fled from him, the whole lot of the quivery-livered night patrol taking themselves off to the far side of the parapets as soon as he threw open the stair tower door and strode out into the mist-hung evening.

Not that he blamed them.

In recent days, even his favorite hound, Ferlie, had begun to eye him as if he'd run mad.

And perhaps he had, he was willing to admit, stopping his pacing to stand before one of the open square-notched crenellations in the parapet wall.

Full mad and unable to do aught about it.

Lusting after a *dream*.

"Blood of Saint Columba," he growled, his folly cutting into him as sharply as the razor-sharp steel of his sword. Thoughts of her bestirred him even now, filling his mind with the warm smoothness of her skin and the fine, plump weight of her breasts, her nipples beautifully puckered and begging his caress. The damp, silky-soft heat between her thighs and her sweet moans of pleasure whene'er he touched her there.

Her fiery passion. For him, his land, and everything he stood for.

He saw it in the way she would reverently touch his plaid or run a finger over the intricate Celtic designs on his sword belt. How her breath would hitch, her eyes filling with wonder when his world intruded on their dreams and he knew she'd caught glimpses of his tapestried bedchamber, the glowing peat fire across from his bed or the black cliffs of Wrath Isle, visible through the room's tall, arch-topped windows.

Marvels, she called such things, shaking her head as if she'd ne'er seen the like.

As if she loved them as much as he did.

That passion blazed inside her, too, and knowing it made him appreciate her in ways that had nothing to do with how good she felt in his arms. How just looking at her made him burn.

His loins heavy and aching with wanting her, needing her *now*, he jammed his fists on his hips and glared into the thick swirls of mist gliding past the battlements. Chill, cloying, and impenetrable, the mist seemed to mock him, its gray-white swaths blotting everything but the damp stone of the crenellated wall right before him.

Just as his dreams had begun throwing up an unbreachable barrier, keeping him from reaching her and letting him see only the great void that loomed without her.

Until tonight.

Casting one last scowl at the mist, he started pacing again, as keenly aware of her as he'd been earlier, sitting at the high table in his hall, holding council with Tavish and several of his most trusted men, planning their surprise raid on Conan Dearg's Ardcraig, when a jolt had ripped through him and he'd sensed her.

Felt her presence, so vibrant and alive he would've sworn she'd somehow stolen into Castle Wrath and was suddenly standing right behind his chair.

Her sweet feminine scent, so fresh and clean, had swirled around him, filling his senses and making his heart slam against his ribs. A scent with him still, even here in the cold dark of the parapets.

To be sure, it wasn't his.

And with certainty not his guardsmen's, the fools still busying themselves on the other side of the battlements. Each one of the impressionable buffoons doing their best to pretend he wasn't there.

Nay, it wasn't coming from them. Their scent leaned toward armpit and old leather. Wool and linen that hadn't been washed in the saints knew how long, the whole charming effect enhanced by a slight whiff of stale ale, horse, and dog.

"Och, aye, 'tis you, my sweet," he breathed, certain of it.

His dream vision, *tamhasg*, or whate'er she was, was near.

So near he could almost taste her.

See her eyes light when she caught that first glimpse of him, feel her arms slide around him, drawing him closer, urging him to make her his.

"*Lass.*" The endearment came choked, burning his throat as he clenched his hands, willing her to appear.

When she didn't, he bit back a roar of frustration and whirled around, turning away from the empty night and striding toward the stair tower. The curving, torchlit steps that would take him back to his bedchamber.

The massive oak-framed bed and the sleep awaiting him there.

The dreams.

His last hope of finding her this night.

Several hours later, he believed he had, stirring in his sleep when soft kisses bathed his cheek, warm and wet, and hot breath hushed sweetly across his ear, waking him.

But instead of his *tamhasg*'s shining eyes greeting him, the eyes meeting his were brown and soulful. Perhaps even a touch worried.

Canine eyes.

"Ach, Ferlie." He sat up and rubbed a hand over his face, his love for the great beast keeping him from letting his disappointment show. "She was here—or somewhere close."

But her scent was gone now. His bed most definitely empty, save himself and his huge, shaggy dog.

Only his surety remained.

Something in his world had shifted. A current in the air, a ne'er-before-there ripple in the wind. He knew not, but whate'er it was, he'd wager his best sword it had to do with *her*.

If the saints were kind, he would learn the answer soon.

Chapter 4

She was really here again.

Kira Never-Give-Up Bedwell, finally returned to the Trotternish Peninsula on the Isle of Skye.

Castle Wrath was no longer her dearest longing, distant and intangible, but a reality. Better yet, she was already halfway across the high three-sided promontory that held the ancient stronghold's ruins. A trek she was finding much easier than years before, since this afternoon was calm and bright, without the fierce wind gusts that had made her last visit so treacherous.

The sheep pats were still everywhere, though. A distinct quiver of *ick* slid through her, but she ignored it. She'd just watch her step and pretend the piles of black goop weren't quite so prevalent.

Not that she really cared.

She blew out a breath that fluffed her bangs as she shot a sideways glance at the nearest such obstacle. Fact was, she'd march right through the stuff if need be.

If doing so meant catching another true glimpse of her Highlander.

Savoring the possibility, she inched as close to the

edge of the cliff as she dared and peered down at Wrath Bay. Its waters glistened blue in the autumn sunshine, the deep scorings in the smooth flat rocks of the small, crescent-shaped strand staring back at her just as she remembered.

Furrows that, according to Wee Hughie, tour-guide-cum-author, were caused by the keels of countless Clan Donald galleys being drawn onto the shore.

War galleys. She was sure.

Greyhounds of the sea. Their heyday marked by grooves that must've taken centuries to form. Deep indentations in stone that might not even have been visible in her Aidan's time.

But they were there now—telltale remnants of long-ago days.

Kira's pulse quickened. Much as the past beguiled her, there was only one part of it she ached to seize.

If only she could.

Her heart pounding, she edged even closer to the precipice, a sheer and dizzying drop to the stony beach below. She squinted to see better, her gaze focused on the tide as it surged up and over the rocks and kelp. Brilliant sunlight glinted off the incoming swells, making the water glitter like jewels, but it was the ancient keel marks that continued to hold her attention. Each centuries-old groove was a not-to-be-denied reminder that *he* once walked there.

He'd been a part of this place where she now stood, and knowing that made her want to pull the clip from her hair, throw off her jacket, and run the rest of the way.

Fly across the grass until she reached Castle Wrath's tumbled walls and moss-grown arches, then collapse before the remains of *his* stairwell. The dark, downward-winding stair that led, she was sure, straight into Aidan's great hall.

There, where for a brief, torchlit moment she'd seen him.

Heard him speaking to her as he ascended the tight, corkscrew steps. She shivered, remembering how he'd reached for her, pulling her against him and lowering his head to kiss her, only to vanish before her eyes.

A feat he could not possibly do again, she saw, reaching the place where she'd looked into his stairwell.

The steps were gone.

The inky darkness that had stared back at her only to suddenly blaze with torchlight was no more. Even the gap had vanished, leaving only a narrow crevice in its place. No longer yawning, it taunted her. A mere slit in the grassy, nettle-covered earth, the whole of it barely a foot wide and hardly adequate to peer into.

She gaped all the same, shaking her head at the pathetic little opening.

She put a hand over her mouth, disbelief slamming into her, freezing her heart. She'd been so certain, so sure nothing would have changed. Not after the stairs must've stood undisturbed for hundreds of years.

Only the briskness of the cold, clean Highland air remained the same. The incredible age of Castle Wrath's broken stones and the roar of the surf crashing into its jagged, impervious cliff foot.

"Oh, no." Kira dropped to her knees, sagging against what should have been the threshold to Aidan's world.

Instead, fallen debris and rubble filled the darkness,

the lichen-and-weed-grown rocks blocking the ancient steps, each cold, silent stone and layer of rich, peaty earth an impassable barrier.

The way to Aidan's great hall—*to him*—was sealed.

Closed off for all eternity.

Unless she possessed enough spirit to brave the cliff's maze of underground tunnels, stairwells, and rooms, much of which were said to be crumbling into the sea.

Dangerous places where one false step could send her hurtling to certain death.

She blew out a breath, frustration warring with her refusal to give up.

She *did* have spirit.

And she thrived on challenges. Each broadsiding kick in the shins only made her roll her sleeves higher, more determined than ever to besiege whom- or whatever would hold her down. As if to prove it, she swiped a hand through her hair and kissed her palms for luck. Then, reaching deep into the crevice, she grabbed hold of the first chunk of weedy, nettle-stinging rock she could get a grip on.

Unfortunately, when she pulled, the rock didn't budge.

A second and third effort cost her two fingernails. Not that she cared. What mattered was not the attractiveness of her hands, but getting into Aidan's great hall. If the stairwell of their previous encounter was to remain off-limits, she would just have to find another way to reach him.

Beyond the wisps of a mere ghostly encounter, she'd felt him here so strongly on her last visit, as if he truly were flesh and bone and raw masculinity. As if he'd been waiting for her, just as she hoped he was now.

If only her gift, the magic of the place, or *whatever*, would kick in again and let him know she was near.

But first she needed to rest.

Shake off a bit more jet lag and gather her strength for the assault it would mean, creeping down into damp, dank-smelling passages. Icky places where she would be able to see no more than a few feet ahead of her flashlight.

And she was glad she had one. Bright blue, plastic and beautiful, it rested in her trusty backpack, along with two sets of extra batteries.

Thanks to Alex and Mara Douglas.

She also had the perfect place to rest. The great grass-grown arch of what she was sure had once been the entry into Castle Wrath's bailey. It, at least, was still there as she remembered, the top half of its imposing bulk rising up out of the cliff-top to wink at her in all its Celtic rune-incised glory. A medieval wonder, undisturbed by time, the arch looked as inviting now as it had twelve years ago.

Strangely beckoning.

Kira frowned. Regrettably, the tangle of brambles and nettles surrounding the arch didn't beckon at all. Unlike the caved-in entrance to Aidan's stairwell, the crevices and holes scattered throughout the castle's empty courtyard appeared anything but filled in.

Just the opposite—they looked deep, dark, and dangerous. She wasn't about to search for one with an intact stairwell until her eyes no longer felt like sandpaper and she'd fortified herself with a tuna sandwich and a thermos of tea.

Tea solved everything, the Brits always claimed.

Hoping it was so, she started forward, carefully

avoiding the worst of the brambles and nettles, but especially watching where she stepped. She had no desire to get better acquainted with one of those black-staring holes-in-the-ground until she was good and ready.

Sadly, when she reached the arch and managed to scramble on top of it, Castle Wrath's pièce de résistance proved to have a few cracks of its own. Some looked rather crumbly around the edges, while others had a fern or two thrusting up from their depths. Thankfully, none looked wide enough for her to fall through.

Almost tired enough not to care if she did, she quickly claimed the most solid-looking spot the arch top offered, pleased because her chosen picnic site also seemed to have the thickest, most cushiony grass.

Soft, cushiony grass was good.

A crackless resting place even better.

Proud that she'd made it to the arch without mishap, she shrugged off her backpack and pulled it onto her lap, eager to dig out her treasures. A tightly rolled tartan picnic rug, waterproof on one side and just one of several souvenirs picked up at One Cairn Village. Her tea thermos and packed lunch. Her father's borrowed mini-binoculars and her two special books.

The Hebridean Clans and Wee Hughie MacSporran's *Rivers of Stone: A Highlander's Ancestral Journey.*

Thinking of the tour guide—no, *author*, she corrected herself—reminded her of the other treasure in her backpack. The most special one of all. A fine MacDonald dress sporran she'd plucked off the wall display in Innes's soap-and-candle craft and workshop.

Now hers to cherish, she meant to have it altered into a handbag when she returned to Aldan.

Not wanting to think about her return journey, she unrolled her tartan picnic rug and spread out her goodies, determined to enjoy her afternoon despite her disappointment over the collapsed stairwell.

Filling her stomach and taking time for a soul-soothing glance through her books would do her good. Then she'd be ready to search for access into Castle Wrath's heart.

Or rather she'd be ready if the words on the page stopped blurring before her eyes. The book, Wee Hughie's little self-published tome, also felt heavier than it should. In fact, the thing slipped right from her fingers, bouncing off her knee to disappear into the nearest crack in the arch top.

"Oh, sheesh!" Too late, she lunged for it, a sudden wave of dizziness making her clumsy.

The book was gone, and it was her fault for being such a butterfingers.

Frowning, she sat back and rubbed a hand over her face.

What she needed was some of that tea.

Cure-all of the British Isles.

Yes, good old Earl Grey would give her a boost.

If only she could remember where she'd placed her thermos and packed lunch. But her mind felt fuzzy and the picnic goods were nowhere to be seen, the smooth stone surface of the arch top pitifully bare.

Worse, the afternoon had darkened and a chill wind now whistled past her ears, its keening making it hard to think. Not that she'd be able to concentrate even if the day had remained as clear and still as it'd been.

Not with all the shouting and dog barking going on around her.

Loud shouting and dog barking.

Even if she couldn't see anyone or their frenzied canines, the noise was deafening enough for her to jam her fingers in her ears and wriggle them. Something she did with great gusto—until she noticed that Wee Hughie's tome and her trusty tea thermos weren't the only things missing.

Her world was missing.

Beginning with her tartan picnic rug and ending with her father's much-prized mini-binoculars. Most alarming of all, the thick carpet of grass covering the arch top had vanished, replaced by smooth, polished stone. The whole sweeping lot of it not showing a single weedy crack. And, surprise-surprise, the arch now raged much higher than before.

She stared down at the cobbles. Yep, her perch was definitely up there.

She swallowed, little chills beginning to streak up and down her spine.

If the well-swept paving stones were an illusion, the arch's height wasn't.

Never in a million years could she have climbed such a towering monstrosity.

Leaping down was unthinkable.

If she could even tear her gaze away from Castle Wrath's bailey and curtain walls long enough to consider the risk. Castle Wrath's teeming, bustling bailey and its mighty, notably *un*tumbled walls.

Thick, crenellated walls of medieval mastery. Massive, whitewashed, and impregnable-looking, they

soared proudly into the Highland sky, every magnificent foot of them daring her to challenge their exis-
tence.

Kira blinked, not about to do the like.

After all, she decided, clutching her jacket closer
against the wind, there wasn't a need. Her wits had
finally returned, and with them, her heart slowed a
pace. She really was seeing Castle Wrath as it had
once been. She looked about the bailey, ready to appreciate the moment for what it was: another fleeting
time slip.

A tantalizing glimpse into the past, visible for the
space of a blink and then forever gone.

Just as she'd seen flashes of Norsemen landing in
America. Or, more recently, at One Cairn Village,
when she'd caught a look at Ravenscraig's onetime
English lord.

She recognized the moment for what it was because
her gift always let her see time-slip images as real and
solid. Only true ghosts and spirits appeared somewhat translucent.

But this time the image was lasting longer.

Much longer.

She shifted, the fine hairs on the back of her neck
beginning to rise.

Never had she enjoyed such a lengthy viewing of the
long ago. A medieval curtain-walled bailey no longer
teeming with mere chickens, goats, and scurrying
washerwomen, but now also filled with out-for-blood
ferocious-looking dogs. Leaping, barking beasts larger
than some ponies she'd seen at state fairs back home.
Equally oversized and nearly as shaggy were the wild-

eyed, gesticulating clansmen who appeared in the same moment as the dogs, the whole unruly lot of them looming up out of nowhere.

One instant there'd been only barking and shouts. The next, the barkers and shouters were there, bold as life, and wanting her.

At least that was the impression they gave her.

Kira's heart began to race again. Something was seriously not right. She blinked several times, but the men and the dogs remained.

Garrulous, frowning, and garbed in rough tartan clothing, the clansmen poured out of the wooden buildings lining the curtain walls or stormed from the keep, a flood of plaid-hung outrage bursting from a door she recognized as the one leading into Aidan's hall.

Her breath caught when she recognized it, but she had no time to digest the meaning of the stairwell's intact appearance. On and on the men came, hollering as they ran at her across the bailey, some wielding swords, others shaking fists.

All stared.

Looking furious, they crowded beneath the arch, gaping up at her as if she were some two-headed monster.

"A fairy!" one cried, pointing with his dirk.

"Nay, a witch!" another corrected, glowering at the other. "I'd ken the like anywhere."

Kira stared back at them, too startled to move. Never had one of her past-glimpses felt so . . . real.

Or so threatening.

She shuddered.

This wasn't how she'd envisioned her return to Aidan's world. She'd hoped to sneak into the shell of his ruined great hall and catch a glimpse of him sitting there. See him lairding it at his high table, all sexy and magnificent. Perhaps even catching his eye and exchanging glances before the image faded.

Maybe even share one brief *real-time* kiss.

Facing a pack of raving, wild-looking Highlandmen who thought she was a witch wasn't her idea of bliss.

Especially when a great bearlike man with a mane of thick black hair and an even bushier black beard shouldered his way through the throng. He stopped at the base of the arch, where he stretched his arms above his head, loudly cracking his knuckles.

"Come!" he roared at his kinsmen. "If she's a witch, the laird will be wanting us to seize her. I'll hoist any souls brave enough onto the arch to get her."

"O-o-oh, no, you won't," Kira disagreed, scooting away from the arch's edge. She pushed quickly to her feet, knowing from experience that the sudden movement would break the spell, plunging Castle Wrath into splendid ruin and sending its long-ago occupants back into their own day.

To her surprise, nothing happened.

The image, and the angry men, remained.

"You aren't really there," she said anyway, looking down at them. She shook her head against the cold knot forming in her belly. "Any moment you'll be gone—and so will I!"

But the icy wind kept whipping past her, the bailey dogs continued to bark, and the Bear was readying himself to hurl the first sword-swinging Highlander onto the arch.

"No swords, you lackwit!" He snatched the other

man's blade and sent it scuttling across the cobbles, instantly endearing himself to Kira.

Until he swung the other man high into the air, informing him, "If there's any head-lopping to be done, I'll do it myself. Seeing as I'm the laird's own ax-man."

"The laird won't want a hair on the maid's head harmed—whoe'er or whate'er she is."

Kira froze, looking on as *he* cut a path through the crowd.

It was Aidan. Every inch of him just as bold and glorious as she knew him. Even if his eyes currently blazed with anger, not passion. Fury directed at his men, not her.

And o-o-oh was he beautiful in a rage.

Her heart flip-flopping, Kira released the breath she'd been holding and looked on, watching as he scorched the gathered men with a glare, then upbraided them.

"Your chief will have the tender parts cut off any man who'd dare lift a hand against a woman—any woman," he warned, throwing back his plaid to reveal the wicked-looking long sword beneath. "As would I."

His chief? Kira's jaw slipped. She would've sworn Aidan was laird. The history books said so, too.

"Ach, Tavish," the Bear argued, solving the riddle.

Looking disgusted, he set down the man he'd been about to hurl onto the arch. "Where'er your eyes?" the man said. "That be no woman on the arch—she's a witch, plain as day. Have a good look at her."

And he did. This Tavish who looked so like her Aidan that Kira's heart was still galloping madly in her chest. He let his plaid fall back into place and tilted his head, staring up at her with Aidan's own dark eyes.

Intelligent, measuring eyes, she noted with relief.

"I can see she is . . . dressed oddly." His gaze swept her from head to toe and back again. "She's also passing fair and nothing like any witch I've e'er had the discomfort to meet."

"Bah!" Her would-be captor snatched up his fallen sword, resheathing it with a scowl. "The laird's gone off women—as well you know. He won't care how fair the wench is. Witch, or no'."

"He'll care that no woman is mistreated on Mac-Donald soil." The man called Tavish planted his hands on his hips and glared round again, raking the others with a cold stare until, one by one, they backed away.

"Be warned, my friends," he added, "if you value your bollocks."

Then, in a whirring blur of plaid and steel, he vaulted onto the arch, landing on his feet in front of Kira before she could even cry out.

"Have no fear," he said, narrowing his eyes at her all the same. "I mean only to see you to my liege. He'll decide your fate, though it willna be beneath an ax-man's blade. That I can promise you—whoe'er you are."

"I'm Kira." She blinked at him, his resemblance to Aidan unsettling her, making her knees tremble. "Kira Bedwell of Aldan, Pennsylvania."

His brow furrowed. "Pen-*where*?"

"It's a long way from here." She tried to smile, but the way he was studying her made it impossible. "A distant place. You won't know it."

"It matters not, *Kee-rah*." He reached to finger one

of the buttons on her jacket. "Though it wouldn't be wise to let the others see you as closely as I have," he added, whipping off his plaid and swirling it over her shoulders. "This will shield you from the worst of their stares. I shall tell them you were shivering with cold."

"They've already seen me."

His lips quirked. "What men think they see can be corrected," he said, patting his sword hilt. "Dinna fash yourself o'er those blunder-heads below."

"And your chieftain?" Kira wrapped the plaid around her. It smelled of man and woodsmoke. "I can't imagine he'd be easily persuaded."

"Aidan is a fair and reasonable man." He looked toward the keep, then back at her. "Crazed as it sounds, I suspect he might even be expecting you."

Aidan.

The breath froze in Kira's throat.

She said nothing, her tongue too thick for words.

Her champion shrugged, his gaze dipping to her feet and the hill-walking boots she'd bought before leaving on her trip. "Och, aye," he drawled, "I'd wager my soul you won't be a surprise."

Kira took a deep breath. "Why not?"

"Would that I could explain it. 'Tis a feeling I have here." Looking slightly sheepish, he pressed a hand to his heart.

Kira bit her lip, her own heart pounding so wildly, she wondered he didn't hear it.

Showing no signs of doing so, he stepped closer, his expression unreadable.

"Come now, let me get you down from here before you do catch a chill." He reached for her, sweeping her into his arms. "Aidan's in the great hall, holding council, though I doubt he'll mind the disruption," he added, hefting her over his shoulder as he made to jump from the arch.

But not before Kira caught a quick glimpse of Wrath Bay.

Wrath Bay, the incoming tide, and the little crescent-shaped strand.

A strand now crowded with colorful, square-sailed galleys.

Nary a keel mark to be seen.

Aidan slammed down his ale cup, well pleased with the decisions of his war council. " 'Tis settled, then." He lifted his voice so it was heard not just at the high table and on the dais but throughout Castle Wrath's hall. "Conan Dearg's time has come to pass. We ride for Ardcraig on the morrow. At first light and not a heartbeat later."

"Aye, let the bastard's days of bluster and swagger be ended!" someone yelled from the shadows.

"To his capture!" Another grabbed an ale jug, waving it in the air before taking a great swig. "May Wrath's dungeon give him a foretaste of hell!"

Cheers rose to the rafters, the hall resounding with agreement as men stamped their feet and rattled swords. Aidan looked on, scarce hearing them. Only his own voice echoing in his ears. Unable to rid himself of it, he pinned a furious stare on the platter of spiced salmon set before him and did his best to fight back a grimace.

A groan, too, were he honest.

Not a heartbeat later.

Lucifer's knees, but he'd made a poor word choice. A thoughtless mistake that only reminded him that his heart still thundered with thoughts of *her*. Certainty that she was near pounded through him, not letting go despite the impossibility of such a fool notion. He felt her all the same. Even now, when he could so easily swipe an arm across the table, sending feasting goods and ale hurtling to the floor.

At least the dogs would thank him.

And still she'd haunt him.

He scowled, his temples beginning to throb. "God's blood," he growled, snatching his ale cup and downing the frothy brew before such mooning got the better of him.

Now was not the time to dwell on her.

Now was—

The time for his world to upend. Spin around him, stealing his breath. The ale cup slid from his hand, landing on the table with a loud *clack* and spill of gold-tinged foam. Eyes wide, he shot to his feet. Uproar filled the hall, a ruckus unfolding near the shadowed entry. Scores of kinsmen shoved through the door, loud and boisterous. Murder on their faces. His best friend, cousin, what-have-you, led the fray, his *dream woman* clutched in the lout's arms.

"By the Rood," Aidan bellowed, staring. "What goes on here?"

"A witch!" Mundy, his Irish-born ax-man, raised his voice above the din. "We caught her dancing nekkid on the gatehouse arch, a horde o' winged demons flying round her head."

Hoots and guffaws accompanied Mundy's outburst,

one man slapping him hard on the back before leaping onto a trestle bench.

The trestle leaper's mirth vanishing, he peered round, his eyes glinting in the torchlight. "That flame-haired vixen wasn't nekkid and if Mundy saw flying demons, I saw none." He raised an arm to point at the lass. "She *is* garbed like no maid I've e'er seen, and Tavish is the only soul I ken able to vault to such heights. Seeing as she doesn't have wings, there's only one thing she can be—just what Mundy says. A witch!"

"She is none the like." Tavish's face darkened as he mounted the dais steps, Aidan's beauty still cradled protectively in his arms. "Ne'er have I carried a more *womanly* female," he vowed, setting her on her feet in front of the high table.

"I daresay you'll agree," he added, his gaze seeking Aidan's.

"Without doubt!" Still staring, he tamped down the urge to challenge his friend to a round in the lists for daring to touch his woman.

A thought that brought an immediate jab of guilt when he caught a closer look at his kinsmen's faces. Murder wasn't the only emotion painted on the fierce and bearded countenances he loved so well. Ranging from suspicion, to fear, to bloodlust, their expressions made it clear he owed Tavish much for coming to his *tamhasg*'s rescue.

"Where did you find her?" He glared at Tavish all the same, the blood roaring in his ears making it hard to think. "How did she get here?"

"I don't know how I got here." His *tamhasg* answered, brushing at the plaid slung loosely about her shoulders. "Not exactly. I—"

"She spelled herself here!" someone yelled.

Others chimed in, those standing near crossing themselves as they edged away from her.

"Cease!" Aidan slammed his fist on the table, jarring cutlery and tipping over wine goblets. "I'll no' have you babbling like women!" he roared, his fury squelching the foul-tempered rumbles.

For good measure, he put back his shoulders and looked round, letting his stare act as a further warning. Fear was something he couldn't condone within his walls. A MacDonald feared nothing. Even if his men seemed to have momentarily forgotten. He folded his arms, watching them. It also appeared to have slipped their minds that he didn't tolerate injustice. Another trait he expected all MacDonalds to adhere to.

Most especially in regard to females.

He drew a deep breath, schooling his features. He knew better than anyone else present that the woman was no witch.

Not that he meant to share how he knew it.

She *was* something he couldn't fathom. Not that he cared. All that mattered was that she stood before him. Scarce able to believe it, he came around the high table and put a hand on her arm, that one touch—her physical nearness—shooting jolts of white-hot flame all through him.

Fighting the urge to clutch her to him, he drew himself to his fullest height, feigning a look of fierceness lest his superstitious kinsmen doubt his ability to deal with a woman they held for a witch.

There would be time enough to win them over to her—if she wasn't an illusion.

Hoping she wasn't, he raised her arm and raked the hall with all the lairdly sternness he had in him. "I can feel this woman's warmth through her clothes. Even"—he jerked a glance at Tavish—"the thickness of Tavish's plaid. All ken witches have blood of ice. If she's of the Fae, or merely a troubled woman here to find succor, it will be for me to decide. No one else shall touch her or even glance askance at her. I forbid it."

Displeased grumbles answered him. A sea of shifting, nervous manhood, all with doubting, belligerent faces. Only a few looked down, swatting at sleeves and hitching sword belts.

"Come, Aidan." A gap-toothed man stepped forward, clearly speaking for them all. "You ken the damage a witch can wreak. Only last year, Widow MacRae's best cow started giving soured milk after the old woman granted a night's shelter to a witch. The same creature caused the widow's daughter to lose her bairn. And—"

"Nonsense!" Aidan cut him off, silencing the rest with another cold stare. "I'll have no such foolery spoken in my hall. The lass is no witch, and it will go poorly for the man who dares say so again. Mark it and be wary."

Beside him, his *tamhasg* sucked in a breath. "Of course, I'm not a witch. Or a fairy," Aidan thought he heard her say, though he couldn't be sure because the scent of her was clouding his wits. The closeness and heat of her sweet, lush body making him crazy.

"Your name." He looked at her, hoping that only he heard the thickness of his voice. "I would know it at last," he added, the words so low he wasn't even sure he'd said them.

Her eyes widened, the slight tremble of her lips telling him he had. "I'm Kira," she said, saying her name for the second time that evening. "Kira Bedwell."

"Kee-*rah* Bedwell," he repeated, pronouncing the name as her champion had, only with an even richer, sexier burr. " 'Tis an apt name."

Kira blinked, not certain she'd heard a slight emphasis on the last words.

His scowl told her she'd imagined it.

Not that it mattered.

With a voice like that he could set a woman into ecstasy just by reading the back of a cereal box. He'd sounded sexy in her dreams. In person, he undid her. Six feet four inches of pure, wild, and savage Highland masculinity was almost more than she could take. Especially when those inches were put together so well. His tall, muscle-ripped frame made all the more irresistible by the thick, silky black hair just brushing his shoulders and his dark, smoldering gaze.

"Lass." He looked at her, his eyes narrowing ever so slightly. "I'll ask you again—how did you get here?"

"It was a time slip." She lowered her voice, not wanting his men to hear. "One that . . . expanded. Or . . . oh, let's just say I've come a long way," she blurted, too awestruck to manage anything better. "From Aldan, Pennsylvania."

And I think I am going to faint.

Her heart had surely stopped. And with it, her ability to breathe. She stared up at him, everything in her world slamming to a halt. Nothing existed except the man before her. His gaze held hers, commanding and possessive. He towered over her, all medieval male and gorgeous, the look in his eyes melting her.

She blinked, swallowing against the fluttering in her stomach. The bite of so much smoke-filled air. An acrid haze that stung her eyes, while the reek of peat, overspiced food, dogs, and ale made her nose twitch. She stood frozen, taking it all in, her ears ringing with the grumbles of angry, tartan-draped men. Harried servants rushed past, their faces averted, the general, noisy chaos like nothing she could have imagined. It all whirled around her in a great, dizzying cacophony. The wild, torchlit, colorful place she'd dreamt of so long.

Diminished to nothing when compared with the wonder of *his* hand on her arm.

"See that no one disturbs us." He spoke again, his voice smooth, deep, and flowing right through her.

Even if his words were directed at the man called Tavish rather than her. "Settle the hall—even if you must draw blood."

Tavish nodded.

He frowned and turned away, pulling her along beside him. Kinsmen and dogs made way as they passed, heading for the shadowed arch of a nearby stair tower.

"I'd have words with you in my privy quarters," he told her, not breaking stride as he swept her off her feet, scooping her into his arms. "Words long overdue."

Then he was carrying her up the winding, torchlit stair, mounting the steps two at a time. Kira slid her arms around his neck, holding fast and biting her lip. The truth of her situation becoming more clear the higher they climbed up the tight, circular stair.

A very *new*-looking stair, lit by stinking, sputtering rush lights and whatever pale light fell through the narrow, deep-set arrow slits.

This was for real.

She was no longer dreaming about the ancient past—she was in it.

And judging by Aidan's frown, he was anything but pleased to see her there.

Chapter 5

Aidan was no longer scowling by the time he ascended the last few rounds of the stair tower and stopped outside his bedchamber door. Far from frowning, his countenance must now be thunderous. Indeed, he was certain of it, for he could feel the flames of anger licking the back of his neck and scalding his cheeks.

For two pins, he would tear back down to the hall, whip out his blade, and lop the heads off the first loose-tongued kinsmen who dared utter the word *witch* again.

Instead, he blew out a hot breath and kicked open his oak-planked door. Striding inside, his *tamhasg* still in his arms, he took some small satisfaction in slamming it behind them.

"So-o-o, lass." He released her at once. "Tell me, what magic brought you here?"

"I already told you I don't know." She stared back at him, her face as flushed as he suspected his must be. "Or rather, I'm not sure. I think I'm trapped in a time slip, though that's never happened before. All I know is that I was on the top of your arch and—"

"I know that." Aidan frowned, not about to admit

he hadn't understood half of what she'd said. Not just the words, but how she'd pronounced them. A problem he'd never had in their dreams. " 'Tis how you got there that interests me."

If you know me.

Not that he was going to ask. Not yet anyway.

First he needed to know what the blazes was going on.

Doing his best to look as if he did, he folded his arms. "Well?"

"If I knew I'd tell you." She shot a glance at the window arch, her eyes rounding at the dark outline of Wrath Isle. Recognition flashed across her face, her eyes widening even more when she turned back toward him and saw the colorful tapestry hanging so close to the window, his huge four-poster bed placed not far away.

"Holy moly." She pressed a hand to her breast, looking around.

Aidan's frown deepened. He understood *holy*, but *moly* was new to him. Not that the word was of any great import. Her astonishment spoke worlds.

She knew his room.

And that could only mean one thing.

She'd lived their dreams as vividly as he had.

The possibility enflamed him and he reached for her, seizing her shoulders. "You've been here." He tightened his grip on her, willing her to admit it. "I can see it all o'er you."

She twisted free, turning back to the window. Stepping closer, she touched the shutter hinges. She examined them, flattening her hands on the stone of the

embrasure before trailing her fingers down the tasseled edge of his tapestry.

"I can't believe how real all this is." She glanced at
him. "How real *you* are. For this long, anyway."

Aidan harrumphed. "I'm as real now as I was when
I woke this morn. 'Tis you I'm concerned about." He
looked at her, the whole situation making his head
pound. "You're no' making a word of sense."

The admission slipped out before he could stop it,
but rather than laugh at him as he'd almost expected,
she shook her head, looking just as dumbfounded as
he felt.

"It doesn't make sense to me, either," she said,
proving it. Her gaze flitted to his bed and then back
to him. "If this had happened at the Na Tri Shean, I
might not be so surprised, but—"

"The Na Tri Shean?" A chill sped down his back.
" 'Tis a bad place, that. Good folk would ne'er set
foot there."

"I'm not a witch." She drew Tavish's plaid more
tightly about her. "I had *business* at the fairy mounds.
That doesn't make me one of them."

"I ken what you are." Aidan closed his eyes, wishing he did.

He also tried not to breathe in her scent.

He wouldn't have believed it, but it was even more
wondrous than in their dreams. So enticing, it befud-
dled his wits. If he succumbed to it, he'd have her
naked and beneath him in a flash and such a breach
of honor would haunt him all his days.

MacDonalds wooed their women. Winning them
with sensual prowess and charm. With the exception

of a few aberrations like Conan Dearg, ne'er would a
man of Aidan's race take an unwilling female.

And Kira Bedwell wasn't just any female. She was
special beyond words. No matter how many fairy
mounds she knew about. Everyone knew of such
places. What mattered was that he wanted and needed
her to desire him as much now as she did in her
dream state.

Only then would he touch her. And only after a
suitable wooing period. She deserved as much and, as
laird, his dignity required it of him.

Much as the waiting pained him.

He looked at her, his heart thundering. "You've
been here." The truth of it pounded through him.
"Tell me, Kira, tell me you know."

She swiped a hand through her hair, the movement
sending Tavish's plaid fluttering to the floor. "Of
course I know." Color bloomed on her cheeks. "I've
been here in my dreams. *Our* dreams."

Aidan nodded. "Aye, lass. How much do you remember of them?"

Her throat worked. "I remember . . . everything."

"Even this?" He slid his arms around her, forcing
himself to hold her gently. "You must tell me, Kira.
If this, too, is familiar?" He smoothed one hand across
her back and with the other caressed the curve of her
hip, drawing her just a bit closer. "Or this?" He lowered his head to lightly brush her lips with his. "Speak
true, sweetness. I would hear the words. Exactly what
you recall."

Kira's face flamed. "I think you know."

"That's no' an answer." He watched her coolly,
every inch the proud, self-assured laird.

And so flesh-and-blood, staring-at-her real, she was sure she must be one big goose bump.

She shivered. His huge stone hearth and his peat fire ranked all kinds of prizes in the romance department, but those little orange-glowing bricks of turf couldn't compete with central heating.

With the exception of her face, she was suddenly f-r-e-e-z-i-n-g.

He blazed like a furnace.

Somehow her hand had become trapped between them, her splayed fingers pressed against the rough weave of his plaid. Heat poured off him, warming her even through the heavy wool. She could also feel the steady thumping of his heart and, a bit lower, the hard buckle of his sword belt digging into her belly. A discomfort as tangible and eye-opening as the cold and one that underscored that he wasn't just a real living and breathing man, he was a *medieval* man.

If she discounted Halloween, there weren't too many times a man in her world walked around with a giant broadsword slapping his thigh.

Aidan MacDonald looked like he was born wearing his.

She swallowed, just a bit daunted by so much muscle and steel.

"I'm waiting, Kee-*rah*."

"Ahhh . . ." The words lodged in her throat.

No way was she going to recite the explicit details of their nightly encounters.

She slid another glance at the tapestry near the window. The one she knew from her dreams. Moon glow slanted across it, the silvery light gilding each bright-gleaming thread and breathing life into the nude and half-clad figures artfully blended into an idyllic forest scene.

Figures entwined in intimate embraces that couldn't hold a candle to the kind of wild, uninhibited love-making they'd enjoyed in their dreams.

Unfortunately, at the moment she did feel a bit . . . inhibited.

And who wouldn't?

Getting down and dirty with a dream man was one thing, but getting all touchy-feely within minutes of a first real meeting, was a whole 'nuther kettle of fish, as her mother would say. Her mother also loved reminding her that no man bothered to buy a cow if the milk was free; whether Aidan had *dream-sampled* her offerings or not wasn't the question.

She'd never been a first-date-bedding kind of girl and she didn't want to start now, no matter how strong and wonderful his arms felt around her.

No matter how kissable his lips.

How good he smelled.

Or how badly she really did want him.

So she lifted her chin and met his stare, hoping she didn't have take-me-I'm-yours flashing on her forehead.

To her dismay, his arched brow and the heated look he pinned on her indicated she just might.

"So, will you say the words? Tell me true what you remember of our dreams?" He smoothed her hair back from her face, his touch sending a cascade of pleasure through her.

Pleasure so sweet, each shivery wave of tingles put a major dent in her jitters.

She clamped her lips together, not quite ready to admit it.

He angled his head. "Come, lass, I already know you to be a bold-hearted maid."

Kira glanced aside. If she looked at him, she'd be a goner. He was that intoxicating.

"Well?" He lifted a handful of her hair, letting the strands glide over his fingers.

Unnerved, she jerked her head back around. "There are no *wells* about it. No wondering, either. You know what I remember. Every bit of it, I'm sure!"

To her annoyance, he smiled.

Another of those conquering alpha-male hero smiles.

"O-o-oh, I believe I know well enough," he admitted, his smooth, whisky-rich burr making it all the more difficult not to throw her arms around his neck and cling to him.

He was, after all, a very *clingable* man.

So curl-her-toes-clingable that she slipped out of his arms before she made a spectacle of herself. Much better to give herself a little space and do some pacing.

Besides, it wasn't every day she got to walk on medieval floor rushes. Not knowing how long she would remain in his time, she dug one toe into the thick layer of fragrant meadowsweet or whatever such herb-strewn rushes were called, then took care to step beyond his reach.

"You canna deny it, lass. Wearing a track in my floor willna change anything." He folded his arms, watching her. His *voice* poured over and into her, the beauty of it making the impossible so incredibly real.

"I know that," she said, pacing anyway. "But moving around helps."

And she definitely needed help. Never would she have believed such a thing could happen.

A single fleeting glimpse . . . oh yes.

But never this.

She slid another glance at him, half expecting him to be gone, but he hadn't budged. He was still there. Bold as day and looking more fiercely handsome than the hottest hero she'd ever seen on the cover of a historical romance novel. Above all, he seemed so amazingly real, and she just couldn't wrap her mind around that.

Her Aidan. His Castle Wrath no longer a confused tumble of stones and broken walls, but a thriving, *living* place where he reigned supreme and had just tossed her over his shoulder and carried her up winding castle steps and into his bedchamber. An act that made the centuries between them as meaningless as a dust mote.

Her throat began to thicken and she swallowed. Never had she felt so overwhelmed.

She stopped her pacing to look at him. "You looked angry in the hall. As if you weren't pleased that I—"

"Angry?" His dark brows arced upward. "Precious lass, I was furious, but no' at you. I was wroth with my men and their foolery. What might have happened had Tavish not crossed the bailey when he did."

He stepped close to caress her face. "Ach, sweetness, you thought wrong." He smoothed his thumb over her lips. "Seeing you appear was like having the sun and the stars burst into my hall. I've burned for you, searching nightly. Waiting, always waiting, and ne'er giving up hope."

Kira's breath caught, something inside her stirring as never before.

Making her bold.

"Hoping what? That I would appear?" She looked up at him, his touch melting her. Heating her. Even the room's chill seemed less biting. In fact, it was almost beginning to feel stuffy. Sure of it, she slipped out of her heavy waxed jacket and let it drop onto the discarded plaid.

He looked at the jacket, then at her. "O-o-oh, lass." His eyes darkened. "You ought not ask what I hoped for—not if hearing the answer will frighten you."

"I'm not frightened." She flipped back her hair and assumed her most unfrightened expression. "I . . . only need time to adjust."

His expression told her he wasn't buying her denial.

Would a kiss put you at ease?

Kira blinked, not sure she'd heard the softly spoken words.

"A kiss?" She spoke quickly before her courage fizzled.

He nodded.

"I don't think a kiss is a good idea just now."

In fact, she knew it wasn't. Just his thumb sliding back and forth across her lips had her hormones on fire. Each word he spoke in that deep, smooth-as-sin burr took her breath and made her fear she might even drown in its richness. A *kiss* would be the end of her.

"No kisses," she emphasized, shaking her head.

"Ach, lass, dinna think it willna cost me, too," he purred, pure male possessiveness rolling off him. "If I kissed you but once, I'd burn to kiss you for hours. Even days. But know this"—he paused to glide his knuckles down the side of her face—"I mean to court you properly, as is fitting. For the now, I'll only kiss you. Naught else until you're ready."

Kira almost choked.

She glanced aside, not wanting him to see how very ready she was.

He captured her chin, forcing her to look at him. "I also mean to chase the worry from your eyes. You ought to know I would ne'er let anyone harm you."

Kira's heart skittered. "It isn't a person I'm worried about."

"Then what?"

"Something far more impossible than our dreams."

He frowned. "It canna be as impossible as you being here."

"It has everything to do with me being here."

She looked down, searching for words, and ending up plucking at her clothes. The fine weave of her top and the stretch wool of her pants at such odds with his rough Highland garb. Her wristwatch, a gleaming incongruity in his world of rush-strewn floors and smoking torchlights, his massive timber-framed bed and the erotic tapestries covering his walls.

Tapestries she'd only ever seen on her one long-ago visit to Scotland. Or, more often, in the glossy colored pages of coffee-table books on castles.

Ancient castles that belonged to a world as distant from hers as the moon.

She nudged the floor rushes a second time, remembering with a pang the times he'd loved her so fiercely that the power of their joinings ripped away her apartment walls, letting her see through her dreams and into the time and place he called his own.

This place, where she'd never thought to stand.

She bit her lip. Any moment she could be whisked away, swept right out of his arms and back to her time. The place she *did* belong, but that would feel so empty now—now that she had finally felt his arms around her for real.

However briefly.

She swallowed and broke away from him, not wanting him to see her concern. But he must have, because he moved with lightning speed, his strong fingers clamping around her arm and yanking her back against him.

"You needn't look so troubled, Kee-*rah.*" His embrace almost crushed her. "Whate'er it is that fashes you has yet to face a MacDonald."

She shook her head, about to tell him that all of Clan Donald's medieval might couldn't conquer the hands of time, but before she could, his mouth crashed down over hers in a searing, demanding kiss.

A deep, soul-slaking kiss full of hot breath, sighs, and tangling tongues. A beautiful melding to cross time and space and ignite a man and a woman in a pleasure so exquisite that she would have melted into a puddle on his rushy floor if he hadn't been squeezing her to him in such a fearsome hold.

Clutching him just as fiercely, she opened her mouth wider, welcoming the deep thrustings of his tongue. The hot glide of his hands roving up and down her back, exploring all her curves and hollows, the way his skilled fingers sought and held her hips.

"Och, lass. I knew you were near." He breathed the words against her lips. "I've felt you close for days, looked for you."

"Yesss . . ." She moaned, tangling her fingers in his hair, pressing her breasts against him.

Time stopped, no longer of importance. He tightened his arms around her, his kiss making her forget everything except her hunger. The raging need to be one with him and have him touch and taste her, to forget all caution and just lose herself in the madness of his raw, sensual heat.

Heat she knew so well and wanted again.

This time for real.

She sighed, the heavy silk of his hair spilling through her fingers as he kept kissing her, each delicious swirl of his tongue against hers making her burn.

Sweet, hot tingles raced across the softness between her thighs, igniting a fire that made her wild. She leaned into him, the feel of his thick, rigid arousal electrifying her. The sexy Gaelic love words he whispered against her throat driving her beyond reason.

Until one of his roaming hands slid across her wristwatch, his seeking fingers hooking around the elastic metal watchband. His frown returning, he peered at the timepiece, lifting her arm to the light of a softly hissing oil lamp.

"It's a watch," Kira breathed, his scowl making her stomach clench.

Clench, and growl.

Loudly.

After all, she hadn't eaten since leaving Ravenscraig's One Cairn Village. Substantial as her full Scottish breakfast had been, she was now so ravenous, she'd gladly devour every crumb of Lindsay's crushed and crumbling organic chocolate chip cookies.

Instead, more pressing matters plagued her.

Namely, Aidan's furrowed brow as he eyed her bargain-basement imitation of a Swiss masterpiece.

"Where did you get this?" He fingered the smooth glass of the watch face. "You didn't wear it in our dreams."

"It's my watch." Kira glanced at it. "I take it off before I sleep. That's why you've never seen it. It tells the time."

He scoffed. "I'm no fool, lass," he countered, his sexy burr still making her burn, no matter how fiercely he glowered at her watch. "I know it's a timepiece. My grandfather had one no' unlike yours. A second-century bronze Roman sundial, small enough to fit in the scrip he wore from his belt."

"*Scrip?*" This time Kira blinked.

He slanted his mouth over hers in another swift, bruising kiss. "Yon is my scrip." He broke the kiss to jerk his head toward an iron-studded strongbox at the foot of his bed.

A rough-leathered sporran rested atop the chest's domed cover, the sight of it only reminding Kira how far back in time she'd spiraled.

And of the fine MacDonald sporran she'd hoped to make into a purse.

Something that would have made a fine gift for Aidan, had it not gone missing when she'd been swept back in time.

She stared at the scrip for a long moment, then looked down at her watch, not wanting to think about the centuries dividing them.

Apparently feeling the same, he unlatched the watch with surprising ease and tossed it onto her jacket. "It willna do if my men see you wearing suchlike." His voice came low and husky, a deep purr that made a little thing like an imitation Swiss watch seem ever so insignificant. "While I might no' have trouble accepting the Fae can fashion such a timepiece, my men might disagree. To be sure, they'd see it as proof you're a witch."

Kira swallowed, the significance of her watch returning like a fist to the gut.

"I told you," she said, amazed by the steadiness of her voice, "I am neither a fairy nor a witch. I'm Kira Bedwell of Aldan, Pennsylvania. I'm a far-seer. A paranormal investigator. And I come from the future. The early twenty-first century, to be exact."

He arched one raven brow, clearly not believing her. "Sweetness, I already ken you aren't of these parts and I'll personally take down the first man who calls you a witch. But there's no wrong in being of the Fae. I doubt there's a Highlander walking who'd deny them, and many are they who've even wed with them. We all ken the tales."

He pressed two fingers to her lips when she tried to protest. "Be that as it may, I'd warn you not to say aught about them to anyone but me. Above all, dinna mention any tall tales about para-*whate'er* or the future. If my men heard you speak the like, even I might have difficulty controlling them."

"But it's the truth." She puffed her bangs off her forehead, the last of her tingles flying out the window. "If you believe in witches and fairies, why can't you accept someone who can look into the past? Or see ghosts?"

"I've no problem with bogles." He waved a dismissive hand. "These hills are full of haints. 'Tis this far-seeing and Penn-*seal* business I'm concerned about."

Kira sighed, a hot, tight knot forming at the base of her neck, just between her shoulder blades. "Far-seeing is a gift I have—as do many others. It runs in my family, on my mother's side, though I'm the first to have it in generations. I only learned I'd inherited it when I saw you years ago, that very first time. Now, I use it to look into haunted sites and legends. Supernatural phenomena. *Destiny Magazine* employs me and I—"

"You're wearing those wretched raiments again." He stepped back and folded his arms, the medieval laird in him blocking his ears to everything she'd said. "All I care about is how it is I saw you at the top of my stair all those years ago only to have you vanish out of my arms. Then"—his gaze held hers, dark with smoldering passion—"you appear in my dreams, night after night, making me burn for you and no other. And now you're here."

Kira moistened her lips, certain she would moan out loud if he kept that smoldering stare on her.

"I've been trying to tell you. My *gift* let us see each other on the stair." She tried not to squirm. "How can I explain it to you? I'm able to see things . . . to look into the distant past. I don't know how the dreams worked. Or why I'm here now. I never really believed in time travel until—"

"Time travel?"

She nodded.

His lips curved into a slow, sensual smile. No, an indulgent smile. The kind that would have been insulting were he not, well, medieval.

"I think you should sleep," he announced suddenly, clearly tired of their conversation. "Aye, a good long sleep will serve you well."

Definitely meaning it, he scooped her into his arms and carried her across the room, lowering her onto the soft fur coverings of his bed. "A good sleep without those raiments. Ne'er have I cared for the like, and you canna wear them here."

"I don't think I'll be around long enough for them to bother anyone."

He cocked a brow. "Och, lass, you'll no' be going anywhere," he said, looking sure of it. "I'll no' allow it."

Kira frowned at him. "I don't think that would matter much. Not against Father Time."

"As for your raiments," he said as if she hadn't spoken, "they bother *me* enough to twist my head in knots. I'll no' have my men going gog-eyed o'er them."

He reached to finger the button above her zipper, his brows snapping together when the thing popped off and arced through the air.

"By the Rood!" He jerked his hand back, staring first at the suicidal button, resting so innocently on the floor rushes, then at the metal teeth of her zipper.

Kira cringed. She could well imagine what it must look like to him.

"It's just a zipper," she said, the strange word making his head throb even more.

She clasped her hand over it and scooted away from him across the bed. Almost as if she feared he'd harm the thing. Aidan almost snorted, and would have, had the wee disk flying off her hose not rattled him to the core. Ne'er had he seen the like. He frowned and rammed a hand through his hair. Och, nay, by a thousand red-tailed devils, he wasn't about to touch the zip-*her*.

Nor would it do to let her see how much her outlandish garb unsettled him.

He was, after all, a man with a reputation to uphold. A brave-hearted chieftain who'd faced death on the battlefield more times than he could count. And he'd defy the flames of Hades and all its winged demons to keep this woman safe, flying disks and zip-*hers* or nay. So he attempted his most worldly pose, standing as tall as only a MacDonald could, his hands clasped loosely behind his back.

"Have done with these garments and sleep," he ordered, the commanding tone a wee nod to his fierce Highland pride. "I'll keep my back turned the while, then take my own rest in yon chair." He indicated his resting chair, a great oaken monstrosity beside the hearth fire.

Not that he meant to sleep this night.

O-o-oh, no.

This night, at least, he'd keep a sharp eye on her. Anything else struck him as extremely unwise. Perhaps he'd even shove his strongbox in front of the door later. Every female he knew could unbolt a drawbar without difficulty, but he knew nary a one who would be able to budge his heavy iron-banded coffer.

Feeling better already, he stretched his hands to the fire, warming them. Behind him, he could hear her scrambling out of her clothes, then settling beneath his covers. O-o-oh, how he ached to join her there— but such pleasures would come soon enough.

Perhaps even sooner than was wise if the twitchings in his tender parts were any indication.

Trying his best to ignore them, he stood unmoving, waiting until he was sure she slept before he moved to his chair. A chair that suddenly struck him as uncomfortable as the stirring at his loins. Why he'd e'er deemed it his *resting chair* he didn't know.

How he expected to sleep in it was well beyond him.

Scowling once more, he leaned his head back against the hard, cold wood and threw a spare plaid over his knees. Only then, safely hidden from possibly prying glances, did he ease one hand beneath the plaid and squeeze a certain part of himself until his eyes watered and all desire left him.

A drastic measure he suspected he might have to employ more than once before the night was over.

Sleep was certainly out of the question.

Especially since the fool night wind was picking up, its wretched blasts rattling the window shutters. A persistent, ongoing racket, the likes of which would've kept a deaf man from a good night's slumber.

He cursed beneath his breath and shifted on the chair.

Unfortunately, his best efforts at ignoring the noise only caused the din to increase. Even yanking the spare plaid over his head proved futile. The wind's howling rose to a teeth-grinding pitch, and the banging shutters became so loud he considered ripping them from their hinges the instant he felt awake enough to see to the task.

Awake enough?

He blinked, the thought jarring him so thoroughly that he sat bolt upright.

He *had* fallen asleep.

And though a fuzzy-headed glance at the bed showed that his lady yet slumbered deeply, the new day broke in a wild cacophony around him.

"By the saints," he grumbled, rubbing his hands over his face. Chaos rang in his ears, loud and penetrating. Poor Ferlie's howls, which he'd mistaken for the wind, and the sharp rapping at his door that wasn't rattled shutters at all.

"Sir!" came the voice of one of his squires, followed by another burst of knocking.

Ferlie gave a piercing bark and charged the door.

Aidan swore and leapt from his chair. Still half-asleep, he grabbed for his clothes and his sword, then bounded across the room, the name Conan Dearg pounding through his mind in rhythm to his squire's door hammering.

This was the morn they rode to Ardcraig.

The day he was sure they would finally capture his dastardly cousin.

Aidan scowled, his pleasure in the deed dampened by the thought of such a cur beneath the same roof as Kira—even with the craven secure in Castle Wrath's dungeon. Pushing the notion from his mind, he reached for the drawbar, only to stub his toe on his strongbox.

"God's mercy!" he scolded, absolutely refusing to acknowledge the pain shooting up his leg.

Furious, he unbolted the door. Flinging it wide, he realized too late that he'd latched his sword belt around his naked hips.

His plaid lay bunched around his feet, where he must've dropped it when he opened the door.

Not that his slack-jawed squire paid his appearance any heed.

Far from it. The youth's stare shot past him, homing in on a naked form far more pleasing than his own. And thanks to the carelessness of sleep, a ripe, well-made nakedness that left little to the lad's red-faced imagination.

Or Aidan's.

His gaze, too, flew straight to Kira's bared and creamy breasts, the lush triangle of flaming curls plainly visible between her slightly parted thighs.

"You've seen nothing." He whipped back around, fixing the squire with his sternest laird's look. "No' if you wish to properly enjoy such sweetness yourself when you're old enough."

Not giving the lad a chance to see it was an empty threat, for he'd ne'er harm a youth—certainly not for ogling a fetching, bare-bottomed female—Aidan stepped into the doorway, making sure his shoulders blocked the view.

"Tell Tavish to see our men mounted at once," he ordered, trying to maintain as much dignity as he could, garbed as he was in naught but his great sword. "I'll join them anon."

As soon as his big toe quit throbbing and he was more suitably dressed. He also had to see to a few other urgent matters. Things that bit deeply into his conscience but that he deemed necessary.

Indeed, vital.

Things that would ensure that his *tamhasg* would find it difficult to leave him.

Chapter 6

Kira awoke to absolute stillness.

She also had a raging headache, a twitching nose, and, she'd bet on it, horribly swollen eyes.

Frog eyes. Red, bulging, and achy.

O-o-oh, yes, even without the luxury of a peek in her bathroom mirror, she knew she must look like death warmed over served on icy-cold toast.

She felt that bad.

Not an unusual occurrence in recent times, considering her perturbation with the media hounds who'd persisted in dogging her every step since she'd owned up to the discovery of the Viking longship and its New England moorings. Truth was, every new morning had seen her reaching for the aspirin and glass of water she kept handy on her night table. Just as sleepless nights spent tossing and turning resulted in aching, puffy eyes.

Annoyances she'd grown accustomed to.

But the thick and furry covers tickling her nose *were* beyond the norm, as was the undeniable scent of dog. No, *dawg*. Much more than a mere hint of dander on the cold, peat-tinged air, the smell was overpowering and definitely there.

A big, smelly dog odor as real as the massive, richly carved medieval bed in which she found herself.

Even if the beast himself wasn't anywhere to be seen. He'd been there. That stood without question. Just as the bed was certainly real, its heavily embroidered curtaining parted just enough to give her a view of tall arch-topped windows and the burgeoning morn. A new day that was *not* breaking over the crowded parking lot of Aldan, Pennsylvania's low-budget Castle Apartments.

Nor the small and cozy car park of the tiny Skye inn she hadn't even spent a night in.

Indeed, she couldn't be in a more different place if she'd stowed away on a rocket to Mars.

Kira's heart began to pound and her mouth went dry. Her headache worsened, and although she would have preferred not to admit it, she feared her time of the month was about to play havoc with her as well. Rarely had she felt so miserable. If she didn't soon feel better, she'd suspect she was allergic to time travel.

Or medieval Scotland.

Much as the notion displeased her.

There could be no doubt that she'd landed there. Even if she weren't peering through the bed curtains at the proof, the lack of noise was a giveaway. There *was* a stiff wind. It blew and moaned, and from somewhere above her came the snapping of what might have been a banner flying from the parapets. She also heard the muffled barking of dogs and the repetitive wash of the waves on the rocks below.

What she didn't hear was the twenty-first century.

The maddening blare of leaf blowers and you-ride-'em-cowboy lawn mowers or deaf old Mr. Wilson's television droning through her apartment's bedroom wall. No rattling of garbage trucks or distant sirens. Not even the low hum of her computer or the weird pops and shudders her ancient refrigerator was always making.

She heard . . . simply nothing.

She listened hard, the silence almost hurting her ears. Half certain that her admittedly wild imagination was conjuring the stillness, she squeezed her eyes shut and opened them again, but the quiet remained. As did the whole medieval-y room, the doggy smell, and the great, dark bulk of Wrath Isle so visible through the tall, arched windows.

Her stomach gave a funny little dip. Last she'd looked, Aldan, Pennsylvania, couldn't claim such a view.

Nor could Castle Wrath—leastways not in the ruinous state she knew it.

Her heart still thumping, she held the furry covers to her breasts as she peered through the gap in the bed curtains. In addition to the window alcoves and view, she was greeted by whitewashed walls and the erotically decadent tapestries that had so startled her the night before.

Her first true indication that she stood in the medieval bedchamber she recognized from her dreams.

Now, some hours later, she swallowed hard. The room's not-so-savory-looking floor rushes and the torchlights in their heavy iron wall brackets took away any last doubt that she was still in Aidan's world.

Trapped there and . . . naked.

Unless time traveling had not just given her a shattering headache but affected her memory as well. She dug her fingers into the pillow, considering the possibility. To be sure, she remembered undressing beneath the covers, but a quick scan of the floor refused to reveal where she'd dropped her clothes.

Or, better said, where she'd flung them.

In particular, her panties and her bra.

Neither bit of crucially important underwear was anywhere to be seen. And for the life of her, unless she was horribly mistaken, the rest of her clothes had gone missing as well. Everything was gone. Including her beloved hill-walking boots, and even her bargain-basement Swiss watch.

Nothing remained to remind her of her own left-behind world.

Even more alarming, Aidan had vanished, too.

Heaven help her if she'd only imagined him.

Conjured his hot-eyed stares and his heart-stopping kisses, the old-fashioned, take-charge sense of chivalry she found so utterly endearing.

Woo her, indeed.

He'd made only one mistake. Hiding her clothes wasn't the way to her heart. Nor was leaving her behind in a strange, doggy-smelling bedchamber, even if she did know the room from their dreams. Too many big, hairy people here seemed to want a piece of her, and not the way she knew their laird did.

She bit her lip, her pulse beating rapidly. It was one thing to be stuck in medieval Skye with Aidan at her side during the day and guarding her come nightfall, and something else entirely to be stranded here alone.

Nearly as distressing, she was hungrier than she could recall being in her entire life and—gasp! horrors!—she felt an urgent need to visit what she knew medieval people called the jakes. If the fates were kind, she would find one of the minuscule water closets tucked away in a discreet corner of Aidan's oh-so-lairdly bedchamber.

If not, she'd simply have to find something to wrap around her nakedness and go looking for one. But first she took a deep breath and peered around the room one more time, just to make sure the *dawg* wasn't lurking in some dark and musty corner, waiting for her.

Not that she didn't like dogs.

She loved them.

But the ones she'd seen barking at her in the bailey weren't the garden-variety, toddle-down-the-sidewalk-looking-happy kind of dogs she was so crazy about. The shaggy, fang-toothed beasts that had gathered beneath the gatehouse arch had looked anything but friendly.

Shuddering at the memory, she slipped from the bed, certain she didn't want anything to do with such monsters. She could still feel their agitated stares.

Or someone's.

A disturbing sensation that came at her from two places—the other side of the closed oak-paneled door and, oddly, from outside the tall arched windows.

The back of her neck prickled, and she grabbed a pillow, holding it in front of her just in case the room was outfitted with one of those peekaboo *squint holes* she knew could be found in medieval castles. Half afraid that might be the case, she crept around the corner of the huge curtained bed, relief washing over her when she spied the mound of clothes piled on top of Aidan's massive iron-banded strongbox.

Not her clothes, unfortunately, but clearly meant for her.

If she could figure out how to wear them.

Not sure that was possible, she picked up what could only be an *arisaid*. "A *yarusatch*," she breathed, pronouncing it as she knew was correct for the female version of the ancient belted plaid.

But whether she could say the thing's name properly or not, it still looked like an overlong bedsheet, finely made of a white-based plaid shot through with thin stripes of black, blue, and red. There wasn't any way she could manage to drape it on without ending up looking like a ghost.

Despite the heavily carved silver brooch someone had thoughtfully tucked into its folds.

"No-o-o, I think I'll pass." She shook her head, then carefully refolded the cloth and placed it on the bed. Celtic shoulder brooch and all. Exiting the room dressed like Casper-in-drag would only have Aidan's scowling-faced clansmen growling at her again.

Sure of it, she examined the other garments, pleased to see that they appeared easier to slip into. A basic-looking woolen gown in a rich shade of dark blue and an emerald green overdress that could only be made of silk. It spilled across her fingers, cool and luxuriant to the touch. The third gown, clearly a lightweight cotton undershift, proved equally delicate.

Regrettably, it also appeared to be the only underwear in the pile.

She frowned. Hoping it wasn't so, she searched

through the garments again, only to have her dread confirmed. Underwear as she knew and appreciated it apparently didn't exist in Aidan's world, even if he could afford fine silks and silver brooches.

At least there were shoes.

She stared at them, not surprised that she'd over-looked them, for in the shadow cast by the bed, the deerhide *cuarans* were difficult to see against the floor rushes. Little more than longish, oval-shaped slippers laced all around with a thin leather cord, they would have reminded her of moccasins if they hadn't looked so ridiculously big.

Big or not, she had to *go*, so she pulled on the silk undergown and the remaining clothes as quickly as she could, pointedly ignoring the *arisaid* and its brooch. She also tried not to notice how awkward the soft-soled, giant *cuarans* felt on her feet.

She wasn't even going to think about her lack of underwear.

Instead, she steeled herself and took a few trial steps in the clumsy shoes. Nothing like her comfortable hill-walking boots, they flipped and flopped with every step, making it next to impossible to walk, as did the long, loose skirts swishing around her legs. Frowning again, she hitched them above her knees so she could march to the door and sail through it on her quest to find a latrine.

She had a pretty good idea where one might be located, but when she yanked open the door, sweeping through it proved impossible.

A tartan-hung boy stood there, a huge platter of food clutched in his hands. He gasped, his face beet-red and his eyes darting any which way but in her direction.

"Oops!" Kira dropped her skirts at once, the near collision only causing the boy to flush all the deeper. Delicious smells wafted up from his food tray, making her mouth water, but *other urges* took precedence.

Even over politeness.

"Sorry." She forced a smile as she tried to squeeze past him. "If that's breakfast, I thank you. Just put it anywhere and I'll dig into it when I get back."

"There'll be no need to be a-getting back as you willna be going anywhere." A burly, great-bearded Highlander stepped from the shadows, the steel glinting all over him underscoring the authority of his deep, don't-argue-with-me voice. "The laird gave orders you are no' to leave his chamber."

A second man snorted. Every bit as well built and ferocious-looking as the other, he snatched the food tray from the boy's hands and narrowed his eyes at her, suspicion rolling off him. "If you even eat the like, you can break your fast alone. We'll keep watch that no one disturbs you."

Kira bristled. "*You* are disturbing me," she shot back, planting her hands on her hips. "I have to go to the ladies' room. The *loo*, if that makes more sense to you!"

Apparently it didn't—the two men merely stared at her, blank-faced and clearly not willing to budge.

Realizing retreat wasn't an option, she held her ground. "Your laird wouldn't wish me to be so . . . discomforted," she said, trying for a more medieval tone. "He'd—"

"Lord Aidan isn't here." The man with the food tray stepped closer, seeming to swell in size as he loomed over her. "He's charged us to see to your comfort, and we have—by bringing you sustenance."

"We can take it away as easily," the other informed her. "If the offerings don't please you."

Kira pressed her lips together, trying hard not to shift from foot to foot. "It isn't that," she began, wondering if she could make a run for it. "I have to—"

"I think she has to use the jakes," the boy chimed in, his embarrassed gaze flicking from one angry-looking Highlander to the other. "The laird said she might have to—"

"The laird isn't himself of late." The first man grabbed her arm and dragged her back inside the room. "If she has suchlike needs, the pot beneath the bed will suffice."

"Not with you looking!" Kira jerked free of the man's grasp and glared at him. "With *no one* looking," she added, rubbing her arm as the *dawg* shuffled into the chamber and plopped down beside the fire, his milky gaze watching her every move.

"No one," she insisted, folding her arms.

The second man plunked down her breakfast tray on a table near the window embrasure. "Watch your tongue, lassie. The laird loses interest in wenches sooner than an autumn wind blows leaves from the trees."

Kira sniffed. Not about to show any weakness, she put back her shoulders and strode over to the hearth, where she ruffed the dawg's head, taking courage from her firm belief that such an ancient creature, however fearsome-looking, was well past the days of biting.

Proving her right, the beast licked her hand.

Kira smiled, as did the red-faced youth still hovering on the threshold.

The two burly Highlanders frowned at her. "We'll be outside yon door," the first one said, jerking his head in that direction. "You won't be winning o'er the rest o' us as easily as old Ferlie."

As if on cue, the dog bared his teeth and growled at the man, his protectiveness earning a scowl. "The laird ought be returned by nightfall," the second man announced, already moving toward the door. "See you dinna cause us any trouble, lest you wish to meet his dark side."

And then the two men were gone, closing the door behind them and leaving her with a full-laden breakfast tray, a moony-eyed geriatric dog, and a pee-pot she couldn't wait to get her hands on.

Fortunately, once she knew where the thing was, it didn't prove difficult to find. Or use. Not that she could imagine ever growing overly fond of such quaintness. All things considered, there were worse annoyances in her own world.

Leaf blowers came to mind.

Or the persistent shrill of the telephone whenever she sat down to concentrate on one of her stories for *Destiny Magazine*. O-o-oh, yes, by comparison, a chamber pot was definitely the lesser evil.

Even the dawg, a creature that looked like a cross between an Irish wolfhound and a donkey, no longer seemed quite so daunting. She'd reserve judgment on his buddies down in the bailey.

"You're not quite a Jack Russell, but I like you," she said, watching him watch her.

Still feeling someone else's eyes on her, she shivered as she washed her hands with cold water from a ewer and basin. She hadn't noticed such amenities earlier, but enough gray morning light was now seeping in through the windows for her to quickly spot what she'd missed. Not just the ewer and basin, but also a small earthen jar of lavender-scented soap and even a comb. A short, folded length of linen she assumed was a medieval drying cloth.

Whether it was or not, she made good use of it.

Just as she would do justice to her breakfast, even if she wasn't quite sure what everything was. Determining to find out, she sat at the table, pleased to recognize oatcakes and cheese, while a green-glazed pottery bowl appeared to be filled with mutton stew. Another dish of the same type held what she suspected might be spiced and pickled eels, a delicacy she doubted she'd try. A small crock of honey and a jug of heather-scented ale rounded out the offerings.

Not too shabby, and certainly more edible-looking than some of things her sister Lindsay tried to palm off on her at times, even though just looking at the eels made her feel like gagging.

Her new four-legged friend suffered no such aversion. His scraggly ears perking, and wearing the most hopeful look she'd ever seen on a dog's face, he pushed to his feet and crossed the room to circle the table, eyeing everything on her breakfast tray as a potential tidbit.

"Okay, Ferlie." She handed him an oatcake. "You win this battle, but the war's not over."

Pasting on a smile for his benefit, she helped herself

to one as well, smearing her own with the soft cheese and honey. Unfortunately, despite her best efforts at trying to stay upbeat, waves of ill ease kept sluicing through her, and the odd prickling at the back of her neck increased tenfold just since she'd sat at the table.

Someone really was staring at her.

And she could no longer deny where the sensation was coming from. Not now, sitting so close to the source. Chills running up and down her spine, she stood, her gaze on the tall arched windows.

Whoever—or whatever—was staring at her was out there, beyond the opened shutters.

"Aieeeeeeeeeeeee!" The piercing scream, a woman's, proved it.

Heart pounding, Kira ran into the window alcove, horror slamming into her when she leaned out the first arched opening to see a woman bobbing in the rough waters beneath Wrath Isle's deadly perpendicular cliffs.

"Dear God!" She clapped a hand to her throat, disbelief and shock stopping her breath.

The woman thrashed frantically and appeared to have a rope tied around her waist—a rope with dead seabirds dangling from its entire length!

Not trusting her eyes, she leaned farther out the window, but there was no mistake. Even through the scudding mists, she could see that the poor woman was encircled by dozens of seabirds-on-a-rope, their buoyant white bodies keeping her afloat as the swift current swept her out to sea.

"Eachann!" the woman wailed, her voice full of despair. "I canna reach the rocks!"

"Get help! Anyone! *Please!*" a second voice cut through the morning, louder and deeper. A man's cry, his terror sounding even greater than the woman's.

"Hold, lass. I willna let you drown!" he yelled, and Kira saw him then, dashing back and forth along Wrath Isle's cliff-tops.

Waving his arms and staring her way, he clearly hoped someone at the castle would see or hear and send help. A boat and men to rescue the woman Kira knew instinctively was his wife.

No, she was the man's life.

His everything, and his anguish seared Kira to the bone.

Waving her own arms, she called to them. "Hang on! Help is on the way!" she shouted, even as she whirled and raced for the door.

She reached to yank it wide, but she needn't have bothered, for it flew open in her face. Her two guardsmen stood there, hands fisted on their hips and glaring at her.

"Have you lost your wits?" The bigger of the two stared at her as if she'd sprouted horns. "Making a din and ranting like a madwoman. The laird—"

"The laird will have your hide if you allow a poor woman to drown!" Kira gave him an adrenaline-powered shove and streaked down the corridor, shouting as she ran. "Help! Someone get a boat! There's a woman in the water!"

"Ho! Come back here, you!" The men bounded after her, their pounding footsteps spurring her on. Yanking up her skirts, she careened around a bend in the dimly lit passage, the flapping, oversized *cuarans* making her clumsy.

"Damn!" she swore when one of them went sailing off her foot. Snatching it, she raced on, but the guardsmen caught up with her, the bigger one grabbing her arm.

"Saints of mercy! That was ill done." He glowered at her. "Think you we'd no' aid a drowning woman?"

"If she saw one." The other man stood panting, fury all over him. "I dinna believe her."

"Of course, I saw the woman," Kira insisted, trying to jerk free. "She'll soon be dead if you don't stop arguing and go save her!"

The bigger man shot the other a glance. "I'll no' stand by and have a woman drown. I say we make haste to look for her." Hefting Kira off her feet, he tossed her over his shoulder and hurried for the stair tower. "Someone in the hall can keep an eye on this one until we return."

"She'll have slipped away by then," the other scoffed, huffing after them. "No woman within these walls is fool enough to fall off the cliffs."

"Bah!" the first man disagreed. "She could have slipped on the rocks down at the landing beach. Perhaps one of the laundresses or—"

"No." Kira twisted in the man's arms. "She fell from the cliffs of Wrath Isle."

The man carrying her stopped short. "That canna be," he said, dropping her to her feet. "No one lives on Wrath Isle. 'Tis a scourged place."

Kira lifted her chin. "I didn't see her fall from there, but I know she did. I saw her husband running along the cliff-top. She called him Eachann."

The big man's eyes rounded. "*Eachann*, was it?"

Kira nodded.

The two men exchanged glances. "Would there have been anything else you noted about the woman?" the big one wanted to know. "Something . . . odd-looking?"

Kira swallowed. She didn't like the way they were watching her. "The woman had a rope tied to her," she said anyway. "A rope with dead seabirds attached to it."

"By the Rood!" The big man jumped back and crossed himself.

The other turned white as a ghost. "I told you there was something no' right about her!"

"No, please." Kira looked from one to the other. "You must help the woman. She'll drown if you don't."

"That's no' possible." The big man shook his head. "Eachann MacQueen's wife already drowned. Her life-rope broke when he lowered her down the cliffs to gather seabirds. Happened nigh onto a hundred years ago. The bards still tell the tale."

Kira's blood froze. She should've realized she was far-seeing the tragedy. But the woman's cries had sounded so real, and she'd tasted the man's terror, alive and coiling around her, squeezing the breath from her.

Somehow, having already gone so far back in the past, she hadn't expected to catch any glimpses of an even more distant time.

But apparently she'd guessed wrong, and although her two tormentors hadn't yet said the *w*-word, their opinion of her was plain to see.

"I am not a witch." She put up her hands, palms

outward. "Please don't be afraid. I can explain every-thing."

The big man crossed himself again and took another step or two backward.

The other snorted. "Aye, and you will, but no' to the likes of us. 'Tis the laird who'll want to know how it is you saw something that happened before any of us were even born. Lest you're indeed a fairy or one of those other creatures we've been forbidden to call you."

"I'm neither," Kira protested, her eyes flying wide when the man yanked a dirk from beneath his belt and began prodding her down the corridor, away from Aidan's bedchamber.

"Where are you taking me?" she demanded, scoot-ing along ahead of his jib-jabbing dirk all the same.

Bravado went only so far and hers stopped at a knife edge.

Apparently the two guardsmen's willingness to speak to her had also ceased. A glance over her shoul-der showed them stony-faced and tight-lipped. Not that she needed any clues as to her destination. They were herding her into a narrow side corridor, a slop-ing, dank-smelling passage with a small, unpleasant-looking door at its end.

Kira's heart began to thunder and her mouth went dry.

She'd seen such passageways on her long-ago tour to Scotland and she knew exactly where they always led.

"O-o-ooh, please!" Pride forgotten, she dug in her heels and braced her hands against the cold, slime-coated walls. A sharp prick of the dirk to her back got her moving again. "Please don't take me down there," she pleaded. "I won't bother any of you, I promise. Just let me go back to your laird's room. Please. You won't even know I'm around."

One of the men snorted.

The other opened the door and dragged her across its threshold. Mercifully darkness hid the things she knew she didn't want to see, but the *squish-squish* beneath her feet was bad enough. Especially since one of them was still bare. As for the scurrying sounds of what could only be rats, she'd just do her best to pretend she hadn't heard them. Or the *drip-drip* of what she was sure would be fouled and rancid water.

The smell was blinding.

She shuddered, thinking that now would be a very good time to be zapped out of medieval Scotland.

Instead, she found herself shoved into a pitch-black cell, the heavy-sounding door slamming shut behind her before she could even blink.

"Wait!" She spun around to pound on the door as one of the men slid home the drawbar. "Please listen to me!"

"Och, you'll be heard soon enough," one of the men assured her. "As soon as the laird returns from warring."

"Warring?" The ground dipped beneath Kira's feet. Medieval warring could take ages. Heaven help her if he didn't return. "Where did he go? I thought you said he'd be back by evening."

No answer came.

Panic gripping her, she strained to see through the small hole in the door, but it was impossible. The men were already gone, leaving her alone in Castle Wrath's dungeon.

So she did what Bedwells were famous for when faced with adversity.

She blew out a breath and began pacing, doing her best not to cry.

Chapter 7

About the same time, Aidan stood in the middle of
Ardcraig's smoke-hazed great hall and struggled to ignore the softly crying women huddled together by the
hearthside. Pale-faced and hand-wringing, they posed
a trial to his already thin patience. He shot another
glance their way, then scowled, dignity alone keeping
him from thrusting his fingers in his ears. Truth was,
he couldn't bear to hear any women cry, especially
when he bore the brunt of causing their grief.

A weakness Conan Dearg's womenfolk were using
to their fullest advantage.

Sure of it, he paced the length of his cousin's hall,
cursing under his breath. Something was sorely amiss,
and if his foe's teary-eyed females would cease their
sniffling and sobbing long enough for him to think
clearly, he'd surely figure out what the devil it was.

In any event, it had little to do with despairing
women and even less with the sad state of Ardcraig's
dingy, foul-smelling hall. O-o-oh, nay, it was the same
niggling sense of *not-rightness* that had ridden him the
last time he and his men had come here, the whole
lot of them scouring Conan Dearg's keep from dun-

geon to parapets, searching pointlessly and making fools of themselves in the process. An embarrassment he wasn't going to endure again.

Especially if it meant having to admit failure to Kira.

Flashing a glance at the blackened ceiling rafters, he clenched his fists in frustration. Truth be told, he was also growing mightily weary of the sideways looks his men had been giving him ever since he'd left his chamber to join them that morn. Their silence rode his last nerve, but he'd deal with such annoyances later. After he'd routed his nefarious cousin and tossed him into Castle Wrath's dungeon.

The blackguard was here somewhere.

Aidan could smell him.

Furious that he hadn't yet found him, he strode over to the dais end of the hall, where Tavish and a few others guarded those of Conan Dearg's garrison who'd had the misfortune of sleeping too soundly when Aidan and his men burst into the hall, swords at the ready and flashing.

Surprisingly, though naked and weaponless, not a one amongst them seemed concerned. They certainly didn't appear sleep-befuddled. If anything, they looked smug. And that was what gave him such an uneasy feeling. Almost as if they'd let themselves be caught unclothed and defenseless, knowing any Highland chieftain with a smidgen of pride would refrain from wielding steel on an unarmed man.

Aidan blew out a breath and slid a glance at them, their bare-bottomed, muscle-bound bulk limned by torchlight and the reddish glow of Conan Dearg's hall fire.

Nary a one of them could meet his eye, each one glancing aside whenever he wheeled to fix him with a penetrating stare.

He shivered, drawing his plaid against a cold that had little to do with his cousin's crowded, untidy hall.

The bastard's men were hiding something.

And he was certain that *something* would prove to be Conan Dearg. The chill creeping up and down his spine left no room for doubt, even if they had searched everywhere. Half expecting to see the craven come crashing out of some hidden corner, swinging a battle-ax, he scanned the shadows, but saw only emptiness.

Even so, his every nerve ending hummed, his warrior instincts screaming with each indrawn breath. He tightened his grip on his sullied blade, his heart heavy with the need to stain his steel with the blood of kin.

Tavish stepped closer and put a hand on his shoulder. "Kin or no, the deaths couldn't be helped," he said, as always seeming to read Aidan's mind.

"The bastard is here," Aidan seethed, anger shielding him from the morning's horrors. "He's sacrificed his men, hiding behind them as he would a woman's skirts."

Tavish shrugged. "They should not have refused us entry." His gaze flicked to Aidan's sword, then to his own. Its blade, too, dripped red. Looking back at Aidan, his lip curled. "Better they died nobly than lying silent and feigning sleep."

Aidan arced a brow. "So you agree something is amiss?"

"To be sure." Tavish lifted his sword, eyeing its

bloodied edge. "I just canna grasp where Conan Dearg is hiding. We've upturned every stone and peered into each corner."

Aidan rubbed the back of his neck, thinking. "We're missing something, but it will come to me soon."

Frowning, he glanced again at the captured garrison men. Others were joining them, men brought in by the patrol he and Tavish had sent around Ardcraig's perimeter. Men now stripped of arms and clothes, just as their brethren from the hall. Their leader was nowhere to be seen. To a man, they stood sullen and defiant, some shifting restlessly, others exchanging glances. All refused to talk, a stubbornness Aidan secretly admired, not that he cared to admit it.

Instead, he shoved his reddened sword into its scabbard and folded his arms. Sooner or later, one of them would let his guard slip, revealing the truth through a gesture or a glance, a word spoken too quickly. Moving to the high table, he settled himself in his cousin's chair, deigning to wait.

"You will grow cold, standing there naked," he observed, speaking to the men but pretending to study his knuckles. "Yet stand you shall, for I will have the bollocks cut from the first man who dares sit."

He leaned back in the chair, watching them. "I am a patient man. It willna cost me the least to while here for days if need be. Indeed, I intend to stay put until one of you tells me where my cousin is keeping himself."

None of the men said anything, though several tightened their jaws and glared at him.

One spat into the floor rushes.

Another slid a nervous glance at the screens passage and the arched entry to the kitchens.

The kitchens.

At once, the hall tilted and dipped, spinning around Aidan as the answer hit him like a fist in the gut.

"God's holy truth!" He leapt to his feet, his own words echoing in his head: *He's sacrificed his men, hiding behind them as he would a woman's skirts.*

He wheeled to face Tavish, triumph surging through him, hot and sweet. "I know where he is!" he cried, and slapped his mailed thigh. "The bastard is in his kitchens—disguised as a scullery wench!"

Tavish's jaw dropped. "By the Rood! The unfortunate creature we saw sitting in a corner, querning corn. The big-boned woman with a head veil and her face turned away from us!"

Aidan nodded. "That'll be him. I'd bet my life on—"

"Your life is over!" One of Conan Dearg's men lunged forward, snatching the sword of Aidan's youngest guardsman. " 'Tis you who shall die!"

"I think not." Aidan whirled with eye-blurring speed, his own sword already drawn as the man rushed him, swinging his blade in a stroke that would have been deadly against any other foe. As it was, steel met steel, the clang of clashing metal and angry snarls filling the air as Aidan parried the man's every slashing blow, then closed in, his arcing blade cutting a mortal wound in the other's side. The man folded in a pool of his own blood, his roar of pain echoing in Aidan's ears.

Jerking his sword free, he swept Conan Dearg's men with a heated stare.

"Should any others amongst you feel honor-bound to defend my cousin, come forward now or hold your peace," he challenged them, bile rising in his throat that he'd been forced to cut down yet another kinsman. "I'll see that you're given a blade and even a shield to counter my blows, but I'd have it a fair fight. No' the likes of what just transpired."

A sea of hostile gazes met his own cold stare, but no one made a move to accept his dare.

"You have no right to speak of fairness when you'd have us ride to Castle Wrath only to be slaughtered by your allies on the journey!" An older man pushed past the others, glancing hotly at the fallen guardsman before turning his glare on Aidan. "Your treachery is the reason we—"

"My treachery?" Aidan stared at him, a chill dread icing his blood. Suspicions too blasphemous to consider. He strode forward, clutching the man by the arms. "What is this you'd accuse me of? If we have our differences, every man within these walls is of my blood. Ne'er would I harm a kinsman without due reason."

He paused to shove the hair from his brow, taking heart in the doubt beginning to flicker in the man's eyes. "I see you know it," he said, releasing him. "I would think every man in these isles knows it as well."

"Your words spoke otherwise." The man rubbed his arms, his face darkening again. "One of Conan's riders intercepted the courier you sent to the Mackenzies of Kintail. Your missive fell into Conan's hands.

He told us of your perfidy. How you planned to invite us to feast with you and how the Mackenzies would lay in wait, falling upon us when we passed through the narrow gorge not far from your holding." The man put back his shoulders, fury blazing in his eyes. "Your orders were to give no quarter, that not a one of us should be left alive."

Heat swept Aidan, scalding the back of his neck. He felt his face flush, well aware that his jaw was working, but no words were coming out.

"By the blood of Christ," Tavish swore beside him, "ne'er have I heard a greater pack of lies."

Aidan's accuser set his mouth in a grim line, his gaze angry and unflinching. Behind him, others surged forward, their own faces red with outrage. "He speaks the truth," one of them called. "The Mackenzies were to ambush us—"

"Who amongst you saw these orders?" Aidan thundered, his temper fraying. "Speak up and prove your lies. Here and now, that I might dispel them."

"I will speak." A young man barely sporting a beard elbowed his way to where Aidan stood. Ignoring the disapproving glances of his fellow guardsmen, he straightened his shoulders and drew a great breath. "We did not see the missive," he said, his tone respectful. "We but believed what our lord told us he'd seen. He claimed his fury was so great upon learning of your plans, that he tossed the parchment into the hearth fire. All know of the strife between the two of you, so why should we have doubted his word?"

He paused to clear his throat, his cheeks reddening a bit. "I ask you, sir, would you not expect the same trust from your own men?"

"Indeed, I would." Aidan folded his arms and did his best not to scorch the louts with a listen-and-learn-from-this-lad glare. "I would know your name." He eyed the boy, judging him to be not more than fifteen summers. "Your name and if you are skilled with horses."

"I am Kendrew. I was orphaned and left at Ardcraig's gates, or so I was told." The boy flushed anew, his gaze darting to Conan Dearg's silent, set-faced men, then back to Aidan. "And I am good with beasts, aye. Especially horses," he added, shifting legs already longer than those of most of the men crowded near him. "I also know my letters and am handy with both a blade and a battle-ax."

Aidan nodded. "So-o-o, Kendrew"—this time he did flash a narrow-eyed glance at his men—"are you afraid of witches?"

The boy blinked, then shook his head. "I do not fear them, no. From my experience, the older ones are naught but healers and the young ones are often women who've fallen out of favor with powerful men. There are some who say my mother was such a woman, but I canna believe she was bad. Were that so, I think I'd feel it here"—he paused to clap a hand over his heart—"though I'm sure there are many things in these hills we'll ne'er understand."

Under other circumstances, Aidan would have smiled. As it was, he made a swift decision. Turning to the man at his left, he ordered, "Mundy, see Kendrew's clothes returned to him and give him a blade." Before the oversized Irishman could protest, he took the boy's arm and drew him forward. "You, lad, shall hie yourself outside and help my men tend their horses. Then you'll return with us to Castle Wrath, where I have other duties in mind for you."

The lad's flush deepened, turning as bright a red as his hair. "But, sir, I canna leave Ardcraig." He pulled back, clearly torn. "I am Conan Dearg's man. I—"

"Go, and dinna make me regret my rashness." Aidan turned from him to Mundy. "See him into the bailey, then set others to gathering my cousin's horses and weapons. We'll be leaving anon. With Conan Dearg."

"No-o-o, please!" One of the sobbing women ran at him, clutching his sleeve. "You canna take the laird from us! See you, I carry his child." She ran her hands down the front of her skirts, displaying the bulge at her middle. "Several of us are heavy with his seed," she added, gesturing to the clutch of females. "We need him—"

"My regrets." Aidan cut her off, wishing his cousin's manhood was long enough to be tied into a knot. Unfortunately, he knew from earlier years that it wasn't.

Frowning, he disentangled himself from the woman's grasp. A comely wench with fiery red hair and a lush, creamy bosom fair spilling from her low-cut bodice, she smelled fresh and sweet, her scent reminding him of Kira and what would happen to her should she land in his cousin's hands. He shuddered at the thought, thanking the saints he knew her to be safe and guarded in his own bedchamber.

"Please, sir," the maid wailed again.

Aidan schooled his features, not wanting to frighten her.

"You shall have all you need and more, my lady," he promised, hoping she'd believe him. "My own patrols will guard your walls, and I will make certain your stores and fuel remain plentiful."

He didn't add that he would also attempt to find more suitable *fathers* for her and the other maids' bairns.

"No one here will suffer—lest you repeat my cousin's mistakes," he added, turning back to the captive men. "I give you my word."

"Your word!" A swarthy man spat at his feet. "A snake's honor," he sneered. "We'll no' have your leavings."

Great shouts of agreement rose from his fellow men and the older man stepped forward again, anger rolling off him in waves. "Hear me, Aidan of Wrath, I am Walter of Ardcraig and have dwelt here since before your birth. I, too, share your MacDonald pride. You may well slay us here where we stand if you mean to leave us unable to defend ourselves. We do not want or need your men riding our lands." He glared at Aidan with withering scorn. "In your place, Conan Dearg would ne'er—"

"Let us speak plainly, Sir Walter." Aidan lifted his voice now that the woman had scurried back to her friends and young Kendrew was out of earshot. "My cousin would and has done many things—including deceiving you." Reaching beneath his plaid, he withdrew the rolled parchment, penned by Conan Dearg's own hand.

The blackguard's seal, cracked and broken, still dangled from the thing, attached to the end of a crumpled bit of red ribbon.

Red as blood and just as damning, as were the words inked inside.

"Read this and then tell me I've no right to put an end to my cousin's villainy once and for all time." Aidan thrust the scroll into the man's hands, then stepped back to wait. "Read it aloud if you will."

Walter of Ardcraig glanced at the scroll, looking up as quickly. His face was ashen. "My lord—this is beyond reason."

"Reason was ne'er one of my cousin's better points," Aidan agreed. "Nevertheless, I'd have his words known. Read on, and loudly enough so all may hear."

Looking miserable, Walter complied. A great silence descended when he finished. Again, Conan Dearg's men avoided Aidan's eye, but this time shame stained the faces of most. Regrettably, not all, so he took back the parchment and tucked it carefully into his plaid.

Then he cleared his throat. "Since my cousin intended to slay me and any of my clan who cared to accompany me to his feast, there will be some amongst you who knew of his plans," he said, his voice ringing. "Be glad I am not him. I willna damn innocent men for the dark deeds of others, but I *will* keep your horses and your weapons until I've decided I have no further reason to distrust you. Or until those brave enough to throw yourself on my mercy step forward and admit your guilt."

"I canna think of a man present who'd be party to the like." Walter spoke up again. "Not a one."

"Then so be it." Aidan gave him a curt nod. "I charge you to ensure I have no cause to return here in anger. If I must, not a stone will remain uncharred."

Before the other could reply, Aidan turned on his

heel and strode for the screens passage and the arched kitchen entry, quickening his pace as he neared the torchlit steps spiraling down into Ardcraig's heart.

He took them two at a time, Tavish and a few others fast on his heels. At the bottom, his heart bounded as he found a cluster of his best guardsmen, standing at ease as they watched over the seemingly innocent kitchen scene. Young boys stirred the cook pots, and a straight-backed graybeard kneaded bread at a table laden with butter, milk, cheese, and other goods obviously meant for the evening meal. Conan Dearg still sat quietly in the corner, his back angled to door as he ground his corn, clearly unaware his hours were measured.

The old man looked up, his expression as tight as his posture. "Can we not be left in peace to tend our work?" he demanded, his voice thrumming with indignation. "Your guardsmen frighten the wee fire laddies and I'm too old for the likes o' such scrutiny!"

"Indeed," Aidan agreed, stepping deeper into the kitchen, the zinging *hiss* of his sword leaving its scabbard announcing his purpose. "We are not here to plague you or yon laddies, though you'd be wise to stand clear lest you get injured in the fray."

"There'll be no fray! Only your death!" Conan Dearg yanked his sword from beneath a pile of grain sacks and leapt to his feet. He lunged forward, overturning a bench as he swung wildly, his movements hampered by his skirts. "You'll no' leave here alive," he snarled, crashing into the table before he regained his balance and attacked again.

Aidan's mouth twitched. "But you shall—leave here

alive," he shot back, easily sidestepping the other's charge. "You'll meet your end in my dungeon, where you'll need neither corn nor a woman's skirts."

Conan Dearg lunged again, his blade meeting Aidan's with an earsplitting *clang*. "You're mad," he bellowed, jumping back when his sword went flying. His face red with fury, he dived for the table, grabbing a kitchen knife, but Aidan was on him in a heartbeat, knocking the knife from his hand before he could even blink.

"Och, I'm no' mad." Aidan tossed aside his own sword, then slammed his fist into his cousin's nose. "I'm reminding you that no one threatens my own and lives to tell the tale." Another blow sent Conan Dearg to his knees, where he pressed a hand against his nose and gaped up at Aidan for a split second before sprawling facedown on the floor.

Satisfied, Aidan glanced at the grim-faced old man and the three wee boys. They cowered in a corner, their distress only deepening his anger. Wiping his hands on his plaid, he turned to Tavish.

"See that someone looks after them." He started toward the kitchen door arch, snatching up his sword on the way. "As for Conan Dearg, we are cousins no more. Have someone get him out of those skirts and properly clad. I'll no' have him shaming us on the journey back to Wrath."

He just hoped he didn't shame himself by dragging Kira into his arms and having his way with her the instant he returned.

After the ordeal he'd just put to an end, his need for her was that great.

*   *   *

Unfortunately, when Aidan and his party approached Castle Wrath a few hours later, all such urges were swiftly replaced by an odd sense of ill ease. Nothing he could put his finger on, but something out of place all the same. A muscle began to twitch in his jaw, and a hard, tight knot started pulsing somewhere deep inside him.

Willing the twitching to cease, he adjusted his plaid to better shield him from the sudden cold he suspected only he'd noticed.

Were he a superstitious man, he might fear someone had hexed him, feeling such an uncanny chill twice in one day. As it was, and just for the sake of good Highland prudence, he shot a glance at Conan Dearg, half thinking he might be attempting to blast him with the evil eye, but the double-dyed blackguard sat ramrod straight in his saddle, his expression stony and his gaze fixed stubbornly on the back of the man leading his steed.

Tavish, his other men, and even young Kendrew appeared oblivious. Some of Aidan's younger kinsmen even whooped and jested with each other before kicking their beasts into flat-out gallops in their eagerness to reach Castle Wrath's looming walls and the warm welcome of its great hall. The promise of a seat beside the fire, free-flowing ale, and a trencher piled high with fine roasted meat.

Perhaps, too, the celebratory feasting he'd sworn would mark Conan Dearg's capture.

Aidan frowned. He'd hoped to enjoy a bit of celebratory *wooing*, perhaps steal a few sweet kisses or more from his dream woman. A quiet evening spent in bliss that would help him banish the distastefulness of the morn.

Instead, he grew more apprehensive the farther he rode along the steep and twisting track leading out to his cliff-girt home. And for no apparent reason, as the day had turned fair, with a fine deep blue sky and a bracing autumn wind. Not far ahead, Castle Wrath with its square keep and high curtain walls stood tall and proud as ever on its pinnacle of rock, Aidan's own banner raised and snapping in the breeze. Everything looked as it should, and from what he could see of the landing beach and the little harbor below his stronghold, naught was amiss there, either.

He turned in his saddle, craning his neck to make certain. The seas were running steep, but his flotilla of longships and galleys appeared safely moored in the choppy, sun-dazzled water. Several of the galleys had been drawn up onto the strand for repairs and the fires of the beachside smokehouses looked well tended, with the usual number of men going about their business drying fish and mending nets.

Even so, something wasn't right.

Sure of it, he placed a hand over the worn leather scrip hanging from his sword belt, hoping the clutch of freshly picked heather tucked within would banish his dark thoughts and put him back in fine fettle.

But as so much of his luck seemed to be going of late, Tavish caught sight of the movement and cocked a knowing brow. "Think you a handful of crushed heather will win a lady's heart?" He edged his horse nearer, his implied superior knowledge of wooing only worsening Aidan's mood.

Leaning close, he lowered his voice, "You'd be better served to seat her next to you in the hall, pouring her wine and hand-feeding her fine morsels. Whispering sweet nothings in her ear and letting your men see—"

"It would seem my men see all too much!" Aidan shot back, glaring at him. "Since when can a man no' pause to tend nature's call without some long-nosed kinsman who claims to be his friend spying on him while he's at the deed?"

Tavish chuckled. "Mayhap since it was the first time since I've known you that I've seen you call for such a halt on such a short journey?"

Aidan harrumphed. "Mayhap I drank too much watered-down ale before we left Ardcraig. The morn's doings left a bad taste in my mouth and I but sought to wash it away."

"Then why not tend such matters standing beside your horse as you usually do? Why sneak off behind a great outcrop where a particularly bonny patch of heather is known to bloom?"

Aidan bit back a curse.

"I'm not the only one who saw you," Tavish continued, making it worse. "Perhaps it's a good thing for the men to know you're so smitten. They've been worried about you."

"They've been grinding on my patience." Aidan flashed him a dark look. "You most of all!"

"You wound me, my friend."

"A God's name! I'll do more than that if you dinna soon leave me be," Aidan groused. He clamped his lips together, refusing to be goaded any further.

"Ho!" Tavish called, leaning over to thwack him on

the shoulder not a breath later. "We've been seen. The drawbridge is down. But isn't that Geordie and Ross with the gatehouse guards? I thought you'd ordered them to guard your lady."

"I did." Aidan's stomach dropped.

He stared ahead, squinting against the afternoon sun. Disbelief washed over him, but there could be no doubt. The drawbridge had been dutifully lowered and the gatehouse's heavy iron portcullis was rattling upward even as they approached, his best guardsmen hastening to swing open the second, inner gates.

As was expected of them.

Them, and *not* Geordie and Ross, two of his most trusted men.

The apparent lackwits who'd sworn they'd watch over Kira with their very lives.

A score of dire possibilities making his head reel, Aidan spurred his horse across the last stretch of rough, cattle-dotted grass. But when he thundered over the drawbridge's hollow-sounding planks and through the arched gatehouse pend, the only men crowding the open guardroom doorways were the ones he'd assigned duty there.

His relief great, he swung down onto the cobbles, tossing his reins to a running stable lad. "The sun must've blinded us," he said, striding over to Tavish the instant his friend dismounted. "I should have known Geordie and Ross could be trusted not to leave their post."

"The sun?" Tavish snorted. "My vision has yet to fail me, though I'll agree I see nary a sign of them now." He jammed fisted hands on his hips and glanced round, wearing a frown as dark as some of Aidan's own. "What I *do* see isn't pleasing. Too many of your men are still avoiding your eye."

"They will think more kindly of me when they see my cousin hauled into the dungeon."

Looking doubtful, Tavish glanced to where a handful of Aidan's stoutest guards were already escorting Conan Dearg across the bailey.

"Then let us make certain he's put in a cell he canna escape," he said, starting after them.

Hesitating, Aidan threw a last look at the gatehouse, pleased to see his younger men crowding around Kendrew, Conan Dearg's man or no. He had no wish for the lad to witness his former liege laird being hustled away.

"Come you." Tavish signaled, waiting for him. "I want surety. We've both seen the bastard wriggle himself out of the worst scrapes and come back to jeer at us."

"He'll no' have the strength this time." Aidan kept pace with him. "No' living on salt beef and soured water."

" 'Tis you who'll wither away on the like—and in your own foul pit." Conan Dearg twisted round to sneer at him. Arrogant and contemptuous as always, he spat on the ground, showing no fear as Aidan's men tightened their grip, bundling him through the low-ceilinged door that led to the steep stone steps winding down into the dungeon.

"The sun will ne'er rise on the day you get the better of me," he boasted, squaring his shoulders to walk proud along the cold and dank passage.

"Some might say that day came this morn." Aidan fell in step beside him. "Salt beef and soured water ne'er sustained any man for long and I've yet to meet one who can live on bluster alone."

Conan Dearg snorted. "I am a hard man, *Cousin*. Rancid victuals and darkness will not break me. Soon I shall prove it to you."

Aidan glanced over his shoulder, not surprised to see the dirk raised in Tavish's hand.

"That isn't the way," he warned, hoping *his* way wasn't a mistake. "Each hour he spends in his cell will repay one of the lives he's taken. We both know how great the number is. A swift death is a mercy he won't find here."

"I dinna trust him." Tavish frowned, but thrust his knife back beneath his sword belt all the same. "He'll charm the water rats into bringing him cheese and wine."

Despite himself, Aidan chuckled, his spirits lifting for the first time that day. His cousin *was* a charmer. And even with a blackened eye and swollen nose, his looks were still dazzling enough to blind any woman who caught a glimpse of him.

That his flashing smiles and swagger would be lost on all but scuttling vermin and whate'er nameless creatures slithered in the matted rushes scattered across the dungeon floor, was a meet end for a man of Conan Dearg's vanity and stature.

Aidan opened his mouth to say as much, but shut it the instant they rounded a corner, entering the oldest and dankest part of the dungeon. A familiar smell hit him square in the face and he stopped short, blinking into the musty, dimly lit passage even as a pitiful, canine wail filled the darkness.

"Saints o' mercy!" Aidan hurried forward, almost slamming into his guardsmen and Conan Dearg, who'd stopped a few paces ahead, their passage blocked by the howling beast's great bulk. Aidan stared at his dog, his jaw slipping. " 'Tis Ferlie!"

An absolute impossibility, for the dog feared the dark and especially avoided the dungeon.

Yet there he was, sitting on his shaggy haunches beside one of the blackened, iron-hinged doors, and clearly intent on staying there.

"Heigh-ho! So you've arranged a mourner for me." Conan Dearg hooted with laughter. "A pity you couldn't have chosen a less offensive creature."

Ignoring him, Aidan snatched one of the rush lights out of its wall bracket and stepped forward, his surprise complete when the sputtering torch illuminated not just his afraid-of-the-dark dog, but two sets of masculine legs standing in the shadows behind the beast.

Legs, as a lifting of the rush light revealed, that belonged to none other than Geordie and Ross.

"What mummery is this?" Aidan thrust the torch at them, his blood icing. "You swore to guard my lady, vowing to see to her safety even if Saint Peter himself came calling for you."

"Ah. See you, we . . . m'mmm . . ." Geordie, the larger of the two twisted his hands, looking uncomfortable. "Your lady, sir, is—"

"*His lady?*" Conan Dearg looked on with interest. "I'd heard he'd gone off women."

"You'll hold your tongue or lose it," Tavish growled, his own face dark with anger as he rammed an elbow into Conan Dearg's ribs, then pressed the tip of his dirk beneath the lout's chin. "Be silent if you know what's good for you."

Scarce hearing them, Aidan felt his knees water, sure as the day that for whatever reason he'd found his two guardsmen and his dog in the deepest bowels of his dungeon, it had something to do with Kira.

Something he was not going to like.

"What has happened?" he demanded, laying on his sternest tone to mask the sick feeling spreading through his gut. "Where is she? And why aren't you guarding her?"

The two men exchanged glances, their misery palpable.

"Um," Geordie tried again, sweat beginning to bead on his brow.

Ross drew a deep breath. "We're guarding you, sir. Not the lass. She doesn't—"

"Guarding me?" Aidan's eyes flew wide.

"Aye, sir." The man bobbed his head. "She did something that proved our suspicions about her. We brought her down here for the good of the clan," he added, speaking quickly now. "Her powers—"

"You brought her down here?" Aidan roared, blood thundering so loudly in his ears that he scarce heard himself shouting. "She's here? In the dungeon?"

The two guardsmen nodded.

Or so Aidan thought, whirling away before he could be sure. He'd already wasted too much time, should have guessed the truth the instant he'd spotted Ferlie and seen the fear in his guards' faces.

Fear for his dream woman squeezing his heart, he

shoved past Tavish and leapt over Ferlie, fumbling at the heavy drawbar of the nearest cell door with fingers that had gone impossibly cold and clumsy.

"Kira!" He yanked at the drawbar. "Sweet lass, can you hear me?"

"The entire keep can hear you." Tavish grabbed the thing and helped him slide it aside. "Go fetch your lady," he said, shoving Aidan into the cell. "I'll see to Conan Dearg and the others."

But his lady wasn't anywhere to be fetched.

The cell was empty.

Then, peering into the darkness, he saw her standing in a corner, her shoulders straight and her hands clasped tightly before her, her eyes squeezed shut.

"Kee-*rah*!"

Her eyes snapped open. "Aidan!" She ran at him, her arms outstretched. "Thank God! I didn't think you'd ever get back!"

"I'm here now." He crossed the cell in two quick strides, catching her when she launched herself at him. "Shush, lass. I have you."

He pressed her head against his shoulder, absorbed her shiver, then kissed her hair, not caring that Tavish and the others gawked through the door.

Ferlie barked and pushed past them, hurling himself at their legs, his tail wagging.

"He followed when they brought me down here." Kira reached down to pet the shaggy, tail-thumping beast. "He's been outside the door the entire time."

Aidan harrumphed. Only his pride and the knowledge that his cousin looked on kept him from acknowledging that his dog had guarded her better than his men.

There'd be time enough later to reward Ferlie and have words with Geordie and Ross.

Time, too, to discover the reason they'd put her into the dungeon. What terrible thing she'd done to give two burly Highlanders such a dreadful fright.

Heaven help them both if he didn't like the answer.

Chapter 8

"I want to go home."

Not sure if she'd spoken aloud or just thought the words, Kira took a deep, calming breath. She needed calm. The backs of her eyes stung, her misery reaching new heights as she stood near the hearth of Aidan's bedchamber and watched a parade of young, flush-faced boys carry pails of steaming water into the room. Carefully avoiding looking at her, each one tipped his burden into a wooden bathing tub that looked exactly like a sawed-in-half wine barrel.

A linen-lined wine barrel, praise God for small mercies.

The last thing she needed was a medieval splinter in her behind.

Her ordeal in Castle Wrath's dungeon had been torture enough. Almost as bad was having Aidan toss her over his shoulder and charge out of the cell, pounding up the stairs with her and then flying through his great hall, knocking over benches and sending people jumping out of their way, poor Ferlie loping after them and barking furiously at anyone who didn't leap aside quickly enough.

She cringed just remembering. It'd been a humilia-
tion she wasn't sure she could swallow.

Not because he'd rescued her.

And not even because he'd gone so caveman wild.

Far from it—she'd rather liked that part. All wind-
torn and travel-stained, with his sword clanking and
eyes ablaze, he could have burst from the pages of a
book about ancient clan warfare. But when he'd raced
through the hall, cursing and shouting for a bath to
be readied for her, his rubber-necked kinsmen had
gaped at her, bug-eyed and slack-jawed, every last one
of them looking on as if he'd run mad and she was a
two-headed alien.

Maybe even a three-headed alien.

And now she was supposed to take a bath.

Kira frowned and folded her arms. She didn't want
a bath. She wanted to go home. Back to the twenty-
first century where she belonged and where she could
moon all over books about medieval Scotland and
framed secondhand Edinburgh castle tea towels, living
in a fantasy that suited her so-o-o much better than
the real thing.

Across the room, the best *real thing* in this nightmare threw off his plaid and unlatched his sword belt,
then sent the last of the pink-cheeked water boys on
their way, closing and bolting the door behind them.
Turning, he strode over to her, no longer looking so
fiercely angry, but not smiling, either.

"This could be your home, Kee-*rah*," he said, his
words letting her know she had spoken aloud. "I know
well that you love this place. That it means as much
to you as to those of us who have called it our own
since before time. When you walk here, you see more

than rock and heather and mist. Your heart recognizes the true spirit of these hills." He paused, studying her so intently that she caught her breath. "I know this from our shared dreams."

Kira swallowed, not wanting to think about their dreams just now. Or her great passion for Scotland. Last she'd heard, being a card-carrying Scotophile didn't include half the things she'd endured since landing here.

Looking down, she fussed at the folds of her skirts, still finding them as cumbersome and awkward as she had the moment she'd first slipped into them. Even worse, the bottom six inches or so were soiled with *goop* from the dungeon. As were her feet, since somewhere during the awful journey down there, she'd lost the blasted *cuarans*.

"Come, lass, you canna deny you belong here." He sounded sure of it. "I've seen your eyes water just watching cloud shadows drift across the heather."

Kira dug her toes into the floor rushes. "I did love it here," she admitted, glancing up at him. "In my time and, yes, in our dreams. But the reality is wa-a-ay different and it scares me."

"Ach, lass." He smoothed the hair back from her face. "Surely you have seen that I willna let aught happen to you?"

She blinked, hating the way her throat was thickening. "Did you know," she began, "that they brought me food when I was in the dungeon?"

When he only looked at her, his expression unreadable, she went on. "A bowl of slaked oats, I think you call it. Porridge. It didn't look too bad, but I couldn't eat, so I set it in a corner. Within minutes, three mice crawled up out of the floor rushes and ate it." She paused to moisten her lips. "Or rather, they would have, if the biggest rat I've ever seen in my life hadn't appeared to claim the porridge for himself."

He took her hand, twining their fingers. "The like will ne'er happen again. I promise you."

She bit her lip. "How can you? It's impossible for you to be at my side every minute, and your men don't like me. They're afraid of me and think I'm a—"

"Then we shall change their minds." He drew her close, tightening his arms around her. "You already have a strong champion in Tavish, and I've a promising young lad in mind to give duty as your personal guard."

"If only it were that simple."

"I will make it so."

Kira tried to smile, but her smile muscles wouldn't cooperate.

Instead, she sighed and rested her head against his shoulder. "You are a medieval warrior chieftain," she began, trying to ignore how good his arms felt around her. "You live in a world of clan feuding, sword fights, and cattle raids, a time when a mere bad tooth or ingrown toenail could kill someone, not to mention battle wounds and childbirth. You have enough to deal with without worrying about—"

"Do you not trust me to care for you?" He pulled back to look at her, his dark eyes narrowing. "I've dealt with the things you name since I drew my first breath, as has any other Highland chieftain worthy of the style. What I need"—he paused, holding her gaze—"is for you to relax and then tell me what happened with Geordie and Ross. Only when I understand what frightened them enough to take you to the dungeon can I hope to dash the fear from their hearts. Your bath will—"

"I don't want a bath."

"It will soothe you," he countered, the richness of his burr almost letting her believe him.

Smooth, husky, and deep, his voice slid through her, its soft Highland beauty seducing her, making her forget where and *when* she was, lulling her into doing whatever he asked.

Almost.

Biting her lip again, her gaze snapped to the *wine barrel*, its steaming water scented and waiting. Truth was, she did want a bath. Desperately. But taking one meant getting undressed, and she was suddenly more aware than ever that she wasn't wearing any underwear.

She didn't need her sixth sense to know that even if Aidan turned his back, he'd peek before she could clamber into his wooden bathing tub.

He had that look about him tonight.

The feral, hot-eyed-predator look that could mean only one thing, no matter how hard he was clearly trying to play the chivalry card.

As if to prove it, he put his hands on her shoulders, easing her down onto a stool next to the bathing tub before she could even splutter a protest. The determined gleam in his eyes holding her in place, he knelt before her, reaching for a basin and a still-filled pail of heated water.

"Give me your foot." He glanced at her as he filled the basin. "It willna do for you to get into the bathing tub until your feet are clean."

Kira tensed. "I can wash them myself. You needn't help me."

In answer, he cocked a brow and flipped her skirts up over her knees. Making it worse, he flashed her an arrogant smile, then clamped a strong hand around her left ankle, lifting her foot and placing it in the basin.

Frowning, she tried to jerk from his grasp, but he only slanted her a look of lairdly admonishment, his fingers tightening on her like an iron-cast ankle bracelet.

"You can see to yourself once we have you settled in your bath."

She lifted her chin. "There will be no *we* about it. If I use the bathing tub, you can leave the room."

"Och, you will bathe," he said, dipping a soap-smeared cloth into the water and then plunging the thing between her toes, scrubbing vigorously. "I shall keep my back turned."

"I don't trust you."

"Then you shall have to learn. As I, too, am trying to do." He looked up, fixing her with a long, level stare as he carefully washed the arch of her foot. "Do not think it is easy for me to accept a place called All-den, Pen-seal-*where'er*, tiny flying disks, and zip-*hers*."

Kira almost smiled, remembering his expression when her button went sailing through the air. "Okay. You've made your point, but no peeking."

"I do not need to peek," he observed, soaping her other foot. "I already know every inch of you. Including a certain bit of sweetness I can see just now."

Kira's eyes flew wide. "What do you mean *a bit of sweetness*?"

He only smiled.

Her own face flaming, she looked down, embarrassment crashing through her when she saw that her gown had slid much higher up her thighs than she'd realized. Even worse, she'd been sitting with her knees open.

"O-o-oh!" She jumped off the stool. "I don't want to talk about our dream-times and what you think you know about me." Shaking out her skirts, she frowned. "You can't compare something from a dream with the reality—"

"Nay, you cannot," he agreed, standing. "The real you fires my blood a thousand times more than any dream vision." He captured her chin and kissed her. Hard, rough, and fast. "Dinna you e'er forget that, even when we must speak of unpleasant things."

Kira angled her head, regarding him in the flickering glow of the hearth fire. "I think I've had enough unpleasantness for one day."

"Even so," he said, his expression serious, "there are matters we must discuss."

"Does it have to be now?"

He nodded, and then lowered his head to kiss her again, this time gently.

When he straightened, she pulled away, her heart thundering. There was something both unsettling and electrifyingly delicious about being kissed when she wasn't wearing any panties, and now clearly wasn't the time to go all hot and tingly. A sensation that vanished when he began pacing between the *wine barrel* and the window embrasure.

Without breaking stride, he slanted her a dark look, all fierce warrior chieftain. "Remove your soiled clothes now, before the water cools," he said, seven hundred years of authority shimmering all over him. "While you bathe, I would hear about your morning. You must tell me what frightened my men."

"What I must do is find a pair of glittery red shoes," Kira snapped, her fingers busy at her gown's lacings.

He stopped to look at her. "Glittery red shoes?"

"Never mind."

"Ah, lass, but I do." He stood watching her, another frown settling on his brow. "You must've said something the like to Geordie and Ross. Perhaps mentioned this future of yours, or the Na Tri Shean?"

"It was neither, but . . . close."

He arched a brow. "That willna do, sweetness. No' when your *whate'er-it-was* made my men gibber with fright."

"I didn't mean to scare them," she returned. "I just wanted them to save what I thought was—oh, no!" She gasped when the bodice lacings ripped and both her gown and her overdress fell open to her waist.

His eyes darkened with *that look* again, his men's fright clearly forgotten as his gaze snapped to her breasts. Planting her hands on her hips, she glared at him, not needing to look down to know that her thin excuse for a medieval undershift hid absolutely nothing. The thing was practically transparent. Just as bad, the room's chill was tightening her nipples. She could feel them thrusting against the delicate linen, just as she could feel the scorching heat of his stare.

An intense, heavy-lidded perusal that only made them pucker all the more.

She bristled, irritated by his effect on her. "You said you'd turn your back."

"And so I shall." He reached to glide his knuckles

down the curve of her cheek. "Now hie yourself into yon bathing tub, lest I forget my vow to woo you properly."

The words spoken, he wheeled around, clasping his hands as casually as possible behind his back and fixing his stare on the night coming down outside his bedchamber's tall, arch-topped windows. He also tried to close his ears to the furious rustling of cloth and the sloshing of water as she rid herself of her garments and climbed into the bath.

"So-o-o," he began, turning only when he was certain it was safe to do so, "what was it that you wished Geordie and Ross to save?"

She looked at him, clouds of steam from the bathwater rising around her like tendrils of fairy mist. "A drowning woman," she said, jutting her jaw as if he wouldn't believe her. "I saw a woman's death— apparently one that took place nearly a hundred years ago. She had seabirds tied to a rope about her waist and—"

"Her name was Annie," Aidan finished for her, his innards twisting. "Her tale is a sad one and well known in these parts. She was married to Eachann MacQueen, a farmer who scratched a living off Wrath Isle's barren slopes, sustaining his family by lowering his wife down the cliffs to gather seabirds and their eggs whene'er hunger drove them to such privations."

"Whoever she was, I saw her." She peered at him, her naked, soapy breasts jiggling as she gripped the edge of the bathing tub and leaned forward. "I didn't see her as a ghost or because of witchcraft, but as a glimpse of the past. The *once-was*, as my gift of far-seeing reveals to me."

Aidan frowned and began pacing again, too aware of the rivulets of water streaming over her full, well-rounded breasts to wrap his mind around something that had happened so long ago, and what it had to do with her and his gog-eyed, clack-tongued kinsmen.

"So you are a seeress." He paused by one of the windows and stared across the dark water at the black, serrated cliffs of Wrath Isle. "The sight is common hereabouts and shouldn't have fashed my men," he said, keeping his back to her. "I'll wager they fear you because of the way you appeared atop the gatehouse arch. We must find a way to explain that. Then they will accept you."

Behind him, Kira sighed. "I don't have second sight," she argued. "At least not if you mean divination and prophecy. I told you, I'm a far-seer. Sometimes I'm able to look back in time, that's all. Now I have gone back in time and that's the only explanation I can give you. That, and that your gatehouse arch is a portal to the past."

Aidan snorted before he could help himself.

"Scoff all you will," she tossed at him. "If you have a better theory, I'm all ears. Fact is, in *my* time, that arch of yours was half buried in the grass, its top covered with moss and ferns. I was sitting on it, having a picnic, when suddenly my world vanished and I saw your men running across the bailey at me."

Aidan considered telling her he wasn't dim-witted enough to believe the like, but decided against it. The matter of their dream encounters and her zip-*her* was making it difficult for him to doubt her.

Not to mention the wee *flying disk*.

He shuddered, his head beginning to throb with the immensity of it all. "Ach, what a tangle," he muttered, turning from the window and going to his table, where he poured a generous cup of his strongest ale—a fine, rich brew flavored with just a hint of heather. He took a long swallow, then wiped his mouth on his sleeve.

"I will not lie to you, Kee-*rah*." He swirled the ale in his cup, looking down into its frothy, honey-colored depths. "What you claim is no' easy to believe. Even when my heart tells me you speak true."

"Then you believe me?"

Aidan let out his breath slowly. "Let us say I can think of no other explanation," he said, setting down the ale cup. He wasn't about to admit how much the zip-*her* and the little disk she called a button bothered him. Instead, he folded his arms and tried to look worldly.

She put her shoulders back. "There's *not* another explanation because I've told the truth."

"Be that as it may, my men will have to be told a different tale."

Her brow furrowed at that, but before she could protest, he raised a silencing hand. "We will put it about that one of my allies brought you here, spiriting you onto the gatehouse arch as a jest. Many of my friends are bold enough to have attempted such foolery," he said, thinking in particular of the Barra MacNeils.

Hebridean devils to a man, and great ravishers of women as well, any one of his friends from the Isle of Barra could have done the deed. Best of all, if ever his tall tale reached the MacNeils, they'd be quicker to throw back their heads and roar with laughter than to draw their swords and demand that he redeem their honor.

O-o-oh, aye, the MacNeils were the answer.

His aching head beginning to feel better already, he smiled.

Kira Bedwell frowned.

She'd wrapped her arms around her knees and sat staring at him from the bathing tub, clearly not agreeing with a thing he'd suggested. "It means a lot to me that you don't think I'm a witch," she said, her tone proving it, "but whether you believe me or not, I am still out of place here. I—"

"Saints of glory!" Aidan crossed the room in a flash. "Your place is with me and has been since that long-ago day we first glimpsed each other. If there be any truth between us, it is that." He frowned down at her, seeing not her nakedness but the stubborn set of her jaw. "Come, lass, you know it as well as—"

"*If there be any truth between us* are words that prove there can be nothing between us," she returned, staring right back at him. "Just like 'saints of glory.' People don't talk like that where I come from, and they sure don't talk like me here." She looked down then, plucking at the tub's linen lining. "Don't you see? Much as I would have wished it otherwise, my being here is a mistake. A weird quirk of fate—a slip in time—that should only have been a fleeting glance. I'd hoped to catch a glimpse of you in your hall, but in my heart I wanted more."

She looked up again, her eyes luminous. "I think my longing was so strong that it caused a *bump* in our destinies, sort of like when the needle of an old-fashioned record player skipped to the wrong groove."

Aidan dropped on one knee beside the bathing tub. He didn't understand all the words she'd used, but he knew well enough what she meant. "The fates do not err," he told her. "Leastways no' Gaelic ones. If they saw fit to send you here, you can be sure that was their intention."

To his annoyance, she didn't look convinced.

Just the opposite, she snatched back her hand when he reached for it, hoping to gentle her with a soft kiss to her palm.

"I'm not so sure ancient Gaelic gods have much control over Americans," she said, tucking her hands beneath her bent knees. "We're always told we make our own beds, and this one"—she glanced around his sumptuous, candlelit room—"is a bed I'm not supposed to be sleeping in. Especially when my being here is causing you so much grief. I can't allow—"

"Grief?" Aidan shot to his feet, pulling her up with him. Scowling, he lifted her from the tub, then swirled a linen drying cloth around her shoulders as he stood glowering at her. "Misery was the long years without you. The empty nights when I wondered if you were indeed naught but a dream. I thought my heart would split when Tavish carried you into my hall and I recognized you."

She gave him a look that made his head start to pound again. "You looked furious when you saw me," she said, clutching the drying cloth to her breasts. "In medieval-speak, you'd probably say *black-browed* and ready to flay me to ribbons."

"No' you, lass. I was ready to punish my men—as I've told you," he reminded her. "I was wroth with them for their treatment of you."

"And that's the very reason I must leave." She moved to stand before the hearth fire, turning her back to its warmth. "I can't stay on and see my presence cause such disruption in your hall. If I'm gone—"

"If you are gone, there will be no hall, for I should spend my days searching for you." He went to her, putting his hands on her shoulders. "My men would become rovers, broken men without direction—"

"You're trying to make me feel good, but it won't work." She ducked away and snatched up another linen towel, using this one to dry her hair. "If I stayed on, you'd be miserable. You'd end up spending every night like this one, stomping about and scowling, grilling me because one of your men misunderstood something I said or did."

Stomping and scowling?

Aidan shoved a hand through his hair. Was he truly guilty of the like? Half certain that he was, he snapped his brows together, his head now throbbing in earnest. Frowning as well, he turned on his heel and did his best not to *stomp* to the window. Once there, he drew a deep breath of the bracing sea air and scowled all he wished.

Truth was, it felt good.

But he didn't need Tavish Long-nose to tell him that black moods and storming through halls weren't ways to win a lady's heart. What he needed was a clear head and a plan. A new approach, guaranteed to impress.

Stepping closer to the window, he braced his hands

on the cold stone ledge and took another deep breath. And another. The chill air would surely help him think. Hopefully, when the answer came, it would be one he could stomach.

Something that wouldn't make him look foolish.

Not that he'd allow such a trivial matter to keep him from gaining his heart's desire.

He sighed. It was amazing what love could do to a man.

Chapter 9

Aidan stood at his bedchamber window, no longer looking out at the night's mist and murk but down at his own two hands. Still planted firmly on the broad stone ledge of the window arch, they were hands a man could be proud of. Strong, large, and capable, they'd swung swords, wielded axes, and were no strangers to hard, backbreaking work.

And, it finally occurred to him, neither were they the hands of a man incapable of claiming the woman he wanted.

The *only* woman he wanted.

Despite the small matters of All-den, Pen-seal-*where'er*, and his men crossing themselves each time she walked past. The saints knew, he'd fought and besieged greater battles. With one last gulp of the cold night air, he straightened his back and turned, ready to take on this new challenge.

A formidable foe, she watched him from near the hearth. Across the length of his chamber, to be sure, but after the distance of dreams, so close he could taste her. Without doubt, he could smell her. The scent of clean, freshly washed woman filled the room, a fine, heathery scent laced with just enough *her* to befuddle his senses and torment him.

Truth was, she drove him beyond reason.

She met his gaze steadily, her sleek flame-bright hair gleaming in the torchlight, the drying cloth still clutched tight around her. The thin, damp cloth clung to her, molding her full, round breasts and tempting him with the sweetness of her shapely hips and thighs.

Even more distracting, she was tapping one foot, the rapid movement making her breasts jig, while the flush of irritation on her face only drew his attention to her soft, kissable lips.

Tiny droplets of water glistened on her shoulders and as he watched, one pearled and trickled down her breasts, disappearing beneath the knotted cloth.

When a second droplet did the same, his mouth went dry.

"A plague on it," he hissed, trying hard not to groan or frown. Clenching his hands, he struggled to ignore the sudden heavy pounding at his loins. He raked a hand through his hair, blotting all thought of her lush, warm curves, the fragrant, heated place hidden between her thighs.

A slick, succulent place he couldn't wait to get his hands on.

His hands, and more.

Much more.

"Return my clothes, and I'll be on my way," she said then, her words dashing cold water on his ponderings. "If the gatehouse arch brought me here, it can surely take me back."

"Och, lass, I fear 'tis too late for that," he said, frowning after all. With long strides, he crossed to her.

"There are clothes a-plenty for you here. Fine clothes. Raiments my sister left behind when she wed a Border chieftain. I'll also have new ones made for you. As for the gatehouse arch, I canna let you near it. Leastways unescorted. No' that I think there's aught amiss with it, but—"

"What is this?" Her eyes flashed. "First you take my clothes and riddle me with questions, and now you'd deny me access to the one place—"

He grabbed her shoulders, silencing her with a fierce, bruising kiss. "Ach, lass," he panted, releasing her. "It was my hope to *woo* you this e'en. My questions were so I can understand what we're facing. I need to know so we can find a way to make things work, together."

"You have a strange way of wooing a woman," she said, hitching up the drying cloth where it had dipped to reveal a pert nipple.

"Perhaps because I dinna do the like every day," Aidan shot back, his frown blacker than ever. "I have ne'er met a woman like you. One I so wished to please. A *future woman.*"

She blinked, then sank onto a stool before the fire. "You wished to please me because I come from the future?"

"Nay!" Aidan almost roared. "Because you are *you*. And dinna tell me it's no' possible to know you that well. Sweet lass, I have lived with you day and night for years now, though I canna explain what brought us together."

He paused, looking at her deeply. "All that matters is that we *are*. No' how we came to be."

She blinked again and bit down on her lip, her eyes

sparkling suspiciously. "You sound like you mean that, MacDonald."

"I do. More than anything," he owned, remembering the handful of heather tucked into his scrip.

Wondering why he hadn't thought of it before, he wheeled about and strode across the room, making for his discarded plaid and sword belt.

"Here!" he announced, seizing the ratty-looking leather pouch and waving it at her. "Now I shall prove to you how I meant us to spend this e'en."

Kira swallowed, not sure she wanted to know.

She'd already resigned herself to leaving him. If she even could. She took a deep breath, forcing herself not to think about how much she would miss him. She would even miss his world, wine barrel baths, stewed eels, and all. Shivering with a cold she suspected had little to do with the room's temperature, she scooted her stool closer to the fire and focused on keeping a neutral look on her face. What she needed to do was concentrate not on how crazy she was about him but on how much better off he'd be once she was gone.

A feat she was mastering beautifully until he plunged his hand into his ancient scrip and withdrew a fistful of crumpled purplish-brown heather, thrusting his prize beneath her nose with as much glowing pride as if he were offering her a dozen long-stemmed roses.

"O-o-oh, no," she cried, her heart squeezing.

She rose slowly to her feet, her every refusal melting away as he pressed the crushed heather into her hands, closing her fingers around the dried, brittle stems.

Closing her fate, too, for the instant her fingers tightened on the heather, she knew herself lost. She opened her mouth to thank him, but shut it as quickly, the thickness in her throat making it impossible to speak.

She looked down at the heather, touching a finger to the tiny, bell-like blooms until they began to swim before her eyes. Blinking furiously, she pressed the gift to her breast, more delighted than if he'd showered her with diamonds and gold. Love, happiness, and wonder swept her, filling her with sweet, golden warmth that chased all else from her mind.

Certainly the Castle Apartments in distant Aldan, Pennsylvania, and even her love's grumbling, grim-faced men and their giant, porridge-eating rats. The three mice that surely lived with a gazillion twitchy-nosed pals beneath the dungeon's matted floor rushes. Even those great annoyances of her own time, every hapless landscape worker who ever wielded a leaf blower.

They were all banished. Gone, as if they'd never been.

Nothing mattered but the tall, fierce-looking Highlander standing so proudly before her. He took a step closer, his dark eyes watching her, waiting.

"You brought me heather." She looked at him, her voice cracking. "Th-thank you."

Aidan humphed, her pleasure affecting him more than was seemly. Tavish, that great gowk of a self-professed *wooing expert*, would no doubt place his hand o'er his heart and declare himself ready to lay all the heather in Scotland at his fair maid's feet.

He was so besotted, he'd throw in every Highland sunset and all the stars in the heavens if such were possible. As it was, he reached for her, gently brushing his lips back and forth over hers, letting his kisses and the fine heat crackling between them say the fancy words he couldn't.

As if she heard them, she slid her arms around his neck and twined her fingers in his hair. "I know the significance of heather," she said, her eyes shining. "You wouldn't have given me such a gift if you didn't care."

"Care?" He jerked, his entire body tight with longing, so ready and needful he could scarce breathe. "Have you no' been listening to me? Lass, I burn for you," he said, bracketing her face and kissing her. "I've waited for you so long."

"We've both waited, but we're together now." She touched his face. "Maybe we really were meant to be."

He lifted a brow. "No more talk about returning to that future place beyond our dreams?"

Kira shook her head.

He stood quiet for a moment, the night breeze coming in the windows riffling his dark, unbound hair, the look in his eyes letting her know there'd be no going back.

Her throat was burning now, her emotions almost overwhelming her, but she kept her back straight, her chin lifted. Not that it was easy. She could so easily lean into him, let him catch and hold her forever. She'd almost swear he made her soul tremble. She knew she could still feel his kisses, the shivery tingles each one sent spilling through her.

"I will ne'er let you go, Kee-*rah*." He glanced at the crumpled heather, then back at her. "You say you know the significance of heather," he said, watching her carefully. "Do you also know that if a woman accepts it from a man, she has as much as bound herself to him?"

"No, I didn't," Kira admitted, her heart pounding. "But it wouldn't have made any difference."

His eyes lit with triumph. "Ach, lass, you will ne'er regret it. I promise you."

She moistened her lips, sure she'd regret it indeed, but the heather felt so *right* in her hand. Almost like magic, something had changed the instant she curled her fingers around the little clutch of blooms, the tiny purplish flowers not just making her heart soar, but giving her courage and hope.

The faith to believe in miracles.

No, the impossible, a voice inside her chided. Ignoring it, she took a deep breath, the warning spiraling away when he pulled her to him and slanted his mouth over hers, kissing her until the room spun.

When he released her, she gasped and touched a hand to her lips. No man had ever kissed her so hotly, dragging her hard against him as he plundered her, slaking his hunger for her as if he wanted to devour not just her lips but the very essence of her.

She drew a shaky breath. "O-o-oh, my."

He gave her a slow smile as he took the heather from her and placed it on the table. "That, sweetness, was only the beginning," he purred, the simmering heat in his eyes making her tingle with anticipation. "I have told you how much I want you. Now I will show you."

His burr turned her knees to jelly. Surely a sexier, more provocative man had never walked or breathed. And the trappings of his medieval bedchamber only heightened his appeal. Fire glow bathed him in a sensual, gold-flickering light, while the impressive length of his broadsword and his massive curtained bed reminded her of certain huge things he had. Everything about him excited her, and she burned to rub herself against him, forgetting her cares and just running her hands over every hard, muscle-ripped inch of him.

Especially his most magnificent inches, the most impressive such inches she'd ever seen.

She flicked a glance in that direction, a very different kind of heat scalding her cheeks. The old adage *tilt in a kilt* flashed through her mind and her face flamed hotter. *Tilt* didn't begin to describe it. If the real Aidan was anything like the dream one, she might climax just looking at him. He was that much of a man and she was wet already. Heaven help her when he touched her.

Really touched her.

"Have you studied me enough, Kee-*rah*?" His eyes darkened as he grasped his tunic and pulled it over his head, tossing it aside. "I hope so, for I would now look upon you."

Not taking his gaze off her, he rid himself of the rest of his clothes faster than she could blink. At ease in his nakedness, he flashed her a smile and stretched his arms above his head, cracking his knuckles.

"Ah-h-h, that's better," he said, tossing his hair over his shoulders. "Look your fill, lass, for I'm no' shy. But have done quickly for I canna wait much longer."

"*Look?*" She stared at him, doing just that. "I can hardly breathe."

His smile turned wicked. "That's good, lass. Then I shall give you a few moments more," he said, clasping his hands behind his back, his steely self-control clearly not extending to *that part* of him.

Kira's eyes widened as her gaze settled there, a fierce need pulsing between her thighs. "Holy moly," she breathed, watching in amazement as he ran even harder beneath her stare. Her mouth went dry and she gulped. Nothing she remembered from their dream lovings had prepared her for this.

She'd been right—*tilt* didn't begin to cover it.

He could be some mythic Celtic sex god and, heaven help her, the longer she gaped at his blatant male perfection, all she could think about was her overlarge breasts and the not-bad-but-definitely-there roll at the top of her belly.

"Oh, dear," she blurted, tightening the knot in the drying cloth as discreetly as she could. Her breasts still swelled over the top of the thing, but at least her tummy and her hips were covered.

Turning away, she dipped her hand in the bathwater, twirling her fingers in it as cheerily as she could. "The water's still warm," she said, risking a glance at him. "If you don't mind sharing, it just occurred to me that maybe you'd like a bath, too?"

His smile faded. "I had a quick wash at a spring when I collected your heather. It was enough."

"You might enjoy a real bath more."

He seized her water-swirling hand and pressed a kiss to her fingers. "You know well what I'd enjoy. What I need."

She jerked back her hand and scooted around the tub. "Still, I think—"

"God's bones!" He was on her in a heartbeat, swooping her off her feet and carrying her across the room. "Have done with such nonsense," he said, lowering her onto his bed. "You ought to know how much I desire you."

Kira pulled a pillow on top of her belly. "I do know . . ." She trailed off, remembering how he'd almost worshipped her curves in their dreams, calling her *lush* and claiming that her *soft, warm body* would fire his blood on even the coldest Highland nights. How he'd smoothed his hands all over her as he said the words, kissing her everywhere. Even so, this was now and no dream, and her belly was definitely a tad too soft.

Angry that she hadn't taken better care of herself, she dug her fingers into the pillow, holding it firmly in place.

"What is bothering you, Kee-*rah*?" He glanced at the table, then back at her. "Shall I bring you an armful of heather next time? I will if a few sprigs weren't enough to properly woo you."

Her heart dipped. "I loved your heather. One sprig would've melted me. It isn't that." She paused, struggling to find the right words. "It's that I've gained a bit of weight since the last time we *dreamt together.*"

His brows shot upward. "Saints! Think you I'd want a stick-woman in my bed?"

"No, but—"

"Ne'er have I desired another woman more than you." His gaze slid across her breasts and her pillow-padded belly, then swept down her thankfully good legs. "Alas," he added, rubbing his chin with the back of his hand, "it would seem I must prove it to you."

He stepped closer, pure male heat pouring off him. Her pulse jumping, Kira watched as he pried her fingers from the pillow. He set it carefully aside, then stood back and folded his arms.

"Now the drying cloth." He waited, every fierce, muscled inch of him daring her to defy him.

No, every fierce, muscled, *scarred* inch, for standing this close and beneath the blaze of a well-burning wall torch, she could see a scoring of faint, silvery scars winking from his hips and thighs. A rather fresh one slashed the side of his left arm. Sword marks, Kira knew. Battle tokens that she'd not noticed in their dreams. Not surprisingly, they only made him look all the more irresistible.

Dark, dangerous, and bearing marks of medieval warfare.

Kira swallowed, the notion making her pulse quicken. She looked up at him, her tummy roll forgotten. "Your sca—"

"My battle scars are no' near as interesting as the sweetness beneath that drying cloth," he said, his burr thicker than ever before. "Have done with it—I would see you naked."

With trembling fingers, Kira obliged. She untied the knot and yanked the thing from beneath her, letting it fall to the floor. Cold air swept her, bringing gooseflesh and tightening her nipples, but she resisted the urge to reach for the covers. She couldn't have moved if her life depended on it. Not with him looking at her as if he wanted to devour her whole.

He was *not* looking at her as if tummy rolls mattered to him.

"You take my breath," he said, proving it. "Every luscious curve of you. Your breasts"—he paused, his gaze latching onto them—"are magnificent." He reached for them, lightly caressing her nipples, then splaying his fingers across her fullness, palming and squeezing. "I will ne'er get enough of you," he vowed, the words sending delicious shivers spilling all through her.

Especially there where he hadn't yet looked.

Tingling flames of pleasure danced and pulsed between her legs, the fiery ache making her burn for more. She writhed on the bed, rocking her hips and biting back her cries, not wanting to rush the moment, the sweet savoring of this first real joining. Then a single whimper escaped her and something flared in his eyes. Something primal and untamed, and so arousing she nearly choked on her need.

"That's my Kee-*rah*," he praised, gliding one hand over her belly, then tracing a finger right down the center of her, the intimacy of his touch electrifying her, shattering her control.

"I *am* yours," she cried, bending her legs and opening her knees, all reservations fleeing.

"Jesu God!" He looked down at her, his nostrils flaring as he swept his hands beneath her buttocks, his grip firm and demanding. "You, lass, ought e'er be clothed in naught but your skin and moon glow," he breathed, his fingers digging into her smooth, plump flesh.

"And you—I've ached for you since the first moment I saw you," she confessed, her throat getting thick again. "I dreamt of you even before our dreams began."

"Och, sweetness, if you only knew how I longed for you, too. How I searched for you." He leaned down to kiss her. A ravenous openmouthed kiss so incredible it was all she could do not to drag him down on top of her, wrapping her legs around his hips and then plunging her hand between them, closing her fingers around him and guiding him home.

There, where she needed him so badly.

Instead, he pulled back to rain kisses down the side of her neck. He nuzzled his face against her breasts, rubbing back and forth, losing himself in her scent and warmth, the smooth, satiny feel of her. "Lass," he breathed, teasing at her nipples with light, barely-there touches before he shoved his hair out of the way and drew one peak deep into his mouth, tasting and savoring her. Losing his soul. Each sweet suckling pull enflamed him more, the blaze of his need rivaling anything he'd ever felt in their dream-passions.

Dream-lust.

Nay, *love*, a bold voice shouted in his head.

He groaned and sucked harder on her nipple, grazing it with his teeth, the immensity of his need for her almost stopping his heart. Whate'er it was, love, lust, or both, it filled him now. A great roaring hunger inside him, all-consuming and out of control, its fury blinding him to all else. Only the naked woman on his bed mattered. His need to make her his scorching him to the bone.

"This is how I need you." He looked up, locking gazes with her. "Just so," he vowed, smoothing a hand down her hip, then tracing light circles across her abdomen, his fingers just brushing the lush, flame red curls of her sex. "Naught but skin and pleasure between us."

She gasped, her body quivering beneath him. "Yes,

just skin to skin," she agreed, lifting her hips until his fingers were on her sleek, damp heat, the silky-soft feel of her breaking his restraint.

"Och, lass, you shouldna done that," he warned, his mouth curving in just the kind of smile he knew would make her burn. "See you, now that I'm touching you with my fingers"—he slid his middle one right inside her—"I've a powerful need to feel you with all o' me."

"I want all of you." She writhed on the bed, her breath hitching. "Love me for real this time. I told you, I've ached for that since the first time I saw you."

He looked at her for a long moment, not missing the flush of arousal staining her breasts or the brilliance of her eyes. Her kiss-swollen lips and the way she kept rocking her hips, pressing against his hand.

"You truly want this?" He had to ask. "There will be no regrets?"

"Yes! And no!" she cried. "No regrets ever."

Something inside him wound tight on her words, a hot-spinning fire that set him hard as granite. "Then so be it," he breathed, stretching his fingers across her slick heat, cupping her intimately. He rubbed with just enough pressure, circling his thumb over her most sensitive spot.

"O-o-oh!" She arched her back, nearly shooting off the bed.

Exultation flashed through him, making him even hotter and harder than before. "Now, sweetness, you will see just how *real* I am," he promised, straddling her. "A more real man ne'er walked and breathed. Nor one who desires you more."

He smoothed her hair back, wanting to see her face

as he touched her. "You are mine." He made the words an oath, his voice roughened by passion. "Now, and for all days to come. I will ne'er let you go."

"I don't want to go anywhere." She peered up at him, her gaze slipping right inside him. "Not anymore."

"The only place we're going is where we've already been in our dreams." He wound his fingers in her hair and claimed her lips in a deep, slaking kiss.

She pulled away, her face troubled. "But our dreams are over," she protested. "What if—"

"A MacDonald doesn't allow what ifs." He looked at her, willing her to believe him. "We've already walked a long path together. Now, this night, we join at the meeting of our destiny."

Certain of it, he lowered his head to her breasts again, swirling his tongue over first one nipple, then the other. He needed the taste, feel, and scent of her, couldn't live without drinking her in.

She was his destiny.

His life.

His heart fell wide with the knowledge. Everything about her felt so familiar. He couldn't remember having ever felt this way about a woman before. It was an intimacy deeper than their dreams, almost as if he'd spent lifetimes holding her. And this was one he wasn't going to let pass without her.

No matter what keeping her might cost him.

Need and longing filling him, he rained soft kisses across the swell of her breasts, her shoulders, and neck. He wanted to savor her so fully that he would forever carry her scent, wouldn't be able to breathe without the essence of her flooding his senses.

A husky moan rumbled low in his chest. A strangled sound some might call capitulation. Maybe even surrender. It mattered not. Only that he never again blink or waken and find her gone, his bed cold and his arms empty.

"Dinna e'er say what if again." He breathed the words against her skin. "Our joining is writ across our souls. Ignoring such a truth would be like trying to stem the tide with one's bare hands."

"Oh, I believe." She locked her arms around him, holding him close. "I think I always have."

"Then let me love you, lass. Now." He reached down between them, nudging her thighs wider as he covered her body with his. *"Mine,"* he vowed, his throat too thick for anything else, his vitals so tight he half feared he'd burst before he could thrust into her.

But then she arched her hips and did some reaching of her own, curling her fingers around him and angling him closer. So close that her slick female heat pulsed hotly against him, the silky-slippery wetness too tempting to resist.

He plunged into her, his soul splitting when she cried his name. Again and again, he kissed her, matching the strokes of his tongue to their mating, riding her harder and deeper and faster until she screamed and tossed beneath him, her nails scoring his shoulders. A woman on fire, she clung to him, her every gasp of pleasure a deeper satisfaction than his own spilling seed.

The room tilted and whirled, the little flames of the oil lamps and the glow from the hearth fire blending into a crazed blur of fast-wheeling stars until his heart slowed and his breath came easier.

Even then, his body still shuddered and her tight, female heat kept convulsing around him, the mingled scent of their pleasure a heady, intoxicating proof of the realness of their loving.

As was her soft, quiet breathing as she nestled close, her warmth and the damp, sated feel of her as reassuring as the solidness of his bedchamber's walls. The sturdy thick-timbered frame of his great curtained bed and the familiar night darkness filling the tall arched windows. All was as it should have been.

He hadn't even realized he'd fallen asleep until he felt a persistent tapping on his shoulder.

He rolled off the bed and leapt to his feet, groping for his sword until he spied the still-bolted door. Relief flooding him, he wheeled around—and knew instantly why he'd been having such sweet dreams.

She sat peering at him from the middle of the bed, beautifully naked and tempting, her hair sleep-tousled and her every curve limned by moonlight and shadow. The shadows prevailed, but there was enough silvery light to catch tantalizing glimpses. Now fully awake, he swept her lush breasts and pouty nipples with his gaze, dipping briefly to her fine legs, curled sweetly beneath her, before settling on the tangle of red curls between her thighs.

He drew a sharp breath, instantly hard.

She shifted on the bed, that one move giving him a quick flash of *all* of her.

Aidan's blood ran burning hot. He stepped closer, his mouth curving in a devilish smile. "I would ne'er have believed you'd be more eager than in our dreams," he said, tossing a glance at the window,

where the stars hadn't even begun to pale. " 'Tis nowhere near daylight and already you want—"

"I couldn't sleep." She glanced aside, something in
her tone freezing his smile.

"What is it?" He sat on the edge of the bed, looking
at her. "Dinna tell me you're sorry we mated?"

"Oh, no, it isn't that," she said, her eyes troubled
all the same.

He reached over and touched her face, then sifted
his fingers through her hair. "I dinna like seeing you
fashed, sweetness. Tell me what's worrying you."

She hesitated only a moment before she seized his
hand, gripping it hard. "I remembered your men saying you'd gone warring. You didn't mention it, so I
worried."

Aidan's smile returned. "Ach," he said, lifting her
hand for a kiss, "I wasn't *warring*, only chasing
vermin."

She blinked. "You mean rats?"

He laughed. "So you could say, aye. But he's caught
now and whiling in my dungeon, so you needn't concern yourself o'er him."

"Oh," she said in a relieved voice, "you mean rats
of the two-legged variety?"

"Indeed," Aidan confirmed, kissing her fingertips.
"My own cousin, Conan Dearg. A blight to our clan
and the worst scourge to e'er walk the heather."

She gasped.

Aidan's smile faded.

"Conan Dearg?" She stared at him, wide-eyed.
"Did I hear you correctly? He's the man in your
dungeon?"

"Unless the weasel's transformed himself into another, aye, that'll be him. Conan Dearg, my cousin. Only remaining son of my father's baseborn half brother." He looked at her, not liking the way her face was paling. " 'Tis rumored he had done with his sire, then his own brothers, one by one, hoping to lay claim to Ardcraig Castle. With that ambition long accomplished, he's set his sights higher in recent times, casting his eye on Wrath as well."

"Dear God," she whispered, even whiter than before. "I can't believe I forgot him. I should have warned you straightaway. But everything happened so fast and I—"

"Whoa, lass." Aidan pushed to his feet. "How can you know Conan Dearg?"

"I don't know him," she said, scrambling off the bed after him. "I know *of* him. From books."

Aidan frowned, one of his best. "You've read of him in books? In this future time of yours?"

She nodded, looking miserable. "According to Scottish history, he's the man who killed you."

Aidan stared at her, feeling the floor give way and the room spin wildly.

This time not in bliss.

Chapter 10

Several hours later, Kira sat in a heavy oaken chair in Aidan's privy solar, once again properly dressed in fitting, period-suitable clothing, up to and including a fresh and floppy pair of oversized *cuarans* and not a stitch of underwear. Most importantly, she was more convinced than ever that she now knew the reason she'd been sent back in time. She also had a pretty good idea of what she was supposed to do about it, even if a certain fierce and stubborn warrior chieftain felt otherwise.

She knew.

And all his pacing and bluster wouldn't change a thing.

Pointedly ignoring the tempting platter of bannocks, butter, and honey winking at her from the table beside her chair, she folded her hands in her lap and waited calmly for the next barrage of questions.

When they didn't come, she took a deep breath. "It must be as clear to you as it is to me." She lifted her voice just in case Aidan couldn't hear her where he stood across the solar, glaring out a window. The day had turned cold and dark, with a sleety wind blowing off the sea. Not that she'd let howling gales and glowers stop her from saying what needed to be said. "There can be no question," she contended. "I was sent here to save you and—"

He huffed. "I dinna need a lass to save me."

Kira pressed her lips together and stared at his back, willing him to be reasonable. "I believe the gatehouse arch will work in reverse. My purpose is to return us to my world."

He spun around. "Us? Why would I be wanting that?" he demanded, his hands curling around his sword belt. "I like my world fine and dinna want to leave it. Nor, I thought, did you." He narrowed his eyes at her, his look challenging. "Or did my ears fool me when you said you wished to stay?"

"That was before you reminded me about Conan Dearg." Kira sighed. "Now things are different. Besides, I meant I wished to stay with *you*. It doesn't matter to me in what time that is."

"It matters to me." He strode to the hearth and took an iron poker to jab at the glowing peats. "I canna just . . . disappear through some *time portal*, as you call it. I have duties here," he said, straightening. "A chieftain's life is no' just filled with cattle raiding and leading men into battle. Teaching the young lads to swing a sword and stand unafraid no matter what comes at them. We must also speak true at all times, keep our promises, and honor the clan elders. We care for the weak and ill, and give shelter to our widows and orphans."

Setting aside the poker, he clasped his hands behind his back and began pacing. "We hold councils and are allies, e'er ready to support our friends when they need us, just as we punish those men who behave badly."

Kira frowned and reached down to stroke old Ferlie's head. Newly washed and pleasant-smelling, thanks to her insistence, her used bathwater, and two somewhat reluctant *water boys*, the great beast lay curled on the floor rushes beside her chair, snoring contentedly. Unfortunately, sweet-smelling or no, his shaggy, medieval-looking bulk, as well as the smoking, hissing flames of a nearby wall torch, only underscored the harshness of Aidan's world. As did the solar's thick whitewashed walls and the eye-stinging *peat-haze* tingeing the air.

The discreet but there-all-the-same door to the one-holed chute garderobe tucked into a hidden corner of the room. A tiny, foul-reeking chamber that had never seen the likes of petal-soft toilet paper or spring-scented air freshener. Yet the soft golden glow from the many beeswax candles and the jeweled colors of the richly embroidered tapestries lent an irresistible air of the distant and faraway.

It truly was a world so like the romantic whimsy of her dreams, yet so different, too.

A world that belonged to Aidan, not her.

Just as her world was a place where Conan Dearg couldn't reach him.

"Clan Donald's name has e'er been a testament of greatness." He glanced at her, his gaze heated. "I will no' pass from history as the first to break such a noble line."

"I know you have duties, and pride." She looked up, not caring for the tight set of his jaw.

"They are more than duties and go deeper than

pride." He dropped to one knee before her, taking her hand with both of his. "I have responsibilities that my honor will not allow me to turn my back on."

She blew out a breath. "Your responsibilities won't matter a whit if you are dead."

To her annoyance, he squeezed her fingers and flashed one of his smug, alpha-male smiles. "Then tell me again, Kee-*rah*, how the books say I died."

"Exactly as I've already told you." Kira shoved a lock of hair away from her face and tucked it behind her ear. "Every book I have says you died at the hands of your cousin, Conan Dearg. One, a self-published book by a man called Wee Hughie Mac-Sporran, goes into greater detail, claiming Conan Dearg locked you in your own dungeon, leaving you to starve on a diet of salt beef and fouled water."

The alpha-male smile turned triumphant, spreading across his face. "Och, lass, dinna you see? You are fashing yourself for naught." He sprang to his feet, pulling her up with him. "Your books erred, though the self-published one, whate'er that means, is closer to the truth than the others. Conan Dearg did not lock me in my dungeon. 'Tis the blackguard himself who whiles there, wasting away on salt beef and soured water. Wee Hughie MacSporran, whoe'er he claims to be, mistook us, switching my fate with my cousin's."

Kira smoothed back her hair again, fighting the desperation beginning to spin inside her.

Looking bolder and more confident than ever, he folded his arms. "I am no' concerned about this Hughie man."

He made a dismissive gesture. "It matters not. His book is wrong."

She hesitated. The image of Wee Hughie's book flashed across her mind, his name and the words *historian, storyteller, and keeper of tradition* almost larger than the slim volume's title. She suppressed a shudder, memories of the self-inflated tour-guide-cum-author's preening on her long-ago coach tour flooding back to her.

Never would she forget his grand camera poses in front of the Robert Bruce statue at Bannockburn and how he'd gone on and on about being directly descended from the well-loved hero king, as well as every other great name in Scottish history.

Including Clan Donald!

She winced, hearing the swellhead's boasts as clearly as if she'd last seen him yesterday.

Too bad for her, she also remembered Mara McDougall-Douglas's husband, Alex, claiming that *Rivers of Stone: A Highlander's Ancestral Journey* was a "fine book" and that Wee Hughie MacSporran was exceptionally well versed in Highland legends and lore.

A notion that made her stomach twist into a cold, tight knot.

Alex Douglas hadn't struck her as a man who would give praise where it wasn't due.

Wishing she felt otherwise, she turned to the table and poured herself a cup of the odd-tasting medieval wine, just another difference she hadn't yet adjusted to. But wet was wet, and she needed to do something about her dry mouth before she could speak.

Draining the cup, she set it down with a *clack*, then

turned back to face Aidan, not at all surprised to see him still wearing his smug look.

"I hate to say it," she began, bracing herself, "but I think the book is right and you're wrong."

He lifted one brow. "And why would you be thinking that?"

"Because I've met the author." She lifted her chin, ignoring how the cold knot inside her was drawing tighter, even starting to pulse. "He was a tour guide on my first trip to Scotland, the one I saw you on. He's even related to you, if he wasn't lying. Either way, I didn't like him. He struck me as being quite full of himself, but he did seem to know a lot about Scottish history."

Aidan humphed. "I'll wager he was full of naught but too much Highland wind."

"He was, as far as boasting about his illustrious ancestors," she agreed. "A shame, because he was also filled with fascinating anecdotes about the places we visited. He's the one who told us about Castle Wrath as our tour bus approached your cliff. If his tales hadn't been so stirring, I might not have felt such an urge to trek out here and have a look. Had I not, we might never have met."

She paused. "Even so, the real reason I believe his book is right is because someone I trust praised his knowledge. I stopped near Oban on my way here, at Ravenscraig Castle, and—"

"*Ravenscraig?*" He looked at her, his brows almost on the ceiling. "That place is a den of cross-grained MacDougall devils. They can't be trusted farther than the length of a sword."

"They were nice to me." Kira bristled. No one bad-talked her friends, no matter how hunky or good in bed. Or even medieval. "Mara McDougall is American like me. She's a friend of my family and just happened to marry a Highlander. His name is Alex, *Sir* Alex Douglas, and they own Ravenscraig in my time. He's the one who gave me a copy of Wee Hughie's book. It was in their gift shop."

"Ah, well, that's good to hear—a Douglas lairding it at Ravenscraig," he announced, not looking a bit remorseful. "Theirs is a fine name, one of the strongest in the land. After MacDonald, of course."

"You'd like Alex. He reminded me of you. He has this air about him, almost as if he could stride right into your time and be instantly at home." She glanced aside, surprised by a sudden rush of emotion. Images of Ravenscraig's One Cairn Village whirled across her mind, her throat thickening as she remembered the warm welcome she'd received there. "If you met Alex, you'd understand why I trust his word on Wee Hughie's book."

Aidan humphed again, his admiration for the great Clan Douglas clearly not going that far.

Kira sighed. "I wish I could have showed you the book, but I lost it when I time-traveled. It slipped from my fingers and fell into a crack in the top of the gatehouse arch."

"I would hear of Ameri-*cains* and tour buses," he declared as if she hadn't spoken. He helped himself to a cup of wine, then eyed her over its rim as he sipped, clearly no longer interested in discussing Wee Hughie and his book. "Are these tour buses only used by Ameri-*cains* and are they anything like the flying machines you told me of earlier?"

She frowned.

This conversation wasn't running in the right direction.

Wishing she'd never let him maneuver her from modern-day books on Clan Donald to airplanes, she put back her shoulders and lifted her chin. "Tour buses are like the flying machines, but on wheels and without wings. They're smaller and never leave the ground. And, yes, lots of American tourists use them. In the Scotland of my time, they're called *coaches*."

Aidan nodded sagely.

"I thought as much," he said, clearly attempting to appear knowledgeable.

"*A-hem.*" Tavish's deep voice cut in, surprising them both. "Pardon the intrusion," he said, stepping out of the shadows by the door, "but Cook is in a dither o'er the preparations for the feast to celebrate Conan Dearg's capture. He wants your permission to dip into the better spices and—"

"If you didn't mean to disturb, you could have knocked." Aidan flashed a frown at the gaping door, then at his long-nosed friend. "Yon door was closed, if I recall. No' that the like has e'er bothered you."

The lout feigned a look of innocence. "Had I known you weren't alone, I would have called out before I entered."

"And had I not seen you standing in a niche in the stair tower, kissing one of the laundresses as my lady and I made our way down the steps, I might be inclined to believe you. As is"—Aidan looked down to flick at his plaid—"I caught your quick, sideways glance as we passed."

Tavish gave a half shrug. "That was hours ago."

Aidan glared at him, his frown deepening when Tavish lifted his hands in mock surrender, then crossed the room to kiss Kira's hand with an unnecessary flourish.

An exaggerated flair that almost made Aidan forget how much he loved the man. Displeased all the same, he eyed him. "I think you have better to do than skulk about plastering your ears to doors and hiding in shadows."

"Be that as it may," Tavish said, straightening, "Cook is driving everyone in the kitchens half mad with his rantings. I thought you ought know."

Not believing a word, Aidan slung an arm around his friend's shoulders and led him toward the table. Pouring a brimming cup of wine, he thrust it into the other's hands. "Cook has ne'er cared to consult me on kitchen matters so long as he's wielded his stew ladle. We both know he'll be fussing about something on the day we lower him into God's good earth."

"That may well be," Tavish agreed.

Folding his arms, Aidan watched him take an all-too-leisurely sip of wine. "Out with it, my friend. How long were you standing there, straining your ears?"

"He only just walked in. I saw him out of the corner of my eye." Kira defended him, lying just as surely as Tavish.

"See?" Tavish smiled and set down his wine cup. "You insulted me for naught."

Aidan grunted. " 'Tis impossible to insult you. Your hide is thicker than an ox's. Further, even if Cook wished my consent to plunder our stores of spices, he would have sent a kitchen lad. So tell me why you're here."

Tavish's jaunty smile vanished. "Would you believe

to save your hide? Leastways, to inform you of certain stirrings in the hall."

Aidan sighed, believing his friend indeed.

Not that he was wont to admit it.

Instead, he folded his arms and cocked a brow, waiting.

To his credit, Tavish didn't squirm. He *did* cast an uncomfortable glance at Ferlie. "Your men are no' pleased about having been ordered to bathe the castle dogs," he said, a frown marring his handsome face. "I suspect they fear they'll be next."

"Oh, dear." Kira spoke up. "That's my fault—"

Aidan held up a hand to silence her. "Nay," he said, snatching up a choice bannock and tossing it to Ferlie. "The time is long past that Wrath's dogs stop fouling the air with their stink. My men, too, now that I think of it."

"As you wish." Tavish didn't bat an eye. "Shall I see that they cease their bickering?"

In answer, Aidan took him by the elbow and ushered him toward the door. "Just tell them that any that are no' bathed and clean-smelling within two days will find themselves scouring the cesspit and then scrubbing each other until their buttocks shine like a bairn's. Now off with you, and dinna return unless we're attacked."

Tavish nodded, but jerked free just before Aidan could shove him out the door. Twisting round, he looked across the room to Kira. "The parchments and scribing goods you wished have been left in Aidan's bedchamber," he said, making her a slight bow. "If you need more, let me know."

Then he was gone.

Disappearing into his infernal shadows before Aidan could have the pleasure of closing the door on him.

He shut it, regardless. Even sliding home the drawbar, though there really wasn't any need. What he needed was to get to the bottom of the goings-on in his castle. Things he wouldn't mind at all had a certain flame-haired, big-bosomed vixen taken the time to mention them to him.

"When did you ask Tavish for scribing goods?" he demanded, turning to fix her with his best I-am-laird-and-you'd-best-answer-me-now stare.

She jutted her chin, not looking a bit impressed. "This morning," she admitted, her gaze bold. "But I didn't ask Tavish directly. I asked the woman who brought me new clothes when you stepped out of the room to leave me to my ablutions."

Aidan nodded. "One of the laundresses, then."

Kira shrugged. "Whatever. I wanted the parchment and ink to keep record of my thoughts."

She blew out a breath of relief when he nodded again, apparently believing her.

Not that she wished to deceive him, but at the moment she didn't wish to discuss her need to put together a story for Dan Hillard. *Her story*, though she'd add a caveat at the end never to reveal her identity.

Whether she ever made it back home or not, she didn't want to be plunged into the limelight. Heaven forbid, to be made an object for dissection on the Internet. The Viking affair had been bad enough. If ever her account of her experiences came into Dan's hands, he need only have the parchment carbon-dated to prove the validity of her tale.

Such a story would thrust *Destiny Magazine* into the big league and bring Dan a fortune.

A good turn he deserved, even if it meant being a bit secretive.

Aidan, too, had his duties and loyalties, as he'd said himself.

So she took a deep breath and squared her shoulders, preparing to use her mother's best strategy for avoiding sticky wickets.

Diversion.

"Are you really going to hold a feast to celebrate your cousin's capture?" she asked the instant he rejoined her beside the solar's hearth fire.

Aidan slid his arms around her, pulling her close. "Aye, I must," he said, resting his chin on her head. "My people expect and deserve it. Locking him in the dungeon is no' enough. They need the *forgetting* of a feast. With luck, a fine and rollicking one can be arranged within a fortnight."

"Your cousin is that bad?" Kira couldn't believe it.

"He is worse," Aidan owned, his gut clenching at the thought of all the souls on Conan Dearg's conscience. "He has but one redeeming quality, though I am at a loss to explain it."

"What?" Kira angled her head, peering at him. "Is he a horse whisperer or something?"

Aidan frowned, not sure what a *horse whisperer* was, but knowing full well that wasn't what he'd meant. "Och, nay," he said, shaking his head. "Conan Dearg is none the like. What he is, is a charmer. There hasn't been a maid yet born who can resist him."

"I don't think he'd impress me." She flicked an invisible speck off her skirts. "From what I'm hearing about him, I'm surprised women even look at him."

"Och, they look." Aidan refilled his wine cup, drinking deeply. "They look and flock to him like bees to a hive. He's a great fiery-haired devil, bold and handsome, and strong as a wild Highland bull."

"It sounds to me like he needs to be de-bulled."

Aidan threw back his head and laughed, then caught himself, stunned to realize he hadn't laughed in longer than he could remember. "Aye, lopping off his bits should've been done long ago," he agreed, serious again. "But he's suffering a meet end now. No' that his passing will bring back the victims of his viciousness."

Dismay flickered in Kira's eyes. "There were many?"

"More than a soul can rightly count." Aidan leaned a hip against the table, considering how much he should share with her. "He used to send large stones sailing down from the battlements of Ardcraig's keep onto the heads of any unwelcome visitors who'd some-how slipped past his gatehouse. The saints only know how many hapless wayfarers seeking no more than a night's lodging were brained in such a manner. He'd designed a special stone-throwing device and tied ropes around the stones, using his contraption to haul them up to be dropped again if the first aim failed to flatten a man."

Pausing, he sighed deeply and looked away. The gusting wind was lessening now and great swaths of mist rolled past the solar windows, turning the night into a shifting mass of chill, damp gray.

"Dinna worry—the career of his stone-throwing device was short-lived," he said, rubbing the back of his neck. "Those days ended when he accidentally dropped a stone on his favorite mistress, killing her. She was the wife of one of his best allies and had taken it upon herself to pay him a surprise visit. Sad for the lady, she disguised herself as a man, and although she gave her identity to the guards, passing unhindered through the gatehouse, in the dark of night Conan Dearg mistook her for a stranger. Someone he didn't care to be pestered by."

He turned back to Kira, not surprised to find her staring at him with rounded eyes.

"Good heavens." She pressed a hand to her breast. "Too bad the husband didn't kill him."

"Och, he tried, well enough," Aidan told her, stretching his arms over his head and cracking his knuckles. "He rode hotfoot to Ardcraig to challenge him as soon as he heard. Their clash lasted all of a heartbeat, with Conan Dreag cleaving the man in two before he'd scarce whipped his blade from its scabbard." He lowered his arms, looking at her. "My cousin is an expert swordsman."

Kira shuddered. "I think he's also crafty," she said, now more determined than ever to persuade Aidan to return to her time with her.

"Aye, that he is," he agreed, glancing at the windows again, his expression hardening. "Cunning and devious as the wiliest fox."

"I've always liked foxes." Kira smoothed the soft, red-gold wool of her skirts, thinking how much the rich color resembled a fox pelt. "I once read a book where a really cute one with magical eyes was a meddling wise woman's familiar. I think his name was Somerled."

"Somerled?" Aidan shot a sharp glance at her. "I dinna think my like-named forebear, who styled himself *King of the Isles*, would've cared for that. And you, sweetness, wouldn't care for my cousin's kind of foxing," he said, reaching to pull her against him. "With surety, not."

"No doubt." Her heart began to thunder as he took her in his arms, drawing her close.

"Indeed." He slid a hand beneath her hair, gently massaging the back of her head. "Conan Dearg's craftiness would put Satan's most devious minions to shame. Once, many years ago, he took a dislike to one of his younger garrison men. The lad was a bit of a rogue and bonny enough to catch the eye of one of my cousin's ladyloves. Much to Conan Dearg's annoyance, because of the lad's sunny disposition and ready laughter, he was also popular with the other men."

She shivered, guessing the outcome. "Don't tell me he ended up in two pieces?"

Aidan shook his head. "Nay, praise the saints, he was one of the few to escape my cousin's grasp. But only by the grace of a passing Mackenzie galley and the good eyes and ears of those who happened to be on board."

Her jaw slipped. "Did your cousin set him adrift in a leaky boat or something?"

"Or something, aye," Aidan told her in a voice like steel. "Because of the lad's popularity, he bided his time, not wanting to rouse suspicion. Opportunity fi-

nally arose when a ewe tumbled off a cliff, landing unharmed on a narrow rock ledge halfway between the cliff-top and the sea."

Releasing her, he pushed away from the table to pace again, distaste making it impossible to stand still. Even with his sweet *tamhasg* pliant and warm against him.

"Agility was another of the lad's many talents, and so my cousin approached him, saying he'd chosen him to fetch the poor ewe," he continued, a chill passing through him as he remembered the deed. "Together with two other men, they went out to the cliffs, a remote place far from prying eyes and where a call for help wouldn't be heard. Eager to please, and just as keen to rescue the ewe, the lad let himself be lowered on a rope down the cliff to the small foothold of a ledge."

"Ropes and cliffs again?" Kira looked at him with a frown. She didn't shudder, but her opinion of his world rippled all o'er her.

His mouth twisted. "Ach, lass," he said, wincing inside, "such is our way of life. The cliffs hold a rich harvest for us. Seabirds, with their eggs and oil, the latterly being a fuel we use to light our lamps. When a beast loses its footing and slips o'er an edge, if it survives the fall, we fetch it. Men here learn to brave the cliffs soon after their first steps. Some women as well, as you know from Annie MacQueen's fate."

"So what was the young man's fate? Did he, too, plunge into the sea?"

"Nay . . ." He hesitated, wishing he'd ne'er mentioned the lad. "He reached the ledge with ease, but before he could secure the end of the rope around the ewe, the rope went slack in his hands. Looking up, he saw its other end sailing down toward him, and the two other men, apparently sacrificed to guarantee their silence."

Kira gasped. "That's horrible."

"To be sure." He came back to her, crossing the room with purposeful strides. "Had it not been for the Mackenzies hearing his cries when they sailed past, a shade too close to the cliffs, he'd surely have died there," he said, putting his hands on her shoulders. "As it was, the Mackenzies anchored in the next cove, sending men to climb the cliffs and then toss down a fresh rope, rescuing both the lad and the ewe."

"Thank goodness." Kira exhaled. "But how did you find out? Did he come here after his rescue?"

"Ach, nay, he had more sense than that and sailed on to Kintail with the Mackenzies, settling and eventually marrying there. The tale did not reach us here at Wrath until some years later when a wandering bard mentioned having met him at a feast at Eilean Creag Castle, the Mackenzie stronghold."

He paused to stroke her cheek. "You needn't look so worried, sweetness," he said, lighting a finger across her lips. "The bard told us the Mackenzie chieftain, a man styled as the Black Stag of Kintail, took a great liking to the lad and saw that he received every comfort and a warm welcome into that clan."

"But—" Kira broke off, frowning. "Didn't anyone wonder what happened to the three missing men?"

Aidan arched a brow. "You mean before the bard's arrival?"

She nodded.

He gave a half smile. "I told you my cousin is cunning," he reminded her. "He crafted an explanation no one would question, claiming the men set sail for the Isle of Barra, hoping to enjoy a bit of carouse and wenching with our allies, the MacNeils. They are generous, openhanded hosts and notorious wenchers. Many of the younger clansmen hereabouts enjoy paying calls there. Some of the older ones, too."

"And you?"

"Me?" Amusement sparked in his eyes. "I will no' lie to you, lass. To be sure, I've enjoyed visiting the Barra MacNeils. And, aye, I've savored the lustier revels they offer their guests, but"—he took her hand and pressed a quick kiss to her palm, another to the back of her wrist—"the MacNeils have no' seen me in recent times."

She blinked. "Why not?"

"Ahhh, sweetness, I think you know," he said, his half smile broadening into a grin.

"Maybe I'd like to hear the words."

"Then you shall have them." His gaze dipped to her breasts as he carefully undid her gown's laces, then eased open her bodice, allowing him to caress her naked skin. "My world isn't all harshness and cruelty," he said, his touch causing an immediate melting between her thighs. "Many are the pleasures, including those that men find on the Isle of Barra. *You* are my pleasure and have been since that first day I saw you. Since then, my only reason for e'er sailing to Barra has been to quench my need for you."

"With other women—oh!" Her breath caught when his fingers brushed a nipple.

Squeezing it gently, he looked down, watching as the nipple tightened beneath his lazy toyings. "With.

Other. Women. Aye." He spoke the words slowly, his still gaze riveted on her breasts. "Poor substitutes for the one woman I burned to have for my own."

"Oh, Aidan." She bit her lip, her *heart* melting this time.

He looked up at her, the blaze in his eyes scorching her soul. " 'Tis you I want, Kee-*rah*. You and no other for the rest of my days."

She nodded, her blasted throat once more too thick for words.

"I canna recall the names of those other women, nor even their faces, save that I sought out ones that minded me of you," he said, cupping her breasts with both hands now, kneading and plumping them. "All I can remember is the emptiness I felt inside each time I left their beds. That, and my gnawing need for the woman in my dreams."

Aidan! Her voice sounded strange in her ears, urgent and roughened, blurred by the roar of her pulse, the wild thundering of her heart. "I couldn't bear to lose you," she tried again, wrapping her arms around his neck, willing to plead. "Please come back to my time with me. You can't stay here. I know your cousin will kill you. He—"

"Will no' have me running away with my tail between my legs like a frightened and whipped cur," he finished for her. "MacDonalds do not flee from their foes. They fight them and win the day. Conan Dearg's days are past."

Kira glanced away. "He doesn't sound like someone easy to defeat," she said, worry squeezing her chest. "You said he's an expert swordsman."

He snorted. "You doubt that I am as good?" He

arched a brow, all arrogant chieftain again. "Sweet lass, I am better."

"Even so—"

"He is in my dungeon and powerless." His mouth crashed down over hers, claiming her lips in a deep, searing kiss. Hot, hard, and demanding. "And all this talk of him has left a bad taste on the back of my tongue," he vowed, breaking away to look at her. "I've a powerful need to banish it with something sweet!"

In a blink, he was on his knees, her skirts shoved up to her hips and his face but a breath away from that-part-of-her-that-should-be-wearing-panties.

Kira froze, unable to move. Not wanting to. She looked down, the way he was staring at her there, making her wet.

"Oh, no," she gasped.

"O-o-oh, aye," he purred, his voice deep with passion. "*This* is the sweetness I crave. You, all hot, wet, and slippery."

He glanced up, the heat in his gaze sizzling her as he jerked her skirts up even higher, then leaned close, nipping and kissing his way up the inside of her thighs before he buried his face between her legs and licked her.

Crying out, she fisted her hands and threw back her head, arching into him and almost climaxing the first time he flicked his tongue over her clit.

"Don't stop," she breathed, her knees nearly giving out on her when he replaced his tongue with a circling finger and then licked along the center of her, plunging his tongue right into her. Deep, deep inside her. "O-o-oh, my God! Aidan—"

Aidan!

The rough and urgent voice again, not hers at all, and this time followed by a loud pounding on the door.

They both froze, passion doused.

Tavish shouted, "Come, man! Open the door!"

Aidan shot to his feet, his face a mask of fury. "I'll kill the bastard," he snarled, storming across the room and yanking open the door. "Did I no' tell you—"

" 'Tis the young lad, Kendrew," Tavish panted, bursting into the room. "He's been hurt, out by the gatehouse. Men just carried him in the hall."

Aidan swore. "The gatehouse? What happened? Was there trouble with the other lads?"

"He had a skirmish, aye. But not with any lad."

"Then who?"

Tavish looked uncomfortable. "If he's to be believed," he said, slanting a look at Kira, "it was your cousin."

"Conan Dearg?" Aidan stared at him. "That's no' possible."

Tavish shrugged. "Aye, it canna be. Conan Dearg is still in the dungeon. I checked myself."

"What exactly happened?" Kira put in, joining them. "Kendrew was in a scuffle at the gatehouse? Could he have mistaken one of the guards for Aidan's cousin?"

"My guards wouldn't fall upon the lad." Aidan shot her a frown.

Tavish snorted. "That, my friend, is what Kendrew claims happened."

Aidan's eyes widened. "What? That Conan Dearg *fell* on him?"

"Nay." Tavish shook his head. "He said the black-guard *leapt* onto him. From the top of the gatehouse arch. Kendrew babbled that he saw the blackguard up there, creeping about on his hands and knees. When he called to him, he says the lout jumped down on top of him, knocking him into the mounting block before running away across the bailey."

Aidan rubbed his jaw. "That doesn't make sense."

Kira looked at him, Kendrew's tale making perfect sense to her.

Aidan's cousin had an accomplice at Wrath. Some-one willing to let him in and out of the dungeon. Even scarier, he'd learned about the gatehouse arch.

And was trying to find out how to use it.

Chapter 11

Kira noticed two things the instant she followed Aidan and Tavish into the smoke-hazed, torchlit great hall. How quickly two plaid-wrapped, sword-toting Highlanders could plow their way through a teeming, jam-packed crowd of men, and the sharp, metallic smell of blood.

Trying to close her nose against the latter, she hurried after them, not missing the way half the men in the hall hastily glanced aside as she dashed past them. Not surprisingly, the other half gaped at her openly, their bearded faces filled with suspicion.

Or hostility.

Only one soul ignored her.

A portly, ruddy-faced giant of a man who needed only a furred, sleeveless jerkin and a winged helmet to look like one of the Vikings who'd once ruled Wrath. Tall, broad-shouldered, and with a wild mane of reddish blond hair, he would've looked genial dressed in anything but his somber, dark robes. Maybe even like a merry, red-cheeked Norse Santa, were he not so focused on the strapping youth sprawled on his back across the rough planks of a trestle table pushed close to the hearth fire.

Clearly a *healer*, the man stood at the head of the table, gently probing an egg-sized lump on Kendrew's forehead. He glanced up at Aidan's approach. "He's not by his wits," he said, the words loud in the quiet of the hall. "The blow to his head is making him spout foolery. He'll fare better once he's rested."

Aidan humphed. "I'd hear what happened. From the lad, or whoe'er. And someone—anyone—send men to comb the castle and grounds." Stepping up to the table, he frowned when Kendrew moaned. "The lad didn't end up like this from tangling with a mist wraith."

The healer shrugged. "The sharp edge of the mounting block could've cut his shoulder. The knot on his head might be from the block's stone as well," he suggested, pulling on his beard. "Depends on how he fell."

"Pah!" quipped an older woman hovering close. "He didn't fall. Conan Dearg attacked him. The lad swore it."

A second, equally grizzled old woman clucked in agreement.

She held a laver while the other dipped a rag into the bloodied water, then swabbed at the gash in Kendrew's shoulder. "Aye," she gabbled, turning bright eyes on Aidan, "the laddie said your cousin waved something strange at him, laughing that he'd now 'best every foe, because he'd see them coming before the battle began.' " Straightening thin shoulders, she flashed a gap-toothed smile and lowered her voice to a conspiratorial whisper. "Conan Dearg then leapt down from the arch, knocking the poor laddie into the mounting block and dashing him on the head wi' the object."

"The object?" Aidan folded his arms.

"The thing he claimed would let him see any foe's approach," the other old woman chirped, once more dipping her rag into the laver.

Kira stared at the two women in horror, scarce hearing their babbling. She saw only the youth's shoulder gash and the filthy rag clutched in the woman's gnarled and age-spotted hand.

Medieval healing at its finest.

Hygiene at its worst.

Shuddering, she clutched Aidan's arm, pulling him back from the table.

"Make them stop," she urged him, her voice rising when the rag-dipping old woman tossed the dripping cloth onto the floor rushes, then produced another, promptly blowing her nose into its ratty-looking folds before plunging the thing deep into Kendrew's wound. "He'll get an infection! Maybe even die. Those filthy rags are full of germs."

"Hush, Kee-*rah*." Aidan patted her hand. "Nils and the birthing sisters know what they're about."

"Oh, no, they don't," she shot back, her whole body trembling. "They'll only make it worse."

"Kee-*rah*, leave be," he warned again, but three startled faces were already looking her way.

The tiniest, most wizened woman peered sharply at her, her lips tightening to a thin, disapproving line. The rag-dipper appeared confused, her knotty hand still pressing the offending cloth against Kendrew's shoulder until Nils puffed his broad chest and plucked the thing from her hand, tossing it not onto the rushes, but into a pail at his feet.

"Lass!" he boomed, fixing Kira with a twinkling blue-eyed stare. "I dinna understand half of what you said, but what I did grasp is just what I've been trying to get through the thick heads of certain she-biddies for years!"

Planting beefy hands on his hips, he cast a frown on the two old women. "To think they call themselves midwives," he scolded, his tone good-natured all the same. "Me, having seen the work of the great healers of the East, and some here still choose not to heed me when I tell them to use clean lengths of linen and fresh water on wounds."

"Fresh, *boiled* water," Kira allowed, sensing an ally in Nils the healer.

Even if the so-called clean bits of linen he was now pulling from some hidden cache in his robes looked anything but snowy white.

They'd surely never been bleached or disinfected.

But they were a vast improvement over the ghastly rags the birthing sisters seemed so fond of.

A chill running through her, she opened her mouth to say more, but glanced at Aidan first, relief sweeping her when he jerked a quick nod, giving her his approval.

At his elbow, Tavish grinned. "Nils learned the healing arts in Jaffa," he disclosed, edging close so only she could hear him. "He went there as a lad, tagging along on an uncle's pilgrimage to the Holy Sepulchre, but the poor man succumbed to the journey. Nils was stranded there for years, learning much before he could return. Naught you might say will shock him."

No' even talk of flying machines and tour buses filled with Ameri-cains? Kira was sure she heard Aidan mutter beneath his breath.

She hesitated, her gaze flicking from the healer, to Tavish, to Aidan.

The she glanced at Kendrew, his pale face and glittering eyes deciding her.

"These, too, should be boiled." She indicated two impossibly large-looking bone needles lying on a nearby stool, a suspicious coil of horse-tail thread revealing their purpose. "Kendrew could catch an infec— . . . I mean, it could go bad for him if these things aren't properly cleaned before they're put to use."

The two old women sniffed in unison.

The same men who'd narrowed eyes at her when she entered the hall crowded round, looking on expectantly. Those who'd averted their gazes shook their heads and grumbled, but pressed forward just the same, curiosity winning out over stubbornness.

Nils the Viking hooted and grabbed her arm, pulling her closer to the table, thrusting one of his almost-clean cloths into her hands.

"She'll bespell him!" someone objected from the throng.

"Be wary, Nils!" another agreed. "You might find those healing cloths turned into snakes next time you reach for one!"

Ignoring them, Nils handed her a bowl of unsavory-looking paste. " 'Tis woundwort," he told her. "My

own special betony healing salve. If you aren't faint
of heart, you can apply it to Kendrew's shoulder. It'll
help draw out the evil."

"Of course," Kira agreed, steeling herself. "I should
wash my hands first." She forced a smile, not wanting
to offend. "You should, too. Anyone who touches—"

"Ho, Nils! You speak of evil. I say *she* be evil." A
female voice cut her off, rising clear and angry from
somewhere near. "Telling a healer and his helpers
how to care for the lad!"

Spinning about, Kira almost collided with the
speaker, a beautiful woman with the creamiest skin
and brightest hair she'd ever seen. Flame-bright hair
that glistened in the torchlight, her braid swinging as
she plunked down a basket of fresh linens at Nils's
feet, then whipped around to disappear into the crowd
without a further word.

Kira opened her mouth to protest, but the rag-
dipper scuttled forward then, snatching the cloth and
bowl. "Sinead and the others speak true." She shunted
Kira aside with a bony elbow. "With so many strange
goings-on these days, it willna do to have *you* poking
and prodding at the laddie."

Bristling, Kira rubbed her ribs. "I only wanted to
help," she said, amazed the tiny old woman could
pack such an elbow jab. "I know you mean well,
but—"

"And what do you know?" another clansman demanded. "You dinna look like a healer to me!"

"My father was a healer." Kira lifted her chin, hoping the lie wasn't flashing on her forehead. But better
a lie than tell them she knew what she did from life in
a future century. "He worked for a king," she added,

borrowing the name of her dad's boss, Elliot King, at the Tile Bonanza.

An uproar rose from the hall. Men pushed closer, scores of bushy brows snapping together as they glared at her, skepticism in every eye.

Aidan was frowning, too. He stood watching her, his arms still folded and his dark expression saying exactly what his tightly clamped lips didn't.

He'd warned her to keep out of it and she hadn't.

"My father *did* work for a king." She put her hands on her hips and glanced round, letting her own dark look dare any of them to challenge her. "I helped him sometimes."

She left off that her helping consisted of long-ago summer jobs at the tile shop's checkout.

"Then prove it." One of the men edged closer, clearly unimpressed. He pointed at Kendrew, sleeping soundly now. "Do something for the lad."

Kira swallowed.

Heat was beginning to bloom inside her. Any minute now it would sweep up her throat and burst onto her cheeks, revealing her for the liar she was.

"It isn't that easy." She straightened her back, aware of every stare. "My knowledge isn't very fresh. It's been years since I helped my father," she added, almost choking on the words.

It was more than years.

Considering where she was, her father hadn't even yet been born!

And even if he were here, he was a ceramic tile salesman, not a healer of kings.

She bit back a groan. She'd really flubbed it this time. Aidan had every right to be frowning at her.

"Good lass." He stepped forward then, slinging an arm around her shoulders. "I will have water boiled for the cloths and stitching needles," he said, nodding to Nils and the two birthing sisters. "Now tell us what else you know. Perhaps something that will ease young Kendrew's pain?"

Kira sighed and shoved a hand through her hair.

What Kendrew needed was morphine and penicillin. A clean, freshly laundered bed in a sterile-smelling hospital, with cute and smiling nurses cooing over him, rather than being cared for by a dark-robed giant who looked like a Viking and two tiny, birdlike women who smelled like they hadn't bathed in a hundred years.

If ever.

She slid a glance at them, hoping Aidan's threat to make his men bathe applied to them as well. Not that their stares would be any less hostile if their bodies were sweet-smelling.

"See?" The rag-dipper pointed at her. "She canna answer you, my lord," she gloated, beaming at Aidan.

"Well, lass?" He squeezed her shoulders, the gesture giving her courage. "Prove to Ella and Etta that you know what you're about."

Kira took a deep breath and closed her eyes, concentrating.

Silence filled the hall as everyone waited. A great, ominous silence, unbroken until a long-ago memory flashed through her mind, filling her ears with her dad's grumbles and groans. His endless fussing the day he'd been brought home from work with a huge lump on his head after a heavy box of tile had tumbled off a shelf, striking him.

Kira almost smiled, remembering, too, how her mother had immediately slapped a cloth-wrapped bag of frozen peas onto his head and given him two aspirins.

Her eyes snapped open and she did smile, certain she had the answer.

"I know how to care for that lump on Kendrew's forehead," she announced, pitching her voice to sound like a healer's daughter. "I'll need something cold. Really cold." She slipped out from under Aidan's arm and faced the crowd, hands on her hips. "What can you bring me that is cold as winter ice?"

A sea of blank faces stared back at her.

"The siege well in the kitchen has cold water," Tavish spoke up. "Would that do?"

Before she could answer, Mundy the Irishman pushed forward. "There's a wee spring out near the byres with water much colder than the kitchen well. One sip is enough to make a man think his teeth will crack."

"That's it!" Kira clapped her hands. "Go, and bring me buckets of it. And"—she glanced at Aidan—"send someone to the kitchens for several small sacks of dried peas."

He looked at her, his brows starting to pull together again. "Dried peas?"

"Yes." She nodded. "Just make sure the sacks are as clean as possible," she added, hoping ice packs made of dried medieval peas soaked in spring water would decrease the swelling as quickly as her mother's bags of frozen veggies.

A muscle jerked in Aidan's jaw. "Right. Peas," he said, not looking entirely convinced.

"Don't worry. I know what I'm doing." Kira reached to touch his plaid, willing him to trust her. "We'll soak the sacks of peas in the icy water," she explained. "When they're cold enough, we'll place a cloth-wrapped sack on Kendrew's forehead, leaving it there until the sack isn't cold anymore. We'll apply a new sack every two hours, so someone will have to keep bringing chilled water from the spring."

"Tavish! Mundy!" Aidan swung around to the other men. "See that her orders are followed," he said, nodding in satisfaction when they took off at a run.

He glanced back at her. "Aught else?"

"Only that we need to get the icy sacks onto Kendrew's forehead as quickly as possible."

"It will be done." He looked at her and something flared in his eyes.

Something heated that went straight to her toes.

"Aye, it will be done," he repeated. "Whate'er you want."

She blinked, her heart pounding. What she wanted was to continue what they'd started in the solar.

But now was clearly not the time.

So she touched a grateful hand to Nils the Viking's sleeve and gave Ella and Etta her best smile, hoping they'd accept a truce if poor Kendrew's goose egg went down as quickly as she hoped.

Aidan looked hopeful, too, and that pleased her more than she would have believed.

Folding his arms again, he raked his men with a triumphant stare. "Soon, Kendrew will be well," he announced, his voice ringing.

Almost as if *he'd* suggested the chilled pea sacks.

Not that she minded.

O-o-oh, no, she didn't care at all. Not as long as he made it up to her the instant they were alone again. Then she would tell him exactly what she wanted.

Judging by the way he'd just looked at her, he was more than ready to give it to her.

She smiled. For a night that had soured so quickly, things were definitely looking up now.

Several hours later, Kira sat alone at a heavy oaken table in Aidan's room, frowning at a stack of parchment sheets. Moonlight slanting through a nearby window arch and two large wax candles illuminated the unwieldy scrolls. Her efforts to record her time-traveling experiences for Dan. Everything that had happened to her since arriving in Scotland, up to and including Kendrew's mysterious scuffle and how she'd subsequently introduced ice packs to the good folk of Castle Wrath.

Unfortunately, she couldn't yet write about whether they'd worked or not, having gladly let Aidan usher her from the hall when Nils the Viking placed a smooth bit of wood between Kendrew's teeth just before the birthing sisters set to work with their bone needles and horse-tail thread.

She shuddered, certain she'd been wise to leave.

At least, thanks to Aidan's nod and the healer's open-mindedness, the sisters had used sterilized needles.

Not sure that they would make much difference, all things considered, she helped herself to a small sip of the wine someone had thoughtfully left sitting beside her parchments. Still not fond of the rather piquant taste of medieval spirits, she wrinkled her nose, restricting herself to a very small sip.

A cloud passed over the moon, dimming her vision. She blinked and edged the two candles closer, needing better light to see. Ink splotches blotted some of her words, the sight of them making her head pound with annoyance. Rubbing her temples, she peered down at the squiggled lines, not sure if she should credit the messiness of her scribbles to the awkwardness of using an inkwell and quill or if working on a keyboard had just ruined her handwriting.

Either way, she could only hope that if ever the parchments reached Dan, he'd be better at deciphering her script than she was.

She also hoped Aidan would return soon.

The moonlight was making her ache for him, its pale glow spilling not just across the table and her blasted parchments, but across the luscious coverings of his great timbered bed on the other side of the room as well. Every time she glanced that way, a delicious curl of anticipation warmed the deepest part of her, making her tingle with excitement. He'd promised to hurry back, the swift, heated kiss he'd given her at the door suggesting even more.

Shivering, she took a deep breath, her scribblings forgotten as his words from earlier circled through her like heady, honeyed wine.

Whate'er you want.

Chills sweeping her, she smiled. The words sent heat coiling through her even as her body trembled. Her breath quickened, and her heart began to thump with a slow, erratic beat. She could almost feel him striding into the room, claiming it and her as his own as he crossed to her. Possession in mind, he would yank up her skirts and settle himself beneath them, telling her that he knew what she wanted so badly and that he wanted it even more.

Hot and cold in turns now, she bit her lip, not wanting to get too worked up before his return. She also needed to write more. Now, with everything so fresh in her mind. But it was hard to concentrate, and the squiggly lines were beginning to look even squigglier, some of them seeming to dance and swim before her eyes.

"Was your father truly a healer of kings?"

"Oh!" She jumped, her heart skittering. She looked up, the quill slipping from her fingers, its ink splashing across the parchment.

Pushing to her feet, she swayed, nerves or the lateness of the hour making her clumsy. "Sheesh!" She frowned and grabbed the chairback, grateful for its support.

She swallowed hard, pulling up all her strength to stand tall and look normal.

Unfazed by tiredness and immune to moon glow. Wholly unaffected by his dark, penetrating gaze, or whatever it was that had her mouth so dry and her legs feeling like rubber bands. The way he changed the very air just by being there.

She blinked, her fingers still clutching the chair. "Is Kendrew okay?"

To her relief, he smiled.

"The lad sleeps." He looked pleased. Equally good, holding her gaze as he did, he didn't seem to notice her death grip on the chair. "Nils gave him a strong sleeping draught after Ella and Etta did their stitching. I doubt he'll wake till the morrow's noon."

"And the lump on his forehead?" She was almost afraid to ask. "Did it go down?"

Bemusement lit his eyes. "Och, aye. With remarkable speed, much to everyone's astonishment."

Kira released a ragged breath. "Thank goodness."

"So tell me, lass." He stepped back and folded his arms, once more assuming his most lairdly tone. "Was your father truly a healer? And of kings?"

"Ahhh . . ." She trailed off. She'd meant to tell him the truth, but her tongue wouldn't form the words, even felt too big in her mouth.

She swallowed and tried again. "No, he isn't a healer. It just seemed like the most diplomatic thing to say. He's a ceramic tile salesman."

One raven brow lifted. "No royal connections?"

Kira shook her head. "Only through a name. He works for a man named King."

His smile returned. "Hah!" He gave a short laugh. "I thought as much."

"You aren't mad? Not even a bit . . . disappointed?"

She'd thought he would be.

At least until she explained herself.

Instead, he stood looking at her, his smile slowly broadening into a grin. A *warm* grin that slid right into her, wrapping around her heart and making her rubbery knees even more unsteady.

"You, lass, could ne'er disappoint me." He spoke softly, his voice almost a caress. "And, nay, I'm no' mad."

"You didn't want me to interfere. I saw it on your

face in the hall." She swallowed again, still finding it hard to form words. "Then . . . then I lied, making my father something he's not."

He touched a finger to her mouth, tracing the curve of her lips. "You delighted me this e'en and have won o'er my men with naught but a few sacks of dried peas and icy water from a spring."

"What?" She blinked. "They're no longer calling for my head?"

"They think you most wise. Even Ella and Etta paid you grudging respect."

"The birthing sisters?" She could hardly believe it. "What about the redheaded woman? The one with the milk-white skin?"

He frowned, looking puzzled. "Ach," he said after a moment, "you must mean Sinead, the laundress?"

Kira nodded, even now feeling the stab of the woman's resentful stare. "She doesn't like me at all."

"She isn't fond of any women." He gave a half shrug, dismissing her. "Especially beautiful ones who are far more desirable than herself."

His words made her heart soar. "I think you are a flatterer."

"I speak but the truth," he said, leaning close to lightly kiss her brow. "Sinead is of no consequence. You needn't fret about her."

"Then why is she here?"

He sighed. "She is laundress, and . . . more. In a castle with so many unmarried men, such women are a necessity. She means naught to me."

"Oh." She should have known.

Wishing she'd never mentioned the woman, much less *seen* her, she took a deep breath. As deep as she could with her chest feeling so tight and achy. She pressed a hand to her breast, trying to ease the pressure.

"Forget the woman. There are one or two others like her here. You needn't pay heed to any of them." He kissed her again, on the cheek this time. "Every man in Wrath's hall drinks to your health this night. Even Ross and Geordie."

"They were that pleased to see Kendrew's swelling go down?"

"Och, to be sure, though I'd wager their pleasure is more self-serving." He drew her to him, sliding his arms around her back. "You wouldn't believe what they're doing just now. Nor would I, had I no' seen it myself."

He pulled back to look her, a smile hovering on his lips. "If you were to slip down there, you'd find at least half of them lying about with chilled sacks of dried peas pressed to whate'er body parts they claim ails them. The others are glaring at them, impatiently waiting their turn because there aren't enough pea sacks to go around."

Kira let go of the chair to wrap her arms around his neck. His smile was getting to her, the dark gleam in his eyes making her breath hitch.

"You look surprised."

His voice was deep, low and soft with a richness that strummed her soul. Holding fast to his shoulders, she leaned into him, certain she'd melt at his feet if she didn't. Her legs *did* feel seriously like rubber.

She frowned. "I think there's something wrong—"

"Naught for you to fash yourself about." He caught one of her hands, bringing it to his lips. "My men are no' bad, Kee-*rah*. I knew they would warm to you in time." Releasing her hand, he smoothed the hair back from her face. "Any who still bear doubts will lose them soon. I promise you."

Not so sure, she looked at him, trying to focus. She wished the clouds would stop blotting the moonlight. Or the candles on the table would burn brighter. At times, his face seemed to blur, lost in the darkening shadows.

She blinked, then squinted, relieved when the dimness receded. "Maybe I should tell your men about hot water bottles?" she offered, her voice sounding far away.

Almost *tinny*, as if she were speaking in a drum.

"Hot water bottles?" He looked amused. "Are they another future healing method?"

She nodded, regretting it instantly for the swift movement nearly split her head. "They are like the heated stones you put in beds to warm them, only better. You need only fill a small leather pouch with boiling water to have soothing heat wherever you need it."

His smile turned wicked. "I can think of a different kind of *soothing heat*." He took her hand again, this time pressing a kiss into her palm. "A slick, slippery-wet heat I've been hungering for all e'en."

"Oh." Kira caught her lip between her teeth, the *heat* he meant pulsing in hot response. "I—"

"I need you naked," he finished for her. "Need us both naked. I've an urge to kiss and lick every inch of you."

"Oh, God, yes!" She leaned into him, the hot tingles between her legs so intense the room began to spin.

Heavens, she tingled everywhere. Even her mouth and lips, her fingers.

This was what she wanted, needed.

His smile positively wolfish now, he reached for the large Celtic brooch at his shoulder, unclasping it faster than her eyes could follow. He whipped off his plaid with equal speed, his sword belt, tunic, and everything else vanishing in a blur until he stood naked before her.

Naked, proud, and leaving her no doubt about how much he wanted her.

He raised his arms over his head, cracking his knuckles, then tossed his hair over his shoulders, the look in his eyes making her wet. "I am ravenous for you," he growled, reaching for her and stripping off her clothes so quickly, she was naked in his arms before she could even blink.

Crossing the room with swift, easy strides, he lowered her onto the bed. He joined her, kissing her long and hard, one hand kneading her breasts while he slid the other between her thighs, rubbing and probing the sleek, damp softness there. Groaning, he cupped her firmly, her hot wetness and the musky scent of her arousal making him run hard as granite. She went soft and pliant against him, her sweet moans and the way she opened her mouth beneath his firing his blood, making him burn for her.

"I must taste you," he purred, covering her body with his and turning his attention to her breasts, smoothing his face against their fullness. He licked and laved them, flicking her nipples with his tongue, then drawing one deep into his mouth, suckling, as he continued to rub her silken heat, taking special care to keep a circling finger on her most sensitive spot.

She whimpered, rocking her hips and pressing herself against his hand, then went limp again, a great shudder rippling through her. "Don't stop," she begged, her voice a mere whisper, her legs opening, giving him greater access.

"Och, lass, I may no' stop for days." He pushed up on his elbows to look at her, the sight of her parted, kiss-swollen lips and passion-heavy eyes making him even harder.

His heart pounding as fiercely as the hot throbbing in his loins, he returned to her breasts, once more licking her satiny-smooth flesh before moving lower, trailing hot, openmouthed kisses down her stomach, stopping only when he reached her triangle of soft, fragrant curls, the rich, musky scent of her almost splitting his soul.

"Jesu God!" He reached down and gripped himself, squeezing hard until the sharp edge receded, not wanting to spill before he'd had enough of her.

"*Aidan . . .*" Her voice came even softer, a faint shiver in the air, a barely-there gasp in the wild thunder drumming in his ears.

But she opened her legs wider, giving him what he needed, her slick woman's flesh wet, glistening, and beautiful in the candlelight, his for the taking.

Needing her badly, he stared down at her, drinking in her beauty as he slid his hands up and down her inner thighs, again and again, urging them even wider apart with each possessive pass of his hands. Far from resisting such intimacy, she only moaned softly, allowing him to open her fully.

Then, just when he was sure he'd burst no matter how fiercely he might squeeze himself, he plunged his face between her legs and nuzzled her roughly, pulling in great, rousing breaths of her hot, womanly scent. Groaning, he opened his mouth over all of her, sucking hard, needing the taste of her, craving and burning for her with a madness he'd never felt for any other woman.

"I will ne'er get enough of you," he vowed, breathing the words against her pulsing heat. "Ne'er in a thousand lifetimes. You are mine . . . forever."

She said nothing, but another little quiver sped through her. And, he'd swear, the scent of her arousal deepened, as did the wetness of her slippery-sleek flesh.

"Ach, but you are sweet!" He rubbed his head back and forth against her, tasting, licking, and nipping.

Most especially licking.

Long, leisurely broad-tongued strokes, each greedy sweep of his tongue thorough and claiming. The fierceness of his desire enflamed him, his need so powerful he thrust his hands beneath her, digging his fingers into her buttocks as he lifted her hips, needing her even closer to his questing, licking tongue.

The same tongue that would have had her writhing in ecstasy were he licking her in their dreams.

Only this time, she wasn't writhing at all.

Truth was, she wasn't even moving.

The wild pounding of Aidan's heart slowed a beat, the furious thunder of his blood in his ears quieting just enough for him to note that her sweet moans and whimpers had stopped too.

Frowning, he slowed his licking, his tongue coming to rest in the sleek dampness of her slick heat. Something was wrong.

Horribly wrong.

His passion ebbing, he sat up, his pride stinging to see that she'd fallen asleep! Her lips were still parted, but her eyes had gone shut. Eyes, he now suspected, that hadn't looked at him with lust-heavy need, but had been weighted with imminent sleep.

"By the Rood!" He pulled a hand down over his face, then blew out a breath. Frustration warring with his wounded pride and a certain still-aching *problem*, he considered helping himself to ease but cast aside the notion at once.

Kira slept too deeply.

His curse alone should have wakened her.

Yet she slept on, her sweet body still as stone, her face pale in the moonlight.

"Kee-*rah*!" He leapt from the bed and reached for her, shaking her by the shoulders, but she remained limp, her eyes closed and her head lolling to the side.

"Saints, lass, speak to me!" He shook her again, his blood once more roaring in his ears and his heart galloping, each fearing beat slamming against his ribs. "What ails you?"

But only silence answered him.

"Damnation!" He eased her back against the pillows, relief flooding him when he pressed his ear to her breast and heard the steady beat of her heart.

Faint, but steady.

Her skin felt cold, her soft breath tinged with something he hadn't noticed before. Trying to place it, he rammed a hand through his hair, dismissing the first thought that came to mind.

Ne'er would he have been so crazed with lust not to have noticed such a piquant scent.

He frowned again.

He'd been *wild* with wanting her.

Wild enough that the hot scent of her musky womanliness must've swept his senses, blotting all else.

Dread piercing him, he sniffed her breath, then ran across the room, grabbing the ewer sitting so innocently beside her parchments. The half-filled cup of wine she'd clearly been sipping from.

Both the wine in the ewer and the cup smelled strongly of monkshood. The same herb in the potion Nils had given to Kendrew.

A fine painkiller and sleep-bringer, but a deadly poison if dosed by the wrong hands.

Cold terror racing up his spine, he threw the ewer and the cup into the hearth, then snatched up his plaid. Grabbing his sword as well, he pounded from the room, two things on his mind. Saving Kira and murdering whoe'er had tried to poison her.

But most of all, keeping Kira alive.

Anything else was unthinkable.

Chapter 12

"Nils! Tavish!"

Aidan burst into the shadowed hall, thundering names and frowning darker than ever. With the castle already settled for the night, scarcely a torch remained lit, but he strode over to one of the few and grabbed it from its wall bracket, raising it high. Even so, he could barely see beyond the thing's wavering, smoky glare.

A fury on him like ne'er before, he stormed past sleeping, snoring men, not stopping until he reached the middle of the hall. If he stomped on someone, woe be to them for being in his way. But all was silent save his men's assorted night noises and a few muffled but telltale rustlings and moans floating out from the darkened window alcoves.

"Hellfire everlasting!" he roared when no one stirred.

The fools carousing in the window embrasures had surely heard him.

Blessedly, the castle dogs did. Their sudden barking and his own shouts soon had men jumping from their pallets, pea sacks and ale cups flying everywhere as they scrambled to their feet, grabbing swords and blinking through the shadows, their sleep-bogged eyes searching for the source of such clamor.

Satisfied, he thrust the flaring torch into the startled hands of a spluttering, half-naked kinsman, then leapt up onto a trestle bench, scanning the darkness for the two men he needed most.

"Tavish! Nils!" He jammed fisted hands on his hips as he looked round, trying to penetrate the shadows. "You!" He wheeled toward the torch-holder. "See that every torch is relit. Each candle. I need to see faces!"

The guilt that would show him whose head needed lopping.

But as the man hastened to do his bidding, the only souls to peer back at him were gaping and confused. Men startled from deep, innocent sleep. Nary a one looked blameworthy. They all merely gawped at him as if he'd spouted horns and a tail.

And lost his wits in the bargain.

"Where is Tavish?" He glared back at them, not caring what they thought. "Nils?"

"I am here." Tavish emerged from one of the window alcoves, his voice raised above the dogs' frantic barking. "Where I e'er sleep," he added, starting forward.

Aidan scowled at him, not missing the lout's disheveled state, or Sinead's bright head gleaming in the depths of the alcove, her naked breasts and a length of bare leg revealed by the newly blazing torches.

"If you were sleeping, I am a suckling babe!" Aidan jumped down from the trestle bench at his friend's approach. "Where is Nils?" he demanded, grabbing his arm. "Kira's been poisoned—with monkshood!"

Tavish's swagger vanished immediately. "Good God!" He stared at Aidan, eyes wide. "*Monkshood? You're sure?*"

Aidan snorted. "She lies abed still as the grave and with the damnable herb on her breath." Letting go of Tavish's arm, he glanced round. "Where is Nils?" he repeated, seeing the healer nowhere. "He'll know a cure."

"But who would—"

"Devil if I know! Only that someone served her tainted wine." Aidan swept his gawking men with another glare. "I must find Nils before I—"

"If the culprit were here, your bellowing would've put him to flight already." Tavish tugged at his tunic, smoothed his rumpled plaid. "I heard your hollering before you reached the hall. Sinead—"

"How long has she been with you?" A dark suspicion whipped through Aidan's mind. "Did she carry wine abovestairs?"

Tavish's eyes rounded. "Come, man, you canna think she had aught to do with it?"

Aidan dragged a hand through his hair. "I dinna know what to think. But I *will* hear where she was. From you or the wench herself—if need be!"

"If you think to put a scare in her, you won't be—dressed as you are," Tavish declared, his gaze flicking the length of him.

The nearly bare length of him, not that he cared.

A hastily donned plaid and well-honed steel were more than enough. His bare hands would do the job—once he knew who bore the guilt.

Male or female.

Putting his hands on his hips, he gave Tavish a look that said so. "Where was she?"

"With me," Tavish owned, his gaze unwavering. "As were Maili and Evanna."

"All at once?" Aidan's brows flew upward.

Tavish shrugged. "Until a short while ago, aye. Only Sinead remained with me after—"

"Enough." Aidan raised a stilling hand. "Where did the other two go?"

"Who knows?" Tavish rubbed his beard, considering. "They are lustful wenches. I saw Maili and Evanna with Mundy earlier, but I think they went to the kitchens to see to laundering Kendrew's bloodied linens. Nils should be there, too. He was after fetching a bite to eat, having watched over Kendrew all night. He—"

"Now you tell me!" Aidan spun on his heel, racing for the screens passage to the kitchens before his friend could finish. "Find the birthing sisters and send them abovestairs!" he called over his shoulder as he ran. "Tell them what happened."

He'd assume they had no hand in poisoning Kira's wine.

Unfortunately, when he barreled into the kitchens, skidding to a halt on the slick, stone-laid floor, he once again encountered a scene of innocence. Panting, he dragged a hand across his brow, immediately dismissing the two wee spit laddies sleeping on pallets before the double-arched hearth. Cook stood beside them, calmly stirring a fine-smelling mutton stew in his great iron cook pot, while a tired-looking graybeard scrubbed the wooden surface of the bread table, quietly conversing with a second equally ancient man who sat nearby, plucking feathers from a plump hen.

None of them looked like evildoers.

"Where is Nils?" he boomed, regardless.

Cook wheeled around, his stew ladle flying from his fingers. "You'll curdle my stew with your yelling," he scolded, casting him an indignant glare as he stooped to swipe the spoon off the floor.

Stalking forward, Aidan snatched the spoon from him and tossed it aside, letting the thing fall where it may. " 'Tis more than stew that will go bad if I do not soon find Nils or learn who sent tainted wine to my bedchamber!"

"Tainted wine?" Cook hitched up his belt, his considerable girth jigging even as his eyes widened. "Ne'er would I send fouled spirits to you! To anyone."

Aidan glowered back at him. "It would seem no one has, yet my lady lies abed near death! I'll have the heads of any bungling fools who—"

"Heigh-ho, lad! What are you shouting about?" Nils strode out of the murk of a hidden corner, Maili the laundress trailing after him, her tumbled flaxen curls and loose bodice leaving no doubt as to what had been going on in the deep shadows of Wrath's kitchens.

"He'd accuse us of serving bad wine." Cook snatched up his stew ladle a second time.

"No' bad wine, *tainted* wine." Aidan ignored him, whirling to Nils. "Someone laced the wine with monkshood and my lady drank it."

The healer's bluster evaporated. "That's not possible. Only I have access to my herb stores," he said, jangling a ring of keys at his belt. "I mixed Kendrew's sleeping draught myself. Here in the kitchens, then locked away my medicines in yon strongbox."

"No one but Nils has touched those herbs," Cook put in, pointing his spoon in the strongbox's direction.

Aidan glanced at the large dome-topped coffer. Not one but two heavy locks held it secure.

As long as Nils's keys remained safely in his possession.

The healer *was* fond of women. By his own accounts, he'd been fleeced more than once by light-fingered lassies, taking advantage of his need for a snooze after pleasure.

Aidan looked at Maili, not surprised that she hadn't bothered to re-lace her gown. Of Wrath's three *laundresses*, she loved her craft best, baring her flesh often and freely. Using her charms to win favors and trinkets from the most jaded, hardened men.

Nils was anything but hardened. Beneath his Nordic bluster, the healer was a lamb.

And, Aidan was sure, Maili craved her comforts too much to risk losing her position at Wrath.

Cook stepped forward, his bearded chin jutting. "I say the lady simply guzzled too much wine! Aye, I doubt the wine was bad at all!"

Aidan frowned. "I smelled the monkshood on Kira's breath, even stronger in the wine."

"How much did she drink?" Nils's brow crinkled, his face as dark as Aidan's own.

"I canna say. There was a half-full cup on the table."

Nils drew a sharp breath. "A sip would be enough."

"Enough for what?" Aidan didn't really want to know.

"If she's had more than a pinch . . ." Nils shook his head, not needing to say more.

Aidan grabbed his arm, propelling him out the door. "Come!" He was running now. "Her heartbeat is steady and she yet breathes. Make haste so you can help her!"

"Would that I could!" Nils threw him a grim look as they dashed for the stairs. "There isn't a cure for monkshood."

Words filtered through the blackness enveloping Kira. Unlikely words like *monks* and *hoods*. Then Ameri-*cains* and tour buses. Grumblings about lairdly duty and love. Gaelic mumblings that sounded like low, softly muttered prayers, then sharp, furious bursts of anger. Heated words she couldn't decipher, only the outrage behind them. Clucking tongues, hurrying footsteps, the banging of doors. Sometimes, she was certain, the soothing patter of rain. It was a strange mishmash that made no sense, sounds flaring briefly in the darkness only to blur and dim as quickly.

Images came and went, too.

Frightful things, mostly. A gnarled hand plucking what looked to be fat garden slugs from an earthen jar, then dangling the icky beasties above her, only to have a larger, stronger hand sweep into view, knocking the slugs from curled, ancient fingers. Two sets of bright, beady eyes peering at her through the mist, a glimpse of grizzled gray hair, or the weaving flame of a candle held way too close to her face.

A bold swirl of plaid and a glint of raven black hair, proud, wide-set shoulders, and the silvery flash of a flourished sword, the bright red jewel in its pommel shining like a sunburst.

And then there was the cold.

Never had she felt so frozen. Buried under an icy avalanche of snow. A heavy, weighty drift of the white stuff that seemed to come and go, chilling her to the bone, then easing slightly, only to freeze her anew before she could gather strength to crack her leaden eyelids to see where all the snow had come from.

Or if she'd been thrust forward in time again and had accidentally landed inside a giant hotel ice machine. The kind that always seemed to be right outside her hotel room door and that made weird popping and *grrr'ing* noises all night. Not to mention the clatter and commotion when someone just *had* to fetch a bucket of ice in the wee hours.

Thinking about it now, though, made her laugh.

Or rather, she'd have laughed if she could.

Too bad for her, her mouth felt drier than a dustbin and her tongue had turned to sandpaper.

Just as bad, she still couldn't seem to open her eyes.

"Sir!" cackled a high-pitched voice just above her ear. "I do believe she's trying to speak."

"No, you fool," chimed a second voice. " 'Tis *laughing* she is!"

"Saints be praised!" A third voice filled the room, this one deep, rich, and very masculine. The joy in it made her want to weep. "Kee-*rah*! Sweet lass, speak to me!"

She couldn't do that, so she blinked—or tried to. Especially when her eyes began to water and burn, hot tears damping her lashes and trickling down her cheeks.

Bedwells didn't cry, dammit.

But apparently she was, because not one, but *two*

pairs of knotty old hands were suddenly dabbing cloths at her cheeks. Gentle old hands, so caring, she swallowed against the emotion welling in her throat. Unfortunately, dry as her mouth was, her swallow caused an odd rasping sound, ghastly even to her own ears.

So awful it was almost a croak.

No, it was worse.

Kira grimaced. That, she could do.

"You she-biddies are hurting her!" A second male voice boomed, some distant corner of her mind recognizing it as belonging to Nils the Viking. "I told you she didn't need bleeding!"

"Pah!" One of the old women sniffed. "You said she might survive the monkshood if she didn't catch a fever. Her own chilled pea sacks prevented that, but who's to say our leeches didn't draw off whate'er other evils might've been in her?"

"The only evil in her was the poison she drank!" a third manly voice declared.

Mundy, the great black-bearded Irishman, if Kira wasn't mistaken.

But poison? She started to ask about that, but her tongue stuck to the roof of her mouth.

As if sensing her discomfort, one of the knotty hands returned, this time to dab a cool wet cloth at her lips.

"Aye, 'tis the leeching that saved her," the owner of the knotty hand insisted. "That, and the powder of newt we sprinkled on the hearth fire. Everyone knows powdered newt fumes cleanse the air o' bad vapors."

"Hah!" Nils the Viking snorted. "Newt fumes do naught but make good men sneeze."

Knotty Hand teetered. "Be that why *you* haven't done?"

"Cease! All of you." *His* voice came again, sweet as a dream. "Away with you, the lot of you. I'll watch o'er her alone now. 'Tis clear she'll soon be waking." Then, in a sterner, don't-argue-with-me tone, "I'll no' have her frightened if she opens her eyes to see so many ugly faces peering at her! And—Tavish! Take Ferlie with you. I willna have her upset by his whining."

"And your bellowing? Ferlie's whimpers and groans are nowise as loud. She's fond of the old beast and might be pleased to know he's pined for her," another deep male voice shot back.

Tavish's own. Her champion the day she'd found herself perched atop Aidan's gateway arch.

She smiled, remembering, but the smile made her lips crack. Even worse, she suspected they were bleeding. "Owww," she moaned before she could stop herself.

"See?" Aidan roared, bellowing indeed. "You're upsetting her! Now begone—all of you!"

A great ruckus followed. The departure, Kira assumed, of those souls at Wrath who'd cared to look in on her. From the number of trudging feet and muttered complaints as Aidan ushered them from the room, it must've been a goodly number indeed.

But only one mattered so much to her that she wanted to throw her arms around him and tell him how glad she was that he was there. How her heart had nearly burst when she'd heard his voice.

And listening to that voice now, she judged he was close.

Possibly on his knees by her bedside. Hoping it, she tried to thrust out her arm and reach for him, feeling a great need to touch him. But her arm refused to move. Her fingers still tingled a bit. In fact, she'd done a lot of tingling, if she remembered rightly.

Just not the *good* kind.

Far from it. Every inch of her throbbed and ached with mind-numbing intensity. A nightmarish stiffness worse than the time she'd tried to cram a year's worth of gym workouts into two days and ended up nearly creeping around her apartment on all fours, finding it too painful to stand and even worse to move.

She felt that bad now.

Having enough of it, she struggled to open her eyes, then tried even harder to raise herself on an elbow. Instead, all she managed was heaving a great, trembling sigh.

He leaned close and kissed her cheek. "Hush, sweet, and lie still," he said, smoothing the hair from her brow. "You'll feel better once we get some broth into you."

Broth?

She tried to smile again. She knew he didn't mean chicken noodle soup, but as long as it was hot broth, she'd feel better indeed. Even lukewarm would do. Her feet felt like a block of ice and even the tips of her fingers were tingling-numb with cold.

"I-I'm f-freezing," she rasped, her teeth chattering.

"You won't be for long." He put a hand to her forehead and she could see his relief through her lashes. "There isn't a fever, and if you're awake now, there's no longer a need to keep you mounded with these chilled pea sacks."

Her lips twitched. So that was why she'd felt buried under an avalanche. It was funny, really. But what she needed was water, not frozen peas.

"I'm thirsty . . . please." Her voice was thick again, hoarse and unintelligible.

She tried to will him to understand, but the concentration only made her head throb harder.

"Saints, but you gave me a fright!" He shoved a hand through his hair, looking almost as haggard as she felt.

Then, leaping to his feet, he threw back the covers and began removing the ice bags, pitching them into a large wooden tub nearby, another cut-in-half wine barrel-y bathing contraption, this one apparently empty.

But what really caught her eye was the flashy sword propped against a chair near the wine barrel. Much longer and definitely more magnificent than his usual one, its blade reflected the flames of the hearth fire, the whole length of the thing shining and sparkling like a well-polished mirror. An elaborately scrolled inscription was inlaid along the blade's fuller, the blood-channel running down from the hilt, but she couldn't make out the letters. The inscription just made the sword look special.

Magical or enchanted.

Much like what she imagined King Arthur and his knights would've carried.

She squinted, trying to see it better. The cross-guard looked rather straight and plain, and the hilt was leather-wrapped and worn. As if it had been used often, and hard. Her breath caught when she focused on the sword's pommel. That was the real attention-getter.

Hers anyway.

A circular, *wheel* pommel, its centerpiece was an enormous bloodred gemstone. Polished smooth and brilliant, dazzling rays of bright, ruby-colored light streamed in every direction from its jeweled surface, the radiant bands dancing crazily on the room's white-washed walls and ceiling.

It was definitely the sunburst blade.

The one she'd seen whipping through the blackness as she'd slept.

She moistened her lips, her heart pounding. Her eyes fluttered completely open.

"I saw that sword." She peered at it now, looking from the blade to Aidan. "You swung it—I saw you in my dreams."

"I raised it, aye." He spoke after a hesitation. "Once."

She blinked, remembering the blade's great sweeping arc through the quiet and darkness. A flashing, lightning-quick arc, the memory of it brought a horrible thought.

"You weren't trying to put me out of my misery, were you?"

Aidan felt his jaw slip. "I was trying to *save* you." He stared down at her, the neck opening of his tunic suddenly so tight he could scarce breathe. "That sword has been in my family for centuries. Some claim it brings us good fortune. I thought its presence might—"

"Help me?" She pushed up on her elbows, her gaze

flitting to the sword again. "Like a good luck talisman or something?"

Aidan nodded. "Many clans have the like," he admitted, hoping that would suffice.

He wasn't about to tell her how he'd dropped to his knees and raised the sword to the Old Ones, vowing on the bloodred pommel stone that he'd grant Kira any wish if only they'd intervene and spare her life.

He knew well what her greatest wish might be and even if the Ancients smote him for it, now that she was clearly back amongst the living, he'd prefer not to tempt fate any further.

It was one thing to hear about Ameri-*cains* and their flying machines and tour buses, and something else entirely to be surrounded by such impossibilities.

Pushing them from his mind, he poured her a small bit of water. "Drink this," he said, slipping his hand behind her head, steadying her as he held the cup to her lips.

She took a few sips and fell back against the pillows. "I must've been in pretty bad shape if you thought only a magic sword could cure me."

"It isn't a magic sword, but a *family* sword. In these hills, we see strength in family. The continuity of our clans." Aidan tossed aside the last of the pea sacks. "I wanted to share that strength with you, that was all."

She still looked skeptical. "There isn't any mumbo jumbo running down the sword's blade?" she asked, slanting another glance at it. "Those cryptic letters aren't a charm or a hex or anything?"

Aidan laughed despite himself. "The inscription reads 'Invincible,' " he told her, speaking true. " 'Tis the blade's name. Family tradition says it came to us from one of the great Somerled's sons, though we cannot say which. The red of the gemstone is supposed to be his blood, frozen forever inside the pommel stone. That, however, is questionable."

"Who knows . . ." She trailed off, her attention on the sword.

"It doesn't matter." He reached for her hand, not liking the shadows beneath her eyes. "Only that you are well now."

Her gaze returned to his. "How long did I sleep? One night? Two?"

"Four." Letting go of her hand, he took a large plaid from the end of the bed and swirled it over her, taking care to smooth it into place. "Tonight would have been the fifth." He touched her cheek, not wanting to frighten her. "You will be fine, Kee-*rah*. Dinna you worry."

But she did.

Especially since learning he'd tried some quirky medieval voodoo to save her. No matter what he cared to call it, that's what it had been.

Frozen ancestral blood indeed.

Not that such a notion was any wackier than time travel. Or ghosts. She certainly knew both existed. She also knew someone must've tried to poison her.

Or him.

She glanced at the water cup, grateful when he picked it up immediately, once more helping her to drink. Before he could take it away, she lifted a shaky hand and grasped his wrist. "The wine I drank," she began, then needed another sip to finish. "It was laced with something, wasn't it?"

He nodded. "It was a careless mistake, Kee-*rah*," he lied, the twitch in his jaw giving him away before he even finished the sentence. "Nils mixed a sleeping draught for Kendrew and someone mistook it for simple wine."

"You aren't fooling me." She struggled to a sitting position, every inch of her screaming protest, but determination made her strong. "Someone here tried to kill me. Or you."

"It willna happen again." He folded his arms, no longer denying it. "I'll no' have you worrying."

She blew out a breath, puffing her bangs off her forehead. "I've been worrying ever since I remembered reading about your cousin locking you in your own dungeon to die."

Aidan frowned.

Her worries couldn't compare to the concerns splitting him. No matter how he turned it, he'd failed her. Conan Dearg wallowed in Wrath's deepest, darkest pit. Every man within Aidan's own walls feared, respected, and, he hoped, loved him. Yet someone he knew, someone close to him, had tried to take Kira's life.

And he'd been unable to prevent it.

Indeed, while she'd sipped the tainted wine, he'd stood laughing in his hall, looking on as his men gallivanted about, making merry with her pea sacks!

Thinking all was well with his world.

It was inexcusable. A mistake he couldn't allow to happen again.

He drew a deep breath, hoping to convince her it wouldn't. "I've ordered my cousin placed in a different part of the dungeon. He's in a larger, more comfortable cell, but there's an oubliette running through its middle. He—"

"A what?"

Aidan sighed and began to pace. "An oubliette is a bottle dungeon," he told her. "A narrow crack in the floor just wide enough for a man to fall through. When he does, the chutelike opening widens into a small round space only large enough to crouch in. There's no escape unless someone is hauled out by a rope."

"That doesn't change the history books."

He glanced at her, annoyed that she kept harping on that string, but pleased to hear her voice sounding stronger. He paused at the table to pour himself a measure of ale, downing it in one quick swallow.

"What it changes is that my cousin may well be tempted to use the oubliette to end his misery. He's a vain man, fond of his appearance and comforts. He'll weary of confinement. The lack of baths and a comb for his hair. If he managed to sweet-talk his way out of the dungeon to climb up onto the gateway arch the night Kendrew claims to have seen him, or if he persuaded someone to taint your wine, he'll have no further chances to do so. He—"

"How do you know?"

Aidan closed his eyes. "Because I will do all in my power to keep you safe."

But as soon as the words left his tongue, his stomach clenched and he fisted his hands.

Truth was, he didn't know.

Not when someone at Wrath conspired with his cousin.

He could only hope.

He started pacing again, well aware that Conan Dearg had been known to wriggle through crevices too tight for a mouse. The bastard had more charm than a whore had favors. But no matter what Kira's history books might say, Aidan didn't want her to become one of Conan's victims.

Even if keeping her safe meant putting certain plans into action.

Things he'd discussed earlier with Tavish and hoped would ne'er be necessary.

He closed his eyes again and ran a hand over his face, forcing himself not to worry about that road until it loomed up before him, leaving him no choice.

After a moment, he drew another deep, lung-filling breath and put back his shoulders, schooling his face into his best expression of lairdly confidence before he strode back across the room, ready to ply his lady with sweet words and kisses until Cook finally sent up a kitchen laddie with her long-overdue broth.

But when he reached the bed, he saw that she'd fallen asleep again.

A restful sleep this time, praise the saints.

Sweet color tinged her cheeks, and for the first time in days her breathing sounded soft and easy. No longer labored and harsh.

Leaning down, he smoothed his knuckles along the side of her face. His heart catching, he kissed her brow. He burned to stretch out beside her, gathering her close and holding her against him all the night through. But she needed her rest and he needed a distraction.

Something to take his mind off that road he did not want to journey down.

It'd been bad enough discussing such eventualities with Tavish.

Frowning at the memory, he made certain Kira was comfortable, then went straight to the table, meaning to help himself to another generous cup of ale and then settle in his chair for the night.

He'd spent the last four nights in its cold embrace. One more wouldn't make that much difference.

But when he reached for the ale jug, he noticed something amiss. There was a new parchment sheet resting atop Kira's stack of scribbled notes.

A parchment he was certain hadn't been there before.

Nor were the boldly inked words slashed across it anything like Kira's.

They were hateful, fate-changing words.

As he looked at them, his eyes narrowed. He snatched up the parchment and held it closer to the flame of a candle, just to be certain. Unfortunately, he'd not been mistaken. The words didn't change and the threat remained the same. *Next time it will not be monkshood in Kira's wine but cold steel in her back.*

"Nay, it will be neither." Aidan stared at the words until his blood iced.

A surprising calm settling on him, he walked across the room and dropped the parchment into the hearth fire. He looked on as the thing curled and blackened, disappearing as surely as its meaningless threat. Whoe'er had penned and delivered it wouldn't be able to reach Kira where he meant to take her.

Perhaps she'd been right all along and they were meant to be together in her time, not his.

How he fared there mattered not.

Only her safekeeping.

Quickly, before any niggling doubts could assail him, he dusted his hands and settled himself in his chair. There'd be much to do on the morrow and a good night's sleep would serve him well. With Tavish's help, the upcoming feast night would likely be their best opportunity to slip away unnoticed.

His mind set, he curled his fingers around the hilt of his family's precious sword, wondering if fate had caused him to prop the thing against his chair. Or if he'd brought them to this pass by vowing on its ancient, bloodred pommel stone.

Either way, he would not fail.

Not with Kira Bedwell as the prize.

Chapter 13

A full sennight later, Aidan stood in the shadows of the great hall's entry arch, oddly detached from the chaotic preparations for the evening's celebratory feast. Everywhere, men bustled about, laughing and jesting, their arms laden with long, streaming garlands of autumn leaves and bright red rowanberries, which they took great pleasure in hanging on the walls and draping wherever they could. Harried servants ignored them, too busy themselves, spreading white linen over row upon row of trestle tables while red-cheeked kitchen laddies dashed after them, looking excited and self-important as they laid out trenchers, ale and wine cups, and knives. Delicately carved spoons of bone that had been his mother's pride. Extra torches already blazed, too, as did a well-doing log fire in the hall's massive hearth.

Tempting aromas drifted from the kitchens, enhancing the hall's smoke-hazed air with mouthwatering hints of what was to come: a bountiful parade of roasted meats, simmering stews, and freshly baked breads. Not to be overlooked, at least two silver candelabrums gleamed on every table, each one boasting fine wax candles waiting to be lit the instant Aidan gave his nod. Even the floor rushes had been replaced, the fresh new layer fragrant with sweet-smelling herbs and dried lavender, much to the frustration of the castle dogs, used to scrounging for scraps of food buried in the matted older rushes.

Not that the new rushes kept them from looking. They did, capering and getting underfoot, barking wildly each time someone paused in their work to shoo them away. Wagging tails, running in circles, and creating general mayhem. As did Aidan's men, their zeal for the day breaking his heart.

Steeling himself, he drew a deep breath and released it slowly. Whether it pained him or nay, he remained where he stood. The saints knew this might be the last time he looked on such a scene. It was wise and good to brand the memories into his soul. With all respect to Kira's world, he doubted it could be as colorful and joyous as his.

Despite the dark bits that were driving him away.

As if to prove it, a great burst of ringing laughter rose from the far side of the hall and he glanced that way, not surprised to see Nils and Mundy holding court with Sinead, Evanna, and Maili. The maids wore rowanberry sprigs in their hair and were dancing gaily around the two laughing men as they balanced on trestle benches, trying in vain to festoon the ceiling rafters with bold swaths of tartan.

Nearby, at the high table, young Kendrew did his part as well. Sitting quietly, he busied himself folding the linen hand towels that would be offered to each celebrant, along with a bowl of fresh, scented washing water.

Watching him, Aidan frowned. He'd grown fond of the lad and had plans for him. A muscle twitched in his jaw and his throat thickened. An annoying condition that worsened when the two birthing sisters hobbled past, sprays of ribbon-wrapped heather clutched to their breasts. Adornments he knew they'd made with great care, intending to place them before Kira's seat at the high table.

In her honor, too, they'd bathed. More than one soul had commented on that fact to him and he'd noticed it now himself, catching the scent of rose-scented soap and fresh, clean linen wafting after them.

Putting back his shoulders, Aidan swallowed hard and blinked. He was a hardened warrior chieftain, after all, and had no business going soft around the edges just because a young lad he scarce knew sat folding hand towels at his table and two bent old women chose this day to bathe for the first time since he'd known them.

The stinging heat piercing the backs of his eyes had nothing to do with the like.

Nothing at all.

And it *especially* had nothing to do with how difficult it was to see his people so ready and eager to finally welcome Kira into their hearts. Now, when the time had come for them to leave.

A cold nose nudged his hand then, and the fool lump in his throat almost burst. "Damnation!" He started, reaching to stroke Ferlie's head when the old dog pressed against him, whimpering. "Ach, Ferlie. Dinna you go making me feel worse."

"You needn't *go* anywhere, you know."

Aidan jumped at the sound of the deep, well-loved

voice behind him. Whirling round, he glared at the only soul besides Kira who knew his plans.

Tavish, good and trusted friend, cousin, possible half brother, and soon to be new laird of Wrath, stood lounging against the wall, his arms folded and his dark eyes glittering challenge.

"You, of all people, know why I must leave. Why it must be tonight." Aidan met his gaze, trying not to see the hurt behind his friend's piercing stare. "No one will miss us if we slip away when the revelries are at their highest, everyone deep in their cups. And"— he glanced out an arrow-slit window—"it will be full dark tonight . . . no moon."

"Ach! How could I forget?" Tavish slapped his forehead with the ball of his hand. "The night's blackness and the mist will shield you from curious eyes when you clamber up onto the gatehouse arch, looking for your time portal."

"Saints, Tavish." Aidan grabbed his friend's arm, gripping hard. "Dinna you start on me too," he said, keenly aware of Ferlie's sad, unblinking stare. "We canna stay. I'll no' have Kira's life threatened."

Tavish arched a brow. "Since when has a MacDonald e'er run from a foe?" He flipped back his plaid, patting the hilt of his sword. "Together we can protect your lady. Here. Where you belong. Both of you."

Aidan shook his head. "I am no' running away. I'm seeing Kee-*rah* back where she belongs and where I know she'll be safe." Whipping back his own plaid, he displayed the Invincible's proud hilt, having asked Tavish earlier to give his old sword to Kendrew once he was gone.

Curling his fingers around the sword's ruby red

pommel stone, he willed his friend to understand. "Have you ne'er loved a woman, Tavish?" He spoke as plain as he could. "Loved her so much that you know you'd no' be able to breathe without her? Enough no' to care about your pride? So much that you'd do anything to keep her safe? Even if the doing might rip your soul?"

Tavish just looked at him.

"That is how I love Kee-*rah*." He let his plaid fall back into place, covering the ancient sword. "Too much to trust even a blade as worthy as the Invincible. No' when my foe is invisible and dwelling within my own castle walls."

Tavish shrugged. "Kill Conan Dearg. Let me kill him. There has to be a connection. Once he is no more, whoe'er it is will surely slink into the shadows."

Aidan sighed. "You know I canna do that."

The weight of the Invincible seeming to increase at his hip, Aidan held his friend's stare, amazed that Tavish could forget how, many years ago when they'd been boys, his father had accidentally slain his own brother, not recognizing him in the fury and bloodlust of a fierce battle melee.

The tragedy had marked Aidan's father for life, and he'd made both boys kneel with their hands on the Invincible's jeweled pommel, swearing on its sacredness ne'er to take up a sword against a kinsman.

No matter the reason.

'Twas an oath Aidan had broken a time or two, much to his sorrow. But he'd ne'er acted in cold blood, and he simply couldn't. Not when he remembered how haunted his father's eyes had been all his living days.

And now he'd made yet another vow on his family's holiest relic, this time calling on the Ancient Ones to save Kira from death by poisoning.

A plea they'd answered.

He couldn't risk their anger by breaking not one but two such pacts.

As if he guessed, Tavish glanced into the festive hall, then back at him. "You truly mean to leave us? Nothing will change your mind?"

"My mind was set the instant I found that parchment. 'Twas no empty threat, but penned with true venom."

"Then I shall go with you." Tavish clapped a hand on his shoulder, looking quite taken by the notion. "I wouldn't mind seeing those flying machines and tour buses."

"Nay, you must stay here to laird in my place." Aidan reached up to press his friend's hand. "The clan will follow you well. Our friends and allies respect you. Equally important, our foes know not to cross you."

"There are others. Good and worthy men—"

"It will ease my mind to know Wrath is in your hands. Yours and no one else's." Aidan paused, needing to swallow. His damnable throat was closing on him again. "I'll have your word, Tavish. Only so can I go in peace."

Tavish scowled at him and turned away, only to swing back around and grab Aidan by the arms, dragging him into a swift, crushing embrace. "Saints, but I shall miss you!"

"Ach, chances are we'll be rejoining you in the hall—back before the sweet courses are served."

Aidan almost wished that would be the way of it. "We canna be sure anything will happen. It is a chance, naught more."

"Nay, it is more. You will be sent forward to Kira's time." Tavish pressed a hand to his heart. "I feel it here."

"We shall see," Aidan said, trying to make light of it.

Truth was, he felt it too.

Almost as if the air around him was already shifting and the cold afternoon mist beginning to drift across the bailey was lying in wait, silent and watching. Anticipating just the right moment to thicken, swirl, and speed him away.

A chill tripping down his spine, he grabbed his friend's shoulders, pulling him close one last time. "I must see to Kira," he said, releasing him. "I've returned her old clothes and she may need help hiding them beneath proper raiments for the feast."

Tavish nodded. "How long will you remain with us? Before you go?"

"Not long." Aidan glanced back into the hall. It was more crowded now, and louder, some of his men already carousing. "Perhaps you can help by making sure the ale flows a bit faster than usual?"

Again Tavish nodded. "As you will."

"So be it, my friend." Aidan turned away, suddenly needing to be gone. "Live well."

But before he'd gone three paces, Tavish halted him with a hand to his arm.

"There might be one unexpected difficulty," he said, looking pained.

Aidan waited. Something told him he wasn't going to like whatever his friend had to say.

"Well?" He looked at him. "What is it?"

"Not it, her."

"Kee-*rah*?"

"Nay." Tavish shook his head. "The MacLeod widow. She—"

"*Fenella MacLeod?*" Aidan's brows lifted. He hadn't heard word of the she-devil since he'd spurned her attentions some long while ago. "What of her?"

"She is here and will surely expect a welcome at the feast."

"How can she be here?" Aidan rubbed the back of his neck, the thought of the predatory widow making his flesh crawl. "The MacLeod holding is on the other side of Skye. I didn't send her word about tonight's celebrations."

"Be that as it may, she is here." Tavish looked miserable. "Down on the landing beach with one of her galleys. She sent word a short while ago, claiming her vessel has sprung a leak. I was coming to tell you when I saw you standing here, looking into the hall."

Aidan snorted. "MacLeod galleys ne'er spring leaks. Their fleet is almost as well kept as our own."

"My thoughts exactly," Tavish agreed. "The woman is curious. She's heard of Kira and wants to see her."

"Ah, well." Aidan considered. "There we have your first duty as Wrath's new laird."

Tavish blinked. "My first duty?"

Aidan nodded.

"You must keep the MacLeod woman occupied tonight. By fair means or foul."

Hours later, Kira sat beside Aidan at the high table

in Wrath's crowded great hall, worrying about what might or might not happen when they finally managed to sneak away from the feast and out into the bailey. Beyond that, only a few other things really concerned her.

How wonderful it was to finally have good-fitting, comfortable shoes on her feet again.

That the panties she'd missed so much now felt constricting. That wearing her medieval garb over her regular clothes made her look fat.

And that if the big-breasted, raven-haired siren sitting with Tavish at the other end of the table didn't stop sending slow, knowing smiles Aidan's way, she and Aidan would be on *their* way well before he intended.

A departure she would truly regret, because if everything went as planned, she'd likely never again have the chance to experience this kind of medieval pageantry.

Not for real, anyway.

And she knew without having ever attended one, that a twenty-first-century *medieval banquet* place couldn't hold a candle to Aidan's feast. No matter how flashy and fancy, how expensive, or how many supposedly hunky male models they engaged to play at being knights.

"Aidan." The siren's low, husky voice slid around the name like a caress. "You didn't tell us your good news," she purred, leaning forward just enough to display the generous swell of her breasts. "How proud you must be—an heir for Wrath at last."

Kira's face flamed.

Aidan, man that he was, fell for the ploy.

He blinked, his gaze flitting to Kira, then back at the woman. "Heir?"

The woman's gaze dipped pointedly to the bulge at Kira's middle. She said nothing, her red lips simply curving in another slow, intimate smile.

A nasty, catty smile that lasted only until Maili materialized beside her, a huge tray of stewed oysters and cooked herring balanced on one hand—a hand that flicked just enough to the side to send the tray's wet, steaming delicacies spilling into the beauty's lap.

"Ohhh!" The woman leapt to her feet, her eyes snapping with fury. "You careless chit!" she cried, swiping at her ruined skirts, her scoldings and jigging drawing all eyes.

Then, before Kira knew what was happening, two strong hands were lifting her to her feet, releasing her almost as quickly to thwack Aidan roughly on the back, then give him a great shove toward the deep shadows at the back of the dais.

Tavish, she saw, barely catching her breath before he yanked back a tapestry and swept open a door she'd not known existed. "Fair means or foul," he said, practically pushing them through it, into the cold, sleety dark of the bailey.

True to the end, he'd created a diversion for their escape.

Then the door slammed behind them and they were alone, running hand in hand across the deserted courtyard, the swirling night mist so thick around them that Wrath Castle and its sturdy walls already seemed little more than a long-ago dream.

Somewhere, muffled and distant, a dog whined and

howled, but otherwise the night was eerily quiet. Great rolling curtains of mist damped all sound, even the pounding of their feet on the bailey's dark, rain-slick cobbles. Then, as they reached the gatehouse, for once emptied and silent, its heavy oaken doors closed and barred, the impassable iron portcullis lowered to keep out any unexpected intruders, even the dog's howls faded away, dwindling until not even a faint echo remained.

What did remain was a ladder, tucked into the deepest shadows in the concealing lee of the curtain wall and giving access to the top of the gatehouse arch.

Looking at it, so real and *waiting*, Kira felt her mouth go dry and she began to tremble.

"Aidan . . ." She pulled him back when he grabbed hold of the ladder, his foot already on the first rung. "I know you ordered men to take turns on the battlements," she said, scanning the wall-walk but seeing only swirling mist and thin curtains of fine, slanting rain. "What if one of them sees us?"

"They won't." He kept his hands on the ladder, already ascending. "They know to keep their eyes trained on the cliffs and the sea. No' on the empty bailey and the gatehouse arch behind them."

Even so, Kira cast a last glance at the top of the curtained walling, so difficult now to see in all the thick, whirling mist. And even if she could make out the battlements, somehow she doubted she'd see any men there.

Not now.

The queasy feeling in her stomach and the prickles at the back of her neck told her it was already too late.

Aidan's men were gone.

Blessedly, *he* was still there. On top of the arch now, and reaching down for her, encouraging her. "Come, Kee-*rah*, give me your hand and I will pull you up."

Kira blinked. She hadn't even realized she'd already scrambled nearly all the way up the ladder. Her heart pounding, she felt his hand grasp hers even as the ladder rung seemed to vanish from beneath her feet.

"Oh, God!" Her breath caught as she hovered just a split second in thin, empty air. But his arm swept around her like a band of steel, his strong hand heaving her up onto the arch top with him. "I think it's happening already," she gasped, clutching at him. "The ladder disappeared beneath me."

"Aye, lass, I know." He kept his arms locked around her, holding her so tight against him she could hardly breathe. "I canna see much through all this mist, but I think more has disappeared than the ladder."

Kira wrapped her own arms around him, clinging to him just as fiercely. She pressed her head against his chest and closed her eyes, not really wanting to see whatever it was he'd meant had disappeared.

It couldn't be helped that they'd find Wrath in ruin if indeed they returned to her time, but she'd come to love the *real* Wrath and didn't want to watch it dissolve before her eyes. It would be difficult enough to see Aidan's face when he saw what had become of his proud home.

She winced.

That was something she should have thought about before. Something she might not have to worry about now because nothing was happening.

Nothing at all.

Even the light patter of the fine, misty rain was no more. Total silence swelled around them, almost like the proverbial quiet before the storm, a thought that made her shudder, then cry out when her foot slipped on the slick stone surface of the arch top.

"Hold, lass!" Aidan's arms tightened around her, righting her before she lost her balance. "Try no' to move, Kee-*rah*. Just hold on to me."

"I will—Iieeeee . . ." Her foot slipped again, this time plunging knee-deep into a mossy, fern-lined crack in the arch's stonework.

Crumbling, ancient stonework, grass-grown and riddled with cracks—just as she remembered.

Equally amazing, her tartan picnic rug and her backpack were wedged in a clump of ferns near her ankle.

"Aidan!" She pulled her foot from the crack, her heart thundering. "We're here! My things, too!"

Her entire body shaking, she reached into the crevice, her fingers closing around a strap on her backpack just when all hell broke loose. An earsplitting *boom* shattered the quiet, knocking the breath from her as wave after wave of brilliant white light flashed across the arch top, ripping away the mist and darkness until every tiny age line and lichen pattern stood out in bold relief on the ruined stone.

Then the world went black.

Total darkness.

Even the cold was gone. The fine, sleety rain. She felt and heard . . . nothing.

Until a great blaring blast pierced her ears and she slammed down onto the stone again, this time landing on her buttocks with a hard, bone-jarring *thunk*.

"Bloody hell, woman! Have you gone daft?"

Kira jerked, a man's angry voice ringing in her ears.

An angry Scottish voice, burred and all, but so unpleasantly startling it took her a moment and a few mad eye-blinks to realize that the owner of the voice was standing beside the open driver door of a bright red car.

"Damned tourists, anyway!" He glared at her, tapping his temple with a forefinger. "I could've hit you! Flying across the car park like there was no tomorrow!" he huffed, jumping back in his car and roaring off.

Car park?

She blinked again, only now fully grasping that she *was* in a car park and not on Wrath's gatehouse arch. Far from it, she was sitting right smack in the middle of a large paved and graveled car park crammed full with cars, square-shaped recreational vehicles, and tightly packed rows of coach tour buses.

Her stomach beginning to do funny things, she recognized the place as the Spean Bridge Mill, a popular tourist trap on the scenic A-82, just north of Fort William and not far from the turnoff to Skye.

This was definitely her time, but something had gone wrong.

They weren't supposed to return here.

Nor was it autumn anymore, but late spring or early summer. She'd lost six or seven months. Her palms starting to dampen, she hoped she hadn't lost more.

Aidan was gone.

Trying not to panic, she pushed to her feet and looked around, searching for him. Her backpack was still clutched tight in her hands and her tartan picnic rug lay a few feet away, unharmed. But her medieval clothes were gone, as was he.

"Aidan!"

A family of four turned to give her weird looks. She scowled at them, not caring what they thought. "Aidan!" she called again, her mouth going dry now, blood starting to pound in her ears.

There was no sign of him anywhere.

Only other people.

Lots and lots of other people. Mostly American and English tourists, from the looks of them. They streamed in and out of the mill-and-tea shop, weaving through the parked cars, and crowding the pretty arbored walkways. An especially noisy bunch blocked the entrance to the mill's busy public restrooms.

Separated from the main gift shop by a flower-lined walkway and a series of dark-wooded pergolas, they were the cleanest and finest public restrooms along the entire A-82. An insider tip for those in the know, complete with a lovely view of the Spean River's rushing, tumbling rapids.

They were also where she needed to go. *Now.*

Not for the usual reason, but because panic and dread were making her ill. Gorge was rising in her throat, hot, bitter, and scary. Worse, she was finding it increasingly difficult to breathe.

She needed to splash cold water on her face and calm down.

She needed to *think.*

Find a way to find Aidan, wherever he'd landed. Or get back to him if he was still standing on his gateway arch top, possibly just as panicked and looking for her!

Moving fast now, Kira headed straight for the restrooms. If need be, she'd use her elbows, or even swing her backpack, to plow a way through the tight knot of tourists blocking the entrance.

She needed a clear head more than they needed to *go*.

But when she neared them, she saw they weren't waiting to get into the fancy restrooms at all. They were taking pictures. Snapping away like mad, oooh'-ing and ahhh'ing over something she couldn't see.

Then two of them moved and she did see.

They were photographing Aidan!

He stood ramrod straight between two wooden bar-rels of spring flowers, the Invincible raised threaten-ingly, and such a fierce glower on his face he would have scared *her* if she hadn't known him. Unmoving and unblinking, he could have been a life-sized statue. The tourists apparently mistook him for a reenactor, posing for their benefit.

A little old lady on the edge of the crowd gave Kira a gentle tap on the arm. "He's been standing there like that for at least ten minutes," she gushed, aiming her diggy camera at him. "My granddaughters back in Ohio will swoon when they see his picture. He's just the kind of wild Highlander they're always dreaming about."

Don't I know it, Kira almost said.

Instead, she gave the woman a tight smile and pushed her way forward. "Aidan! There you are. Come, we're late." She laid on her most businesslike tone. "Your appearance at the Loch Ness Medieval Festival is in an hour." She grabbed his arm, his mus-cles tight and tense and ready for battle. She flashed an apologetic smile at the crowd as she pulled him away. "We'll just make it if we hurry."

"Wait!" A family father with three little kids hurried after her. "There's a medieval festival at Loch Ness today?"

Kira nodded. "All day," she lied, praying Aidan wouldn't contradict her.

Not that he looked keen on saying much of anything.

His mouth was still set in a firm, hard line, and he'd clamped his jaw so tight she wouldn't be surprised if he never got it open again.

He also refused to let her pull him farther than a few yards from where he'd been standing. His scowl darkening, he sheathed the Invincible with such force, the English family father and the rest of the crowd scattered at once, leaving them alone on the walkway.

Others, those just now exiting the gift shop, made a wide circle around them.

"Wise souls." Aidan spoke at last, eyeing them as they scuttled past.

Planting his legs apart and folding his arms, he assumed his most regal mien. A posture that lasted until one of the monstrous *things* he assumed was a coach tour bus rumbled past them, only to come to a shuddering, smoke-belching halt, then disgorge a small throng of chattering, oddly garbed people who looked very much like the ones who'd cornered him the instant he'd landed in this horrid, dreadful place.

One turned to gape at him—a female, and not unattractive, all things considered—but when she paused and aimed one of those little silvery objects at him, he smiled wickedly and whipped the Invincible a foot or two out of its sheath.

It was enough.

The woman ran away faster than he would have believed.

"Aidan, please. That was just a camera. She *liked* you and wanted to take your picture." Kira put a hand on his arm. "You can't do things like that here. Times are different. You're scaring people."

He closed his eyes and drew a deep breath, trying to ignore the way the foul-smelling smoke from the tour bus tainted the pure Highland air.

"I am sorry, Kee-*rah*," he said, the words costing him much. "I—"

"You aren't sorry you're here with me, are you?" She looked at him, the worry in her eyes lancing him. "Or . . . or mad at me?"

"Ach, lass." He rammed the sword back into its sheath and grabbed her, crushing her to him and slanting his mouth over hers in a ferocious, demanding kiss that would surely set the gawkers' tongues wagging.

Not that he cared.

Setting her from him at last, he straightened his plaid and tossed back his hair. "Sweet Kee-*rah*, where'er you are is where I need to be. I am no' sorry, nor mad. Just . . ."

Terrified.

He couldn't say the word, but he could see in her face that she knew. Her eyes filling with the tears she was e'er swearing she ne'er shed, her whole expression softened, and she slid her arms around him, pressing close.

"It will be okay," she said, her voice thick, husky.

"You'll see. But we can't stay here and I don't think it's a good idea to go to Wrath. Not yet, anyway."

Aidan nodded, his own throat tightening.

Hearing the name of his home spoken aloud in this strange place that his beloved Scotland had become pinched his heart just a bit more than was good for a man.

But he *was* a man. A fine, braw one, he hoped. So he drew another deep breath of the odd-smelling air, then braced his hands on his hips and looked round, once more assuming his lairdly airs.

"So-o-o, Kee-rah!" he boomed. "Where shall we go?"

She considered a moment, then beamed. "I think . . . I think south to Ravenscraig."

"That MacDougall nest?" His brows snapped together—until he remembered she'd told him a Douglas now lairded it there. "To your friends?" he amended, silently thinking a journey to people she knew would be wise indeed.

"Yes. To Mara McDougall Douglas and her husband, Alex." Still smiling, she looked down and opened her travel pouch with one of those infernal zip-*hers*, then plunged her hand inside it and rummaged about until she withdrew a tiny gold piece of parchment.

A thin, bright, and shiny thing that she waved at him.

"My credit card," she said, clutching it as if it were made of gold indeed. "It will get us a rental car . . . I think there's a small local agency somewhere here in Spean Bridge. Maybe Roy Bridge. If not, I'll find one in Fort William and ask them to deliver the car."

Aidan nodded again, trying his best to look . . . sage.

Truth was, he hadn't understood a word she'd said.

He did, though, have a very unpleasant suspicion that getting to Ravenscraig—near distant Oban, by all the saints!—would entail a journey in one of the smaller tour-bus-looking things crowded so thickly across the Spean Bridge Mill's busy courtyard.

He certainly didn't see any stables about.

Indeed, horses didn't seem to exist in her world. Which left his original notion.

The one that he didn't care for at all.

Needing to know, he put back his shoulders again and cleared his throat. "Ahhh, Kee-*rah*, lass," he began, pleased by the strength of his voice, "this *rental car* you mention? Would it be anything like these small tour buses sitting about here?"

To his dismay, she nodded. "Yes. Those are cars." Then, starting forward, she added, "There's a call box just down the way. I'll phone Mara McDougall and let her know we're coming. Then I'll find us a car. Don't worry—we'll be on our way before you know it."

Aidan nodded again, beginning to feel like a head-bobbing fool.

But he dutifully followed her down the road, away from the frightful Spean Bridge Mill and its horrors.

Hoping worse ones weren't awaiting him.

If the speed of the rental cars whizzing past them on the road gave any indication, the journey to Oban would be a nightmare.

Something he became absolutely certain of when, a short while later, she stopped beside a tall, bright red metal and glass container and opened its door. Popping inside, she punched at tiny numbers on a metal plate, then spoke rapidly into a strange silver thing she pressed to the side of her head.

Just watching her made *his* head throb and ache.

When two earth-shaking, earsplitting *flying machines* zoomed past just overhead, he knew for sure this modern Scotland was not for him.

"They were RAF military jets," Kira told him, stepping out of the red-and-glass box at last. "They fly over like that all the time. Even in the most remote parts of Scotland." She smiled. "Just ignore them."

Aidan gave the most casual shrug he could. "I scarce noticed them," he lied, glad his knees hadn't buckled when they'd sped across the sky.

"Anyway, we're all set." Looking pleased, she stretched up on her toes to kiss him. "Mara and Alex are delighted we're coming and they can't wait to meet you."

He grunted. "And the *rental car*?"

"It's called a 'hire car' here, and we'll have to go back to the Spean Bridge Mill to wait for one," she said, hooking her arm through his for the walk back to that awful place. "Someone will bring it up from Fort William shortly."

Aidan harrumphed this time, having never heard of Fort William either.

"There's just one thing you should know." She stopped just before they reached the large courtyard with all the tour buses and rental-hire cars. "I'm not very good at driving on the left."

"It doesn't matter, Kee-*rah*," he lied again.

Something told him *driving on the left* might be very important in this place.

Not that he was in a position to do much about it. Instead, he did what he could.

He walked proud and curled his hand around his sword's ruby red pommel, taking comfort in the blade's name.

Sooner or later, he would surely be able to convince himself that he was just as unshakable.

Chapter 14

A surprisingly short while later, considering how long such journeys took in his day, Aidan decided he liked Fort William even less than the Spean Bridge Mill. Unfortunately, he was also quite sure he'd prefer walking the town's crowded, strange-looking streets to spending much more time trapped inside Kira's rental-hire car.

She hadn't been exaggerating when she'd claimed she wasn't very good at driving left, and he strongly suspected she might even have similar difficulties driving right if such a thing existed.

He had no idea and didn't really care to know.

For himself, once they were settled where'er that might prove to be, he would secure himself a fine and capable steed. Perhaps even a whole stable of them. Cars, tour buses, and the rolling nightmares Kira called recreational vehicles were not for him.

And from what he'd seen of her *RAF military jets*, he knew without doubt that flying machines would disagree with him even more.

But for now, he had other worries. Another huge, square-shaped recreational vehicle was heading straight at them and he didn't need to sneak a glance at Kira to know she'd spotted it, too, and was fearful.

Each time one of the monstrosities approached, she gritted her teeth and tightened her hands on the thing she called a *steering wheel.* Even more alarming, he was certain she also shut her eyes at the critical moment when the things thundered past them. Considering the narrowness of the road, he understood her distress.

Sadly, her ill ease only worsened his own.

Frowning, he wished the Invincible had fit inside the car rather than having to be stashed in the storage area she called the trunk-boot. He felt naked and vulnerable without the great brand at his hip. Aye, to his mind, there weren't many advantages to this driving.

No matter how quickly the rental-hire car might get them to Oban.

If they even arrived alive.

Something he wasn't all too sure would be the case.

Casting a cautious glance at his lady, he wriggled his jaw as unobtrusively as possible. He'd been clenching it since they'd left the Spean Bridge Mill and his teeth were beginning to ache. His head ached even worse. Truth was, even though Kira had taken great pains to explain her world and tried so valiantly to ready him for her life before he'd landed in her time, none of those details and descriptions could have prepared him for what he was facing now.

He doubted even Tavish would have been pleased by Kira's Scotland.

Much as the lout declared his eagerness to see it.

Thinking of his friend made his heart hurt, so he fixed his attention on the road ahead, regretting it immediately when he spotted another recreational vehicle in the distance, heading determinedly their way. Dreading Kira's reaction as much as the coming encounter, he looked down at the wee bit of tartan cloth clasped so tightly in his hands.

An *eye mask*, Kira had called it.

She'd plucked it from her travel pouch and offered it to him when he'd balked at being strapped into the rental-hire car. Naturally, he'd refused to use it, preferring to see death coming rather than hide behind such a fool thing.

Even so, if they didn't soon reach their destination, he might reconsider.

"Why don't you put that in your new sporran?" Kira glanced at him, and he immediately ceased fiddling with the thing.

Driving left was danger fraught enough without him distracting her. But apparently it was too late to worry about it, because her gaze dipped briefly to the eye mask.

"If you haven't used it by now, there'll be less need soon," she said, blessedly returning her attention to the road. "We're almost to Ballachulish now. After the bridge, we'll leave the A-82 for the A-828, the coast road that'll take us right down to Ravenscraig Castle. That road won't be as busy."

Aidan harrumphed.

He wasn't at all sure driving left on a less-traveled coast road would prove any less harrowing than constant encounters with recreational vehicles on a busy one. Coast roads presented other hazards, as even he knew.

Things like cliffs and sharp, hair-raising turns.

He frowned. If either one caused Kira to shut her eyes as she did each time a recreational vehicle or tour bus whizzed past them, he would insist she halt immediately. He would then wisely proceed to Ravenscraig on foot, whether she laughed at him or nay.

"I thought you liked the sporran." She reached over to flick one of the scrip's tassels, clearly misinterpreting his scowl.

"I like it fine." He hoped the quick answer would get her hand back on the steering wheel.

Relieved when it did, he looked down, admiring her gift. He did like it. Indeed, he was more than pleased. Ne'er had he seen such a fancily fashioned scrip, all fine leather and fur and decorated with flashy silver-beaded chains and tassels. It even boasted the MacDonald crest. Had he possessed such a treasure in his time, he'd have been the envy of every other laird in the Highlands.

A notion that pleased him.

"So you *do* like it?"

His frown returned. "To know I smiled means you took your eyes off the road again, Kee-*rah*." It was high time to warn her about such things. " 'Tis a mighty fine gift and I am proud to wear it."

"I wish I'd been able to give it to you at Wrath."

He swallowed. He wished that too. But there wasn't any point in being sad about something they couldn't change. So he forced a smile, aiming for a wolfish one.

Just in case she was peeking at him again.

"If your friends at Ravenscraig give us private quarters, I shall show you exactly how much your gift pleased me, Kee-*rah*. How much *you* please me." He glanced at her, deliberately deepening his burr. "A man might even think this time-traveling business makes a body ravenous."

Kira's heart flipped to hear him sound like himself again. Another, entirely different part of her tingled. She knew just the kind of *ravenous* he meant and she couldn't wait.

"Don't make me think of such things while I'm driving," she said, only half meaning it. "I might just pull over and demand you take care of that hunger now. But we're almost there and Mara said they have a big surprise for us, so we'd best keep going."

"As you wish, my lady." He sat back, her tartan eye mask still clutched tight in his hands, his white-knuckled grip letting her know how much his bravura cost him.

Kira bit her lip and drove on, pretending not to notice.

With any luck, Mara McDougall's surprise would be something special enough to take his mind off all he'd left behind. Make him less sad and help him adjust better to her world. From Mara's excitement on the telephone, she could almost believe that might just happen.

Then, about an hour and a good stretch of lonely coast road later, Ravenscraig Castle's double-turreted gatehouse finally loomed ahead and she did believe it.

A large banner stretched across the gatehouse, welcoming them with the traditional Gaelic greeting *Ceud Mile Failte!*

A Hundred Thousand Welcomes!

Aidan snorted. "The MacDougalls have grown friendlier since my day."

Kira glanced at him. "I told you—they *are* friendly. To everyone."

But the greeting made her smile. Even if she suspected that the banner remained in place all summer,
there to greet the scores of MacDougalls and others
who visited Ravenscraig from all over the world, eager
to enjoy One Cairn Village's *Brigadoon*-ish charm or
to take advantage of Mara's state-of-the-art genealogi-
cal center.

The welcome banner wasn't the surprise.

A cluster of signposts lining the drive and the overlarge placard in front of the rhododendrons flanking
the gatehouse had to be it. Bold and colorful, the signs
announced the second annual Ravenscraig Highland
Games.

Not that they wouldn't have discovered the day's
significance the instant they drove beneath the gatehouse's raised portcullis and through its dark, tun-
nellike *pend*. The castle came into view as soon as
they did, but only the tall, parapeted towers.

Everything else was blocked from view, the entire
expanse of endless, emerald green lawn crowded with
colorful tents and tartan-draped platforms. Rows of
refreshment booths and trinket stalls lined the perimeter, as did a large U-shaped area of bleachers.

Chaos reigned, with competing pipe bands standing
in tight circles everywhere, playing their hearts out,
while solo pipers stood on the scattered platforms, giving skirling accompaniment to young girls performing
the Highland fling.

On the far side of the lawn, the kilted heavies were
already in full swing, throwing hammers and weights,
and tossing the huge, telephone pole–like caber.
Closer by, more kilties engaged in a fierce tug-o'-war,

much to the delight of the female spectators. From their flushed faces and laughter, Kira suspected they were more keen on catching beneath-the-kilt flashes than watching to see which team of huffing, straining tuggers actually won.

Kira beamed as she drove past them, slowing to a snail's pace as she followed the parking instructions of a young, freckle-faced lad in a kilt. Beside her, Aidan was silent, but she caught a suspicious gleam in his eye when he clambered out of the car.

A gleam that was getting brighter by the moment. So she held her silence, not wanting to embarrass him by saying anything he'd have to comment on. Not until she was sure he'd caught himself.

Her throat was thick too.

Pipes always did that to her. She knew, too, that such games went back well over a thousand years. That medieval chieftains like Aidan used the competitions to select the clan's strongest and fastest men. Those with the most stamina and the greatest hearts. Men who became the chieftain's personal *tail*, or bodyguards. His most prized fighting men.

Trusted friends.

She shivered. The medieval games must've been full of pageantry and color. Things she was certain Aidan was remembering now. She could tell by the way his hands shook just a bit as he refastened his sword belt, then smoothed his plaid, his head held high.

Looking proud.

And so out of place against the backdrop of milling T-shirted, sneaker-footed American tourists that she could have sat down and wept.

"Aidan, my love." She reached for his hand, lacing their fingers. "We can leave now. No one yet knows we've arrived. We can go back—"

"You call me your love." He looked at her, his gaze going so deep she'd swear he'd brushed her soul. "Am I, lass? Do you love me as much as I love you?"

Kira's heart burst. He'd never yet mentioned love, but she'd guessed, hoped. "Oh, Aidan, you know I do." She slid her arms around him, squeezing tight. "I love you more than there are sands on the shore. More than all the stars in the night sky. I have always loved you. I think since that very first day."

He nodded, taking her hands and kissing both palms. "Then all is good, Kee-*rah*. We shall stay here and visit your friends. Then . . . I canna say. But we are no' going back to Wrath. No' so long as Conan Dearg breathes and a faceless enemy threatens you in my own bedchamber."

Kira looked down, nudging at a pebble on the graveled path. She'd almost hoped he'd say they *would* go back to Wrath. Her world felt funny to her, too, now.

She never would have believed it, but she was actually homesick for the fourteenth century.

"Nay, lass." He shook his head, almost as if he'd read her thoughts. "We are here now and shall make the best of it."

"And if—" She broke off, her jaw dropping.

Just ahead a small book stand claimed pride of place in the middle of the Games' row of trinket stalls. Two large flags flew above it, the red and gold Lion Rampant, so often associated with Robert the Bruce, and the blue and white Scottish Saltire. Both snapped proudly in the afternoon wind, but it was the giant

poster of RIVERS OF STONE: A HIGHLANDER'S ANCES-
TRAL JOURNEY and the many teetering stacks of the
little book that drew attention.

As did the tall, kilted Highlander preening beside
the book table, surrounded by a clutch of female Australian tourists. Loud and giggly, they wore their national flag on the backs of their sweatshirts. All except
one, a brassy-looking older woman who appeared to
be hanging on to every word the Highlander said.

In addition to the Australian flag, the back of her
sweatshirt declared that she was ELIZABETH: WORLD
CHAMPION KILT-TILTER.

Kira almost choked. "Oh-my-Gawd! It's him!" She
grabbed Aidan's arm. "Wee Hughie MacSporran."

Aidan stopped. "The scribe who claims Conan
Dearg locked me in my dungeon to starve to death?"

"The very one—I think. He's a bit heavier and has
less hair than the last time I saw him. But"—she
squinted, straining to catch a better look at him
through the clustering Aussies—"Yes, I'm sure now.
It's him."

Aidan narrowed his eyes at the man, then smiled.

His wickedest smile. "Then come." He started forward, his hand on the Invincible's hilt. "I shall give
him a history lesson."

Reaching the little book stand, he whipped out the
sword and plunged it into the earth a few inches from
Wee Hughie's feet. "Greetings, kinsman!" he boomed,
clapping the startled Highlander on the shoulder. "I'm
told you're of good Clan Donald blood?"

The Aussie women giggled.

Wee Hughie's face colored, but he nodded, his
Adam's apple bobbing. "I—"

"He's related to Robert the Bruce," the Kilt-Tilter trilled, eyeing Aidan with equal interest.

Kira frowned at her.

Aidan arched a brow. "Indeed?"

Wee Hughie stepped back a pace, brushing at his kilt. "The Bruce was my great-great-great-grandfather. Eighteen generations in a direct line."

Aidan closed the space between them. With a wink at Kira, he lowered his voice. "I canna claim eighteen generations from the man, but I have fought and wenched at his side. Welcomed him at my table and hearth."

Wee Hughie lifted his chin, clearly annoyed. "Ancestral roots should not be mocked. I can document my lineage back through two thousand years of Scottish history."

"Lad, if you do have Clan Donald blood, I *am* your history."

"Come, let's move on." Kira put a hand on his arm, not surprised when he brushed it away.

"And"—he yanked the Invincible from the ground, resheathing it without taking his gaze off the author— "I am here to tell you that your book is wrong. Aidan MacDonald of Wrath didn't die in his own dungeon. That was his cousin, Conan Dearg."

Wee Hughie puffed his chest. "You, sir, are the one who has your history skewed. I never wrote that. Conan Dearg drowned."

Aidan frowned and picked up one of the books, tucking it inside his plaid. "I shall read this and see what other errors you've made," he said, once more clapping the author on the shoulder. "If I find more, kinsman, we shall meet again."

"Spoken like a true Highlander of old."

A tall, darkly handsome man fell into step beside them the minute Aidan turned and pulled Kira away from the book stand. Dressed like a prosperous knight of old, he made them a gallant bow, clearly taking pains not to dislodge the studded medieval shield he held in front of his groin.

A beautiful Highland targe, round and covered with smooth, supple-looking leather, it was the finest example of a medieval shield Kira had ever seen outside a museum.

"You must be one of Sir Alex's reenactor friends," she said, certain of it. "I'm Kira. Of Aldan, Pennsylvania." She glanced at Aidan. "And this is Sir Aidan. The MacDonald of Wrath," she blurted, his true identity somehow spilling from her.

The dark knight's casual, easy grace could have pulled even more from her had she not been careful.

There was just something about him.

"I know who you are, Lady Kira." He smiled, his gaze passing knowingly to Aidan before returning to her. "You have been expected. Both of you. We are here to help you."

"We?" Kira blinked.

"Many of us." He gave a slight nod, his mailed shirt gleaming in the afternoon sun. "I am Sir Hardwin, onetime companion-in-arms to Alex of Ravenscraig, and late of my own fair Seagrave in the north."

Kira's brow furrowed. "Late?"

He shrugged and flashed her a dazzling smile. "So to speak, my lady."

For one crazy mad moment, she was certain she could see Wee Hughie MacSporran and his fan club of

Aussie women right through the man and his precious medieval targe.

But then a cloud passed over the sun and the illusion faded, leaving him looking as solid as everyone else.

Including the giant bearlike man with a shock of shaggy red hair and an equally wild beard who suddenly appeared at his side.

"Dinna fash yourself, Kira-lass. We are friends." The bushy-bearded newcomer slung an arm around the first man's shoulders, then winked at Aidan. "Friends of . . . old."

Kira slid a glance at Aidan, not surprised to see him eyeing the two men with skeptical, narrowed eyes.

"You have the looks of the MacNeils about you," he said, his gaze fixed on bushy-beard.

"Aye, and I suppose I do!" The man rocked back on his heels, mirth rolling off him. " 'Tis Bran of Barra I am," he added, looking quite pleased about it. "And you are a Skye MacDonald—a son of Somerled, as I live and breathe!"

And then he was gone.

As was the first man, both swallowed up by a new surge of holidaymakers pushing past them into the rows of trinket stalls and refreshment booths.

Nothing of the strange encounter remained . . . until a bright flash of glitter struck Kira's eye and she stooped, examining the grass where the two men had stood.

Two gold rings lay there, glinting in the day's fading light. Celtic rings identically patterned with slender-stemmed trumpets, birds, and delicate swirls. A man and a woman's rings, both looking suspiciously medieval.

So beautifully medieval, her heart dipped the instant her fingers closed around them.

We are here to help you. The dark knight's words came back to her and she suddenly knew.

As she should have known right away, and would have, had the day's trials not taken such a toll.

She turned to Aidan, the rings clutched tight in her hand. "They were ghosts," she said, the wonder of it sending warmth all through her.

"I know that." He snatched the rings and frowned down at them, not about to admit he'd not known indeed.

He'd been about to draw the Invincible again and challenge the cheeky bastards.

As it was, he chose to bow to the greater wisdom of his lady regarding the spirits of her time. He also didn't want to overlook the possibility that the Ancient Ones of his own time might still be looking after them.

If that were the case, the rings had a definite purpose and had best be worn.

Sure of it, he grabbed her hand and shoved the smaller-looking ring onto the fourth finger of her left hand, then worked the other onto the same finger of his own left hand.

And with no time to spare, it would seem, because no sooner were the rings in place than a wild-eyed older couple came tearing across the grass toward them, calling his lady's name.

"Kira!" A tall, slender woman threw her arms around Kira, sobbing and laughing at the same time. "Dear God, girl, *where* have you been? We've been here for weeks, searching for you!"

The balding, potbellied man puffing after her wasn't looking at Kira at all, but at him. "So you're the man who's married my little girl?" he demanded, eyeing him as if he were one of the birthing sisters' newts. "Without so much as a by-your-leave!"

Quick on his heels, a running, panting couple about Aidan's own age burst through a hedge of rhododendron, then drew to a skidding, slip-sliding halt.

Keeping a few paces behind the older couple, they winked and gesticulated, the man's magnificent Highland regalia and the woman's simple flame-haired beauty letting him know they were his hosts.

Mara McDougall of Penseal-*where'er* and her Douglas husband, Alex.

That they'd informed Kira's parents that he and Kira had married was more than obvious. Not that he cared. Far from it, the notion pleased him.

He'd meant to wed her anyway, as soon as he'd managed to settle their future.

It scarce mattered if he claimed her as his wife already.

In his heart, she'd been his since time was.

Mayhap, he sometimes believed, many lifetimes before that as well.

They fit together that beautifully.

Secure in that knowledge, he put back his shoulders and smoothed his plaid, understanding now why the Ancient Ones had sent the ring-bearing bogles.

"Well?" Kira's father glared at him, both his chins quivering. "What have you to say for yourself?"

"The only thing of import, sir." Aidan cleared his throat, regretting the temporary deception. "I am the man who loves your daughter. And, aye, I've taken her to wife."

"Taken her to wife?" The man's face reddened. "That's a queer way to put it."

"He's a reenactor, George." Kira's mother spoke up. "Don't you see his costume? He's speaking *in period*. Like the guides at Pennsbury Manor back home. Or Colonial Williamsburg."

George Bedwell glared at his wife. "I'd have him speak to me as my daughter's father, not some tourist!"

"Oh, George, calm down," the woman returned. She threw Aidan an apologetic smile. "You know how long we've waited to see Kira settled. I'll not have you scaring the boy off before the ink is dried on their marriage license."

"I hope to God he has one." George produced a small square of white linen and mopped his brow. "I'll have answers if he doesn't."

"We are properly wed." Aidan extended his hand, showing the man his ring.

George peered at it, looking only somewhat mollified.

Aidan nodded, then did his best to assume the most respectful mien he could manage.

The only consolation he was willing to give, considering his position.

"My sorrow, sir, that we were unable to inform you until now. It simply wasn't possible."

"Not possible?" George's face went red again. "In this day of high-speed Internet and e-mail? Good old-fashioned telephones?"

Aidan sighed and pulled a hand down over his face. "Where my home is, we do not have such amenities."

Kira pulled away from her mother to hasten over to him. "You don't understand, Daddy," she began, sliding an arm around Aidan. "Aidan is—"

"Aidan?" Her mother pressed a hand to her throat, her eyes rounding. "Dear God, it's him!"

"What do you mean *him?*" Her husband shot another angry look at her. "Have you met this man already? Met him, and not told me?"

Blanche Bedwell shook her head. "No. I've never met him, but I've heard of him. For years. He—"

"Years?" Kira's father's gaze flew from her mother to her and then back to her mother again. "You've known of him that long and I wasn't informed?"

His wife pursed her lips. "You weren't informed because there was nothing to say. He was a dream. An obsession of Kira's since her graduation trip to Scotland. He's a legendary historical hero who lived over seven hundred years ago."

Kira's father laughed. "Are you telling me my daughter married a ghost?"

Blanche shrugged.

Alex Douglas chose that moment to stride forward, placing a hand on both their shoulders. "Aidan of Wrath is no ghost." He spoke in a level tone. "Trust me, I can sense spirits within a hundred paces. Your new son-in-law is a good man."

He paused, his gaze dropping to the Invincible's hilt, lingering there, before he fixed Aidan with a deep, knowing stare.

"He simply hails from a distant time."

"From seven centuries ago?" George frowned at

him. "Look," he added, glancing first at Kira, then the others, "our family has had its share of oddballs. Far-seers, ghost-seers, and other assorted fruit-loops. But I've yet to hear of anyone marrying someone seven hundred years dead."

Mara McDougall Douglas coughed. Joining them, she put a hand on George Bedwell's arm. "I know it sounds impossible," she said, her voice so calm *anything* sounded possible, "but you have to remember this is Scotland. It's an ancient land, full of magic. I've had to learn that myself. Strange things can happen here that you'd never hear of elsewhere."

She exchanged a quick glance with her husband. "Strange and wonderful things."

George grunted. "I don't see anything wonderful about my daughter marrying a dead man."

"Oh, Daddy. He's not dead." Kira reached for Aidan's hand, grasping it hard. "You can't imagine what he's sacrificed for me."

"Seven-hundred-year-old men have to be dead." George insisted it, bent on being belligerent.

"Nay, that is not so. I can prove it to you . . . if you desire." Aidan spoke with his laird's voice. "But I warn you, it is not wise to tamper with such things. The consequences can be dire and wreak more harm than your simple doubts can stir in a lifetime."

"And where—*how*—do you intend to live your life-time?" Kira's father eyed them. "Even Elliot King at the Tile Bonanza wouldn't hire you on a résumé that says you're a seven-hundred-year-old legendary histor-ical hero."

Aidan swallowed, unable to answer him.

Worse, he understood the man's outrage.

Given the circumstances, he would have reacted in a similar fashion. Nay, he'd ne'er have tolerated such a discussion in the first place and would have silenced the upstart young man with a swift, swinging pass of the Invincible.

Kira, apparently, had other thoughts.

Shrugging off her backpack, she undid the zip-*her* and withdrew a bundle of rolled parchments. No longer fresh and supple as he knew they'd been at Wrath, the scrolls now appeared ancient. Thin and brittle, they crackled in her hands, the frayed red ribbon tying them looking ready to crumble to dust.

"Here." She thrust them into her father's hands. "This is a record of my time in medieval Scotland. I wrote it for Dan Hillard and would appreciate it if you'd see he gets it. He can have the paper and ink carbon-dated. That'll prove the year it was written, and you, Daddy, cannot deny that it's in my handwriting."

Her father grunted again.

Some of the angry red color left his face as he peered down at the parchments. "That still doesn't tell me where you mean to live? And how?"

Kira glanced at Aidan. "We'll stay here in Scotland," she said, knowing that would please him. Turning back to her parents, she hugged them both. "You know it's always been my dreamland. Now it is also the home of the man I love."

She kissed them each on the cheek, willing them to understand. "Someday . . . maybe . . . we'll return to Aidan's time. If such a thing is even possible. But if we did, you will now have seen us together and will know how happy we are. If it came to that, I'd try to somehow let you know we made it back. That we were okay and thriving in Aidan's world."

"Humph." Her father pressed his lips together and scowled, reminding her so much of Aidan that she would have laughed had the circumstances allowed.

"You are well and truly married?" He grabbed her hand, examining the ring Aidan had slipped onto her finger only an hour before.

"Yes," she lied, knowing in her heart that they soon would be.

"And you love my daughter?" He shot another glance at Aidan. "Have the means to keep her fed and clothed? Happy?"

Aidan smiled, sensing the man's softening. "She is my life, sir. I'd be honored to have your blessing . . . but I'm keeping her whether it pleases you or nay."

"Then take good care of her, by God." Her father marched over to him, thrusting out his hand.

"I will, sir," Aidan said, meaning it. He surprised himself by ignoring the older man's hand and, instead, grasping him by the shoulders for a quick, tight embrace. "Ne'er worry about her. I would kill the man who'd even glance sideways at her."

There are some men who deserve killing, he thought he heard Alex Douglas speak low at his shoulder. But when he released Kira's father and looked at Alex, his host stood across the little clearing again, one arm slung casually around his wife.

"We've readied the Heatherbrae for you," he said.

Looking so like the men of Aidan's own day that his heart squeezed.

"It's the same cottage Kira had before." Mara McDougall Douglas slipped away from her husband.

Coming forward, she handed Aidan a key. "I think you'll find it comfortable. It's a bit old-fashioned, but has everything you need."

Unfortunately, when he took himself there a short while later, hoping to give Kira some time alone with her family, he found himself unable to enjoy the luxuriously appointed cottage's amenities.

The *lights*, as a cheery young man named Malcolm had called the bright-glaring contraptions, hurt his eyes. And the chattering little moving people in the so-called *telly* unsettled him so much he was sure his head would soon burst just trying to comprehend the thing.

Almost as bad, when he'd tried to use the *shower* he'd scalded his back. Then, a short while later, he'd raised a blister on his finger when he'd touched one of the *lights*, trying to see how the fool thing worked.

But none of those horrors came anywhere near to the nightmare spread across the bed in the Heatherbrae's tidy bedchamber.

Going there now, he stared down at the books he'd examined earlier. Wee Hughie's *Rivers of Stone: A Highlander's Ancestral Journey*. Kira's other little volume, *The Hebridean Clans*, and several others.

Eight altogether. Kira's two, plus six he'd plucked from a shelf on the wall.

Each one said the same thing.

Conan Dearg drowned.

Not that he'd really care—were it not for the rest.

Sinking onto the edge of the bed, he picked up his kinsman's little tome, once more opening it to the damning passage. Tracing the words with a blister-tipped finger, he swallowed against the thickness in his throat and wondered how the fates could be so cruel as to let him save Kira only to cause Tavish's death.

Aidan closed his eyes and groaned. Never had he felt more helpless and miserable. Until Alex Douglas's cryptic words came back to him.

There are some men who deserve killing.

His eyes snapped open. When the first thing that leapt into view was the Invincible, its bloodred pommel jewel glittering like a dragon's eye, he knew what he had to do.

Leaping to his feet, he grabbed the sword, feeling better, *stronger*, the instant his fingers clenched around the leather-wrapped hilt.

Power—and rage—swept him, heating his blood until it was all he could do not to throw back his head and shout his clan's battle cry.

Instead, the words he'd said to Tavish the morning of the feast echoed in his ears: *Chances are we'll be rejoining you in the hall—back before the sweet courses are served.*

He closed his eyes again, his heart thundering. If they could manage that, all might not be lost.

It was a risk he had to take.

Chapter 15

"You want to go back?"

Kira slowly closed the door of the Heatherbrae behind her, then set down the glossy monthly, *Scotland Today*, that she'd brought back from the Ravenscraig library. She stared at Aidan, her initial euphoria on hearing him declare he wanted to return to his time giving way to queasiness and dry mouth now that she looked at him more closely.

He no longer looked like Aidan-out-of-water, but rather the fierce laird of Wrath she knew so well from his own time.

His jaw was set in a formidable line and his eyes blazed. Most telling of all, he'd strapped on the Invincible.

Crossing the cottage's little sitting area, she slid her arms around him. "What's wrong? What's happened?" She looked up at him, not surprised when he disentangled himself and started pacing. "Why do you want to go back now? I know things aren't ideal, but we just got here."

"It's no' that I want to go back, though the saints know I do." He whirled to face her, his expression giving her chills. "We *must.* According to your history books, our leaving caused Tavish's death."

Kira's eyes widened. "What? How can that be?"

He disappeared into the bedroom, returning a moment later with an armful of books. Dumping them onto a tartan-upholstered armchair, he snatched up one and began flipping through its pages.

"Here! The lines in the middle of the page." He thrust the book at her, pointing to a brief paragraph on page 57. "Read it and you'll understand."

Kira looked down at the clear black print, her stomach dropping as she read the words. "Oh, God." She tossed down the book and pressed a hand to her chest. "Conan Dearg slew Tavish while escaping Wrath's dungeon? Then drowned? With that MacLeod woman?"

"So the books say." Aidan folded his arms. "All of them. Even that fool, Wee Hughie's. Some just say Conan Dearg killed *the laird of Wrath*, but the result is the same. After we left, Tavish took my place. Had we remained, he would still be alive."

"And you'd be dead." She didn't like that possibility either.

Aidan snorted. "Nay. Conan Dearg would be dead, and by my sword. No' from drowning."

Kira dropped onto a chair. "I don't get the drowning part. Or the connection with that awful woman."

"That's because you don't know my cousin. Or Fenella MacLeod." He gave her an alpha-male look, all medieval chieftain again. "I wouldn't be one of the most respected warrior lairds in the Highlands if the answer weren't clear to me."

Kira looked at him. It wasn't clear to her at all.

" 'Tis simple, lass." He picked up Mara McDougall Douglas's welcome decanter of single malt and poured himself a hefty dram. Tossing it down in one quick swig, he wiped his mouth with the back of his hand. "Lady Fenella devours men faster than I just swallowed that whisky. Conan Dearg will have attracted her like a lodestone. Especially since she was grieved with me."

"She didn't like you?" Kira lifted a brow.

"She liked me too much. Some while before you came to Wrath, she visited, offering her men and her fleet of longships to help me to search for Conan Dearg." He paused to toss back his hair, a look of distaste passing over his face. "Not surprisingly, she offered other services as well. When I declined, she left in a fury."

"And you think she then hooked up with your cousin? To get back at you?"

He nodded. "I'd bet my sword that was the way of it. I should have thought of it before, but I was . . . distracted."

Kira swallowed. She knew he meant her. "I still don't understand the drowning part. Especially if the MacLeod woman is supposed to have drowned with him."

"I can only guess, but I'd vow Lady Fenella helped him escape at some point during the feast and they tried to leave Wrath Bay in her galley." Coming over to her, he placed his hands on her shoulders. "Tavish and I suspected her of damaging her own craft as a ploy to pull up on my landing beach. If her flight with Conan Dearg caused as much confusion as I suspect it might have, and my men pursued them, in the rush to get away she may have set sail in her own galley rather than taking one of mine as I imagine she'd planned to do."

"You think her boat sank?" Kira blinked up at him. "As they tried to sail away?"

"I was told when she arrived that there was quite a hole gouged in her galley's hull. They wouldn't have made it past Wrath Isle if they sought to flee in such a vessel."

Kira shuddered. "If this is true, I'll bet she was behind my poisoning."

"I thought the same," he agreed, shoving a hand through his hair. "Though if she'd been slipping into Wrath to visit Conan Dearg, or harm you, someone there must've been helping her."

"That has to be how your cousin got up onto the arch that night." Kira bit her lip, a hundred thoughts churning in her head. "I suspected he'd somehow learned about me. How I got there. Someone must've helped him sneak out of the dungeon so he could examine the top of the arch."

"Indeed. You're a wise lassie." A touch of admiration lit his eyes. "Poor Kendrew must've startled him—and suffered the consequences."

"But who would've helped your cousin?" Kira couldn't wrap her mind around it. "Your men can't stand him. And the women, those laundresses—" She broke off, suspicion making her breath catch. "Do you think one of them did it?"

He frowned. "Help my cousin?" He started pacing again, rubbing the back of his neck as he walked.

"Could be. I've told you, Conan Dearg exerts a weird influence on women. But I can't see any of the laundresses doing Lady Fenella any favors."

Stopping by the table, he helped himself to another dram of whisky. "It doesn't matter, Kee-*rah*." Confidence rolled off him. If she hadn't known better, she'd have sworn he'd grown several inches. That his powerful shoulders had gone even wider. "Now that I know what to be wary of, I'll get to the bottom of the matter when we go back. Hopefully we can get there the same night we left. If so, I'm sure I can save Tavish."

Kira's heart sank. "Oh, dear," she said, half certain the shadows in the room had just deepened, turning as dark as the blackness she felt bearing down on them. Her gaze slid to the little pine table by the door. The slick and colorful issue of *Scotland Today* lying on the tabletop. "I don't think we can get back."

She hadn't wanted to say so yet, but now, watching and listening to him talk about saving his friend, she couldn't keep quiet any longer. "The gatehouse arch—"

"Worked once and will serve us again." He set down the little crystal dram glass. "You just need to *left drive* us back to Wrath. We'll leave in the morning, as soon as you've said your farewells to your family and friends."

"You don't understand." Kira pressed her fingers to her temples. "It won't matter if we go back to Skye. Even if we did, we wouldn't be able to get to the arch top. Not even the outermost ruins of your castle."

He looked at her, uncomprehending.

"The site's under construction," she tried to explain, pushing to her feet. Going to the little table near the door, she grabbed the *Scotland Today* and waved it at him. "It's all in here. You can even see pictures. In the months I've been away, Wrath has gone to the National Trust for Scotland. That's a historical preservation society and they're currently developing the ruins into a tourist exhibition. They—"

"A what?" He stared at her, the blood draining from his face. "You mean a place overrun with Ameri-*cains* and tour buses?"

Kira nodded, hating that she had to tell him. "Mother said they tried to go there weeks ago when they first arrived, but it's all roped off and guarded. Even at night. No one can set foot on the property."

"I see." He looked at her, all the flash and gleam in his eyes, vanished. "Put that thing away, Kee-*rah*," he said, glancing at the magazine in her hands. "I dinna want to see the images. No' now."

Turning away from her, he went to the cottage's front window. The one with the view of Mara McDougall Douglas's One Cairn Village memorial cairn. Its stones and great Celtic cross shimmered silvery blue in the pale luminosity of the late-summer night, the beauty of it twisting Kira's heart.

Aidan seemed to be staring at it, too, his shoulders sagging more the longer he stood there, stiff and silent, his hands clenched tightly at his sides.

Kira moved to join him, but stopped halfway there, her stare shooting past him to the big memorial cairn, a smile splitting her soul the instant she made the connection.

"Oh, God!" she cried, starting to tremble. "I know what we can do!"

Aidan whipped around, the hope on his face making

her heart soar. "You know of another *time portal*, Kee-*rah*? Another way we can return?"

"I might." She couldn't lie to him. "Let's say there's a chance. If"—she snatched Wee Hughie's book off the chair and thumbed through its pages until she found what she needed—"we go here! The Na Tri Shean."

His brows shot upward. "That accursed place?"

Kira nodded. "My boss, Dan Hillard, had reason to believe the cairns there aren't just fairy mounds, but a portal to the Other World and all places beyond and between. A *time portal*." She shoved the book beneath his nose, forcing him to look at the black-and-white photograph of the three piles of stone on their hill. "If we go there, maybe, just maybe, we can get back to Wrath."

"Cnoc Freiceadain—the Na Tri Shean—is far from here, Kee-*rah*." He rubbed his forehead. "Getting there would mean crossing almost the whole of Scotland."

"Does it matter?" She tossed aside the book and wrapped her arms around him, squeezing tight. "It's our only chance."

He drew a deep breath, then hugged her back. "Then we shall seize it. I owe Tavish no less."

Kira grinned. "I can't wait to see the look on his face when he sees you."

That he might not was something she wouldn't consider.

After all, as Mara McDougall Douglas had said, Scotland was a place of miracles.

It was past nightfall the next day by the time they

passed through the tiny hamlet of Shebster in Scotland's far north and finally reached the great grass-grown hill that held the three long-chambered cairns known as the Na Tri Shean. A stout, rib-sticking full Scottish breakfast, a swift but emotional farewell from George and Blanche Bedwell and their hosts at Ravenscraig, along with hope, sheer will, and a seemingly endless ribbon of narrow, winding Highland roads had brought them here. And now, turning off the ignition at last, Kira had to struggle to hide her disappointment.

Dan's supposed time portal par excellence proved nondescript.

Little more than a huge, treeless hill stood before them, outlined against the eerily light late-summer night sky. The hill's summit showed the telltale fairy mounds, said to date back to the third millennium BC, but rather than the massive, well-defined cairns she'd expected, only a scattered jumble of boulders and stones showed that anything really significant had once stood there.

Getting out of the car, she pushed back her shoulders and glanced at Aidan. "Not very impressive, hmmm? I'm sorry. I thought—"

"You are thinking like a woman who no longer believes in magic, Kee-*rah*." Tossing back his plaid, he whipped out the Invincible and held its blade to the soft, silver-glowing sky. At once, the combined light of the bright crescent moon and the pale northern sun caught the sword's edge, making its cold, hard steel shine and glow like a living thing. "The power of a place like this remains through time and eternity. It matters little that the man-made cairns are tumbled.

Besides"—he reached for her hand, then started forward, up the hill—"the stones only marked what was
beneath. It is there, deep under the earth, that we
must go."

"Under the earth?" Kira stopped, digging in her
heels. Suddenly the great grassy hill no longer looked
so harmless. "What are you saying?"

He looked at her, his dark eyes glittering in the
strange silvery-blue light. "I thought you knew what
long-chambered cairns are."

Kira swallowed, not wanting to admit she hadn't
really given it that much thought. At least not as far
as *entering* the cairns and going down into the cold,
dark earth.

"I will be with you, Kee-*rah*. You needn't fear." He
traced his knuckles down the curve of her cheek.
"Now, come. Get out your flashlight, or whate'er you
call it, and help me look for an entrance. There should
be three. They'll be low in the ground, and perhaps
hidden by rocks or underbrush. I doubt it matters
which cairn we enter. The magic will be powerful in
each."

Hoping that he was right, Kira fished the flashlight
out of her backpack and let him pull her higher up
the grassy slope. They found an entrance quickly, with
surprising ease. The dark, low-linteled opening seemed
to stare right at them, an impenetrable-looking black
hole in the hillside, its contours softened by thick-
growing underbrush.

It also looked painfully small.

A rabbit hole she doubted either one of them could
squeeze into.

Her stomach tightening, she flicked on the flashlight

and aimed it into the darkness. A few moss-covered stone steps gleamed weakly in the narrow band of light. Nothing else was discernible except the narrowness of the dank, low-ceilinged entry.

"I don't think anyone above four feet can get down those steps." She turned to Aidan, sure he'd agree. "Especially not you."

To her surprise, he simply shoved the Invincible back into its scabbard and stretched his arms, flexing his fingers. "Once we've mastered the steps and crept through the long passage, we'll come to the inner chamber, Kee-*rah*. We'll be able to stand upright then. You'll see. It willna be so bad."

He pulled her close, tightening his arms around her before he released her and grabbed the flashlight. "Come now," he said, ducking low and stepping into the darkness. "Follow close behind me and keep your head down. Dinna straighten until I tell you."

And then he was gone, the blackness swallowing him as he descended deeper into the cairn.

"Oh, God." Kira threw one last glance at the parked rental car, then dipped her head to hurry after him.

Cold, damp, and silence slammed into her, the smell of earth and old stone.

Grabbing the back of Aidan's plaid, she prayed her feet wouldn't slip on the mossy steps. Then, before she knew it, they'd reached the bottom and were crouching along a tight, cobbled passage, its walls seeming to grow more constricting the farther they went.

"We're almost there, Kee-*rah*." Aidan's voice echoed in the darkness. "Dinna be afraid."

Then he was straightening, pulling her up with him and wrapping a strong arm around her waist, holding her close. They were in a small, oval-shaped chamber with high, stone-slabbed walls and a corbeled ceiling. Kira thought she saw a few tipped-over urns and the remains of an ancient-looking fire, but before she could be certain, Aidan clicked off the flashlight.

"I dinna think it's wise to use your light now, sweetness." He took her hand, easing her down onto the cold stone floor beside him. He gathered her against him, keeping their fingers tightly laced. "We'll just sit here and think of Wrath and hope the magic works."

In the silence, she heard the soft *hiss* of the Invincible leaving its sheath, then the rustle of his plaid as he settled the great sword across his knees. Its pommel stone glowed a faint red in the darkness, but all else was black. A deep, cloying blackness that suddenly zoomed in on them, then snapped back, exploding into a wild, spinning vortex of bright, eye-piercing color.

Icy wind rushed past them and the ground shook, tilting crazily as the tornado-like wind swirled faster. Kira's skirts flew up into her face, covering her head until she yanked them down.

"Aidan—my clothes!" She grabbed his arm, digging her fingers into him. "My medieval clothes are back!" She twisted around, straining to see him, but where he should have been, was only a flash of black and wild glen, the kind that could have been inhabited by witches and demons. Lightning crackled and *zished* across the chamber's ceiling, booming thunder splitting her ears.

"Wha—" she cried out, but the image vanished instantly, replaced by a young girl in peasant's clothing, a willow-wand basket clutched to her hip.

The girl disappeared, too, swept away before Kira even really saw her. More images followed, each one whizzing past at light speed, whirling and whirling, the colors and roar of the wind making her dizzy.

"Kee-*rah*! Hold on, lass!" Aidan's voice rose above the chaos.

Kira felt his arm tighten around her, almost squeezing the breath from her as a yelling, helmeted Viking war band sped past them, followed immediately by a quick glimpse into the splendor of a Victorian great hall, complete with dark-paneled walls hung with stag heads, weaponry, and gilt-framed portraits. A swirl of cloud and mist came next, then a broad, open stretch of empty moorland, thick with heather and broom.

A field of daffodils, giving way to the sudden skirl of bagpipes as an army of Highlanders crested a hill, their swords glinting in brilliant sunshine, their banners streaming in the wind.

Then the cloud and mist returned, the loud wail of the pipes melting into the darkness, leaving only cold and silence, the soft red glow of the Invincible's pommel stone, and the distant howls of a dog.

"By the Rood! That's Ferlie." Aidan shot to his feet, pulling her up beside him. "Kee-*rah*, sweet, it's over. We've made it. We're on the arch."

Kira kept her death grip on his arm, her heart pounding. "Thank God!" She glanced at him. "But do you think it's real? Not like all those images that just whirled past?"

"Och, 'tis Wrath, aye." Aidan laughed. "Sure as I'm

standing here. I can even see my men patrolling the far side of the parapet walk. And the ladder—it's still here, propped against the gatehouse, just as we left it."

Kira swallowed. Joy swept her when she saw the top of the ladder peeping up over the edge of the arch, the two burly guards on the opposite wall-walk. Ross and Geordie, if she wasn't mistaken. The Invincible rested on the smooth stone of the arch top, the red gleam of its pommel now matched by the flickering orange-red glow of the smokehouse fires down on the landing strand.

They were home.

"Come, lass, I've a score to settle." Aidan snatched up his sword, sheathing it, before he turned toward the ladder. "Let's hope we're no' too late."

Scrambling down, he held up his arms for her, helping her descend. He threw a quick glance through the swirling mist toward his keep, relieved to see torchlight glimmering at the window slits. With luck, the feasting would still be in full swing, his cousin yet locked in his dungeon cell.

They pounded across the cobbles and burst into the hall. Aidan skidded to a halt, disbelief stopping his heart. Instead of being full of stir and turmoil, shouts and laughter, the hall was empty. No one sat at the rows of long tables. On the dais, his overturned laird's chair and a toppled bench indicated a hasty departure. As did the many filled trenchers and ale cups, the still-burning candles in the silver candelabrums.

Aidan's blood ran cold.

Now he knew why the hall door had stood wide and poor Ferlie howled somewhere, deep in the bowels of the castle.

The other castle dogs were gone, though by straining his ears, he could hear them now. Barking in the distance, along with the muffled cries of men. A woman's sudden piercing wail, the sound making his gut clench.

"Guidsakes! It's happening!" He grabbed Kira's hand, pulling her with him from the hall, racing to the low arched door that led to the dungeon. "Tavish!" he roared, shouting as they ran. "Hold, man! We're coming!"

But when they rushed down the dark, narrow stair and reached Conan Dearg's cell, the heavy iron-bound door stood cracked, a fresh-looking pool of blood near the threshold leaving no doubt as to what had transpired.

"Dear God!" Beside him, Kira clapped a hand to her throat, her face paling as she stared at the blood. "We're too late."

"Nay! Dinna say it." Aidan whipped around, pressing his hand against her lips. "It could be my cousin's blood. It *must* be—I'll no' allow otherwise!"

Kira looked at him, her stomach clenching. "Then they'll be down at the boat strand—the drowning part."

"That'll be the way of it," he agreed, already sprinting down the fetid passage. "Pray God we get there in time."

Streaking after him, Kira kept a hand pressed to her ribs, half afraid her heart would jump right through them if she didn't. Aidan almost scared her. Never had she seen him look so fierce.

So deadly.

He shot up the stairs and through the hall with ex-

plosive speed, gripping his sword hilt as he ran, not
breaking stride until they'd crossed the bailey and
neared the small postern door in the curtain walling.
As at Conan Dearg's cell, they found the door ajar.
Ferlie paced to and fro in front of the opening, howling and fretting, his lame back legs keeping him from
bounding down the cliff steps to the landing strand
below.

"He's no' dead, Ferlie," Aidan tossed at him, pausing just long enough at the top of the steps to reach
again for Kira's hand. "I can see him! Tavish. And
my cousin." He glanced at her, his eyes wild, blazing.
"They're at the water's edge, fighting."

And they were. Kira saw them now as well. Aidan's
men and a pack of crazed, barking dogs crowded the
little strand, Tavish and Conan Dearg going at each
other in the middle of a small cleared circle. She saw,
too, that the reddish-orange glow she'd noticed from
the arch wasn't caused by the strand's smokehouses,
but came from the torches that many of Aidan's men
held above their heads. The flames gave the scene a
hellish taint, the men's shouts and the clashing shriek
of steel meeting steel filling her with terror.

In Wrath Bay, a lone galley sped seaward, its
hoisted sail declaring the MacLeod colors, the widow's
face as she stood clutching the rail bathed as red as
the torch flames. Her raven hair streamed in the night
wind and her galley was already beginning to founder,
lurching heavily to one side as it raced toward the
rocks of Wrath Isle.

"Oh, God," Kira cried as they flew down the steep
cliff-side steps. "It's just like you said it would be!

That boat's going to hit those rocks any minute, and Tavish—"

"—is holding his own," Aidan panted as they tore down the last few steps and leapt onto the pebbly strand, "and I'm about to relieve him!"

Aidan wrenched the Invincible from its scabbard. Men leapt back, freeing a path as he ran across the beach, sword raised, fury in his eye. Ahead, Tavish and Conan Dearg circled each other, blades feinting and slashing, both men bloodstained and sweating.

His own sword already lashing, Aidan hurled himself at his cousin, sweeping the Invincible in a great, eye-blinding figure-eight motion. "Conan Dearg!" he roared, " 'tis time for a reckoning!"

"A mercy!" Tavish spun around, his eyes flying wide. "Aidan!" he cried, his relief evident. "A God's name! I dinna believe it!"

The distraction cost him. Quick as lightning, Conan Dearg dove, swinging his blade in an wide arc that would've lopped off Tavish's head if Aidan hadn't whirled round, kicking Tavish so hard he flew back against the wall of gathered men.

From the corner of his eye, he saw Mundy catch him, seizing Tavish's sword and tossing it aside as he snaked a quick arm around Tavish's waist, holding him so he couldn't rush back into the circle.

"So it comes down to the two of us!" Conan Dearg taunted, Tavish forgotten. "I've waited long for the day!"

" 'Tis the day you die, Cousin." Aidan lunged, taking a first cut on Conan Dearg's arm. "Breathe your last while you can."

Conan Dearg laughed and came at him, his sword glinting red in the torchlight as it crashed against Aidan's with a loud, arm-jarring *clank*. With a ferocious burst of strength, Aidan knocked him back, grunting with satisfaction when Conan Dearg lost his footing on the slick shingle, his blade nearly flying from his hand.

Aidan smiled, advancing before Conan Dearg could right himself. "You're tired . . . clumsy. Come, let me help you find rest!"

"A pox on you!" Conan Dearg yelled, swaying on his feet. "You will rue . . ."

"That I didn't do this years ago!" Aidan finished, ramming the Invincible deep into his cousin's chest. Hoisting him in the air, he spat on him. "May you find the devil good company."

Conan Dearg stared at him, his eyes bulging, a trickle of blood bubbling from his lips. Glaring at him, Aidan withdrew his blade and resheathed it, grabbing his cousin before he could topple to the ground.

With a great heave, he pushed him into the surf, dusting his hands as Conan Dearg landed with a splash, a flicker of life still gleaming in his eyes as he stared up at Aidan.

"So you die by drowning," Aidan informed him, stepping closer to the water's edge. "As the history books decried."

"The *history books*?" Tavish spoke at his shoulder, looking on as Conan Dearg went limp, his eyes glazing as the tide claimed him.

Aidan drew a deep breath, then slung an arm around his friend, pulling him close. "I'll explain later," he panted, releasing Tavish to drag his sleeve over his forehead. "After I've seen to whoe'er poisoned Kee-*rah*." He glanced round at his men, raising his voice when they pressed closer, their cheers and shouts loud in his ears. "Or do you think it was Conan Dearg? Fenella?"

"It doesn't matter." Kira finally managed to push through the circle of men. She ran forward, flinging herself into Aidan's arms. "All that counts is that we're back here and Tavish is safe."

Tavish looked at her and laughed. "Safe? Me?" Grinning, he jammed his hands on his hips. "I could say the same to the two of you! Saints, but I've worried about you."

"We were fine." Aidan put back his shoulders. "A mere day's . . . journeying. Naught more."

Tavish snorted and thwacked him on the back. "I'd hear all about it, regardless."

But Aidan didn't answer him, his gaze sliding away to probe the crowd, searching faces and finding two missing. Nils, whose fierce Viking looks and great height should have had him standing head and shoulders over the fray. And Maili. She was notably absent from where the other two laundresses stood with a small group of kitchen laddies.

A dark suspicion made his jaw clench. "Love-of-God." He looked over Kira's head to Tavish. "Dinna tell me Nils or Maili had aught to do with all this?"

"Not Nils," Tavish said, no longer smiling. "It was Maili. She helped them, though you should know she's the one who warned me of their escape when Fenella disappeared from the hall not long after you left. Maili followed her and—"

"*Maili?*" Aidan's jaw dropped. "But she helped us get away when she dumped the oysters and herring into Fenella's lap." Glancing to sea, he shuddered. The MacLeod galley was almost gone, its wreckage gleaming dully on the choppy waves. "I canna believe Maili would—"

"She did it for love of a man." Tavish looked uncomfortable. "Apparently, she'd set her sights on one of Fenella's men and the widow promised she'd arrange a marriage between them—in exchange for Maili's help in slipping in and out of Wrath. And, aye, serving Kira poisoned wine."

Aidan shook his head. "But she helped you," he repeated, puzzled.

"To be sure," Tavish agreed. "She also confronted the widow a few days before the feast, demanding to know about the supposed marriage pact. Fenella laughed at her, claiming no MacLeod would lower himself by wedding a laundress."

"I see." Aidan nodded. "And where is she now?"

"In your solar . . . with Nils. He's looking after her." Tavish shoved a hand through his hair, let out a breath. "Maili followed Fenella into the dungeon and they argued. Fenella dirked her in the ribs in front of Conan Dearg's cell. It was Maili's cry that alerted us to their escape. She then told us everything, before she lost consciousness."

"Will she live?"

Tavish shrugged. "Nils says there is a chance. But she'll need care. You may not want—"

"Give her the best care possible." Kira pulled out of Aidan's arms, speaking up at last. "Nothing happened to me and she *did* help us get away."

Aidan looked at her. "You dinna mind, Kee-*rah*? The monkshood could have killed you."

Kira shook her head. "But it didn't." She smiled and blinked at him, her eyes starting to mist and her throat closing. "I doubt she'll do anything like that again. And, besides, I can understand a woman's desperation to win the man she loves." Swiping a hand across her cheek, she lifted her chin. "I might have done the same. If I thought it was the only way to your heart."

"Och, lass." Aidan reached for her, wrapping his arms tight around her. "I lost my heart to you that day I saw you standing at the top of my stair tower. As I have told you!"

"A-hem." Tavish tapped his arm, interrupting just as Aidan was about to kiss her. "There's one more thing."

Aidan glared at him. "By all the living saints! Some things ne'er change. What is it?"

"This." His smile returning, Tavish reached beneath his plaid and withdrew a small black object. Two cylinderlike rolls, topped with two rounds of bright, clear-shining glass. "I found this buried in the floor rushes in Conan Dearg's cell. "I dinna know what it is, but—"

"My dad's field glasses!" Kira grabbed them, her heart pounding. "Oh, Aidan! Conan Dearg must've found them on the arch. That night Kendrew saw him crawling around up there. They must be—"

"The *strange object* he used to hit Kendrew on the head with." Aidan took them from her, peering at them curiously. Lifting them, he looked into the glass part, dropping them at once. "By the Rood!" he cried, bending to pick them up again. He peered into them once more, this time smiling.

"Another mystery solved." He handed them to Tavish. "Now we know what Conan Dearg meant when he said he'd 'see his foes coming before any battle could begin.' "

Tavish nodded, looking equally pleased. "I thought the same when I found them." He clapped Aidan on the back again. "Now *we* shall enjoy that advantage. Woe be to our enemies!"

"And woe be to my men if they don't soon clear the strand and return to the feast," Aidan returned. "I'd have a few quiet moments with my lady before we rejoin you."

"As you wish." Tavish nodded, his smile broadening to a grin when his gaze dipped to the gold rings on their fingers. "Dare I hope the remainder of the feast might be spent celebrating something other than Conan Dearg's demise?"

"You might." Aidan's voice was gruff, husky and thick. "Now get them all back up to the keep before I lose patience."

Tavish laughed, but did as he was bid.

Alone at last with Kira, Aidan took a deep breath. "So, lass," he began, putting his hands on her shoulders. "Shall we give my brave men something to celebrate?"

She blinked, her throat too thick for words.

"Well?" He looked at her. "Dinna tell you're wishing a longer wooing period? No' now, after all we've been through together?"

She swallowed. "Aidan MacDonald, if you're asking me to marry you, you know I'd love nothing more, but—"

"But?" He frowned. "That's another thing you should know by now. I dinna care for *buts*. Though"—he folded his arms, looking quite the fearsome laird again—"something tells me I ought to hear this one."

Kira looked down, nudging her toe into the pebbles. "It's just that . . . well, you know I've always felt that I was sent back in time to save you?"

He nodded.

"Now that I have . . . I mean, now that everything's been resolved, I'm wondering if I won't soon be zapped back to my own time."

His frown deepening, he lifted her chin. "That willna happen, Kee-*rah*. Your place is here with me. I know it."

"How can you?"

He smiled. "Because you are my *tamhasg*, that's why."

Kira's brows lifted. "Your *what*?"

"Och, Kira." He drew her into his arms, kissing her. "I ne'er believed you were sent here to save me. That, too, I've told you. We're together because we were meant to be. That's what a *tamhasg* is."

This time Kira frowned. "I don't understand."

He laughed and kissed her again. "Then I'll speak plainly. A *tamhasg* is the sighting of a future bride or groom. I knew you were mine not long after seeing you that first time. I've always known it and it's why I know *time* isn't going to whisk you away from me."

"Oh, Aidan." She blinked, unable to say more.

Not that it mattered.

She could see in his eyes that he knew how happy he'd just made her.

Proving it, he grinned and offered her his arm. "Come, sweetness, shall we go share our good news with my men?"

Kira nodded, not about to say no.

Epilogue

Castle Wrath
Highland Scotland, Five Modern-Day Years Later

"I knew it was a waste of money to come here." George Bedwell stood in the middle of the National Trust for Scotland's Castle Wrath car park, his resentful stare fixed on the closed Visitor Centre. "We've spent half our vacation time bugging those people, and no one has offered a clue as to what happened to Kira or that man of hers. If he even *was* 'Aidan of Wrath.'"

"You know he was." Blanche Bedwell looked on as the last coach tour bus of the day belched a plume of exhaust fumes before rumbling out of the fast-emptying parking lot. "Just because we haven't found out anything doesn't mean fate wasn't good to them."

Her husband snorted and hitched up his belt. "She promised she'd try and leave some kind of sign for us. With all the nutty far-seeing and time travel she was capable of, you'd think she'd have been able to manage something as simple as leaving us a clue."

"Now, George—"

"Och! A thousand pardons." A tall, dark-haired man bowed courteously. "I didn't mean to run into you," he said, clutching a deep blue National Trust for Scotland gift bag in front of his groin.

Flashing a smile, he straightened, holding the shop bag carefully in place. "I trust this lass can help you. She has the answers you seek."

"What?" George Bedwell put back his shoulders and huffed. But when he adjusted his camera strap, ready to scald the nosy bugger with an angry, all-American stare, he could only splutter and gape.

The man was gone.

In his place, a young girl stared at them, her eyes wide. A badge declared her to be an employee of the National Trust and she held a clutch of business folders pressed to her breast.

"Oh! I'm sorry. I was daydreaming and didn't see you." She smoothed a hand through hair so like Kira's that George Bedwell's jaw dropped.

"It's all right, dear." Blanche touched her arm. "We were distracted, too. That man—"

George stomped on her toe.

The girl smiled, looking more like Kira by the moment. "I don't know who you mean, but maybe I can be of service? It's after hours, but if you have any questions about the site, just ask."

"Ahhh, errrr . . ." George hesitated, the back of his neck flaming.

He'd definitely ingested too much haggis at the hotel ceilidh the night before.

"Your ring." His wife peered at the girl's hand. "I've seen that design before."

George shot her a glare. "Pay her no heed," he said to the girl. Ignoring his wife, he brushed at his jacket, trying to look distinguished.

With luck, Blanche would follow his lead and not say something that would embarrass them.

"Our daughter once had a ring like that," she said anyway. "She—"

"Oh? That's amazing. I wouldn't have thought that possible." She glanced down at the heavy gold ring.

A Celtic-looking ring, engraved with slender-stemmed trumpets, birds, and delicate swirls.

"You see, it's an old family design," she explained. "It's been passed down through the centuries." She cast a glance at the closed Visitor Centre. "An uncle of mine believes it goes back to Aidan of Wrath and his wife, Katherine."

Blanche coughed.

George frowned. "Katherine?"

The name was the reason for his foul humor.

They'd been so close, everything falling into place until they'd stumbled across the archives claiming Aidan of Wrath had wed and lived his long life with a woman called Katherine, not Kira.

The girl nodded, once more looking so much like Kira that their hearts stopped.

"Ach," she cooed, her soft Highland voice drawing them in, letting them *believe*. "Katherine is only the name in the annals." Lifting her hand, she touched the gold ring, her smile going wistful. "There are actually two rings. A man's and a woman's, both with a simple 'A' and 'K' engraved on the inside. No one knows what Aidan of Wrath's wife's name really was.

Unfortunately, history has lost her real name. Scholars replaced it with Katherine because of the K."

"We see." Blanche slid a glance at her husband.

He was frowning again, his gaze on the perimeter wall of the Castle Wrath grounds. "Did this *Katherine* have any children?" he asked, clasping his hands behind his back as he stared down at Wrath Bay.

"Oh, there were many." The girl beamed at him even if he wasn't looking. "Her firstborn was named George."

"Indeed?" George nodded, ready to believe at last.

And when they drove away a short while later, their eyes damp and their hearts content, a shadow materialized in the middle of the car park. A shimmering, crackling *cloud* that took on more density the closer it drifted to the low stone wall at the edge of the castle grounds.

Then, just when it appeared as if all Ameri-*cains* and tour buses were finally gone, a tall, dark-haired man stepped out of the mist and dusted his hands. Then he winked at the burly, bushy-bearded man sitting on the wall.

"That was well done." Bushy-beard slapped his thigh, then stood. "Great fun to watch."

"It was the least I could do." The dark-haired man adjusted the shop bag at his groin. "Though next time, I think *you* should do the honors."

"What?" Bushy-beard wriggled his eyebrows. "And spoil your fun?"

The dark-haired man looked past him to Wrath Isle, his lips curving in a slow smile. "My fun is about to begin."

Bushy-beard looked skeptical. "Down on that accursed isle?"

"Nay, you loon. I feel a need to go have a closer look at our ring."

His friend lifted a brow. "The ring or the girl wearing it?"

The dark-haired man laughed. "If you have to ask, you don't know me as well as you should."

And with that, he clapped Bushy-beard on the arm, then turned and set off across the car park toward the Visitor Centre, his grin broadening with each step he took.

It was good to be *alive*.

Time, space, and even an ancient curse
can't keep this medieval Highlander away
from his modern American beauty.
Turn the page for a sneak peek of
Allie Mackay's next paranormal romance,
on sale November 2008.

Dunroamin Castle
A Registered Residential Care Home
Scotland's Far North
The Present

Someone was watching her.

Cilla Swanner dropped the pullover she'd been about to lift out of her suitcase and stood very still. Something had set the fine hairs on the back of her neck to standing and it wasn't the overall gloom seeming to fill the shadowy, dark-paneled bedchamber. Nor was it the deep midnight silence pressing in on her from all sides, even though it wasn't much later than three in the afternoon. And, considering herself a modern, unflappable woman, she wasn't impressionable enough to be influenced by how much the lavishly furnished, gothic-styled room reminded her of every Dracula movie she'd ever seen.

At least she hoped not.

Especially since the room would be hers for the summer.

She frowned and puffed her bangs off her forehead.

Unfortunately, the way her palms were damping and her heart was knocking, she just might be more suggestible than she would have thought.

Even so, she allowed herself a quick glance over her shoulder, half expecting the latched window shutters to slowly swing open, giving her a glimpse of the thick fog currently rolling across Dunroamin's lonely shore. Pea soup, she'd call such roiling, impenetrable fog, though the local term was *sea haar*. Either way, she just knew that if she did dare to open the shutters, she'd see more than swirling gray mist.

In her present jet-lagged state of mind, she'd likely see a seagull glide past and mistake it for a bat.

Pushing the notion from her mind, she reached again for her pullover, then thought better of it and rolled her shoulders instead. Not exactly a Lilliputian, cramming herself into an economy window seat from Newark to Glasgow had left her feeling stiff, achy, and more than a little cranky.

The long drive north hadn't done much to de-frazzle her, however breathtaking the scenery. Thank goodness she'd had competent escorts and hadn't had to brave the left-sided driving and spindle-thin roads herself. Equally good, she knew exactly how to banish her bodily aches and lingering tiredness.

A long, hot shower was what she needed.

And no matter how Transylvania-like the high-ceilinged, wood-floored room struck her, its spacious and airy bathroom was totally twenty-first century.

Already feeling the restorative pounding of a good, steaming shower, she stripped with light speed, just reaching around to unhook her bra when she noticed the framed poster of her aunt Birdie and uncle Mac on Dunroamin's entry steps.

She had a copy of it in her apartment back in Yardley, Pennsylvania. Hers was mounted in a tartan frame and had pride of place above her living room sofa. This one hung near the shuttered windows, its old worldy-looking frame as dark as the room's paneling.

But at least its familiarity took away some of the room's eeriness. Thankful for that, Cilla tossed aside her bra and went to look at the poster. A Christmas card photo she'd had blown up just last year, thinking that her aunt and uncle would appreciate the way a slanting ray of winter sun highlighted the stone armorial panel with the MacGhee coat of arms above their heads. Their heads, and the dark head of a tall, broad-shouldered man standing a few feet behind them, close to the castle's opened door.

"Huh?" She blinked, certain she was now not just jet-lagged, but going crazy.

The man—who looked roguishly medieval—hadn't been in the poster before.

Nor was he there now, on second look.

He'd only been a shadow. A trick of light cast across the glass covering the framed poster.

She shivered all the same. Rubbing her arms, she stepped closer to the poster. He'd looked so real. And if she was beginning to see imaginary men—handsome, medieval, or otherwise—she was in worse shape than from any jet lag she'd ever experienced.

Certain that had to be it, the mind-fuzzing effects of crossing time zones and lack of sleep, she touched a finger to the poster glass, relieved to find it smooth and cool to the touch, absolutely normal-feeling, just as it should be.

But whether the man was gone or not, something was wrong. In just the few seconds she'd needed to cross the room, the air had grown all thick and heavy. Icy, too. As if someone had set an air conditioner to subzero, deliberately flash-freezing the bedchamber.

She frowned. Unless she was mistaken, Dunroamin didn't have air conditioners.

It *did* have strange shadows in posters.

No, not shadows.

The man was back, and this time he'd moved. Just as dark and medieval-looking as before, he now stood next to Aunt Birdie and Uncle Mac instead of behind them.

"Oh, God!" She jumped back from the poster and raised her arms across her naked breasts.

He cocked a brow at her—right through the poster glass!

Her heart began to gallop. She couldn't move. Her legs suddenly felt like rubber and even screaming wasn't an option. Her throat had closed and her tongue felt stuck to the top of her mouth.

Disbelief and shock sweeping her, she looked on as the man, illusion, or whatever, moved away from her aunt and uncle to lean a shoulder against the door arch. Then he just stood there, arms and ankles crossed as he stared back at her, something that looked like a round medieval shield propped against the wall near his feet.

"You aren't there." She found her voice again, a

pathetic croak. "I am not seeing you—" she broke off, a chill whipping down her spine.

Mr. Not-there was gone again.

Only the shadow on the glass remained.

"Oh, man." Her shower forgotten, she snatched up her bra and the rest of her airplane clothes, tossing them back on even faster than she'd taken them off. She should never have accepted Uncle Mac's welcome dram.

Not after being up nearly thirty hours.

"Miss Swanner?" A woman's voice called through the closed door, accompanied by a quick rap. "Are you awake?"

She almost flew across the room, half tempted to answer that, yes, she was awake, but she was also having *waking hallucinations*.

Instead, she ran still-shaky hands through her hair and opened the door. "Yes?"

"I'm Honoria, Dunroamin's housekeeper. I've come to take you down to tea, if you're feeling up to it." An older woman in a heavy tweed suit and sturdy shoes peered at her, the oversized print of an unusually large badge stating her name pinned to her jacket.

Following her glance, the woman put back strong-looking shoulders and cleared her throat. "Some of our residents have difficulty remembering names. Others"—she looked both ways down the dimly lit corridor, tactfully lowering her voice—"don't see well."

Cilla almost choked. There wasn't anything wrong with her memory, but since a few moments ago, she had some serious doubts about her vision.

About everything.

The world she'd known and understood tipped drastically when she'd peered at that poster.

Hoping the housekeeper wouldn't notice how flustered she was, she stepped into the hallway, gratefully closing the door behind her. "I'd love tea," she said, meaning it. "And I'm looking forward to meeting the residents. Aunt Birdie and Uncle Mac always talked so much about them, I feel as if I know them alrea—"

"Och, you won't be seeing any of them just yet." The housekeeper glanced at her as they moved down the plaid-carpeted corridor. "They'll be having their tea in the library. Your aunt and uncle are waiting for you in the armory."

She blinked, wondering if her hearing was going wacky as well. *"The armory?"*

Honoria paused at the top of a great oak staircase. "It's not what it sounds like, though there are still enough weapons on the walls. Your uncle uses the room as his private *den*—I believe that's what you Americans call it?"

"Oh." She felt foolish for thinking she was going somewhere that would give her the willies.

A *den* she could handle, even if it did have a few swords and shields decorating the walls.

But when Honoria opened the door, ushering her inside, Cilla found the armory unlike any American-style den she'd ever seen. Full of quiet and shadows, medieval weapons gleamed on every inch of wall space and two full-sized suits of standing armor flanked a row of tall windows across from the door.

Cilla froze just inside the threshold, the willies making her stomach clench.

Her aunt and uncle were nowhere to be seen.

Her heart thumping again, she turned to the door. "Are you sure this is where Aunt Birdie and—" She closed her mouth, catching a glimpse of the housekeeper rounding a curve at the far end of the corridor.

"Ach! There you are," her uncle's deep voice sounded from the room's shadows. "Come, have tea with us."

Spinning around, she saw her aunt and uncle at last. They sat in the soft lamplight of a corner table set for tea. Aunt Birdie, with her sleek tawny-colored hair and large deep blue eyes, looked so much like an older version of her mother and herself that she started.

Uncle Mac, kilted as always, wore the bold, masculine room like a second skin.

With his larger-than-life good looks and full, curling beard, not to mention his horn-handled *sgian-dubh*, the ever-present dagger peeking up from his sock, he looked every bit the fierce Highland chieftain.

So much so, Cilla forgot herself and blurted what she really wanted to know. "Uncle Mac—does your castle have ghosts?"

ABOUT THE AUTHOR

Allie Mackay is the alter ego of *USA Today* bestselling author Sue-Ellen Welfonder, who writes Scottish medieval romances. A former flight attendant, she spent fifteen years living in Europe and still makes annual visits to Scotland. Proud of her own Hebridean ancestry, she belongs to two clan societies: the MacFie Clan Society and the Clan MacAlpine Society. Her greatest passions are Scotland, medieval history, the paranormal, and dogs. She is married and lives with her husband and Jack Russell terrier in her home state of Florida. Visit her on the Web at www.alliemackay.com.